SENTINEL

First published in 2014 by
Peridot Press
12 Deben Mill Business Centre, Melton,
Woodbridge, Suffolk IP12 1BL

ISBN: 978-1-909717-09-1

Set and designed by Theoria Design
www.theoriadesign.com

Visit: www.thesentineltrilogy.com
Follow: @SentinelTrilogy
Like: facebook.com/SentinelTrilogy

JOSHUA WINNING

SENTINEL

BOOK ONE OF THE SENTINEL TRILOGY

PROLOGUE

18 AUGUST, 1589

IT WAS MAGIC, ISABEL HAD SAID, but Jessica still didn't quite believe it. She'd pouted at first and turned her head. Isabel's reproach had been hot like a needle in her ear.

"They become confounded in the afterworlds and they wander until time is nothing more than dull heartache. They require our help."

Isabel had looked perfectly sane as she'd said it. Jessica had searched for a tell-tale twinkle in her eye or an uncharacteristic curl of her lip, but there had been nothing. Only that familiar stern brow, those thin, pressed lips and the cobweb crinkles about her eyes.

Now they were sitting hand-in-hand and Jessica was more confused than ever. She felt small, wished she was at home, even if that meant curling into a corner of the bed away from a man she didn't love.

A faint vibration. A grumble of thunder. She was probably imagining it. Here, the only sound she could be certain of was the quick gasp of her own breath.

A crisp blue light quivered before her. It spiraled up from a bowl at the centre of the table, caught between their outstretched arms. The pentagon-shaped room glowed and the hairs on Jessica's arms shivered.

"I have never seen blue fire," she murmured.

She could only just discern the old woman's watery outline through the light.

"It is a gateway," Isabel explained. "A temporary opening between the worlds. Through it we are able to commune with those lost on the lonely roads, guide them toward rest."

Jessica was ready with a tart retort, but the defiance died as it met her lips. A shape had stirred within the light. It looked like… a face. A man's face. Deep-set eyes like wounds.

"Friend," Isabel said. Jessica realised she wasn't addressing her but the thing in the light. "Tell us your name, friend."

Silence. Then–

"Harold Baxter."

The voice convulsed awkwardly and Jessica trembled.

"Harold," Isabel continued calmly. She didn't sound like herself. The usually hard, clipped vowels were longer. Softer.

"Harold," Isabel purred. "Why do you linger here?"

"JEREMY! He looks livid. What have I done? He's- OH GOD! Blood!"

"Harold," Isabel snapped. "Forget that. It is in the past now. You are free of such horrors."

Silence. Then–

"There is another here."

A faint jangle of bracelets. Jessica thought she saw Isabel's face droop. It was impossible to tell through the curtain of light.

"Speak," Isabel uttered.

A moment's quiet. Then–

"Free me."

It crashed like thunder. The voice made Jessica's head pound.

Isabel's grip tightened about her hands.

Choking heat blasted her face. The blue light fizzled and flames erupted.

The column of light blazed red fire.

Twin pinpricks flashed within the gateway and Jessica screamed.

★

She broke out into the night, where the folds of her dress were snatched up by the wind.

Terrified, Jessica collapsed in front of the house. She sobbed with her face in her hands.

Rain drove from above and the storm threatened to swallow her whole.

Caaw! Caaw!

The sound sang over the storm's bellowing and Jessica scoured the shadows uncertainly.

Then she saw it.

Flitting through the darkness on powerful wings was a raven. Barely visible in the night, its keen eyes flashed in response to the lightning. It dropped to the ground a mere foot from the young woman.

They regarded one another for a moment. Overpowered by curiosity, Jessica got to her feet.

Caaw!

The bird took to the air once more and, smiling now, Jessica followed it into the storm.

CHAPTER ONE
ALONE

8 August, 2013

Anita hallow took a deep breath and tried to settle her nerves. At least they were here now. Soon they'd be moving, and the quicker that happened, the quicker she could do what she had to. She'd be home again soon. Her insides shuddered and she searched about for a distraction.

There, in the window: the reflection of a worry-tired woman. Anita changed her focus and peered out at the platform.

Cambridge train station was typically teeming for a Friday night. A tinny voice rang over the tannoy and though the rush hour had long since passed, the station was still alive.

"For God's sake, Bobby!" a voice whinnied, and Anita was plucked from her reverie. She watched in the window as the reflection of a couple trudged down the carriage aisle; a plump woman was waddling along behind a man with spider-like limbs.

"Whatever you do it always goes wrong," the woman shrieked. "I don't know why you even bother, I just don't. If it's not one thing it's something else. You're a walking–"

The admonishments faded into the distance.

Anita shrank further into her seat as the carriage began to fill up. Around her, people hollered into their mobile phones; joking and arguing, shamelessly sharing the most colourful details of their lives. She wondered what those lives were like, dislocated as they were from the worries of her world.

A hand reached out and touched hers.

Anita jumped, then remembered Max. He was sitting across the table from her, his hair a scruff of sandy blond, eyes twinkling wryly. Nothing ever seemed to bother him.

"I told you about worrying." He squeezed her hand warmly.

It would be easy to mistake them as strangers, they made such an unusual pairing. Anita's timid, frowning countenance was thrown into stark contrast by her husband's easy confidence. Yet here they were, eighteen years married. Their conflicting personalities complemented one another in ways that made them both better people. Anita's gentle, compassionate nature ensured that she was able to defuse some of Max's more fiery tempers, while Max's determination meant that he was able to instil in Anita the confidence that she so often lacked.

"I'm not worrying." Anita raised a defiant eyebrow. There was no fooling Max, though, and she sighed. "I just… I can't," she began, but she was aware that the carriage was now groaning with people. A nervous glance about her confirmed that none of the other passengers were taking any notice of them. And why should they?

"Everything will be fine, Nicholas can take care of himself," Max said. "He's not a child anymore. Isn't that exactly why we've been called?"

"But that's just it – we have no idea. It's been fifteen years, what if something awful has happened?"

"All the more reason to keep calm," Max reasoned. "If Nicholas needs anything he's got Tabatha next door. I told you not to have that coffee; it always makes you jittery."

Anita offered a weak smile. "I know."

She turned to peruse the crowds once more. As they sat quietly, Anita's fingers moved absentmindedly to a silver pendant threaded about her neck. She stroked the surface, tracing the familiar contours, finding reassurance in their permanence.

"Pardon me, is this seat taken?"

Anita looked up as a figure paused at their table. He was an elderly gentleman, his stern face creased with experience, silver-rimmed spectacles perched on the end of a large nose. He wore black from head to toe and the only other shade on his person was a slash of white at the neck; a clerical collar that marked him out as a man of the cloth.

"Feel free," Anita said.

"Ah," the priest said pleasantly, seating himself next to Max. "Much obliged." He set a leather bag down on the table.

The blinkered lights above the train doorway beeped, and with a mechanical hiss the doors closed. The train's engine gathered momentum, causing the windowpanes to judder, and finally they began their departure from Cambridge station. Summer air gusted in through the window and Anita peered up into the dark sky where a full moon peered back at her.

Max read his newspaper. Next to him, the priest popped open his bag, retrieving a pen and a pad of paper.

Anita watched him from across the table, observing the pen as it crept over the paper, gripped by knobbly fingers. She had always admired the men and women of the clergy. Though she didn't believe in God – at least not the God that the Christians worshipped – she sensed the ardour of their conviction and respected them for it. What she admired most was the unwavering commitment of their faith. These people had devoted their entire lives to the belief that out there, somewhere, somebody was watching over and protecting them. They put their trust in something that they couldn't physically prove, but rather felt. Faith was a complicated and wonderful thing.

Outside the panorama began to change. Cambridge gave way to a collection of small towns and fields.

"Can we trust her?" Anita murmured, mostly to herself. Opposite her, Max lowered his paper. "Tabatha, I mean," Anita explained. She flashed a look at the priest, who was still absorbed in writing.

"I can't think of anybody more worthy of our trust," Max said. "Except Sam of course, but he'll be with us."

"I know, but at least Sam knows–" She stopped mid-thought, not daring to finish it here, where anybody could overhear them.

"Why don't you get a bit of shuteye? We've a good hour ahead of us." Max offered her a knowing smile. "Don't worry, I won't leave the train without you."

Anita returned the smile, though hers didn't seem to fit right. She sank into the chair; too nervy to think clearly, too tired to sleep. She sat listening to the *click-a-clack* of the train.

She had known this day was approaching, but she hadn't ever expected it to arrive. The shock upon receiving the letter had been unpleasant, and for the first time in a long time she had felt scared.

What if they took Nicholas away from them? From her? What if they considered her unfit to handle him? Bad things always seemed to come at the best of times, like weeds corrupting a bed of flowers. He was just a kid and she didn't want him to be a part of any of this.

Anita had been fighting her entire life. Never the smartest girl at school, she stayed up studying into the smallest hours of the night to keep up with her peers. And now, after so many years of peace and quiet, something had come to set her nerves on edge once more. That old, familiar anxiety returned in a suffocating flood. As the weeks, months and years slipped by, she had almost forgotten that their lives were different. They were nearly (dare she even think it?) *normal*. The letter was the rude awakening she hoped would never come.

It would come eventually, of course. How could it not?

"Sorry, but I don't suppose you saw what that last station was?"

The voice tugged Anita out of her morose thoughts.

The priest was peering at her over the rims of his spectacles.

"Uh," She hadn't been paying attention to the little stations as they periodically whooshed past in the dark. "Newmarket, possibly?"

"Much obliged." The priest's voice was kindly despite his bloodless features.

"Nervous traveller," he explained. "Always worried I'll miss my stop." He held her gaze for a second longer. "Going far?"

"Not really. Just an hour or so."

"I never liked trains," the priest commented. "Even as a boy. Of course they were all steam then, entirely different creatures. My father loved them, but they were too big and loud for me."

Anita nodded politely. The elderly gentleman seemed to detect the worry in her face. "You're leaving somebody behind?" he asked.

Anita looked at him in surprise, and she nodded unsurely.

"Yes."

"Somebody you love dearly," the priest observed. "One of the most difficult things to do in this world; bid farewell to those we hold dear. It happens far too frequently now, I fear."

Anita nodded again, pursing her lips. She could feel the colour rising in her cheeks.

"I'm sorry," the priest said hastily. "I didn't mean to upset you. You'll see him again soon enough, don't you worry."

"How did you know?"

"A mother's love for her son is a powerful thing. One of the most powerful forces in existence, perhaps. That love and ache is written in you plain as day."

Anita frowned, unsettled by the ease with which the priest had read her. Max lowered his newspaper, sharing a look with her across the table.

Harvester.

The thought leapt to her in a burst of panic. No, she told herself. He's just a friendly old priest. No way he could be one of them; unless they were getting very good at what they did.

Calm. Stay calm.

"I'm sorry, have we met before?" she asked.

"I don't believe so. Why, I–"

Whatever the priest had been about to say never left his mouth, because at that moment the train gave a jolt that caused Max to drop his paper.

"What was that?" Anita demanded.

"I don't know," Max said, casting a look down the carriage. It shuddered for a second time and Anita bolted upright.

The windows made a clattering complaint.

A raucous squealing shattered the still night.

"That doesn't sound good," the priest muttered.

"It's the brakes," Anita yelled over the noise. "Someone's thrown on the brakes!"

"Why would they do that?" Max shouted back.

Anita pressed her forehead against the glass, cupping her hands either side of her face. "We're over water," she said. "Why would the driver brake on a bridge?"

Her insides knotted themselves up as she watched orange sparks spew out from beneath the train. They showered down over the side of the bridge and hissed on the river far below.

No, no, no.

Instantly, Anita thought the worst. She attempted to shrink away from the dread that was nipping at her mind, but it was almost impossible.

Next to Max, the priest crossed himself quickly and raised his eyes to the ceiling, whispering what could only have been a solemn prayer.

Other passengers strained to peer out of the windows.

Panicked murmurs rippled through the train.

"A car!" somebody hollered. "There's a car on the track!"

Another voice took up the cry: "He'll never brake in time!"

Anita shot her husband a fearful look.

"Max?"

She watched her husband struggle to answer. He looked paler than she'd seen him in a long time, and despair speared her gut. *Was this it?* They had struggled for so long to be happy; their lives seemed almost perfect. Perfect, at least, in comparison to what they had grown up with. She couldn't let it end here. She wouldn't let *them* destroy that.

Even as determination kindled inside her, Anita watched her husband's jaw clench. She understood in an instant.

"They've found us, haven't they?"

Before Max could reply there came a sudden crunching smash and Anita was thrown against the table.

It was as if somebody had stamped on her chest. She choked, gasping for breath.

Screams and wails littered the carriage. Above them, the lights sputtered and died.

They were plummeted into darkness.

"Lord have mercy on our souls," an elderly voice breathed in the dark.

"Somebody help us!" another voice howled, and there was a frantic surge of movement. People stumbled from their seats, spilling into the aisle.

Anita's eyes began to adjust to the moonlit environment just as a hand grabbed hers from across the table.

"Come on," Max said firmly. "Move." He clambered over the table to join her.

"They're here, aren't they?" Anita said.

They're here for us. Everybody on this train is going to die because of us.

"Go!" Max shouted.

Together they staggered into the aisle, grabbing a hold of each other. The pandemonium closed in around them.

Anita squeezed Max's hand tight as he forged a course through the carriage. Other passengers pushed and pulled their way in different directions, elbows and knees jabbing sharply as they fought to find a way off the train.

Then the train gave another jolt, moving under their feet.

"What's going on?" Max yelled, but his voice was lost amid the shrieks.

Anita attempted to swallow the panic rising up from her gut. She was rusty. Though this was by far the worst situation she'd ever been in, she'd have been far more clear-headed in the past. All she could think about was Nicholas. She had to survive this for him. There was no alternative.

"The exit!" she shouted. "I see the exit!"

They pushed urgently on and Anita forced herself not to look down at where fallen people lay bleeding and unconscious. Trampled. Somewhere, a passenger managed to break a window.

Finally, Max and Anita found themselves at the train door.

Peopled jostled about them like caged animals, frantic for an escape yet too panicked to make any sense of their surroundings.

Max shouldered his way up to the double doors, making sure that Anita was close behind him. He jabbed the button marked 'OPEN' with empty optimism, knowing that it would fail to function.

"The door," Anita wheezed, standing her ground as limbs stabbed her painfully and feet crushed her own. "We have to get it open."

Max cast about the exit swiftly, then gripped at the fissure at the centre of the doors. He strained against them, attempting to drag them apart. They quivered a bit, stubbornly resisting his efforts. Anita moved to help, heaving at the door with all her strength.

Another man who seemed to understand their intentions grabbed at the door. Together they all laboured, and with a submissive sigh the doors finally skated open.

Suffocating summer air rushed keenly inside.

Anita tried to push herself backwards as the wind snatched at her clothes and hair, but the wall of people prevented her from doing so.

She clung at the edge of the doorway, peering down in horror.

The carriage teetered on the edge of the bridge, the world falling away mere inches from her feet.

Below, the river's dark waters swelled hungrily in the moonlight.

"How did this happen?" a tall man asked.

"A car," Anita breathed. "Somebody said something about a car."

Gripping onto the other side of the doorway, Max eased himself out and peered down the length of the train. When he drew back inside, he was shaking.

"Well?" the tall man asked.

"The whole thing's going to go," Max told Anita quietly. "We have to get off on the other side."

At that moment, the train shifted under their feet and Anita was flung into Max's arms.

She buried her face in his chest.

"Nicholas," she whispered.

And then they were falling through the night.

★

The world came crashing down.

As Sam Wilkins observed the shadowy grimace on Nicholas Hallow's face, he knew that everything had changed for the fifteen year old forever. The boy's eyes were fixed on a spot on the lounge floor, unmoving, still absorbing the enormity of what he had been told.

"I'm... sorry, Nicholas," Sam said.

Attired in a scratchy grey suit, the old man's wardrobe was outdated and functional. White hair was thinning at the crown and his face was etched with the cares of seventy-one years of living. Despite this, the elderly man was in remarkable shape – he didn't slouch like so many other pensioners, as if the years were pressing down on his shoulders, nor did he have a catalogue of ailments and prescriptions to contend with. Sam Wilkins had embraced the world all those years ago and he had no intention of letting it go just yet.

Sitting in a sturdy armchair, he struggled to conceal his anguish. He loathed that he was the one to saddle Nicholas with such terrible news – news that the lad should never have to deal with. But he wouldn't have it any other way.

"There was an accident on the railway. A car somehow found its way onto the track and caused a collision."

He spoke slowly so as not to trip over the difficult words. He didn't believe in patronising the younger generations, never had. Bare facts, while sometimes difficult to stomach, were always the best policy in his opinion. Sam knew better than anyone how terrible a creature the imagination could be if only fleeting details of such an awful event were given.

No, he had no intention of burdening Nicholas's subconscious any more than he had to.

"The crash…" he began, and somehow the truth now seemed far worse than anything Nicholas could imagine. "The crash would have lasted mere moments."

Nicholas gave little reaction. His quiet was unnerving. Not for the first time, Sam noted the resemblance the boy bore to his mother. He was sullen-looking, having inherited both her soulful eyes and her dark, tousled hair. There was no doubt that the quick temper was his father's. His face held an almost ghostly pallor that not even the soft lamplight could warm.

"They're both…"

Nicholas's voice made Sam's chest tighten.

"Yes, lad," the old man conceded softly. "I'm afraid so."

He trudged over to where Nicholas was sitting on the sofa. With great care, he moved to kneel down beside him, his knees popping with the strain.

Nicholas barely moved, barely seemed to notice he was there.

"Nicholas," Sam said. "I know this is a lot to take in, lad, but I am here for you."

He reached out a hand and touched Nicholas's arm.

It was as if he had been struck with a bolt of electricity.

Even as the old man touched him, Nicholas shrank back in sudden anger.

"You're lying!" he yelled. He jumped away from the sofa. "You're lying! They're not dead!"

His voice rose to the ceiling and the returning echoes mocked his despair.

Dead! Dead! Ead! Ed!

The boy bolted from the room, tearing up the stairs.

Sam heard his bedroom door slam shut.

The old man put a hand on the arm of the sofa and eased himself up.

A figure entered the room.

"You told him," the newcomer said simply.

Sam didn't look at the speaker. Instead, he walked to the fireplace. Behind him, Tabatha Blittmore fidgeted with her over-sized woollen jumper.

"Yes," Sam puffed wearily. "I have told him."

Tabatha tutted.

"Poor boy," she said sadly. "Such a loss. Such a great, great loss."

"Max and Anita were fine people." Sam stared into the cold fireplace. "The world is a sadder place without them."

"However will he cope?"

"Nicholas is strong, he'll survive. These things are sent to test us."

There was quiet for a moment.

"What'll happen now? He can hardly stay here all by himself."

"The Hallows asked that you keep an eye on Nicholas," Sam mused, "and if you were willing, perhaps you would carry out their wish... At least until an alternative is found."

He turned to face her.

If the circumstances had been any different, the comical sight of Tabatha Blittmore would have amused him. Her tangerine jumper was four sizes too big, hanging almost to her knees, while her brown corduroy trousers tapered down to conceal her bare feet. A mountain of crimped, dirty blonde hair spilled either side of a moon-like face.

She was young – perhaps in her late twenties, he couldn't quite tell; everybody started to look the same once you hit sixty – and naïve, but her kindness was immeasurable.

Even as Sam suggested the arrangement, Tabatha nodded, and the curls fell across her eyes.

"Of course," she said, swiping at the bothersome locks. "I would be happy to."

Sam nodded.

"That's what we'll do, then. I expect social services will be in touch. Just refer them to me."

He retrieved a coat and battered fedora from the armchair, his voice taking on a hushed tone as he began muttering to himself.

"I'll have to make a few phone calls, things will have to be set in motion…"

"I'm sorry?" Tabatha said.

Sam met her bemused gaze.

"I must be off," he said. "I'll visit again in the next few days. Don't worry about the, uh, the funeral arrangements, I'll see to those."

Tabatha hurried to shake his hand.

"Thank you, Mr Wilkins. I couldn't have broken the news to him myself."

Sam gave her a warm smile. "You'll do fine, my dear." The smile slackened thoughtfully. "And if anything… happens, be sure to call me. I'm always about."

"Thank you, I will."

★

Hours later, when Nicholas lay in a fitful slumber, two eyes watched him in a silent vigil from the windowsill.

Almost a part of the night itself, the raven perched there until dawn set the sky on fire.

CHAPTER TWO
The Letter From Beyond

Nicholas coasted numbly through the days following the news of the train wreck. He slept late, wrapped in the snug cocoon of his duvet, and picked at his food with disinterest, preferring the seclusion of his bedroom over all else.

The constant fussing of Tabatha Blittmore – who was originally only meant to keep an eye on him during his parents' absence, but had now all but moved herself in from next door – provided momentary distraction, but was mostly just another source of frustration.

Shock and disbelief reverberated through him, finding no outlet for expression or acceptance.

Up in his room, Nicholas lolled on his bed, peering solemnly out the window. The third floor attic conversion offered an impressive view of Midsummer Common, located in the centre of the city of Cambridge. A great, green expanse of land, the Common rolled all the way down to the River Cam, where the Fort St. George pub nestled by the waterside, its outdoor areas crammed full of sun worshippers.

The summer season was at its peak. Immaculate blue skies graced each bright August morning. The air buzzed with busy insects and fat cats dozed. Whereas other youngsters were playing and laughing on the Common, though, Nicholas hid here.

As he stared out across the Common, he escaped into memory, recalling something Sam had once told him.

Midsummer Common was a place heaving with history; it had seen births and deaths, but it was a strange bylaw from the 1800s that came to Nicholas now. According to the law, any person found beating a carpet or rug, or caught gambling or betting on the Common, would be fined forty shillings. The law had never been repealed, which meant that even today, law-breakers could face the fine.

The anecdote had tickled Nicholas before. Now he didn't care. Rolling over in bed, he flipped open his phone and brought up a photo. His parents beamed at him. He'd taken it at London Zoo earlier in the summer. His dad wasn't fussed about seeing a load of wild animals in cages, but his mum loved the reptile room. She'd spent hours in there cooing over the geckos and they'd dragged her away practically kicking and screaming when the penguin show started.

Their faces brought only confusion now.

As the loneliness inside of him welled, his parents' grins warped, coiling into cold sneers.

Nicholas hurled the phone across the room.

It struck the wall before hitting the floor.

He let it lie there for a minute. Then, when his breathing had calmed, he got up and checked it wasn't broken.

There were texts from his friends. A few missed calls. He didn't reply to any of them. What would he say? Thanks? No worries, anybody fancy pizza?

There were no words.

Restlessly, Nicholas paced the house's darkened halls.

It was a robust, Victorian building with narrow staircases and high ceilings. The last house on the left in a run of three-storey terraces, all of which overlooked the Common, the austere residence was bright by day and cosy by night.

Before moving here, they had lived in an unremarkable semi-detached in Milton where hot water was a luxury and the birds in the roof were an annual menace. Then Nicholas's father had landed a job at a publishing company and they'd moved into the city, away from Milton. With its view of the river and the friendly neighbours – Tabatha had been the first to introduce herself – it was a happy home.

It felt drained, now. The colour had gone out of it and Nicholas felt like he was wandering a tomb. The house had become a powerful reminder of what he had lost.

Before he knew why, the boy found himself outside his parents' bedroom. He stared at the closed door.

Images of his mother and father flashed before his eyes; imagined, blurry conjurations of them battling to escape an exploding train. Snatches of their panic. The pain that they must have endured. The confused emotions inside of him surged. Nicholas found that he couldn't tear his eyes away. Almost independently of his thoughts, his hand reached out to take the door handle.

"Nicholas? Are you there?"

His chest tightened and a smothering hand seemed to clamp over his mouth.

His mother! The boy's mind raced. His mother! She was on the other side of the door!

The door handle burned into his palm. Moulded to his skin. Air refused to enter his lungs. There was a distant rattling sound. His entire arm was shaking, making the metal handle rattle with it.

"M–mum?"

He managed a throaty croak and the sound of his voice sent shivers across the back of his neck, as if a ghostly breath had fallen there.

"Nicholas? Lunch is ready!"

Nicholas's hand dropped to his side, free of whatever madness had seized it.

It hadn't been his mother calling to him; it was Tabatha shouting up the stairs. He couldn't tell if that realisation was a comfort.

Turning slowly to traipse down the stairs, he eyed the closed bedroom door with uncertainty. What had drawn him to it?

He found Tabatha in the kitchen. Her hands were concealed by large, flowery oven gloves and she was heaving a saucepan from the stove by the pantry. She shuffled across the floor, straining under the weight of it, before pouring soup into bowls on the table.

"Blast!" she muttered as a quantity missed the second bowl entirely and slopped across the tabletop. She mopped the mess up with one of the oven gloves, only for a clump of hair to come loose from behind her ear. Juggling the saucepan, she swiped the hair back with the glove.

"Well isn't that perfect, now I've got soup in my hair!"

The saucepan was consigned to the hob with a bang.

Looking annoyed, Tabatha flapped off the oven gloves and pulled at her hair.

Nicholas peered down at the murky contents of his bowl. It looked like watery paint.

"Well, that was a learning process," Tabatha declared, sitting down with a sigh. "Don't look at me like that, young man," she scolded lightly. "How you could call that contraption an oven I'll never know. I might as well have tried to cook on a park bench."

Nicholas stirred the soup with his spoon.

"You should eat something," Tabatha urged. "Don't want you ending up like a skeleton, do we? You're skinny enough as it is."

Nicholas sipped a spoonful, if only to humour the woman, and grimaced.

"Not my best, I admit," Tabatha complied, meekly sucking at her own spoonful. "Maybe it needed just a touch more salt. How are you feeling today?"

Nicholas pushed the bowl away and slumped back in his chair.

"I'm not hungry," he muttered.

"Oh, come, come," Tabatha reprimanded. "What would your mother sa—"

She stopped abruptly, realising what she had been about to say. Her cheeks flushed a violent, guilt-ridden crimson. "Oh Nicholas, I'm sorry," she puffed. "I didn't mean... Oh I am a fool! Curse this stupid trap of mine."

"It's okay."

They sat in silence as Tabatha picked awkwardly at her bread.

Nicholas dug into the tabletop with his bread knife, chiselling out little fragments of wood.

"Mr Wilkins is popping round later," Tabatha told him with strained exuberance. "Won't that be nice?"

Nicholas merely nodded.

In a soothing voice, Tabatha added: "It might help to talk about it."

Nicholas stopped his carving, paused with the blade embedded in the table.

"Sometimes it helps," Tabatha added.

"I don't feel like talking," Nicholas said through clenched teeth.

He felt his throat reddening. Didn't she understand that talking about it only made it more real? Made it something that he couldn't ignore?

"It couldn't do any harm," Tabatha soothed. "You might feel better. Can't keep stuff pent up for long, it goes bad inside."

Nicholas's eyes were fixed on the dents in the table. Unblinking. Then he couldn't bear it anymore.

"I hate them."

The words came out blistering with pent-up emotion, and as soon as he had uttered them, tears came. He couldn't stop them. "I hate them for leaving me here."

Tabatha nodded and leaned in closer to the table. "It's alright," she murmured.

"It's not!"

Nicholas struck the tabletop again, beating the wood angrily with the blade.

"Why did they have to go? They wouldn't even tell me where they were going! They should have taken me–"

"Don't think that." Tabatha took the hand that he was using against the table and held it tightly. "It's okay to hate them, it's okay to feel alone. But you're not alone."

"Easy for you to say." The tears spilled fiercely. "I just wish..."

He fell silent again.

"What do you wish?"

"I want it to stop."

"It will never stop," Tabatha told him shrewdly. "But I can promise that, over time, it will be more bearable."

"You don't know that."

"I do. Five years ago I lost my brother."

Tabatha met Nicholas's stunned gaze.

"At the time I thought the pain and misery would never end. And to a point it hasn't, but I've learned to cope with it. I don't pretend to be wise in anything, and I'm not exactly known for having a clever head... But I know enough about losing a loved one to tell you that you'll start to feel better. It just takes time."

Nicholas wiped at his cheeks and nodded slowly. Some of the weight that had been crushing him seemed to have lessened slightly.

"I know what'll cheer us both up," Tabatha said brightly. She jumped up from her chair and disappeared into the walk-in pantry. Nicholas heard a few crashes and a number of out-of-breath shouts before Tabatha emerged once more. She brandished a worn wooden box, setting it down on the table in front him.

"It's my dad's, he lent it to me especially," Tabatha said proudly. "It contains just about every old magic trick you could imagine. Want a peek?"

Nicholas smiled.

"My, but if that isn't the first time you've smiled in days," Tabatha gushed.

Before he could think anything of it, she opened the box.

★

Sam Wilkins arrived mid-afternoon and Nicholas was grateful for his company. They sat on a bench in the small, sun-dappled back garden. The fresh air, mingled with the giddy perfume of the flowers, improved Nicholas's mood.

"I trust things aren't too unbearable with young Tabatha?" Sam asked, eyes twinkling beneath the rim of the fedora.

"It's fine," Nicholas said, though Sam had a point. Tabatha's incessant fawning had become increasingly trying as the days wore on. Still, her kind words had helped, and Nicholas couldn't bring himself to complain about her, no matter how aggravating she sometimes was.

"Good, good."

Sam removed the fedora and placed it on his knee, wiping his brow with a handkerchief.

"And you're well? No more nightmares?"

Nicholas shook his head. He inwardly cursed Tabatha for telling Sam about the bad dreams; the last thing he wanted was for him to think he was some kind of bed-wetting kid. But Tabatha had heard him crying out in his sleep more than once and clearly felt it important to inform Sam.

"It's a struggle, lad, I can't put it any plainer than that," Sam sighed. "You need anything, you come straight to me."

"I know, thanks," Nicholas said. "I'm okay."

"Good to hear," Sam replied. "You've got your mother's strength. Never let anything get her down, that woman. Not even when she and your father were scraping a living and barely making ends meet." He paused briefly before adding: "As pleasant as your company may be, I must admit to having an ulterior motive. It's rather important, in fact."

Nicholas's insides shrivelled into a ball – he had a nagging feeling that they were about to discuss the funeral.

"Important?" he asked reluctantly.

"Oh, yes." Sam gave him a business-like nod. "You see, I received a letter this morning." He pulled a battered white envelope from his shirt pocket and passed it to the boy. Nicholas turned it over in his hands, the sun catching brightly across the white paper and momentarily blinding him. Then the envelope came back into focus.

"It's... it's my dad's handwriting," Nicholas uttered in shock. He looked at Sam expectantly. "Does this mean–"

"I'm afraid the letter was posted before the incident," Sam explained. "It involves you, however. Go ahead and read it."

With trembling hands, Nicholas pulled a folded sheet of paper from the envelope and began to read.

Dearest Samuel,

As you know, Anita and I are to travel east tomorrow. Though it pains us to leave him, Nicholas is to stay in Cambridge. We had no choice in the matter.

I wish to ask you a favour. Though I hope that nothing hinders this trip, Anita and I worry. There is talk; we have spoken of this before. The rumours have unsettled us both and we fear that something terrible will come to pass.

Samuel, if when you read this news has reached you that something has happened to us, I want you to take Nicholas into your care. We've discussed this before, I know. He mustn't stay in Cambridge; it is too dangerous a place. Take him east – take him to whom we intend to reach.

In you I trust my life, and the life of my son. I pray that all runs smoothly for us, and that I will see you again.

May the Guardian bless you.
Maxwell

Nicholas swallowed the lump that had lodged in his throat.

"Th–they knew?" he murmured. "They knew that something was going to happen to them?"

"Clearly they suspected..." Sam began. He cleared his own throat. "What has happened has happened; we cannot change it."

"But, what is he talking about? Who were they going to see?" Nicholas's head was spinning. "They told me they were visiting an old friend, but they didn't say where or who. And this letter makes it sound like... like they didn't have a choice."

Why hadn't he paid more attention when his parents had left that evening? He knew why. He'd been looking forward to having the house to himself; there had even been talk of a party. He hadn't even bothered to ask where his parents were going. It hadn't interested him.

Sam turned to contemplate the garden for a moment, his quick blue eyes troubled. "There are things in this world that are quite... secret, Nicholas," he began softly. They watched a bird hop from the overgrown pond onto a small boulder in the undergrowth. "Things that most people are oblivious to. Forgive me, it was not my intention to confuse you. But, you see, what your father alludes to in that letter is both very important, and very dangerous. If it had fallen into the wrong hands... I'm surprised he even sent it. An act of desperation, perhaps..." The elderly man shuddered and Nicholas felt a slow, slithering unease creep through him.

He gripped the letter tightly.

"But what is he talking about? What's a Guardian? Where were they going?"

"The lady I believe they were visiting is somebody very special indeed," Sam said, and Nicholas noticed the old man smile faintly. "Your parents knew a lady in the east, though you won't remember meeting her – you were very young. She is your godmother. It is my belief that your godmother and the friend your father mentioned to you are in fact one and the same."

"So... I'm going to have to live with her?" Nicholas asked. He felt more out of control than ever. Everything was happening so quickly and he didn't seem to have a say in any of it. All he wanted was his parents back. He hadn't even noticed the humdrum routine of everyday life before. Now it was gone, replaced with overwhelming uncertainty, he craved it. The lemon squares his mum used to bake. His dad's bad jokes. But they were the one thing he couldn't have, and never would.

Sam seemed to struggle with this for a moment. Then he offered sagely: "I believe it is important that we do as your father asked – he always knew how to best handle situations like these."

"But I've never even heard of her before," Nicholas argued. "Mum and Dad never mentioned her."

"In time, lad," Sam said, a smile crumpling the corners of his mouth. "Don't worry about such things. We're all going to take care of you."

Nicholas frowned, worried. He stared down at the letter, re-reading it quickly, searching for anything that he might have missed. "I still don't understand why, if he knew something was going to happen, all he could think about was me," he murmured.

Sam rested a hand on Nicholas's shoulder. "Love knows no bounds," he said plainly. As he said it, though, Nicholas detected something else in the man's voice, something strained. He couldn't think what it meant.

They sat quietly for a few moments. Nicholas shivered, aware that a chill had entered the garden, and the pair looked up in unison. An angry black cloud was unfurling across the afternoon sun like a colossal inkblot. The day grew dark and thunder grumbled.

"The heat wave has broken, then," Sam commented, returning the fedora to his head. "We had best get inside."

Nicholas got to his feet, hurriedly pocketing the letter as rain began to drum from above. It was only a matter of seconds before they were drenched. Hurrying to the back door, he and Sam hastened into the kitchen and Nicholas forced the door closed against a gust of wind.

"Well, that was rather unexpected." Sam shook water from the brim of his hat. "Our summers really never improve, do they?"

"What a pair you two are!" a voice shrieked behind them. Tabatha was standing in the doorway. "Like a couple of drowned rats!"

"Hello again, Miss Blittmore," Sam greeted her genially. "I apologise for the briefness of my visit, but I had better be moving before it worsens out there."

"Oh Mr Wilkins, you won't stay for a cup of tea?" Tabatha looked disappointed. She seized a tea towel from the counter and began to rub vigorously at Nicholas's tangle of wet hair. He scowled and darted out of her reach.

"Another time, thank you, Miss Blittmore," Sam replied. "There's no rest for the wicked, you know. I must be very wicked indeed; there always seems to be something on the go." He strode to the kitchen door, then stopped and turned stiffly. "Ah, and the matter of the funeral. I've spoken to a priest at a quaint church that I know Anita was fond of. I'll phone you within the day with the necessary details."

"Thank you, Mr. Wilkins," Tabatha said, putting an arm around Nicholas's shoulders. The boy moved away to peer out at the rain-lashed garden.

Sam nodded and then tipped his hat. "I'll show myself out. Goodbye."

"'Bye," Nicholas murmured, still peering through the kitchen window. Snow was fluttering into the garden.

CHAPTER THREE
WHISPERS

SHE HAD MANY NAMES. BUT OF them all, those numerous titles and adoring epithets, the one that He had chosen for her was the one she cherished. It had suited her even before it had been uttered, and as it stung the air for the first time, she had embraced it as her own. From then on it evoked fear and love in the hearts of all who crossed her path.

Malika.

A flash of lightning lit the cemetery. Gravestones erupted from the ground like snaggle teeth to grind at the night air, and in that briefest of moments something was silhouetted amid them. A cloaked figure.

It wove between the stones, twin pricks of light glinting in the shadows cast by a hood.

Above, an elemental purr disturbed the heavens. The winds stirred, moaning about the graves to mock the long-silenced voices of their occupants.

The cloaked form approached a mausoleum and produced an intricate key. It was slotted into a corroded lock, then twisted with a grating protest of metal. With a final *thunk* the lock complied.

Pausing in the open doorway, the figure raised pale hands and the hood was cast back with a sigh. A mass of lustrous red hair slithered over cloak-clad shoulders.

The storm fell silent.

Porcelain skin gleamed. Blood-red lips were full with defiance.

Malika.

She swung the door shut and bent to examine the interior of the crypt.

"Charming, still," she murmured mellifluously.

In this dank place, the walls were infested with unnatural, spiny weeds. They clutched jealously at every stone, having prospered despite the lack of nourishing sunlight.

Malika glided over to a sarcophagus, the tomb's sole resident.

The tip of her tongue dabbed her lips and when she pressed her hands to the cold surface a delicious shiver travelled through her.

"The power has dwindled none," she whispered. "Even when such time has passed."

The colour rose in her cheeks as she studied the symbols carved into the rough surface – a dead language long forgotten. Its mere presence soothed. It was only now, scrutinising these words after so many years, that she realised what had been missing. They reminded her of times long past; back when she had not stalked the shadows alone.

Now was the time to change that. Summoning her strength, she prised open the sarcophagus. The cover-stone skated sideways, hinged at one end.

Malika peered down.

This was no ordinary grave. No rotted cadaver dreamed here.

The sarcophagus was bottomless. A flight of steps plunged down into darkness. Malika breathed in the pungent stink that came roving from below. It was the scent of death and decay, of years of torment and agony. Before she could stop it, a delighted laugh spilled from her throat.

The shadows recoiled.

"How could I forget?" she murmured in caramel tones. "Forgive me my absence, I have returned now, at the waking of the world's darkest era."

Like a ghost, Malika swept over the side of the sarcophagus. The darkness below was solid like a shapeless, living thing, but to her eyes there was no dark. Her cat-like eyes picked out the stairs all the way to the bottom and her footsteps rang out as she descended.

There came no answering sounds; she had not expected any. It had been many decades since her last visit and she had sealed the mausoleum herself. That had been during the Second World War, when the earth had rocked as bombs were sent to scar the face of the world. She had revelled in that time, watching with glee as the petty humans fought, maimed and killed each other. Blood had flowed and she had soaked up the chaos eagerly from the sidelines.

The stone steps came to an end.

She hissed a foreign-sounding word and her command struck out like a whip. Fire erupted in an iron bowl held aloft by stone. There came another eruption. And another. And another, until the cavernous area below the graveyard was at last revealed to her, bathed in angry orange flickers.

It was vast, stretching further than even she could see. Pillars like trees, spreading upwards into a dark canopy of shadow.

Malika stepped into the hallowed chamber, moving resolutely. Water trickled down the columns, and at last she came to what she had been seeking; that which her heart ached to behold.

An immense stone effigy towered over her. It bore the face of a monster – fang-filled jaws snarled, beady eyes stared and horns curved up out of a bulging forehead to disappear into the stone wall.

Malika's breast heaved as she studied the carving. She raised her trembling hands and untied the cloak that smothered her form.

It came away at her shoulders, rippling to the floor. There, before the looming image of her God, she became absolute in her beauty. A crimson dress fell to her feet. Here and there pieces of the fabric were embroidered with tiny diamonds. The firelight ignited her pallid complexion and she was radiant.

Unable to contain herself any longer, Malika threw her arms up, fingers stretched out. She spoke words that few would understand now – a tumult of syllables and rhythms that were both beautiful and tragic. Her voice was forceful, demanding. And in the ghostly draft that made the fires flicker there came an answer.

Malika paused, casting about the cavern. Then, barely perceptible on the air, little more than a whisper, heaved the tone of another voice.

The flames in the black bowls spat. The ground shuddered and stirred even the pillars. The world groaned under a sudden great weight.

Malika fell silent.

Icy waves sighed from the effigy's open maw. There, in the recess of the statue's yawning mouth, two points of white light had appeared.

For a moment, Malika stood frozen, her arms still raised. The blood thrummed deafeningly in her ears. She could feel the eyes watching her. Penetrating. Tasting every inch of her. It took her a moment to compose herself. Such time had passed since she had basked in the presence of a higher being, one greater in power and authority than she, that she momentarily forgot herself.

Dropping her arms to her side, she fell to her knees and uttered: "My Lord."

The bright pricks of light needled out from the dark.

"*Malika*," guttered a throaty voice.

The woman raised her head. "It is I, Lord, your ever-loyal disciple."

"*An age has passed since our last meeting.*"

"Many ages, my Lord," Malika replied.

"*The Light has taken purchase of so many years?*"

"It has," Malika consented. She rose, limbs flexing like a lioness's, gaining in confidence. "But change surges above, carried on a wind of unease. The world is slipping, my Lord. It teeters on the brink. Corruption lays ruin to even the sturdiest of foundations, and the Light's hold on order is loosening."

"*You come bearing agreeable news.*"

"The world is much changed," Malika continued. "The evil of Man blooms and sin stalks the streets like never before."

"*Has the world indeed fallen so?*" A coughing laugh made the flames spit. "*Then my Rising has come not a moment too soon. The world is yet ready for a new array, a new leader and a new chaos.*"

Malika smiled darkly.

"*You have done well, Malika,*" the voice wheezed. "*Many would not have remained faithful when confronted daily with the despicable presence of Man. Such pitiful woes.*"

"It was the knowledge of your return that nourished me through the bleakest of nights," Malika burred softly. "I live only to serve Diltraa."

"*I am indebted for a servant as loyal as thee.*"

In the dark of the open maw a twisted form was hunched.

It sucked in tentative, rattling breaths.

"Even now other servants infiltrate the world," Malika informed him. "Those whose sole desire is to bring forth the bedlam so long ago promised. Across England, Sentinels are being destroyed. And with every one that dies, the blanket of darkness musters its weight. Soon it will eclipse all."

"*It is indeed a time for rejoicing. But not so swift*," said the whisper. The eyes glittered. "*We must exercise caution. The Vaktarin prevails; I feel her presence and power even from here. No doubt Esus still guides her.*"

"But their grip slackens with every Sentinel silenced; we can overthrow them," Malika persisted eagerly, hands clenched into fists. "Without the eyes of the Sentinels, the Vaktarin and Esus are defenceless."

The pinpricks blazed.

In their shallow bowls the flames burst upward, showering livid sparks onto the ground.

"*Do not underestimate Them! Blind confidence will land daggers in your back and poison in your veins.*"

Malika bowed quickly. "Forgive me, my Lord. I will do anything that you ask."

"*You will*," Diltraa spat. The flames dwindled. "*I require a vessel; something that I may travel in undetected.*"

"Anything, my Lord," Malika agreed keenly. "Ask of me anything, and it shall be yours."

"*I sense something quite suitable. It resides in the town above, less than a mile from here.*"

Malika nodded and bowed once more. "I shall obtain it for you, my Lord."

The eyes burned expectantly in the gloom.

★

No matter how many times he re-read the letter, its magnitude refused to fade. It was the final thread, an invisible spider-spun cord that linked him and his parents together. Nicholas couldn't put it down.

The events of the day his parents had left for the train still haunted his thoughts. The last time he'd seen his mother and father, they had been waving from the back window of a taxi. And now Nicholas thought of it, he remembered his mother's strange, stretched smile. The image lingered in his mind's eye – the way she had bitten her bottom lip. Nicholas wondered what it could mean. Was it conceivable that, like his father in the letter, his mother had known something might happen to them on the journey? Was that why she had refused to say goodbye to him?

A chill prickled down his spine. He sensed the air shift behind him and turned, expecting to see that Tabatha had come into the room.

His bedroom door was still shut and he was alone in the room. He shook the chill off, returning to the letter.

It left so many unanswered questions. Who was 'She'? Nicholas had never heard his parents speak of a godmother. And if they had never mentioned her, why were they going to her with such urgency? Why all the secrecy? And why, above all, did they feel the need to send the letter? Nicholas desperately wanted to see Sam again – he was the only person who could provide him with answers.

"*Nicholas.*"

The sound scattered Nicholas's thoughts.

A whisper so soft it shivered on the air.

He turned.

Across the room, his bedroom door was open a crack.

Nicholas frowned, sure that just a moment ago it had been closed. He got up from the bed and walked to the door, peering out into the hallway. It was deserted.

Nicholas turned to walk back into his bedroom.

"*Nicholassssssss…*"

The boy froze. The hairs on his arms stood on end. Slowly, he moved to look back into the hallway.

There was nobody there, only a slash of moonlight filtering in through the window.

"Tabatha?" he called out.

"*Nicholassss.*"

The letter fluttered from his hand and rested on the floor.

"Who's there?" he demanded. He thought he could feel eyes on him, but there was nobody there. Every fibre of his being screamed at him to stay where he was, but his feet – as if alive with foolish curiosity – stepped him out into the hall.

"Who's there?" the boy repeated. "Tabatha?" He walked toward the stairs, his heart hammering.

"*Nicholassss.*"

It was louder this time, closer. Nicholas spun towards the sound.

There was his parents' bedroom door. He chewed on the inside of his cheek, his stomach tied up in knots.

He moved to the door and pressed his ear against the wood.

Nothing.

Not a peep.

Reaching down, he took the door handle just as he had done the day before and twisted it.

The door fell open.

The smell of his parents still lingered here. The comforting scent of his father's aftershave mingled with the heather perfume his mother loved. Grief welled in his chest. Fresh and suffocating. He looked around the room, tidy and modest, rambling roses adorning the wallpaper. The same as it always had been. But somehow more special now, like the letter. Something to preserve.

There was no sign of life here, though. Nothing that might have whispered, anyway.

Nicholas found himself scrutinising the far wall. A picture of a younger version of himself hung there.

There was something strange.

Where the wall met the floor, a long, horizontal crack of light had appeared. He'd never noticed it before.

They didn't want me to notice it before, he thought to himself, though he couldn't explain why such a thought should occur to him.

Going to the wall, he crouched down and felt the base of the skirting. Then he pressed his cheek against the carpet.

A draft sighed through the crack and Nicholas could hear soft murmurs. He strained to make out the words, but found that he couldn't.

The sound of Tabatha's footsteps on the stairs made Nicholas get hurriedly to his feet.

"Nicholas? Are you still up?"

"Yes, I'm coming," he called.

He backed away from the wall, wondering what could possibly lie behind it. Then he closed his parents' bedroom door and joined Tabatha on the landing.

CHAPTER FOUR
Unravelling Threads

THE FIRST MOMENT THAT NICHOLAS KNEW he was outside was when a rough hand touched his bare arm.

"You alright?" a voice asked.

Nicholas blinked.

In front of him, a dilapidated church flexed up into the night sky. Frostbitten and swaddled in snow, its shattered windows gaped like mouths while graffiti-scrawled timber boarded up the entrance. Red and blue lights skipped over the stonework.

"What's going on?" he said.

The owner of the hand took a step forward, blocking out the decrepit structure. He was a tall figure with a wide nose and even wider shoulders. There was a police badge pinned to his chest.

"Had a bit too much to drink?" the officer asked.

"What?" Nicholas repeated. He became suddenly aware that he was freezing. Looking down, he found that he was standing barefoot in the snow, dressed in boxers and a white vest. His feet were muddy and nearly purple from the cold.

"What's going on?" he mumbled again.

A minute ago he'd drifted off to sleep – very much in his bed – and now he didn't know where he was.

"You better come with us," the officer said, drawing Nicholas toward a waiting police car. The lights on top whirred about like they belonged in a fairground ride. Nicholas got into the back of the car and was handed a blanket, which he gratefully wrapped around himself.

His head was swimming. He was at home in bed and he was in a police car. Everything was a fuzzy muddle.

The officer took his address and drove Nicholas back to Midsummer Common.

When they got to the house, Tabatha was already sat on the doorstep, more than slightly resembling a plump pink marshmallow in her fluffy dressing gown. Her face drawn tight with worry, she jumped to her feet as Nicholas trudged up the steps, the policeman just behind him.

They went inside and Tabatha put the kettle on. Nicholas slumped at the kitchen table, confused and vaguely annoyed. The policeman had performed a breathalyser test and was satisfied that Nicholas hadn't downed a bottle of whisky and decided to go for a drunken stroll. But he wanted to know what Nicholas was doing out in the middle of the night dressed, in his words, like he was "partying on a Portuguese beach".

"Don't you think I do, too?" Nicholas mumbled defensively. He felt like a freak, and all this fuss was only making things worse.

"Have you ever sleepwalked before?" the officer asked.

"Not that I'm aware of."

"That's got to be the explanation, though, hasn't it officer?" Tabatha shuffled over in her slippers and set three steaming mugs down on the table. "How else would you explain it?"

The officer ignored Tabatha's question. "I've had sleepwalkers rolling around in their front gardens before, but I've never known anybody to walk five miles into the countryside at two o'clock in the morning without waking up first," he said. "And definitely not barefoot."

"*Five miles?*" Tabatha shrieked. "I'm surprised you didn't catch your death of cold. Do you think he should see the doctor?"

"As long as you're alright." The officer continued to ignore her. Nicholas met the policeman's gaze and saw that he was genuinely concerned. Perhaps it was the embarrassment of it all, or Tabatha's persistent fussing, or the headache-inducing muddle the night had turned into, but the man's pity made Nicholas feel even more pathetic.

"I'm fine," he grunted, shoving his chair back. "Cheers for the ride." He dumped the blanket on the table and trudged out of the kitchen.

Up in his room, everything looked as it should. The duvet was pushed down to the foot of the bed, his bed sheets crumpled where he'd slept earlier. Everything looked normal, and everything was normal – except for the fact that Nicholas had just walked miles into the middle of nowhere while unconscious. As far as he knew, he'd never sleepwalked before. And yet he'd surely just set some sort of sleepwalking record. How – and why?

Nicholas spent the whole night restlessly pondering the conundrum.

Sam arrived early in the morning. It was the day of the funeral, and Nicholas wished he could just sleep through it.

As Tabatha told Sam about Nicholas's night-time saunter, the old man was his usual laidback self, just as Nicholas knew he would be. Sam had barely set foot in the front door that morning before Tabatha swooped on him to inform him of the night's events. She told the story as theatrically as possible, replete with dramatic pauses and an impression of the burly officer. By the time Nicholas found them in the kitchen, Sam was wearing a polite but weary smile – he'd obviously spent the entire conversation nodding.

The old man shrugged the whole thing off with an amiable "we'll have to furnish you with a bell if you're going to start going on midnight wanders", and Nicholas had been grateful for it.

Hours later, he was sitting in another church. The charcoal smudges under Nicholas's eyes were even darker than ever. *They sort of complemented the occasion*, he thought gloomily. Dressed in a black suit and tie, he sat in the front pew of a pretty local church, Sam at his side. The last time he'd worn this suit it had been for a wedding. Now he was at a funeral. His parents' funeral. There was an unpleasant symmetry in there somewhere.

He found it almost impossible to pay attention to what the priest was saying. Rain tapped at the church's stained glass windows and the sound echoed through the melancholy environment. The service blurred into eternity.

After his sleepless night, Nicholas felt numb to everything, like he was wrapped up in that stuff they used to insulate houses. He'd been dreading this day, but now it was here it just felt strange. Like a part of a movie or a really bad soap opera. He'd seen a million funerals on TV before, but it was different to be in the middle of one.

And Nicholas really was in the middle of it. He felt all eyes on him – the poor boy whose young parents had been tragically snatched away from him. A band of Nicholas's school friends were sitting somewhere near the back, but their presence only muddled things further. Nicholas had never seen their faces so serious. The sight of self-appointed class clown Charlie Walker looking so grey was almost crazier than the thought that his parents' bodies were lying in boxes mere feet away.

Nicholas didn't want to look at the coffins, but his eyes were drawn magnetically in their direction. They were surprisingly small, and the more he looked, the harder he found it to believe that his parents were lying in them. Cold. Unmoving. Silent. And they would never move again.

He almost wanted to lift the lids to make sure they really were in there. It was only the thought of what he might find inside that stopped him. What did his parents look like now? After the train wreck? What was even left of them? Nicholas shuddered and pushed the disturbing images from his head, fixing his gaze on the priest, who had said "Hallows" instead of "Hallow" at least twice now. Just another strange addition to the whole macabre circus.

When the service moved outside into the rainfall, Nicholas got a sense of just how many people had turned up to pay their respects. Half of them he didn't recognise, but some he did – his parents' friends mostly, all looking smarter in their Sunday best than he had ever seen them.

As the mourners congregated beside two freshly-dug pits in the cemetery grounds, Nicholas caught the eye of a scrawny woman whose hair had been scraped back into a tight bun. He knew her. Alice Gibbons, one of his mum's livelier colleagues. From across the holes in the ground, Alice fixed Nicholas with such a despairing look of pity that the boy found himself doing the one thing he didn't feel like doing. He smiled. There was just something about that wretched look that jolted a bizarre response out of him – one that both masked his true feelings and endeavoured to reassure the woman, somehow, that all of this was okay. He was okay. Couldn't be better. He looked away before she could respond.

The coffins were lowered into the earth. It swallowed them expectantly and Nicholas sensed the beginning of a horrible finality. His parents were gone, and nothing would ever return them. The rain that pounded the graveyard streaked his face, mimicking the tears that he couldn't shed here. Sam's comforting hand on his shoulder couldn't help.

In a towering oak that spread finger-like branches above them, a raven perched, hunched against the downpour.

When it was all over, Sam drove Nicholas and Tabatha back to the house. There was to be no wake – Sam had explained that it would have taken too much organising, but Nicholas knew that the convention had been skipped for his sake. He wasn't entirely ungrateful for that – at least he wouldn't have to face all of the people from the church who had looked at him with such cloying compassion.

At the house, a bleary-eyed Tabatha mumbled something about making a pot of tea before disappearing into the kitchen. Nicholas stood with Sam in the dim hallway.

"That went as well as can be expected," Sam said, bobbing on his heels. "Quite a good turn-out, don't you think?"

"They knew lots of people," Nicholas said. He felt leaden inside. Heavy and empty at the same time. A used tin can.

"Indeed," Sam said softly. He took a breath, as if mustering the strength to go on. "As we discussed, I have arranged for your departure tomorrow–"

"Tomorrow?!"

Tabatha had emerged from the kitchen, red-eyed with a scrunched up tissue in her hand. Apparently realising her outburst, Tabatha blushed and hastily added: "Meaning no disrespect, but we've only just had the funeral. You don't think it's a bit soon, Mr Wilkins?"

"I admit, things have been put on something of a fast track," Sam mitigated. "But I feel that it would be for the best if Nicholas–" he turned to address the boy directly, "–the best for you if you were with your godmother as soon as possible. I've spoken with social services and they agreed, though it took some convincing that they didn't need to come and see Nicholas. Luckily I know somebody there."

Nicholas was grateful for that. He didn't understand any of the legal stuff that happened in a situation like this, but he didn't fancy having to sit and talk to an overly-friendly therapist about his feelings. He was quite happy keeping them to himself.

"Are you really sure that's the best thing, Mr Wilkins?" Tabatha asked, stuffing the tissue up her sleeve.

"I do," Sam persisted. "It is in the interest of all that Nicholas is given a chance to settle down after all this. I believe that Nicholas is most safe – by that of course I mean safe emotionally – with the people that his parents wished him to be with. Fresh surroundings will do him a world of good."

"What do you think, Nicholas?" Tabatha asked, rubbing his arm.

"If it's what Dad wanted..." Nicholas said. "I want to meet her, whoever she is."

Whether he realised it or not, the mystery of this enigmatic and conspicuously absent godmother was the only thing keeping Nicholas going. He couldn't understand all the secrecy, and he wanted to get to the bottom of whatever his parents had been up to when they died. It seemed like the most important thing in the world now. The only thing.

Tabatha nodded and wiped at her eyes. "I'll go see how that tea is doing."

"You'll be going by bus," Sam told Nicholas. "I have been led to believe that they are quite comfortable. I do regret, however, that I won't be able to accompany you–"

"You won't?" Nicholas was taken aback. "You're not coming?" The thought that he would have to travel by himself hadn't even crossed his mind. Suddenly he felt more alone than ever.

Sam ruffled the boy's hair affectionately. "Oh lad, I am sorry. You know I would if I could."

He would if he could. Now he thought of it, Nicholas couldn't help wondering just what Sam got up to in his spare time – surely a man in his seventies should be taking life easy, playing chess in the park and scribbling poisonous letters to local newspapers about vandals and street gangs. Yet Sam seemed to spend his time constantly running around putting out fires all over Cambridge.

"Don't fret," Sam went on. "A good friend of mine is headed the same way, so he'll be getting the bus with you. You'll get on with

Richard; he's a thinker like you." Sam checked his watch. "Is that really the time? I'm afraid I must be off. I'll be back at nine a.m. sharp to take you to the bus station. Best have everything ready before then, eh? No playing on that x-cite all evening, or whatever it's called."

"Xbox." Nicholas smiled despite himself. "I'll be ready."

"Take care, lad. Get some sleep."

It was only when Sam had gone that Nicholas realised he'd forgotten to ask him about the strange wall in his parents' bedroom.

★

The remainder of the day crawled torpidly by. Hostile clouds lingered in the sky while rain slicked the streets, reducing the snow to mulch. Nicholas despised being cooped up inside, hated the stale air and lying about the house with nothing to do. It gave him too much time to think.

When he could stand the drumming on his ceiling no more, the boy dragged on a grey hoodie and trudged out onto Midsummer Common. It wasn't long before he was soaked through, but Nicholas didn't care. Squelching across the sodden grass, he made his way towards the river, seeing that a number of Red Poll bullocks had been set out to graze on the grassy land. Confronted with the inclement conditions, the cows huddled under a tree, barely moving. Solid mud statues.

At the riverside, Nicholas stood alone and peered down into the cloudy water. Boats that had been moored on the other side rocked against one another, jostled by the current.

In this weather, the Common was a desolate place. Nicholas remembered a story that Sam had told him once about a murder committed here in the late 1800s. A sixteen-year-old girl called Emma Rolfe had met up with a local tailor, a man almost ten years her senior, who took her to a nearby green and slit her throat. After killing her, the wretched man returned to a pub in Fair Street to finish his drink. He was later hanged for his crime at Norwich Gaol.

Nicholas shivered. As the rain battered him, he found it easy to believe such a despicable thing could happen here. When he was a child, he'd marvelled at those macabre tales, thrilling in their bloody ability to chill; but the older he got the more unnerving he found them. Emma Rolfe surely hadn't wanted to die; her fate had been decided for her by a savage drunk. His parents hadn't wanted to die either, but that hadn't stopped it happening. Like Miss Rolfe, their life stories would forever be defined by their deaths.

Nicholas sniffed, wiped at his nose. It felt strange to cry in the rain. The sky darkened and a drone of thunder threatened to tear the heavens in half. It was time to get back inside.

The boy turned, then stopped.

The herd of Red Polls had lined up in front of him, barring his way. They were unnervingly still, staring stupidly at him with goggly eyes that were both vacant and oddly sinister.

"What the—" Nicholas uttered. He knew cows were curious, but he'd never seen a herd brave a downpour like this just to get a closer look at somebody. He was rooted to the spot.

"Shoo!" he yelled.

The cows merely gawped at him. The rain drove into their tough hides and they must be freezing, but the animals didn't seem to care. Hot breath steamed from their nostrils.

Nicholas considered for a moment, then began moving slowly towards them, one hand outstretched in front of him. The cows still refused to move. Every one of those lopsided alien eyes was fixed intently on him, as if the creatures were trying to read the boy's thoughts. Or, Nicholas found himself thinking, wondering what his blood would taste like.

His heart pounding now, Nicholas pushed forward until he was mere feet away from the wall of hide and hoof. Through the mizzling air, the image of the creatures swam. Nicholas wiped at his face.

Then, quite remarkably, as his outstretched hand trembled inches away from the snout at the line-up's centre, the creature began to back away. As if they'd choreographed the whole thing, the beasts parted, and fell clumsily to their knees. The way was suddenly clear.

Nicholas didn't pause to ponder this new oddity. He beat his shoes into the wet ground and ran all the way home without looking back.

Later, Tabatha made them dinner, but Nicholas had no appetite. He put his plate in the sink and slunk off to his room.

When evening arrived, he lazed in the lounge, where the hearth crackled and the double-glazing dulled the thrum of the storm. He sat on the window seat, peering out across the overcast Common. The cows were back under their tree again, sheltering against the showers.

Tabatha was curled up on the sofa reading a women's magazine, the cover of which was ornamented with articles like 'Make Your Own Teapot Cosy!' and 'Try The Sat Fat Diet – Lose Weight In Just Two Weeks!'

"Have you ever made a teapot cosy?" he asked.

"What? Oh, I think I tried once," Tabatha deliberated.

"And?"

Tabatha looked embarrassed. "I use it to clean the windows."

"Nicholasssss."

Nicholas's head jerked as a familiar whisper roved into the room.

"Did you hear that?"

"Hear what?"

"I thought I heard a noise," Nicholas said.

"It's just the storm." Tabatha tutted and shook her head, her spaghetti hair bouncing. "Most bizarre thing I've ever seen in all my life – a whole week of rain and snow, right in the middle of August! Global warming my left bum cheek. I thought we'd be getting some tropical weather out of it, but it seems like the complete opposite."

Nicholas frowned, drawn to the lounge door. He left the window seat.

"I'll be back in a minute," he said.

At the foot of the stairs in the hall, Nicholas found the whispers were even louder.

"Who's there?" he called out. He started up the staircase, following the echoes. Presently, he was in front of his parents' bedroom door again, just as before. He didn't pause this time, pushing open the door.

Silence. The whispers had stopped.

Nicholas stepped inside and closed the door, turning the key in the lock. He moved immediately to the far wall, determination fuelling him. He didn't question what was driving him, didn't stop to wonder what force was pushing him to search the wall so purposefully.

He looked at the framed picture on the wall, as if seeing it for the first time. Normally he'd have kicked himself for being so stupid, but not this time. There wasn't time. Tomorrow he'd be leaving the house, and with it the mysteries that were surely hidden behind this very wall. He reached up and lifted the frame from its hook.

There it was, like he had known it would be.

A small hollow had been chiselled out of the plaster, and in it rested a simple-looking brass lever. Nicholas's mouth went dry. Whatever lay on the other side of this wall had to hold the answers about his parents. It just had to.

Shaking, Nicholas put his hand into the hollow and pushed the lever down. There came a *click*, a muted chugging of chains and a section of the wall fell open like a door.

Dislodged dust puffed out into the bedroom.

Nicholas stepped forward, pushing the door-like part of the wall, and entered the room beyond the wall.

It was a small, shabby-looking study. A smell of air gone stale festered here; that wet, musty aroma that always lingered in places of great age. Pushed against one wall was a lavish oak desk. A writing pad was strewn with papers, and the bureau came equipped with too many drawers to count. The opposite wall was concealed by an enormous bookcase that was crammed full with decrepit-looking volumes. Lastly, the back wall housed an immense oil painting that depicted a forest setting in which strange, squat creatures frolicked and laughed.

Nicholas surveyed the room in wonderment, the stale odours making him light-headed. How had he never known this was here? He wondered if his parents had been aware of it – and then he remembered the framed photo hanging on the wall, and knew that they had. The thought that his parents had kept secrets from him struck him anew, and a curious mixture of annoyance and regret mingled inside of him. Had they created this odd little study themselves? And if so, what for?

Stepping further inside, the boy ran his fingers along the bookshelves. They came away caked in dirt. He didn't notice, instead absorbing the titles resting there: *March Of The Three*, *Esus: A History*, *Dimensions And Damnation*, and finally *The Sentinel Chronicles*, of which there were a great many instalments.

Nicholas didn't know what any of these titles could mean, but there were hundreds more. He pulled *The Sentinel Chronicles, Volume*

IV, October 1983 from the shelf. The cover was engraved with a silver raven, its wings outspread in flight. He flipped through the pages.

15 OCTOBER, 1983

William Harvey of Bridge Street reported a disturbance at approximately 11:30pm. After hearing a noise in his back garden, he carried out a search of the premises, but no intruder was discovered. Harvey did report, however, the detection of a strange black substance around the base of his dustbin. After analysing the samples provided by Harvey, it is our belief that this substance was in fact the same saliva discovered at the scene of the Milton murders not two weeks hence.

Nicholas grimaced. What sort of book was this?

Realising that any second Tabatha could come looking for him, he moved over to the desk. He scoured the papers there, noting a number of different handwritings – some belonging to his parents, others seemingly older and more studied. There were strange diagrams, none of which Nicholas could make sense of, as well as a constellation chart, a dried-up inkwell and an assortment of fountain pens.

His attention bent to a large drawer at the base of the unit – the only one equipped with a lock. He tried the handle, ever optimistic. It didn't open. Curiosity suitably aroused, Nicholas pulled open the other drawers, pushing aside small notebooks and sketchpads in search of a key. There was none.

Nicholas sat on the floor with a thump, irritated. Where would somebody hide a key for a drawer? Struck with an idea, he crouched down to peer under the desk and then reached a hand underneath, feeling the underbelly of the unit. His fingers touched something. Eagerly he pulled, ripping at the masking tape and when his hand emerged from under the desk, a small golden key winked in it. It was a trick his father had used often. Nicholas had told him numerous times that it was stupid to tape a key so close to the lock it fitted, but he was grateful for it now.

He slotted the key into the lock. "Please work," he said quietly to himself. He waited a second. There was a click and the drawer opened.

Nicholas peered inside. Brown paper stared up at him from the bottom of the drawer. A parcel, neatly wrapped. Written simply across it was: *To Nicholas, on his sixteenth birthday.*

It was his mother's handwriting.

Nicholas's body shook with nerves. Swallowing, he reached into the drawer and pulled the parcel out. He sat cross-legged on the floor, setting the parcel on his lap. It would be his sixteenth birthday in a couple of weeks; was this a present from his parents? He stared at it for what seemed like an eternity, wondering at its contents, prolonging the unwrapping so that he could savour the final gift that he would ever receive from his parents.

Finally, he began to pull apart the brown paper. Piece by piece it fell away, until two green velvet boxes were revealed. The first was the size of a cigar case, and he could hear something rattling inside. The second was larger, about the size of a jewellery box, but flatter.

He concentrated on the smaller box first, prising it open. The hinges gave a satisfying creak.

Resting on the soft velvet interior was a silver pendant. It was shaped like a raven, wings spread in mid-flight and laced onto a chain. Nicholas looked at the volume of *The Sentinel Chronicles* resting beside him. It was adorned with the same symbol. He pulled the pendant from the box and it twinkled in the light from the bedroom. His mother had worn one identical to this, he remembered. He wondered what its significance could possibly be. Why had he never asked her why she wore hers? Carefully, he returned the pendant to its box, turning to the second gift.

Except this one wouldn't open. No matter how long he searched for a small fastening, there was none. He tapped it on the floor gently, hoping that an invisible seal would give, but to no avail.

A knock sounded from the bedroom door.

Startled, Nicholas dropped the box.

"Nicholas? Are you in there?"

Tabatha's voice came through from the other side.

Nicholas got to his feet, hurrying back into his parents' room, then to the bedroom door. "I'm here," he said. "Give me a minute."

Panicked, he rushed back into the hidden study. Gathering up the two velvet boxes and the October 1983 edition of *The Sentinel Chronicles*, he placed them under his parents' bed, hoping that Tabatha wouldn't check under there before he could retrieve them later. Then he moved to the door in the wall and went to pull it closed… but it wouldn't move.

His blood froze.

"Nicholas? Is everything alright?" Tabatha called. The door handle juddered. "I can hear funny noises. Why have you locked the door?"

Nicholas put all his weight into pulling the wall-door, but it refused to close.

"Nicholas?" The bedroom door handle jerked violently. "Will you let me in?" There was panic in Tabatha's voice now.

"Come on, come on," Nicholas breathed. Then he remembered the hollow in the middle of the wall-door and he inwardly scolded himself. In all his haste, he had forgotten how he had opened the door in the first place.

Reaching into the alcove, he tugged the brass handle upwards. The familiar sound of creaking cogs came and the door slowly sealed itself up.

Hurriedly, Nicholas placed the framed picture back on its hook.

"Nicholas?"

He hastened over to the bedroom door and unlocked it. It opened from the other side as Tabatha let herself in.

"Is everything okay?" she asked.

"Fine," Nicholas said. "I just… needed a moment in here. Before I leave tomorrow."

Tabatha relaxed, seeing for herself that he was okay. "Thank God, I thought… well I don't know what I thought. Come on down, won't you? The TV's on the fritz again."

Nicholas nodded and they both left the room.

With growing unease, the boy realised he had simply unearthed yet more questions about his parents.

CHAPTER FIVE
House Call

THE DOORBELL COULDN'T HAVE CHIMED AT a worse time.

Richard Walden was standing on the landing, rapping at a closed door with mounting annoyance.

"Dad, are you going to let me in?"

"Go away!" came the muffled response.

Richard sighed and used the doorframe to prop up his exhausted body. A hand went absentmindedly to his glasses, which he rearranged on the bridge of his nose – a habitual sign of his frustration. For a man in his early thirties he looked younger. He was scruffy and unkempt – traits that his fellow university professors deeply disapproved of – and if he'd been younger, those qualities would probably be mistaken for cool. But Richard wasn't cool. In fact, he was deeply uncool.

Richard didn't care about being cool. That was painfully evident in his rebelliously untamed hair and his unfashionable eyewear. He was thin, too. Almost too thin – apart from a swelling belly that hinted he relied on an evening beer to digest the trials of the day.

Richard wasn't cool.

He was, if anybody cared to notice, a despairing man at his wits end.

"Dad, please. You can't stay in there forever."

"I ain't comin' out."

Richard's jaw clenched and he tried not to let the situation rile him as it always did. It was moments like these that made him think Lucy could be right. Perhaps his father should be moved to a hospice. The nurses there were sure to have far more patience than he did. Plus there were more of them. Here it was just him and Lucy. An army of two.

Juggling his father's daily care with a demanding job was beginning to wear them both down. Not only that, it was putting a strain on their marriage. But he'd seen those places, where old people sat around like living dolls and well-meaning nurses mopped their mouths and changed their clothes for them. He wouldn't have his father in a place like that. Not yet, anyway.

"It's only vegetables," Richard persisted. He hoped he was using the soothing voice that Lucy always encouraged him to. "You like potatoes."

"Mutiny!" came the shrill reply. "My own son trying to put the kibosh on his old man!"

Crashes and bangs came through the door – drawers no doubt being ripped from the dresser, objects being stomped into the carpet. Richard dreaded to think what his father was doing and chastised himself for not removing the lock sooner. He supposed it had slipped his mind what with everything that was going on.

"We're not trying to poison you, dad," Richard said. "Just come out and we'll fix you something else."

"Where's Agnes?" the voice raged. "I want Agnes."

Despairing, Richard closed his eyes, resting his forehead against the door. Every now and again his father would forget that his wife was dead, and every time Richard had to explain it to him. The confused expression that clouded his father's features was always heartbreaking.

"She's not here, Dad," Richard said. "Now come and eat, please."

"Never!"

Richard opened his eyes as a hand touched his arm. Lucy was beside him.

"No luck?" she asked. She was, if anything, the complete opposite of her husband. Her blonde hair shone in salon-styled tresses and her cheeks always possessed a rosy just-pinched glow. She was, even to this day, the most beautiful woman Richard had ever met. He used to wonder (and still did occasionally) why she'd ever shown any interest in him – why she'd even noticed him, let alone spoken to him that day at the charity event.

"He hasn't been like this for weeks," Richard said, pushing his glasses up again. "I don't understand what set him off."

"Could've been anything. The doctor said he could turn at any moment, with no real reason That's the way it goes."

"I hate this," Richard said, his face scrunching up. "I hate that my own father doesn't recognise us half the time."

Lucy kissed him. "Don't let it get to you," she said softly. "It'll pass, you know it will. And then we'll have the fun of tidying up!"

Richard tried to smile, but he found it hard to look at her. He was a failure.

"Maybe it's time to give St. Mary's a ring."

Richard pulled away from her. "What?"

"It's been six months, Rich. We've tried our best, we really have. But... I just don't think it's working."

"I don't believe it. He's sick, and you want to stick him in one of those homes?"

"Can't you see what this is doing to you?"

He didn't respond.

"Well I can, and I can't just sit by and watch anymore."

The muscle in her jaw flickered the way it did when she was holding back, trying not to be as forthright as she could be. He was too angry to find it endearing. She reached out for his hand and he moved out of the way, his throat reddening.

"What are you saying?" he demanded quietly.

"I think it's time we thought seriously about moving your father into St. Mary's Hospice," Lucy relented. She sounded as crestfallen as he felt.

It was at this moment that the doorbell chimed downstairs.

Richard paid it no attention.

"I can't believe you're saying this," he said, searching her face for some sign that she was joking, or at the very least that she could be convinced otherwise. "I thought we agreed to look after him."

"We did, and we've tried our best. But things have changed," Lucy said. "This is changing us."

"We knew it was going to be hard..."

The doorbell rang again, this time accompanied by knocking.

"I'm going to answer that... we'll talk about this later," Lucy said. She disappeared down the stairs.

Richard took a breath. He was trembling all over. How could she expect him to abandon his own father like that? It wasn't fair. She couldn't know how he felt. It seemed like she wanted him to choose between the two of them – his wife and his father. He couldn't do it, and he shouldn't have to.

Through his troubled thoughts, Richard realised that the noises that had been coming from his father's bedroom had stopped. Gently, he tapped at the door.

"Dad? Are you okay in there?"

"Richard."

Lucy appeared at the top of the stairs. She looked flustered.

"We have a visitor." She sidled up to him, giving him a meaningful look as another figure bobbed onto the landing.

It was a short, overweight man who looked about sixty, but was most likely still only in his early fifties. His dated brown suit was tailored for a man two sizes smaller, giving the newcomer a bloated appearance. He clutched an official-looking leather bag and wiped the raindrops from his hairless head with a starched white handkerchief.

"Dr Snelling," Richard uttered in surprise. It had completely slipped his mind that the doctor was stopping by for his father's monthly check-up. Another thing he could add to the list of things he'd forgotten.

"Hello Richard," the little man said toothily. "Dear me, this doesn't look good." He gave the couple a look that managed to be as mournful as it was cheerful, his eyes crinkling behind little round glasses.

"Er, yes," Richard said shortly. "You've caught us at a bit of an awkward moment."

"So I see," the doctor said brightly, totally unfazed by the tense atmosphere. "Has he been in there for long?"

"About fifteen minutes."

Richard felt Lucy put her hand comfortingly into his and was glad she was there.

"He's been fine for so long now, I don't understand what could've set him off."

"Hard to tell," Dr Snelling said. He puffed his cheeks out

thoughtfully. "Perhaps he'll respond to me – I've known him for almost as long as you have, dear boy!"

"Might as well give it a try," Richard said. He and Lucy moved out of the way as the little man wobbled up to the door. Richard gave his wife an uncomfortable sideways look – this wasn't good. She squeezed his hand and Richard felt guilty for his outburst. All this really was wearing him down. Max and Anita Hallow's funeral that morning had drained the last vestiges of his energy, and now his father was having one of his turns. Sometimes Richard just wanted to lie down and sleep. He could probably sleep for a hundred years without waking up.

Dr Snelling drummed lightly at the door with the back of his hand. "Patrick," he called evenly. "It's Raymond Snelling, will you let me in?"

Richard watched the door with little hope. A few moments passed with no response. "Maybe you could come back another day whe–" he began, but just then there was the sound of a bolt being drawn back, and the bedroom door creaked open.

"Ah," Dr Snelling cooed happily, as if he'd been expecting this to happen any second. Patience really was a virtue! "How kind of you, Patrick." He stepped inside. Richard and Lucy hurried after him.

The room was in utter tumult. In other circumstances it would have been a pleasant place to live, but not today. Drawers had been flung free from the dresser, a mirror on the wall was skewed at an impertinent angle, and clothes had been strewn everywhere so that the floor was almost completely obscured. Sat amidst the bedlam was Patrick Walden, hunched over on the bed. He was a woeful figure, his thinning grey hair revealing a liver-spotted scalp, and the skin hung slack about his throat.

Dr Snelling toddled over to him, almost tripping on a discarded pair of trousers. He chuckled. "My, my Patrick, what have you been up to?" He set his bag down on the bedside table.

"Can I get you a cup of tea, doctor?" Lucy asked from the doorway. "Might warm you up a bit."

"That would be lovely, thank you. Milk, no sugar." Dr Snelling offered her a bucktoothed smile. "Give us a chance to catch up, won't it Patrick?"

Lucy pulled Richard along with her and they both traipsed down the stairs into the poky kitchen.

"He couldn't have come at a worse time," Richard lamented, slumping against the counter as Lucy filled the kettle. "I dread to think what he's going to write in those notes of his."

They fell into silence as Lucy flicked the kettle on.

"It feels like everything is going down the drain," Richard continued sombrely. "Anita and Max; Dad more unstable than he's ever been..."

Lucy bit her lip. "Do you think we should talk to Dr Snelling about St Mary's?" she asked softly.

"Maybe," Richard relented with a sigh. "Maybe you're right."

The admission left him deflated.

There was a yelp from upstairs.

"Did you hear that?" Richard started.

"Hear what?" Lucy asked, taking a coffee mug down from a shelf.

"I hope Dad hasn't started up his fuss again," Richard groaned. "I'll go and check on them."

As Richard mounted the stairs, another yelp sounded, followed by miserable sobbing. Richard's heart jumped in his chest; it sounded like his father. He'd never heard him make that sound before, even on his worst days. Richard took the stairs two at a time and rushed to his father's bedroom door. He froze.

Patrick Walden was still perched on the bed, his shoulders slumped, but his head was tilted backwards at an unsightly angle, forced there by Dr Snelling's podgy hand. Tears trickled down the sides of the old man's face and his breathing came in short, pained pants.

Dr Snelling's comical, chubby face was twisted into an alarming scowl; lips drawn back so that he appeared quite mad.

"What's going on?" Richard demanded.

Dr Snelling's head whipped around. His eyes no longer contained their usual spark of joviality – they were beady and pig-like, almost popping out of his head.

"Good of you to join us," Dr Snelling burred, his voice an octave lower than usual and betraying no surprise at the interruption.

Richard took a step into the room.

"I wouldn't," the doctor cautioned. He applied more pressure to Patrick's forehead, making the old man whimper even louder. Richard paused, looking at the fleshy hand pressed to his father's head. Some sort of metal device was strapped to the doctor's hand.

"What are you doing?" Richard pleaded.

"Dealing with this snivelling waste of human life," Dr Snelling sneered. "Isn't that what you wanted?"

"What?! What do you want?"

The doctor gave an amused snort. He bared his teeth. "I think you already know the answer to that."

Richard's knuckles turned white as they clenched into fists. He couldn't comprehend what was happening – the family doctor, who he and his parents had turned to for nigh on two decades, attacking his father and grinning insanely as if it was all massively amusing.

"Let him go and we'll talk," Richard breathed.

"Do I look that stupid?" the doctor spat. He forced the old man's head back further, making a gurgling yell stream from his throat. Sparks danced across the fat man's hand.

"Stop it!" Richard shouted. "Do you really think he can tell you anything?"

"I don't expect him to tell me a thing," Dr Snelling said calmly, though his body was shaking. "His brain's like Swiss cheese. *You're* the one who is going to talk."

Richard's mind raced. What could the doctor possibly want to know? Looking at the crazed man, he realised there was only one thing he was interested in, and that was the one thing Richard couldn't tell him. His father had taught him better than that.

"What do you want me to talk about?" he asked.

The doctor snarled. "Tut, tut, Walden. Playing the fool may have worked before, but not with me. Not now."

Richard searched the room for anything that he could use against the doctor. Adrenaline fizzed through him. His father had always warned him that one day something like this could happen. *Would* happen. But Richard had never believed it. He'd always thought that bad things happened to other people – not him, not his family. He wished he'd taken his father more seriously.

He spotted a lamp lying by his foot. He looked at the doctor, weighing up whether or not he could grab the lamp and cross the room quickly enough to strike him. Before Richard had the chance to move, though, there was a strangled bellow, and Patrick lashed out, as if something inside of him had snapped.

Dr Snelling, caught unaware by the assault, was flung back off the bed. He landed on the floor with a thud. Patrick fell on top of him with a shrill screech, flailing his arms madly at the doctor, scratching at his face with arthritic fingers.

Richard charged over just as the doctor, recovering from the shock buried his fist in Patrick's face. The old man fell back, cracking his head against the bedside cabinet and slumping unconsciously against it.

Richard raised the lamp, which he must have taken up as he hurried over. He prepared to bring it down on the doctor's head.

"STOP!"

Richard halted mid-motion.

The doctor stared up from the floor with manic eyes. His right hand – equipped with the metal device – was pointed at Richard's chest.

"That would be very ill-advised," the doctor huffed.

The device in his hand glinted and Richard saw it clearly for the first time. Five metal rings – each embedded with a small orange stone – were attached to each of the doctor's fingers and thumb. The rings were linked by a number of jointed metal stalks that converged over the back of his hand. It was a strange silver gauntlet.

Richard couldn't determine what sort of power – if any – such a device might possess; he'd certainly never heard of anything like it. Still paused in mid-motion, his anger overpowered him and, filled with fury, he brought the lamp swinging down.

In the split second it took Richard to do so, Dr Snelling's arm bucked and white light erupted blindingly from his fingers. It blasted Richard in the chest with the force of a sledgehammer.

He hurtled backwards, right through the open bedroom door, hitting the wall in the landing.

"Dear me, Walden. So you're taking the hard road."

The words spiked in Richard's ears as he lay crumpled on the floor. His head throbbed dully and he gasped for breath, winded. He tried to move, but the pain was too great. A hand gripped his throat as the doctor fell upon him.

"Always the heroes," Dr Snelling hissed, pushing his face so close to Richard's that he could see the beads of sweat clinging to his cranium. "You never learn."

"Wh—what d'you want?" Richard managed to slur.

The doctor squeezed Richard's throat. "You're going to tell me everything you know about the Sentinels," he whispered, his spittle spraying Richard's cheek.

"I—I don't know what... you're talking about," Richard panted, gagging as the doctor's fingers bit into his throat.

Dr Snelling reached down and ripped the sleeve of Richard's shirt with the metal gauntlet. A tattooed raven was on his forearm.

"There," the stocky man sighed, licking his lips. "The time for playing the fool is over, Walden."

"I've... had that for years," Richard gurgled. "Reminds me of... that poem. The famous one."

Without a word, Dr Snelling placed the gauntlet against Richard's forehead.

"No more jokes," he snarled. "Let's see how you laugh when I'm through with you."

Sparks exploded around the metal device once more. White hot energy seared Richard's mind. He screamed.

"Lucy!" he howled. "Lucy, get out of here!"

"She can't hear you, fool," Dr Snelling spat. "She's downstairs right now still stirring my tea. Do you think I'd let her hear you?"

The sparks sputtered and died.

"We are everywhere, and we are many," Dr Snelling growled. "Your confidence in all that is good and true is your ultimate downfall. You would be the wiser man by giving in."

"It doesn't matter... what you do to me... or my family, in the end... we will always win," Richard wheezed.

"It pleases me to hear you so ready to die," the doctor taunted. "I will delight in aiding you in that quest. Now talk!"

The sparks fizzed and Richard's eyes rolled back in his head. Through the blazing light, he felt something cold stirring, pressing against his skull. Where the doctor's hand pushed against his head, a wriggling invader scraped hungrily against his scalp.

Richard screamed again, battling against it, desperate to move his arms, his legs, anything that might push the doctor away. But he was paralysed. The coldness crept over him and he could no longer feel his body. Apart from his head, where the squirming, wriggling thing cracked through his skull and burrowed into his brain, invading his thoughts.

"That's it," the doctor hissed, drool escaping the corner of his mouth. A ravenous grin separated his lips. "Let me in, it'll all be over soon."

Richard fought, but there was no contest. The worm-like thing gnawed its way through the contents of his skull, ripping aside chunks of his mind. It was so strong, and the darkness that gushed over him felt suddenly inviting.

"There." Dr Snelling gave a satisfied sniff, though Richard was beyond the understanding of words. His eyes flickered, his face gaunt.

Through a haze of stars, images surfaced and the worm in his brain had stopped burrowing. The images shimmered with such speed that Richard's failing mind barely had a second to consider them, though they were startlingly familiar: a raven screeched before leaping from a branch; a cloaked, masked figure advanced toward him; his father handed him a velvet box, from which he drew a silver pendant; Lucy stood before him in a white veil; a dim room brimmed with people, adorned in silver, deep in conversation; an old-fashioned bus was parked at a kerb; a teenage boy with curly hair; and finally, lingering with significance, a rambling manor house loomed over a small village in the countryside.

Everything went black.

★

Dr Snelling fell away from his slumped victim, gasping.

"So that's where she's been hiding," he whispered. He gave an unpleasant sniggering laugh and slipped the gauntlet from his hand, casting Richard a cursory glance.

The man's eyes had been burned bone white, his face a sickening shade of grey. He showed no signs of life save the slight rise and fall of his chest.

"I promised you death," Dr Snelling told the fallen man, "but I rather feel this is a greater reward for your services to the Dark Prophets." He pottered into Patrick Walden's bedroom, whistling a jaunty tune as he packed the metal contraption into his bag. With the case in hand, he stepped over Richard's body.

"Take care, old chap," the doctor said. He descended the staircase, reaching the front door. But as he moved for the door handle—

"Dr Snelling!"

He stopped, hearing Lucy's voice behind him. A sinister smile split his lips as he saw her hurrying down the hallway.

"Dr Snelling," she said again, "you're leaving already? Won't you stay for a cup of tea?"

"Oh, I'm all done, my dear," the doctor said cheerily, giving her the toothiest of grins.

"That was quick." Lucy cast a fleeting glance up the staircase.

"Oh yes," Dr Snelling said. "Everything is quite in order, I'm very pleased."

"Is Richard still up there with Patrick?" Lucy asked.

"He is," the doctor nodded. "Why don't you take him the cup of tea you were making for me? I'm sorry I can't stay longer. I really must be off now, there are many other patients to attend to."

"Of course."

Lucy hurried to open the door for him.

"All the best," he said, winking at her from the doorstep.

"Goodbye doctor."

The tubby man lingered on the doorstep for a few minutes, his forehead scrunched up expectantly. Then came what he had been waiting for – a scream from the Walden's landing.

Beaming, the doctor turned and hopped down the garden path, whistling as he plodded down the street and was lost from sight.

★

All was dark. Nicholas lay on his back in bed watching the shadows playing across the ceiling. Twenty minutes ago he'd heard the floorboards in the landing creak as Tabatha made her way to bed, followed closely by the click of the bedroom door shutting. It had taken all of his willpower to remain in bed for this long – he knew that if Tabatha caught him wandering about the house at night there would be no end to her questioning.

His mind was whirling. He'd always felt so close to his parents, and he'd always felt – quite lovingly – that they were rather boring individuals. His father worked for a small publishing company (quite what he did there Nicholas wasn't sure), while his mother had supervised a local nursery. They had played their part in the world, and he had loved them despite their plainness. Yet now he had uncovered a secret chapter in their lives that he knew nothing about, and that for his entire life had been concealed behind a secret door.

Deciding it was safe now, Nicholas pushed back his duvet and went to his door.

Down the stairs he could see the spare room that Tabatha was currently occupying. It was quiet. The coast was as clear as it was ever going to be.

He hurried down the stairs on tiptoe. He had perfected the art of roaming the house at night unheard, having done so for years when his parents were still alive. Stalking down the landing, he found that his parents' door was still slightly open. Not wasting a second, he went inside, bending down to peer under the bed. In the darkness he could make out three distinct shapes – the objects he had left there.

Moments later, the boy returned to his bedroom with the objects in his arms. He pushed his door to and jumped back into bed, shivering in the cold as he spread the horde out in front of him. The silver raven on the cover of *The Sentinel Chronicles* shone in the moonlight. Nicholas flipped to the first page of the book.

To the Sentinel collective, whom we present the most recent journal of events.

Nicholas wondered what the Sentinel collective was. It sounded like some sort of organisation. This book – a journal of sorts detailing the events of every week in October 1983 – certainly seemed to back up that theory. He remembered that the other Sentinel volumes in the hidden room all had years marked on their spines. He wished he could go back and take a few more books, but he didn't dare risk waking Tabatha. Those cogs weren't exactly quiet.

He turned to the first entry and read by the light of the moon.

2 January, 1983

Woodpoint Prison is no more. Esus has called an emergency summit. What follows is an account of the events that led to the devastation of the prison and its inhabitants.

Ten pm Woodpoint Prison, North London. After lights out, prisoner #5532, Arnold Humphreys, reported that his cellmate, Timothy Bull (#6723), was behaving strangely. He was ordered to be quiet by the wardens.

Humphreys fell silent for a time. At 10:24 there were reports of a scream. Wardens unlocked cell #19 – the cell occupied by Humphreys and Bull – and found Humphreys crumpled in a corner with his throat torn out. After a brief tussle, Bull condemned the wardens to the same fate.

Using the keys from the dead wardens, Bull unlocked the remainder of the cells and slaughtered the inmates. He then progressed through the prison, killing anybody in his way, and eventually burned the entire complex to the ground. Of the 50 souls interred there, and the 10 guards on duty, only one of them survived – inmate Joseph Turner (#3625).

11.32am Bull was found by Sentinel Andrew Davis, resident of Croft Heights, a neighbourhood half a mile from the prison. Davis suffered a bite to the neck, but managed to knock Bull unconscious. Later, Bull was restrained, questioned and tested by Davis, who discovered that Bull had mutated. Davis believes the mutation was linked to an insect bite on his forearm. Bull displayed the same symptoms as a rabid dog, and was eventually shot dead after escaping his restraints and attempting to strangle Davis.

Nicholas stopped reading, shocked by the grisly story. The *Chronicles* seemed to be some sort of macabre horror anthology. And yet the nameless author's tone seemed assured enough, as if these were hard facts. Nicholas's insides leapt when he allowed himself to consider that the story was, in fact, true. If it was true, just what sort of organisation was this? And how were his parents involved?

Suddenly tired, he closed the book and fell back onto his pillow, pulling the duvet up around him. He pondered the ceiling and his thoughts turned to what would happen tomorrow. He thought about the bus journey, and how a stranger would be accompanying him. Richard somebody. He realised with a jolt that he didn't want to leave. He wanted to stay in the house where the memories of his parents were most vivid.

He tried to imagine what the next day would hold, but found he couldn't. What worried him most was his godmother, of whom he knew nothing about. He remembered the strange smile Sam had worn when he had mentioned her in the garden. Sam obviously liked her, and yet had remained tight-lipped, refusing to tell Nicholas anything. Would this woman know anything about his parents? Would she have answers? Nicholas knew that his parents had been going to visit her; that much he had learned from the letter. But why had they never mentioned her to him?

Nicholas rolled over in bed, throwing his leg outside the covers. He felt hot and anxious. He didn't think sleep would ever come.

Something caught the corner of the boy's eye and Nicholas's head spun toward the window. He threw himself out of bed and rushed over. A black shape swooped through the air and was lost in the darkness.

It had looked like a raven.

CHAPTER SIX
Due Departure

THE EARLY MORNING HOURS WERE CRISP and cool. The sky was white and stretched taut like a bed sheet. Sam sat at the kitchen table reading the newspaper by the light of a pale dawn. The cuffs of his shirt frayed around his wrists, waiting to be fastened.

He sighed and put the paper down, crunching on a bit of toast. The authorities were still poring over the site of the train wreck. Sam suspected they wouldn't find anything of note. Whoever had caused the crash had been canny enough to plan it, which meant they would also have been canny enough to take precautions. The one thing the authorities did seem to know was that the car that had been on the track belonged to a young man. Clive Kelly. A waiter from Cambridge. Naturally, blame was being heaped squarely on his shoulders. Or, it would be if the police had any idea where he was.

Clive Kelly. Sam rolled the name around his mouth with the toast. It wasn't familiar. Certainly not a Sentinel. Which didn't mean the young man didn't know about Sentinels.

Sam tossed the remainder of his toast onto the plate. It was cold anyway. He couldn't seem to extricate the Hallows from his thoughts. The letter from Maxwell. It had been written on the day of the accident, like a hurried after-thought, perhaps even posted as the Hallows made their way to the station. That would explain why Max hadn't phoned or met with him. It was an act of desperation.

Something wasn't right, that much was clear. Something somewhere had gone horribly wrong, and now Nicholas had no parents. He could expect things to worsen, too, Sam imagined. The train crash felt like a beginning. A prelude. A warning.

At least the boy was leaving today; getting away from the city. To safety. And Sam could concentrate on finding out what really happened to that train.

The old man was just lifting a tepid cup of tea to his lips when the phone trilled. The cup froze and an old maxim Sam's mother had uttered many decades ago spilled to the front of his mind: *No good news rises with the sun.*

Setting the cup down, Sam went into the hall.

"Wilkins," he said gruffly into the receiver. His brow furrowed. "No, I was up, you're not disturbing me. What's the matter?" The frown burrowed deeper. "Don't go anywhere; I'll be there within the half hour."

Shakily, he replaced the receiver. In the mirror above the table, his drawn, tired reflection grimaced back at him.

"Pull yourself together man," he barked. He squinted at his watch and tutted. He had little time, even at this early hour.

Half an hour later, Sam paced up to the front door of the Waldens' semi-detached house, pulling his collar up against a wind that seemed intent on carving him in half.

He stood there for a few moments before knocking, aware that something unpleasant could be lying in wait for him. He dreaded to think what.

He rapped firmly three times.

There came the sound of hurried movement from inside the house, and then the clatter of locks being drawn back.

The change in Lucy Walden was startling. She seemed to have gone from beauty queen to old maid over night. Her hair was scraped back in a ponytail, her make-up free face haggard.

Sam felt the surprise etch his face and quickly attempted to eliminate it. "Lucy," he said, and found no more words would come.

"Mr Wilkins," Lucy said. "Please come in."

He went inside, removing the beaten fedora. He gripped it before him like a shield. Lucy looked so different that he couldn't help but feel on edge.

"Richard's upstairs," Lucy said simply. "He's... Well, he's..." She stopped, pressing her lips together.

"I'll just go up and see him, can't keep the old chap waiting," Sam said with forced cheerfulness.

Lucy nodded and disappeared into the sitting room. Sam rocked on his heels as he contemplated the dim staircase. "Right then," he murmured, setting off.

When he came to the open doorway he stopped. From here he could see into the bedroom, and despite the distance between them, Sam could tell how ill Richard was. The younger man was laid out on his back in bed, a white duvet emblazoned with sunflowers draped over him. His skin was a sickly grey, his cheeks sunken and skeletal. Fine beads of sweat clung to his forehead and deathly groans entered and escaped his throat. His glasses sat watching him from the bedside cabinet.

"Dear, dear," Sam clucked, entering the room furtively. "Richard, old boy, what have they done to you?"

The closer Sam got, the more ill Richard was revealed to be. When he reached the head of the bed, the old man found that his legs would no longer hold him and he sank into the chair at the bedside.

"It was the doctor."

Sam glanced up as a curt voice jabbed from the doorway.

There, lingering in the half-shadows by the doorframe was Patrick Walden. Despite being of a similar age to him, Patrick's mind had quietly fled years ago. Remorsefully, Sam remembered when Richard's father had been the sharpest of their circle. Patrick's strategies had always been the best, and he was the first anybody came to in a crisis. Now he could barely remember his own name. Time was unspeakably cruel.

"Doctor?" Sam asked, finding that his voice came out as if he were addressing a child. He knew that the old, healthy Patrick would have hated him for that, but there was no helping it.

The other man didn't seem to notice. Patrick sucked in his bottom lip and looked like he was about to spit on the carpet. "Filthy doctor tried to hurt me," he said plainly. "My son, him there in the bed–" he pointed to make sure Sam knew who he was referring to, "–tried to save me. He ain't in good shape now, oh no. Foolish lad. Foolish but brave."

"A doctor did this to Richard?" Sam asked, unsure if Patrick's ramblings contained any truth.

"Probably a devil," Patrick snarled. "Can't trust no-one these days, them's all devils."

Sam inclined a humouring nod; the other man had sense enough to realise that at least. His gaze strayed from Patrick to his son laid out on the bed. A doctor abusing his own patients? The very suggestion troubled him to the core. He tried to figure out what possible course of events could have landed Richard, as poorly as he now looked, in this bed. What did this mean?

"Dad, come on now," came Lucy's hushed, weary voice. "Leave Mr Wilkins alone for a bit, will you? He'll talk to you later."

"Filthy doctor." Patrick scowled and disappeared down the landing.

"He said something about a doctor?" Sam ventured.

Lucy sagged against the doorframe. She nodded. "He's known our family for years, even before we got married. We trusted him. But now look at us." She raised a hand to her mouth.

Sam couldn't believe what he was hearing. "I knew evil was insidious, but this…?" He was transfixed by Richard's emaciated face. Blinking, he averted his gaze. "Has anybody been to see him, to help him?"

"You're the only person I called," Lucy said. "The only person I could think of to call. How can I trust anybody after what happened? I don't know who to trust anymore."

"You were wise not to call anyone," Sam said in a hushed tone, as if he were worried he might disturb his friend's slumber. Bitterly Sam realised such worries were redundant. Richard looked all but on the brink of death.

"How about a cup of tea?" he suggested.

Lucy nodded and the old man eased himself from the chair. As he left the room, he cast a sorrowful glance back at the figure in the bed. "Goodbye, old boy," he murmured. Then he closed the door.

In the kitchen, Sam watched Lucy put the kettle on. It steamed up the window, obscuring his view of the back garden.

"Dark times are approaching, there's no doubt," he breathed.

"It's ridiculous," Lucy said, slouching against the sideboard. "All I can think about is that we're meant to be going to the theatre on Saturday, and Richard will be so disappointed. We don't get to go out much, with Patrick. We needed that night. I'm a horrible person."

Sam didn't say anything. He understood all too well the dark net of thoughts that fell with tragedy.

"Who do you think the doctor was? I mean, really?" Lucy asked.

"This was no random attack, that much I think we can be certain of," Sam said. "This has all the markings of a Harvester."

If possible, Lucy turned paler than she already was. "I was worried you'd say that," she said quietly. Her jaw tightened, became stone. "A Harvester, in my own house–"

She banged at the sideboard and the teaspoons tinkled on their saucers.

"Damn them all." This she said through clenched teeth.

"Indeed," Sam concurred. "They're a poison on this Earth. There's no doubt in my mind that the doctor you speak of –"

"Dr Snelling."

"Dr Snelling," Sam continued, "knew you were of Sentinel lineage the moment you stepped foot in his practice. Harvesters are increasingly accurate in their ability to root out those of Sentinel ancestry – perhaps the rumours of their telepathic abilities are not altogether unfounded."

Harvesters. Sam shuddered. He barely believed it himself. Yet that was the only reasonable explanation for Richard's sorry state. He couldn't remember the last time he'd encountered one of their number, but this smacked of their work. The toxic stench of it filled the house. They were bounty hunters. If a Sentinel was one side of the coin, a Harvester was the other. A Harvester's sole purpose was to track down and eradicate Sentinels. They were human, mortal, but corrupted by their devotion to the Dark Prophets, the heinous gods that they sacrificed Sentinels to.

It had been years since a Harvester attack, though. Many in the Sentinel community considered them if not extinct, then resolutely put in their place. If they were surfacing...

"But… Patrick always told me that Harvesters discard each of their identities as often as a snake sheds its skin," Lucy said. "We knew him as Dr Snelling for years. Decades."

The kettle clicked and Lucy made the tea, setting a teacup in front of Sam before seating herself opposite him.

"He had quite a catch in you two," Sam murmured, stirring his tea. "He was trailing you, siphoning information. Perhaps even studying you."

"Are we really that exposed?" Lucy demanded shrilly. "Can we truly be so powerless?"

"The power of the Dark Prophets is growing," Sam said. "I can feel it in my bones, no matter how old they are."

He gulped the tea – the subject left his mouth dry.

"Snelling made his move for a reason. It has been too long since a Harvester surfaced for attack – there must be grounds for it."

"They're getting stronger, aren't they?" Lucy said in a hushed tone. She hadn't touched her own tea. It sat in front of her, steam curling question marks between them.

"Yes. And more assured," Sam said. "The days when the Adepts and their Harvesters feared the authority of the Sentinels are waning, almost extinct if their recent activity is anything to go by."

A grave silence descended on them and they sat with their own gloomy thoughts.

"Do you think what happened to Richard has something to do with the train wreck?" Lucy asked.

"Oh yes," Sam nodded, the two incidents slotting together in his mind like the pieces of a jigsaw. "The train wreck was no accident either, whatever the press believe. Max and Anita were doomed the second they boarded that train; it was they who were targeted on that occasion, along with the other Sentinels on board. I'm still not sure how the agents of the Dark Prophets knew there were Sentinels on the train, though. Perhaps their powers are greater than we give them credit for. They certainly didn't know they were travelling to the summit; if they had, perhaps the Hallows would have been permitted to live so that the Harvesters might follow them to their destination."

"Which, if possible, would have created an even worse situation," Lucy lamented. "Tragedy everywhere," she sighed. "Will it never end?"

"End?" Sam said. "This is just the beginning. Oh, it will end eventually, that we can be certain of. But at what cost? That is the question we should be asking."

The elderly man stared into his empty cup, feeling equally depleted. He couldn't remember ever feeling as disheartened as he did now; not even after Judith's passing. Three friends in just over a week. They had been as much a part of his family as any blood relative. All gone. Or near enough. His mood swung pendulously between angry and dejected in an unbalanced manner that was surely not healthy. But what good was he to anybody in such a sorry state? The dark moments would come, sure as the rain, but then he'd pick himself up again. It wasn't over, not by a long shot.

"Would you like another cup?" Lucy asked, standing.

"Thank you, but no," Sam said, forcing a smile. "I must be off."

"What'll happen about the boy?" Lucy asked, accompanying the old man to the door.

"I'll take him," Sam said. "In Richard's place." He paused to open the front door, then added: "I have a friend. She may be able to help with Richard. I can't promise anything, but there's always a chance."

To his surprise, Lucy took the old man's hand in her own and squeezed it warmly. "Thank you for everything, Mr Wilkins. You're a good friend. We owe you so much."

"You owe me nothing," Sam said, extricating his hand and waving it in front of him dismissively. "When I return I'll pay my friend a visit."

"Well, we'll be here when you get back," Lucy commented dourly.

"Never give up hope," Sam said.

Replacing the fedora, he stepped out into the rain.

★

It had been a sleepless night and Nicholas would have rather stayed cocooned in his bed than face the day. But Tabatha was having none of it. Even as the first shafts of light were edging through Nicholas's curtains, Tabatha had swept them open and badgered the boy until finally, relenting, he had fallen out of bed and traipsed downstairs to eat breakfast. The cooked sausages, tomatoes and bacon merely turned his stomach, though, as his thoughts lingered on what the day would hold.

"Eat up," Tabatha insisted, setting a glass of orange juice down in front of him. "You'll need the energy."

Grudgingly, Nicholas forced the food down and spent the next hour packing. By eight a.m. a large suitcase and a backpack were sitting in the front entrance ready for the journey. The latter contained *The Sentinel Chronicles*, the raven pendant, and the small locked box, which Nicholas had managed to slip in when Tabatha had been occupied cleaning the kitchen.

As promised, Sam arrived at nine o'clock, drenched through.

"All ready, are we?" the old man asked, rainwater pooling at his feet in the hallway.

"Ready," Nicholas confirmed. He eyed the older man — though Sam appeared as buoyant as ever, there was a tightness to his smile. "Are you okay?" the boy asked.

"Hmm? Top of the world, lad," Sam replied, but he turned away to pick up the suitcase as he said it. When he moved to take the backpack, Nicholas seized it quickly.

"I'll get that," he said, shouldering the bag.

The sound of hurried footsteps echoed into the hallway, and Tabatha came rushing down the stairs clutching something in her hands.

"Here," she said breathlessly, "you'll be wanting this." She thrust a battered old teddy bear in front of her. Nicholas eyed it, then Tabatha. The woman was more flustered than he had ever seen her.

"Thanks, don't know how I missed that," he said, stuffing it into his backpack.

Tabatha bit her lip. "You're so brave," she said. "My brave little soldier." As if unable to contain herself anymore, she grabbed Nicholas and squeezed him to her in a claustrophobic embrace. Nicholas's eyes almost popped out of his head. He patted the woman on the back and eased himself out of her clutching hands.

"So this is it," Tabatha gulped.

"Seems that way," Nicholas agreed. He felt an unexpected lump in his throat as he realised that he wouldn't be seeing Tabatha again for some time – he'd grown accustomed to her eccentric ways. He swallowed the lump down. "Thanks for… you know, everything," he mumbled.

"I wouldn't have had it any other way," the woman gushed, wiping her tears on a handful of her blonde hair. "Now just you be careful. Don't go talking to any strangers or anything." She fussed with the scarf about Nicholas's neck, puffing it up under his chin.

"I won't, don't worry."

Tabatha nodded, her cheeks glowing red. It seemed she was fit to burst. Nicholas looked pleadingly at Sam, but found that the old man – who would normally have found Tabatha's fanatical behaviour chuckle-worthy – appeared to be lost in his own thoughts.

"Shall we be off then?" Sam said, opening the front door. Nicholas eyed the dismal day that sat on the doorstep and wished more than ever that he didn't have to leave.

"Seeya," he said to Tabatha.

"'Bye Nicholas, safe journey," the woman returned, dabbing at her tears once more.

"Farewell Miss Blittmore," Sam put in, tipping his hat to her. "I'll be back to discuss the house another day. Just pop the keys through the letterbox."

Tabatha nodded mid-sniffle.

"I'm just going to tidy a few more things then I'll lock the place up," she told him.

Sam directed Nicholas to the black Morris Minor waiting at the kerb.

"There's a slight change of plan," he told him, setting Nicholas's suitcase down on the pavement as he searched for his keys.

"Change?"

"As you know, originally my good friend Richard was to travel with you," Sam explained. "However, this I'm afraid has become an impossibility." Nicholas noticed the strange tone in which the elderly man said this, and wondered if that was the reason he seemed drained today. "In his stead, I shall be accompanying you."

Nicholas's face lit up immediately, and without thinking he flung his arms about the old man. Sam appeared taken aback and coughed deep in his throat until the boy let go.

"Yes, well," he murmured, clearing his throat again and finally pulling the keys from his pocket. "We had best make haste if we are to reach the bus in time."

Grinning, Nicholas got into the car. All his worries seemed to have suddenly evaporated – if Sam was with him, he had nothing to be anxious about. In fact, he couldn't have asked for better company.

The Morris Minor pulled away from the kerb and Nicholas waved out of the window until he couldn't see Tabatha anymore.

CHAPTER SEVEN
Sabotage

SOMETHING STRANGE HAPPENED WHEN NICHOLAS AND Sam went to catch the bus. Instead of clambering aboard a coach at Drummer Street, Cambridge's bustling bus station, Sam drove them to a poky side street just off the green known as Parker's Piece.

He pulled the car up behind an old-fashioned, pillar-box red coach, which Nicholas eyed with interest. It looked like something from the seventies; a squat vehicle with curved edges and a large grille at the front, under which was stamped 'ECW'. The panel above the windshield that usually displayed the bus's destination was conspicuously blank.

"Here we are," Sam said, easing himself out of the car.

Nicholas got out onto the pavement.

"This?" he said, gesturing sceptically at the decrepit motor. "This is our ride?"

"Lovely, isn't she?" Sam beamed, popping open the Morris Minor's boot and retrieving their suitcases.

"It looks even older than, well, you," Nicholas said. Though it was cleaner than any bus he'd ever seen, the vehicle looked like it had been off the road for decades. Less a working means of transport than a tourist attraction, it probably spent most of its time being trundled out at those motor fairs that middle-aged men flocked to with cameras.

"Easy there, lad, you'll hurt her feelings," Sam winked. He locked the car and went to the coach door, then rapped on the glass. A man who was already sitting in the driver's seat pulled a lever by the gearshift. The door folded inward to reveal the driver. He was in his fifties, wearing a faded cap. His top lip was almost completely lost under a bristly grey slug of a moustache.

"Morning," Sam greeted him. "Come on then, Nicholas."

Still regarding the bus cynically, Nicholas followed Sam. The driver, a somewhat dishevelled fellow Nicholas noted when he got a better look at him, squinted curiously up at the boy with pink-rimmed eyes. When the boy returned his stare, the driver quickly went back to scrutinising a map that he'd unfurled on top of the steering wheel.

Nicholas traipsed after Sam down the aisle. They stopped by four bright-coloured and clearly seventies-era seats set around a faux-wood table.

"This'll do," Sam said, slotting his box-like suitcase into the overhead storage space. "Pop your things away and I'll have a word with the driver."

"Why do you—" Nicholas began, but the old man had already marched off to the front of the bus. Warily, the boy stowed his luggage next to Sam's, seating himself by the window. He peered over the tops of the seats, watching Sam converse with the man in the cap. What was he doing? They seemed to be getting on like old friends.

Nicholas squinted, attempting to read Sam's lips, but it wasn't easy. He thought he saw the old man mutter "no stopping no matter what", but that didn't seem right.

Why would Sam be telling the driver what to do?

Patting the other man on the shoulder, Sam loped back to Nicholas and sat down.

"What were you talking to him for?" Nicholas asked.

"Hmm?" Sam murmured, as if he hadn't heard properly. "Oh, just this and that. Old person stuff, boring, you know."

"Do you know him?"

"Oh yes, we go way back. He's doing this as a favour."

"That's a pretty big favour."

Sam didn't say anything and Nicholas regarded the older man doubtfully. He decided to let it lie – for now anyway. He had plenty of other, more important questions to grill Sam with during the journey. It was probably best he didn't rile him before they'd even set off, no matter how odd this all was.

The bus was soon grumbling through the traffic-clogged streets of Cambridge. The day was grim and wet, but that hadn't dissuaded people from leaving their homes – in truth, Cambridge was busier than ever. The fact that the roads had succumbed to the weather didn't help; no end of roadblocks forced the driver to manoeuvre through numerous maddening diversions. It took them almost an hour to reach the city's outskirts, and when they finally left behind the crammed streets, the clear country roads offered a welcome reprieve.

Sam barely spoke at all during that first hour. His tired gaze lingered on the dreary morning sky, his expression as troubled as the heavens. Sighing, Nicholas propped his elbows up on the table. He sensed this was not a good time to bring up the hidden study in his parents' bedroom.

"I am sorry lad," Sam said, scratching the back of his head. "I've not been the best of company, have I? Got things preying on my mind."

"It's okay." Nicholas played with the table edge for a minute.

"Maybe you should get some shut eye, lad. You look tired."

Nicholas nodded, understanding that Sam wasn't in the mood for idle chatter. He shuffled down in his seat and buried his nose in his scarf.

Closing his eyes, he attempted to shut out the sound of the creaking, empty bus seats, but he couldn't help wondering what was bothering Sam. He was usually so animated; a busy person who loved nothing more than being busy. Nicholas had never seen him so withdrawn. Perhaps his parents' deaths had affected Sam more than Nicholas realised. He'd been friends with them ever since Nicholas was a baby. Fifteen years. It was a long time. Fifteen years ago Sam Wilkins would have been in his mid-fifties. Nicholas wondered what had brought the spirited middle-ager into the lives of his young parents. The subject had rarely been touched upon, and on the exceptional occasions that it had, the conversation had always been discreetly steered in a different direction. Nicholas knew that Sam had lost his wife around the same time that he'd met his parents, but that was all.

Nicholas snapped out of his reverie. What was that? At first he thought he'd heard somebody speaking, but as he scrutinised the interior of the bus, he found that Sam was immersed in window watching, while the bus driver was concentrating on the road. Even the world outside seemed quiet, cushioned by lethargic clouds.

Yet Nicholas felt restless. A dull prickling sensation stirred in his belly, and he shuddered.

Then, just like the day he'd found himself drawn to his parents' bedroom door, Nicholas's legs wanted him to move. They positively ached, and he was powerless to deny them. Standing, he swayed towards the back of the bus, as if a piece of string had unravelled from his chest and was pulling him there.

The boy stared out of the rear window. The road was bathed in the eerie scarlet glow of the vehicle's taillights.

Nicholas pressed his forehead against the glass, lightheaded, his breath steaming up the window. He couldn't blink. His eyelids were pinned back and he gawped dumbly out at the road without knowing why.

There's something out there.

He pulled abruptly away from the window, blinking out of the daze.

What had just happened? A wave of nausea cramped his stomach. His emotions were all tangled and he couldn't think straight. Whatever had pulled him to the back of the bus had been the same thing that helped him uncover the hidden study. But what was it?

There was only one thing that Nicholas was sure of, though he couldn't explain how he knew it – there was something out there in the countryside, and it was following them.

Following me.

"What's happening?" Nicholas muttered.

"Nicholas? You alright, lad?"

Sam was craning over his seat.

"Fine," Nicholas managed to say. "I'm fine." He staggered back.

"You look pale, are you feeling alright?" Sam asked, scrutinising the boy's face.

"I'm fine, maybe a bit travel sick," Nicholas said. "These lights are giving me a headache."

The feeble flush of the overhead lights was depressing, and Sam didn't seem to have any trouble believing him.

"I know how you feel, lad." He called to the bus driver. "I say, I don't suppose you could dim the lights?"

The driver said nothing, but blinked at Sam in his rear-view mirror before nodding. He turned a dial and the lights softened.

"Ah, that seems to have done the trick," Sam said. He smiled at Nicholas and seemed to notice that the boy was giving him a particularly intense look. "What's on your mind, lad?"

Nicholas lowered his gaze, then looked back at the old man. "If I ask you something, will you promise to give me an honest answer?"

Sam stiffened ever so slightly at the request, and he didn't blink for a very long time. Then he said: "I'll see what I can do. What do you want to ask me?"

"I was in Mum and Dad's room the other day and I found something, a hidden room behind the wall. It was full of books like this..."

Nicholas reached into his rucksack and pulled out the *Sentinel Chronicles*, handing it to Sam. The older man flicked through the book, his eyebrows arching in what could have been surprise or merely feigned interest – Nicholas wasn't sure which. "Do you know what it is?"

Sam rested the book on the tabletop. "I couldn't say," he said. "It looks like some sort of journal."

Nicholas tried to read the elderly man's expression, but it was like scrutinising a painting.

"I also found these," he continued, retrieving the raven pendant and the mystery box from his bag. "They were supposed to be for my sixteenth birthday – that's what it said on the wrapping, anyway. I remember Mum used to wear a necklace just like this."

"That she did," Sam nodded. He took the pendant and stared down at it in silence. He held it almost reverently, Nicholas noticed.

"Do you know what they're about?" Nicholas asked. "You probably knew them better than me, and I think they were hiding something."

Sam sat very still for what felt to Nicholas like an eternity, his downturned gaze fixed on the pendant. Finally, the man heaved a great sigh and murmured: "I really couldn't say, lad."

His tone was measured and kind.

"Please, Mr Wilkins… Sam," Nicholas pleaded. "If they were going to give me these things when I turned sixteen they were obviously going to tell me what they had been hiding. If you know anything, I want to know. I need to. They were my parents."

He could hear the desperation in his voice and it sounded childish, but he didn't care. Things were happening that he couldn't understand and Sam was his last hope. If Sam couldn't help, nobody could.

The old man peered down at the necklace for a moment longer, then passed it back to Nicholas. "It's a mystery," he said. "If I could help you, Nicholas, I would. You know that."

Nicholas's eyes were suddenly bright with tears. If he could just see what Sam was thinking – he obviously knew something, and he was keeping it from him just as his parents had.

"You know something, I know you do," he said through gritted teeth.

"I know lots of things, that is true." Sam inclined a nod. "But alas, nothing that might shed light on those trinkets of yours."

"I remember you telling me stories when I was younger," Nicholas continued, though despair was quickly flooding through him. "About monsters and heroes, and how the world used to be before–"

"Fiction, lad. Stories," Sam said gently. "Fascinating, yes. Joyous escapes from the drudgery of the real world, certainly. But not real, my boy. You can't put faith in such things."

"No, they were real."

"You're tired, lad. Try to get some sleep," Sam said. He was resigned now – the energy seemed to have left him once more. "We'll be there soon."

Nicholas thrust the objects back into his bag. He wiped hastily at his cheeks and sank down in his seat. Anger and annoyance hammered in his chest. He knew Sam was keeping something from him, and he didn't understand why. It was too much. His parents had lived a whole life separate from him; that much he understood. It hurt that they'd kept it from him. It hurt that they'd never had the chance to talk to him about it, and now even Sam was refusing to tell him anything. Nicholas hated them all.

Outside, the sky hurled snow to the ground.

Nicholas closed his eyes, but he could still feel Sam's presence across the table. For the first time, he wondered why Sam was accompanying him on the trip at all. Why had anybody assumed Nicholas required a chaperone to begin with? Surely a fifteen-year-old boy could manage a coach trip alone. Nicholas's mind probed for an answer, and like the realisation that somebody was following them, an answer suddenly rang through as clear as a bell.

They're protecting me.

Like so many other recent discoveries, the realisation felt heavy with truth. His parents had been protecting him from whatever other life they were leading; his mother had looked sad and scared when she had left him that final morning; Sam knew his godmother, but wouldn't reveal anything about her, just as he knew what the raven pendant meant. All of them – *all of them* – were keeping things from him, and it was all to protect him. But why? And from what?

With these thoughts occupying his mind, Nicholas slithered into a fitful slumber.

★

There were three of them and they were whispering.

About him.

He strained to hear, but the whispers were like the wind. They rose and fell. He couldn't grasp their meaning. He didn't know them. But they were murmuring about him. And they knew everything about him. They knew where he was going. What he meant. What he was.

They knew his purpose.

Nicholas awoke with a start. He gripped the back of the bus seat, the fog of the dream lingering. Then everything came back into focus.

Relaxing, he collapsed back into the seat.

"Bad dream?"

Nicholas looked across at Sam and nodded. "It felt so real. They were whispering about me."

Sam moved in his seat, making the worn leather creak under his weight – it was almost as if he had gone to sit suddenly upright but caught himself at the last moment. In his confused state, Nicholas didn't notice.

"Who? Who was whispering about you?" Sam asked. He looked worried, but for once Nicholas didn't pick up on the tightness in his chaperone's tone.

"The trees," Nicholas said. "Three trees, all huddled together like... women. And they were talking about me. They knew me."

A rumour of a smile crept onto Sam's lips, and the leather seat creaked again as he relaxed back into it. "How unusual," he remarked. "That head of yours is quite the mystery."

Nicholas looked out of the window and was surprised to find that snow was flurrying heavily now. A pallid mantle had settled upon the world, making it appear strange in the gloomy afternoon half-light. Time seemed to linger confused between night and day.

"Snow," the boy murmured. "Again."

"Indeed," Sam commented. "It seems we're to be denied yet another summer."

"Two weeks ago it was thirty degrees," Nicholas said. "We all went to the park for a picnic… I got sunburnt."

Sam chuckled, then grew serious. "The road is beginning to ice over," he said. "I would have advised the driver to stop, but we don't have much further to go."

Nicholas nodded. Then, inexplicably, that dull, prickling pain returned in his stomach.

"Are you alright, lad? You've gone dreadful pale again."

"I– I don't feel right," Nicholas said. A swell of nausea coursed through him. His vision darkened and he put a hand to his forehead. His skin was clammy and cold. He saw red. The hot red of the bus's taillights on the road. And another red. Darker and glittering.

Something's wrong.

"You don't look right, do you want water?" Sam offered.

"I– I think we need to stop the bus," Nicholas said, his vision swimming alarmingly. "There's something–"

BAM!

Before Nicholas could finish the thought, a horrendous explosion rent the air. The bus lurched on the icy road.

Nicholas and Sam were thrown against their seats.

"What's going on?" Nicholas cried.

"It sounds like one of the tyres has blown," Sam said.

The bus careered across the road like an enraged bull. The driver pumped the pedals and spun the steering wheel, but the vehicle skated precariously over the road and he could do nothing to bring it under control.

As the bus pitched over a bump, Nicholas was thrown against the window so hard that the breath was knocked from him.

"He... he can't stop it," Nicholas gasped, clutching at the back of the seat. The jerky motions tossed him about, and the seat's metal frame jabbed him painfully as he was thrown repeatedly against it. The vehicle hit another bump and Nicholas's bags tumbled into the aisle.

"Hold on!" Sam yelled.

Nicholas watched the driver frantically playing with the bus's gears, but still they sped across the frozen road.

"Come on, you clapped out thing," the driver bellowed.

He stopped and squinted, as if he'd spotted something on the road. *What is it?* Nicholas thought uneasily. He saw the driver pumping at the brakes again, but the bus ploughed onwards. The driver said something under his breath, then jerked the steering wheel to the right. The bus's wheels turned on the road but the vehicle failed to change direction, merely skating across the ice.

"What's going on?" Nicholas exclaimed.

"I don't know," Sam replied. "Just hold on!"

Nicholas craned over the seats, attempting to see whatever it was that the driver had seen.

Something was caught in the headlights. Somebody standing in the middle of the road.

It was a woman and she was smiling.

At the last possible moment, she stepped out of the bus's path, her crimson gown billowing behind her. And there, ahead, was a sharp bend in the road.

Sam squinted through the windscreen and his face hardened.

"Get down, boy!" he yelled. "Down!"

Nicholas didn't waste time asking questions. He threw himself down. Under the table he saw Sam do the same.

He squeezed his eyes shut.

The bus pummelled into the bend in the road, hitting the embankment at the roadside and bucking alarmingly upwards. The front of the vehicle ricocheted up into the air, its back wheels still sliding on the icy road. Then with a THUMP the back wheels struck the grassy bank and the bus catapulted forwards.

There was a moment of stillness as the vehicle fell through the air.

Then- CRUNCH. The bus crashed down into the ditch at the roadside. It crumpled on impact, rocking onto its side and rolling over in the wide, muddy ditch. Finally it came to a standstill.

There was blackness. And throbbing pain.

Nicholas lay still. He couldn't move. He couldn't see. All he knew was that his whole body was suddenly heavy. Aching. His clothes pinned him down.

There came a rasping breath nearby, followed quickly by a cough.

Nicholas opened his eyes. It took him a moment to realise where he was, his surroundings had changed so much. Up on the ceiling were rows of crumpled bus seats and tables, and all around him were splinters of glass. Except it wasn't the ceiling of the bus above him; it was the floor. The bus had landed upside down and he was lying on the hard metal of the roof.

The cough came again and Nicholas turned his head. Sam lay a few feet away. The old man looked as beaten up as Nicholas felt – his eyes were closed and there was an angry red slash on his cheek. But he was alive.

"Sam," Nicholas managed to rasp.

He could practically see the old man's mind willing himself to move. Finally, Sam's eyelids trembled open and he struggled to focus groggily on him.

"Nicholas," Sam said, and coughed again. "You... you alright?"

"Been better," Nicholas replied. He tried to move, but his muscles screamed at him to stop. He lay there motionless.

"Agreed. Just try–" Sam's head twitched to one side. "Shhh."

Nicholas held his breath. Then he heard it too – very softly, but with growing clarity. The patter of soft footfalls.

Then a new sound tore into the silence – that of ripping, screeching metal. It made Nicholas's teeth knock against one another.

The bus shuddered and a blast of cold air hit him in the face. The boy squinted down to the front of the bus where the noise seemed to have originated. He frowned. The door had been ripped from its frame. There was another whisper of hushed movement and a silhouette appeared in the doorway.

Somebody's here to help us!

The stranger swept into the crumpled bus.

It was the outline of a woman. Mountainous curls of soft hair framed the silhouetted head, snake-like in the dim light. Nicholas watched the newcomer as she peered at the bus driver's seat above. He could just make out the obscure form of a slumped body, held in place upside down by the seatbelt.

A voice hissed.

"Sentinel pig."

A shiver ran through him, as if icy fingers had caressed his spine. That wasn't the voice of a rescuer. Not any rescuer he'd choose to come to his aid, anyhow. He watched as the woman reached for the slumped body in the driving seat and pulled it by the throat into the aisle.

"Please," a choked voice cried. It was the bus driver. "Please... Help me."

"Help you?" a voice spat in reply, and the curls were tossed back to release a scathing laugh. "Help you?"

"Please... please..."

The face of the silhouetted woman moved closer to that of the man in her grasp so that they were almost touching. Nicholas saw her raise another hand to the man's face and caress his cheek.

Then she tore his throat out.

"NO!" Nicholas cried.

The woman spun and dropped the lifeless body.

Sunlight finally broke through the clouds, illuminating her face.

Nicholas gasped. He couldn't help it. She was the most beautiful creature he had ever seen. Pearly skin shimmered in the light, her proud countenance framed by ruby curls. Her eyes sparkled like the diamonds in her crimson dress.

Nicholas felt like he'd been punched in the gut. Couldn't breathe. Couldn't think.

"There," the woman purred, taking measured steps into the bus. "There you are."

"Stay back!" Sam warned, though his voice contained none of the authority he had surely intended it to.

The woman smiled and her loveliness increased tenfold. "Do you fear me?" she teased, peering down her nose at him. "Am I feared by those who seek my demise?"

Nicholas watched her unhurried approach, his mouth half open. She was mesmerising. He forgot everything. The pain. The bus. The world. It all fell away around her until there was only the woman; stark and red and impossible.

"I do not fear you, hag," Sam sputtered.

"Lies!" she bellowed. Glass crunched under her feet as she loomed toward them. "All men fear me. You're all worms, writhing in pitiful worship."

"I bow to none but the Trinity themselves! Nicholas, stay away from her. Don't look at her."

The woman's eyes slid from the old man to the boy.

"Nicholas," she whispered. "Such a noble name. I wonder if you will die with the nobility it suggests?"

"You'll not touch him, witch," Sam's voice barked. Nicholas could barely hear it.

"We have searched too long and hard to give up now," the woman purred. "How interesting that he was so easily discovered, even after all your efforts." She winked at Sam. "You're losing your touch."

Now she was standing over Nicholas, and he was lost in the depths of her cat-like eyes. Enraptured. Unable to move. She stooped down and cupped his chin in her hand. Her skin was ice cold and he melted into it.

"Just a child," she murmured quietly, searching his young face. "All this time we have feared you, sought you, and you're nothing more than a human child."

"Get away from him!"

Nicholas was unaware of the sound of crunching glass and stomping footsteps behind him. All that existed in his world now was this enchanting creature. He could happily lie here for the rest of his life.

Before he knew what was happening, a dark shape hurtled over him and barrelled into the woman.

Sam and the woman tumbled across the hard metal of the bus ceiling.

Nicholas blinked sluggishly and shook his head. *What was going on?*

He turned towards the scuffle and saw two bodies crash together at the front of the bus. The woman in red landed on top of Sam. One of her hands went to his neck and squeezed while the other pressed down on his chest.

"Fool," she spat. "Nothing will come between me and the boy. Especially not a decrepit old corpse like you." She turned her nails inward against his chest and the sharp tips sliced through his clothing.

Sam gasped and swung upward with his left hand. There came a bone-crunching thwack as he struck the woman over the head with a heavy object, and she crashed backward. She hit the side of the vehicle, a previously intact window shattering under her weight.

"Nicholas," Sam called, "here, lad."

He fumbled with the object that he'd used against his attacker – it was his old-fashioned suitcase. The old man's hands shook as he struggled with the catches on the side.

Nicholas heaved himself to his feet, but even as he did so the entire vehicle creaked. There was the sound of complaining metal as the battered bus roof weakened under the weight pressing down from above.

"Hurry!" Sam yelled. He flipped open the lid of the case.

Nicholas took a step, but before he could advance any further his path was blocked. The woman stood coiled, as if she were about to pounce. The tussle with Sam had left her breathless and glowing – she had enjoyed it.

"Nicholasss," she hissed. "You won't get away. I can smell it on you; in your veins, your skin, your hair. You're different."

Nicholas stopped still, bewitched by the murky spirals of her eyes. "Different," he murmured.

"You feel it," she hummed. "I see it in you. It's printed in every fibre of your being."

"Leave him, she-devil!" Sam's voice roared.

She ignored the old man. "You're dangerous," she whispered. "You're a threat to the world, Nicholas."

Nicholas suddenly felt only four years old. A child in an adult's world. *She knew.* She knew everything that he'd been feeling, all of the strange things that had been happening to him.

BLAM!

A flash of orange lit the inside of the bus and shocked Nicholas out of the woman's grip. And then he saw her face. It had gone blank, one eyebrow arched upwards in angry surprise. His eyes travelled down her body to where dark crimson flowered on her gown.

"What–?" she murmured.

There was another fiery explosion and the woman's body convulsed before collapsing in a heap at Nicholas's feet. Revealed at the front of the bus, blue smoke curling about him, was Sam. He lowered the rifle in his grasp and gave Nicholas a half smile.

"Thought that might shut her up," he said.

Nicholas simply stared back at him.

"We have to move quickly," the old man added urgently. "It won't keep her down for long."

"It won't… what?" Nicholas said.

"Find your things, hurry," Sam urged, already dismantling the rifle and slipping it back into the suitcase.

"O–okay," Nicholas mumbled.

He tried to forget about the body that lay at his feet, pooling black liquid across the ceiling of the bus. He scraped through the shards of glass and quickly found his backpack. Shouldering it, he hurried to the front of the bus, where he found Sam already had his suitcase.

Sam was bent over the crumpled body of the bus driver.

"S–Sam," the driver gurgled, his face covered in blood. "I'm… I'm s–sorry…"

A final breath sighed from the gash in his throat and he was gone.

"Malcolm," Sam said in a hushed tone. "You're in a better place now." He pulled the driver's coat from the wreckage and draped it over the dead man's form. "May the Trinity bless you."

He straightened.

"Follow me," the old man said without looking at Nicholas. "Be careful."

Nicholas watched as Sam stepped through one of the shattered bus windows and out onto the grassy bank of the ditch. He cast a glance back at the shape of the woman, lying motionless in the darkness, wondering what she had known about him. Then he followed Sam.

CHAPTER EIGHT
Footprints

Nicholas had never been so cold in his life. Or scared. If it hadn't been for Sam urging him tirelessly on, Nicholas suspected he might have succumbed to the lure of sleep hours ago, despite the hostile climate. His eyelids drooped and every step made his frozen toes ache inside his boots.

Apart from the occasional bursts of encouragement, Sam was quiet again. The older man frowned against the grey weather. The fedora perched on his brow gathered snow and submerged his features in shadow.

Nicholas didn't know what time it was, but an odd half-light was ebbing into the frosty countryside, picking out the highs and lows of the snow-cloaked landscape. Great expanses of bare terrain huddled under the icy air for what seemed like miles, and the hills resembled the shoulders of great giants who had buried their heads ostrich-like in the ground.

"Can we slow down?" Nicholas asked breathlessly. "I can't feel my feet anymore."

"We can't stop," Sam replied resolutely. "Our only hope is to place as much land between us and that bus as we can. We need to reach safe ground as soon as possible."

"Do you think we'll be attacked again?"

Sam's unwavering stare betrayed nothing and he was moving mechanically, as if a switch in his brain had been flicked to 'auto-pilot'. He'd set a brisk, urgent pace that Nicholas, weighed down by his suitcase and backpack, struggled to keep up with.

"We're not safe out here in the open," the elderly man mumbled.

"Do you think we'll get into trouble because of what happened with the bus? Would they arrest us?" Nicholas asked.

"The police!" Sam's mechanical demeanour stalled momentarily and he uttered a good-natured laugh. "No lad, nothing like that."

"Then what? What are you afraid of?" Nicholas skipped along as fast as he could. Sam may be in his seventies, but if his stride was anything to go by, he was fitter than anybody Nicholas knew.

Sam didn't answer. He pushed on through the snow.

"What is it?" Nicholas persisted.

Sam glowered from beneath the brim of his hat and Nicholas could tell that he'd struck a nerve.

"Can we please slow down?"

"No!" Sam answered gruffly, before adding quietly to himself: "We can't slow down for anything. If that woman reaches us before we get to safe ground we're done for. At least the snow will cover our tracks."

"Woman? What woman?"

No reply came. Nicholas detected in the older man the same inner struggle that he'd observed earlier when he'd confronted him about his parents.

"You can't mean the woman from the bus; you shot her twice, I saw her go down," Nicholas pressed. Grimly, the boy added: "There was blood everywhere."

"You have to trust me," Sam murmured, not looking at him. He scanned the horizon, and the old man reminded Nicholas of a nervous deer who had picked up a dangerous scent, but not yet discovered the whereabouts of the hungry lion.

"Course I trust you," Nicholas said. "You've always been there. I think that woman back there was going to kill me – you stopped her."

"I merely slowed her down," Sam grumbled, again in that quiet tone, as if he hoped that Nicholas wouldn't hear him.

"She was strange," Nicholas commented. "When I looked into her eyes it felt like the whole world didn't exist anymore, and I didn't care." He looked up at Sam, ignoring the set stoniness of his jaw. "She was... different, wasn't she? Not normal?"

"Yes," Sam relented. "You remember I said there are things in this world that are secret. She was one of them."

"Why did she kill the bus driver?" Nicholas probed. The encounter in the upturned bus had left him with more questions than ever before. He'd seen somebody die right in front of him – he was a witness to a murder. He shivered, and for once it wasn't because of the weather.

"I don't know," Sam said flatly.

"You do. You know things, and you won't tell me," Nicholas persisted. "You know things about my parents; about where we're going; about that woman back there in the bus. And I don't understand why you won't tell me anything. You want me to trust you, but–"

"Enough!"

Sam whirled on the boy.

Taken aback by the outburst, Nicholas stared up at the old man. The expression on Sam's face startled him – his eyes were wide with desperation.

"Please, boy," Sam appealed softly, "that *thing* back there in the bus is hunting us, and we need to get as far away from it as possible."

"But... you killed her."

Sam shook his head. "She won't stay down," he said. "I've come across things like her before and they never stay down."

"Was she a..." Now that he had to say the word, Nicholas felt foolish, but there was no other way of putting it. He thought about what he'd gleaned from the *Sentinel Chronicles*, those journal entries that hinted there was something more to this world than he had ever imagined. Sam had always told him stories about monsters. What if they hadn't been stories?

"Was she a demon?" Nicholas asked.

"Near enough," Sam said.

"So all that stuff you said on the bus about monsters not being real was just for my benefit, then."

Nicholas could feel his tenuous grip on reality slipping. Perhaps it was the cold, or the fact that his life had already been turned upside down by his parents, but it felt good to finally have something resembling an answer, no matter how outlandish it was.

"I'm sorry, lad," Sam said, and his apology sounded genuine. "I really think–"

"What's a Sentinel?" Nicholas continued. "Do you kill things like that? Stop them?"

Sam didn't say anything, but he didn't need to.

"I'm right, aren't I?"

Slowly, Sam nodded. Rather than feeling vindicated, Nicholas suddenly felt ill. There were evil things out there. A whole world he knew nothing about. He'd lived alongside it his entire life and he'd never even noticed it.

"And my parents?"

"No more questions," Sam said. "Your parents kept these things from you for a reason. The less you know at the moment the better. Trust me, you're safer that way. You'll get your answers soon enough. First we need to get to safety."

Nicholas held the other man's desperate stare. Sam had kept things from him so far, what made this any different? His shoulders slumped when he realised he really didn't have a choice in the matter. Finally Nicholas nodded and they started trudging through the snow once more.

When a few moments had passed, Nicholas said: "I never knew you owned a rifle."

Sam coughed. "Yes, well... The less said about that the better, eh?"

Nicholas grinned and hurried after him.

★

From the outside, the church looked almost pleasant. Soft scatterings of snow had settled snugly in all the right places, affording the hallowed edifice a festive, Christmas card quality.

Inside, however, was a different matter. Many years had slipped by since those with faith enough had worshipped here. If possible it was even colder inside the building than out – the very stones of the church held a chilly charge that had accumulated through the long lonely years. The wind groaned through the empty window frames, humming between the crumpled pages of the hymnbooks.

Into this forbidding place a figure took a couple of faltering steps. A side doorway gave a creaking objection as it was heaved shut and Malika moved down the church aisle. She got barely three feet before she was forced to lean against one of the pews, clutching at the bloody wounds in her torso.

"*Where is the child?*"

A voice shivered through the building.

Malika's feline eyes flashed to the altar at the other end of the aisle. An unfamiliar emotion stirred within her. Dread. Diltraa did not take kindly to failure and she wasn't looking forward to the consequences. He was an Adept, an emissary of the Dark Prophets, and as his Familiar it was Malika's duty to ensure that his designs were carried out. In that, she had failed.

Sucking the air in through her teeth, a brief, terrible expression contorted her enchanting countenance. The blood that stained her dress began to move of its own accord, snaking upwards and then seeping back through the ruby material, re-entering the gunshot wounds. Presently all traces of blood vanished, and Malika shook her crimson locks out with a sigh. She straightened and glided down the aisle.

"The child has eluded us," she offered softly.

Leaves skated about her feet as she scanned the austere surroundings for her master. She traced the gloom of the pulpit over to the altar before finally settling on the confessional booths that occupied a space beneath one of the few remaining intact windows. There, in the darkness that gathered inside the confessional, her keen sight discerned a shape.

"*Explain*," the figure in the booth croaked.

Malika paused a few feet from the cubicle. She stood with her head held high, but the tones that she spoke in were deferential and melodious.

"He was not alone. Another came to his aid."

"*This was a surprise?*" challenged the rasping voice. "*We knew the boy would not travel unaccompanied, the subjects of the Trinity are not quite so dim-witted as you fancy.*"

"The man was armed," Malika returned frostily. "You would have me snatch the boy while riddled with bullets?"

"*Insolence!*" the voice screeched. The confessional trembled.

Malika bowed her head quickly. "Forgive me."

"*You have squandered a golden opportunity!*" raged the voice. "*The child was all but served on a platter and you flee at the first indication of defiance? Has the fire dwindled in you so?*"

Malika absorbed the scathing words.

"I was foolish," she acquiesced. "Time was that none could face me and walk away alive. It will not happen again."

"*Indeed. Mistakes will not be tolerated. Too much is at stake – already time is running thin.*" There was a pause. Then the rasping voice intoned: "*Step closer.*"

Malika raised her eyes. She attempted to pierce the shroud of darkness within the confessional, yet even her sensitive sight was denied access there. Blinking, she took a step towards the booth.

"*Closer,*" the voice rattled.

Malika edged closer still. The form within the confessional became a little clearer, and two dim lights glimmered frigidly as they observed her.

"I was rash and thoughtless," Malika said, searching to appease the thing within the booth. "I understand the magnitude of our undertaking. I will not fail you again."

"*And yet you failed tonight,*" Diltraa whispered. "*And now my careful plans lie ruined. I should tear the fickle heart from your breast.*"

Finally the demon lord emerged from the confessional. But the face of the creature didn't fit the voice that had lashed from the darkness. It was the face of an eight-year-old boy. Dressed in a fitted, dust-speckled black suit, partnered with a black tie and shoes, the child's features were pale and stretched, cheekbones sharp as razors. There was a confidence and maturity about the boy that is not usually associated with one of his tender age. The dry lips sneered arrogantly and the eyes shone bone white. Here, then, was the vessel that the demon Diltraa had chosen in which to reside – the body of a dead child. Malika had retrieved it from its grave herself. Clawed away the earth and prised open the coffin. She'd been disappointed that the corpse was so fresh – it had barely begun to decompose.

"*You've weakened in the presence of man,*" Diltraa said coolly, observing his Familiar. "*The follies that permeate their pointless lives have left a mark on you. They've sapped you of your effervescence.*"

The demon child sniffed the air and its features contorted in disgust. "*The stench of humanity is all over you*," he spat.

Dropping her gaze, Malika swept to her knees before him.

"The years have weighed heavy," she admitted. "But never for a second did I stray."

The boy circled his prostrated Familiar and slowly drew a rusted dagger from his sleeve. He clenched the corroded blade in his small fist.

"*Have you fashioned a cosy nest for yourself with a mortal man?*" he goaded. "*Does he tell you he loves you? Does he put his hands on you? Is he the one responsible for taming the miserable beast that now cowers before me?*"

Malika trembled almost imperceptibly at the demon boy's needling, but she refused to be riled into anger. Let her lord vent his frustration, she deserved every one of those barbed words. Besides, she'd endured worse.

"*I fear that you have outstayed your welcome,*" Diltraa mourned, pacing slowly. There was something awkward about the way he moved, as if the foul thing that had seized control of the corpse had yet to familiarise itself with the mechanisms of a human body. As a result, the demon's movements were clumsy and ungainly. Ugly to look at.

"*The many years of your immortal life have afforded you a blind confidence and you answer to none but the whim of your own black heart,*" the child spat.

"I am forever indebted to you," Malika returned evenly. "I owe you all."

"*Would you betray me, I wonder?*" Diltraa continued. He paused before her and tugged at her chin with his ashen hand. "*Is that the truth behind your failure? Would you knife me in the back even as you return me to this pathetic world?*"

Malika peered up into those bleached, bottomless eyes, her quick mind searching for anything that might spare her the ultimate demonstration of her master's wrath.

"I have something," she murmured finally.

"*You should have the boy for me,*" Diltraa condemned, sneering at her as he pulled her face closer to his.

"This could lead us to the boy."

Diltraa paused, curious. After a moment, he released his grip on the stooped figure and clasped his hands behind his back.

"*I am waiting,*" he said.

Not daring to stand, Malika reached into the folds of her dress and extracted a small object.

"I discovered this as I stumbled, wounded, from the vehicle in which the boy travelled," she purred. She raised the object before her, seated like a church offering in her hands.

The demon lord took the object and turned it over. It was a battered brown leather wallet.

"*What use is this?*"

"It belongs to the man who protects the boy," Malika said softly, confident that this would pique her master's interest.

Squinting down at the worn object in his grasp, Diltraa flipped the wallet open. He flicked casually through the pockets before discovering a card that bore a photo of a grizzled old man. The name on the license read: SAMUEL WILKINS.

Malika gazed up at the boy, a half smile on her ruby lips.

"Find the man and the boy is ours," she said silkily.

The demon child pondered the wallet for a moment longer, committing the face of the man to memory. Then he turned his glare on Malika.

"*It is possible that my plans are salvageable,*" he mused. "*And it would seem that you have not yet exhausted your uses.*"

Malika nodded, the slash of a smile quivering. Her sharp mind had often served her well; it had sustained her through the years in even the bleakest of situations. Diltraa had been right in his estimation of her confidence; the numerous decades that Malika had shadowed the world had educated her considerably and she had become a mistress of manipulation.

Diltraa stroked his Familiar's cheek and she turned her full beauty on him.

"*The Harvesters have organised in my support; already Snelling has proven worthy. All is not yet at an end.*"

"You shall have the boy and your fury shall rock the Earth," Malika soothed.

"*Yesss,*" the boy whispered, his warped features darkening. He pocketed the wallet. "*Forget the boy, he is beyond our reach for now.*"

The demon child paced before the confessional.

"*I have located the whereabouts of the Rewe; you will obtain it for me. Everything must be set in motion with haste.*"

His youthful face stretched awkwardly, as if something beneath the surface was still reconciling itself with this new form of bone and muscle.

"*I need to feed.*"

★

"I don't get what's going on with this weather," Nicholas grumbled, his tired legs beating an ever-wearied course through the snow. "It doesn't make any sense."

"Not much does these days, lad," Sam said gloomily. Despite this, the elderly man's mood seemed lighter since his earlier outburst – Nicholas expected that the distance they'd placed between themselves and the bus was responsible for his more pliant temperament.

"But it's the middle of the summer, this is insane," Nicholas argued. He was exhausted and colder than he had ever imagined possible. He knew they had to press on, though; the thought of another encounter with that woman was not a welcome one, no matter how unlikely it was that she'd survived the gunshots. His head was still attempting to catch up with everything that had happened. Sam was a Sentinel. Which meant his parents probably were, too. But what did that even mean?

Suddenly gripped by a thought, he rummaged in his trouser pocket. It was empty. Annoyed, the boy realised he'd lost his mobile phone in the scuffle.

Typical. Here they were, trudging out into the wilds of the countryside, frozen stiff and possibly being stalked by some bloodthirsty fiend, and he didn't even have his phone. He probably wouldn't get any network reception out here anyway, he told himself. It didn't help, though. As the cold crept into his shivering bones, he felt completely disconnected from the world.

"Japanese folklore," Sam began conversationally, brushing snow from the brim of the fedora, "tells of a female demon named *yuki ouna.*

A sinister menace, she inhabits snow storms and causes travellers to become lost in their confounding depths, never to emerge again. I wonder if she is to blame for this irksome phenomenon."

Nicholas smiled inwardly, appreciating the old man's story. It seemed an age had passed since Sam had last shared one of his tales.

"Then again," Sam added soberly, "we could simply be experiencing the fabulous fickleness of British weather."

"Let's hope," Nicholas said. "I'm not sure we could handle another demon lady."

Strangely, Sam didn't seem to hear this. He stared off into the distance.

Nicholas followed his line of vision and saw that new wooded outcrops had emerged on the horizon, their snowy outlines merging almost imperceptibly with the sky.

"Not far now," he told the boy.

"Thank g–" Nicholas began. But before he could complete the sentence, Sam grabbed hold of his arm and brought him to a standstill. "Wha–?"

"Shhh," Sam cautioned. He cocked his head to one side, as if straining to hear something.

A familiar pang of apprehension reverberated through Nicholas. Then the sound came to his ears, too – a soft, careful rustling. The boy tensed at the prospect of another attack – he was sure he didn't have the energy for a second confrontation.

The rustling subsided.

"What do you think it is?" the boy breathed. He eyed a nearby hedgerow – the sound could easily have come from there. Every muscle in his body tensed and blood thumped in his ears. Then he noticed that the snowy ground below the hedge had been disturbed, and the boy relaxed as he recognised the marks in the dirty snow. He made to move toward the bush.

Sam squeezed his arm, but Nicholas pulled free. "It's okay," he assured him.

As Sam's hold doubtfully slackened, Nicholas crept over to the bush. Bending down, he reached out a hand and drew aside the lowest branches.

Two impossibly large yellow eyes blinked up at him from a thatch of bunched black fur.

"*Meeeeew.*"

"They were just cat footprints," Nicholas said cheerfully. He held his hand out toward the animal curled up beneath the bush. It shivered against the chill wind. Twigs were caught in its fur and it looked like it hadn't had a good meal in days.

"Easy!" Sam rushed to the boy's side. "Don't touch it."

Huddled in its hiding place, the cat sniffed at Nicholas's outstretched fingers.

"It's just a cat," Nicholas said, reaching toward the animal.

"No!" Sam cried, and the cat recoiled from the outburst.

"What?" Nicholas demanded.

Sam took a breath and rolled his eyes. "Evil takes many forms," he hissed. "We can't trust anything out here."

Nicholas regarded the old man incredulously; had he lost it completely? Whatever Sam was going on about, though, his expression was grave. Bemused, Nicholas looked at Sam, and then the cat, and then back again.

"But…" he murmured. "But it's just a cat. Look, it's freezing."

The creature peered up at the boy and his heart went out to it. There was nothing evil about the pitiful thing.

"We can't leave it out here," Nicholas said. "It'll die." And before Sam could utter another word, he pulled the cat out. It was skinny, little more than a kitten, and Nicholas pressed it to his chest, zipping his jacket up over the animal so that its furry head poked out under his chin. Grateful, the cat huddled against the warmth of Nicholas's torso and purred.

Sam glared disapprovingly. "Come on," he muttered. Nicholas tramped after him.

They walked on, rounding the margins of an immense forest, and found that they were at the crest of a hill. Below them the land dipped to create a large basin-shaped valley that stretched out until the land met the sky. And there, between the trees, nestled a house. The countryside seemed to enclose protectively about it, shielding it from the rest of the world.

"Is that–" Nicholas murmured.

"It most certainly is," Sam replied. He marched off down the sloping ground and Nicholas slowly followed, admiring the impressive building in the distance. Wrapped in his coat, the cat puffed out hot breath as it dozed.

Sam picked his way down into the natural basin and Nicholas hurried after him.

At last they were standing before the regal abode. It towered over them, and Nicholas had to crane his head right back to take in the highest chimneys and turrets. It was an unusual house, sliding into disrepair but still impressive in its dimensions. A flight of stone steps led up to a wide door, while a trellis of bright green ivy softened off the house's austere edges.

"This is where my godmother lives?" Nicholas asked dubiously.

Awake now, the cat sniffed at the house with interest.

Sam smiled for what seemed like the first time in weeks.

"That it is," he said simply.

Still smiling, Sam ascended the steps. Nicholas trailed behind him, suddenly nervous. He hadn't expected anything like this; his godmother must be rolling in it. Not to mention old. He found himself longing for the comfort of Midsummer Common. That, unfortunately, was now out of his reach, and presently the boy was standing next to Sam before the solid front door.

The older man tapped the door knocker and waited, bobbing on his heels. Nicholas swallowed anxiously. Inside his coat, the cat squirmed with anticipation.

From the other side of the door there came the sound of chains rattling, then bolts being drawn aside, and finally the door opened. The light from outside spilled into the dark place that lay beyond the door, illuminating the shape of a young woman. She could not have been any further from what Nicholas had been expecting.

"Greetings Samuel," the woman said. "And hello Nicholas. My name is Jessica. Won't you come in?"

CHAPTER NINE
The Woman In The House

NICHOLAS COULDN'T HELP BUT STARE AT the woman. She was young and beautiful, but in a completely different way to the woman he'd encountered on the bus. There was an innocence to Jessica, something faintly childlike in her heart-shaped face. Sections of her chestnut-coloured hair had been plaited to form a crown about her head, while she wore a white silk dress that skimmed her knees, tiny gold threads twinkling whenever she moved. Though Nicholas supposed she could be no older than twenty, Jessica was relaxed and confident. Her smiling eyes were as warm as they were enigmatic.

"Welcome to my home," the woman said as Sam drew the door closed behind them. Nicholas nodded politely and avoided Jessica's curious gaze by looking about the entrance hall, which was immersed in a soft ochre glow. Little ornamental lamps smouldered faintly. The walls were adorned with intricate tapestries and sumptuous indigo drapes framed the double doors ahead of them. Nicholas felt warmth steal quickly into his freezing limbs.

"I have waited some time to meet with you, Nicholas," Jessica said. "The last time I saw you, you were a baby. You would not remember me."

Nicholas found himself caught in the woman's penetrating gaze once more. The lamplight danced softly about her so that she seemed alternately ghoulish and radiant. It must be a trick of the light, the boy thought, or perhaps he was more tired than he'd realised.

Eventually, Nicholas managed to murmur: "You're… my godmother?"

Jessica laughed pleasantly and shared a look with Sam. "We shall talk of that later, no doubt," she said. "But look at you, you've come a long way, you must be exhausted."

Nicholas shook his head; this was all far too interesting and strange, he couldn't possibly sleep now. But as the house's welcoming atmosphere embraced him, his body began to feel sluggish. Tiredness overwhelmed him.

"Come," Jessica said. "Let me show you to your room."

In a flash of white and gold she spun on her heel and pushed open the curtain-fringed doors. Nicholas and Sam followed her into a circular lobby with an impossibly high ceiling. The marble floor was inscribed with a sprawling motif, while a staircase swept up to bend around the curved walls.

"Follow me," Jessica said, moving to the stairs.

Nicholas looked at Sam, who had paused to consider a painting. The older man gave him a reassuring smile.

"Go on, lad. I'll speak to you later."

Surrendering, the boy followed Jessica up the staircase. For such an old place, the woman's home had been well maintained. The carpets were springy underfoot and there wasn't a cobweb in sight. In some way, the house seemed to be an extension of Jessica herself – pristine and hospitable, yet submerged in an aura of mystery.

They reached the first of the three floors and Jessica led Nicholas down a wide landing lined with doors. She gestured to one sitting open waiting, motioning for Nicholas to go inside.

"This is your room," she smiled.

Nicholas went inside and found a modest room that contained a wardrobe, a dressing table, and a double bed festooned with pillows and cushions. It was immersed in the same friendly glow that warmed the entire house.

"It is perhaps a little dated, I admit," Jessica said, entering behind the boy and surveying the room. "But it will do for now. No doubt you will make it your own soon enough."

Nicholas nodded sleepily.

"Get some rest," Jessica advised. "You'll wake feeling fresh and new."

"Thanks," Nicholas said. Jessica nodded and left the room, pulling the door to behind her. Alone in his new bedroom, Nicholas was too tired to do anything more than sidle up to the bed, unzip his coat to let the cat out, and then crawl onto the mattress. Within seconds he had sunk into the pillows and was sound asleep.

★

"Forgive me, but you seem to have arrived a day later than expected, Samuel."

Sam, who had been admiring one of the lobby's many tapestries, turned toward the voice.

"We have had something of an eventful journey," he returned reverently, watching Jessica as she descended the stairs. "Far more eventful than I would have liked."

"You must tell me all," Jessica said. She led the elderly man from the lobby and down a corridor. Once again Sam was reminded of the grandeur of this most impressive old house. He'd been here many times in his long life, and he'd yet to find a place that filled him with the same sense of awe. Chandeliers winked above his head while marble floors shone underfoot.

"My home has been a place of great activity in recent weeks," Jessica told Sam, leading him down a passageway presided over by solemn-faced statues. "I am not accustomed to such a continuous flow of people – it was perhaps fitting preparation for the arrival of my young house guest."

"Let's hope that his arrival will bring an end to those bearing grievous news," Sam said.

"Indeed."

To their right, an enormous glass cabinet displayed the bones of a colossal creature that – if alive – would no doubt make short work of any unwanted visitors. Its fanged skull grinned behind the glass, its hollow eye sockets following their movements.

Finally, they entered a conservatory. Here, plants with spearing leaves thrived in harmony with the most delicate of azure flowers. Wintry sunlight trickled in through the windowpanes, illuminating a couple of wicker chairs, beside which a table had been set with a polished silver teapot, china cups and a plate of biscuits.

"Won't you take a seat," Jessica offered.

"Don't mind if I do." Sam's feet almost emitted a sigh of relief as he relaxed into one of the wicker chairs, and the conservatory's humid atmosphere warmed him almost instantly. How quickly the body forgot what it was to be cold.

"You must be famished, please help yourself," Jessica said, waving to the table as she seated herself. Sam poured himself a cup of tea and eagerly sipped it, smacking his lips.

"He is so young," Jessica murmured, almost to herself. "I had forgotten how young one is at fifteen."

"I fear that Nicholas will be forced to grow up very quickly in the coming weeks," Sam put in sombrely, dunking a biscuit in his tea.

Jessica nodded, her lovely face suddenly troubled. "That day dawns on us all. We hurry through our young years so eager to prove our worth. And then we spend the rest of our lives attempting to recapture the very youth we have squandered."

"Youth is wasted on the young," Sam shrugged, dipping another biscuit into his cup.

"Tell me," Jessica appealed softly. "You said you'd had an eventful journey?"

Sam returned his cup to its saucer on the table, brushing biscuit crumbs from his chin. "We were discovered," he told her gravely. "I had thought travelling by bus might help us slip under the radar. I couldn't have been more wrong."

"What happened?"

"It was a woman – at least, that's what it pretended to be. She wasn't interested in me in the slightest; she just wanted Nicholas. She knew who he was. And she would have taken him if I hadn't stopped her. She was powerful, too, my goodness. I dread to think…"

The old man trailed off, the thought too depressing to finish.

"So it's true that the Prophets are aware of the child's existence," Jessica breathed uneasily. "That is perhaps the most worrying news of all."

"He's safe here, though," Sam reasoned. "It could have turned out far worse. It's quite remarkable, really – there's barely a scratch on him."

"The same can't be said of you," Jessica said, referring to the livid line on Sam's cheek.

"I believe the Prophets are finding the weak links in the chain and exploiting them," Sam said. "Just a few days ago the Waldens were attacked by their family doctor – a Harvester in disguise. And then that woman on the bus."

"A Familiar?"

"I'm certain of it," Sam said. "Though which of the Adepts she serves remains a mystery."

Jessica sighed. The sun that beamed in through the conservatory windows afforded her a golden aura.

"I pray that my protection will be enough," she deliberated. "The time of peace has almost run its course – there is war on the horizon. The Dark Prophets are readying themselves."

Sam poured himself another cup of tea. "Nicholas was shaken, though he didn't say anything. He's a brave lad. He saw that harlot kill Malcolm; I wish he hadn't. He has many questions. I have managed to stall him this far, but he is no fool. He will keep asking."

"Then he shall have answers, it is only right."

"What will you tell him?" Sam asked.

"Everything," Jessica responded plainly.

"And if he reacts badly?"

"If he is the son that Max and Anita raised, and if he is the one that we have waited for, the answers will not come as a surprise to him," Jessica said. "No doubt he will have realised, at least subconsciously, that he is different to most other boys."

Sam nodded. "He's told me of dreams," he said. "Though he doesn't understand their significance. I remember one year, it was Anita's birthday. Nicholas was three, I believe, and there was a party at the Hallows' home. Whenever Anita's friend Michael came near Nicholas, he started crying. He kept saying something. 'Fire.' The poor child was inconsolable. 'Fire, fire,' he kept saying." Sam shook his head at the memory. "A week later, Michael was dead. His flat burned to the ground; some sort of electrical fault."

"I remember," Jessica said. "Anita was so shaken by it she sought my counsel."

"Those incidents were rare, though, and he has grown up in as normal an environment as any of us could have hoped for," Sam went on. "I think you are right; he has suspicions. No matter how efficiently we protected him, we cannot deny his difference." Sam paused again, adding dismally: "He could not have asked for better parents. They loved him dearly."

"The losses are being felt everywhere," Jessica said. "Esus has been attending Sentinel calls all over the country – things are happening, so many lives are being brought to an untimely end. We can expect things to darken long before the dawn."

"That is the reason I cannot linger here for much longer," Sam said, draining his cup and setting it down on the table. "I have promised Lucy Walden that I will attempt to help her."

"You won't stay?" Jessica asked furtively.

Sam stood. "As always, you have been a most gracious host," he bowed his head deferentially. "Perhaps one day we shall have a conversation that doesn't involve death and disaster."

Jessica nodded. "That sounds most civilised. I pray such a time is close at hand."

"Give my regards to Nicholas when he wakes? I'll see him again soon," Sam said.

"I will be sure of it. Take care Samuel, don't do anything too rash."

Sam bowed and left the room.

★

Malika paused by a streetlamp, wary of the bright neon that the naked bulb cast in a circle at her feet. Hers was a difficult relationship with the urban wastelands that had taken slow, lecherous purchase of the Earth. On the one hand she abhorred the constant noise and fuss, the robotic crowds with their deplorable agendas, the stench of humanity and aimless life. Yet at the same time she respected the corruptive force of the ever-hungry metropolis, sensing here a wickedness that almost twinned that within her own corrupt heart.

Here, on Trumpington Street in an old part of Cambridge, there were few distractions from her task. The daylight hours had long since dissolved into night, and those with sense enough had drawn their curtains against whatever ill deeds might be taking place in the dim streets. The restaurants and cafes that lined Trumpington had all locked up for the night, though a salty tang from the fish grill was still perceptible in the night air.

The slices of black in Malika's eyes trained upon the majestic building across the road. The Fitzwilliam Museum was an imposing place, its substantial nineteenth century structure a rebuff to the modern city that had grown up around it. Malika approached slowly, passing through the unlocked gates and mounting the stone steps. She skirted round the building to where two stone lions stood guard, raised on lofty platforms.

Smiling to herself, Malika drew near to the great beasts and touched the front paw of the nearest creature.

"Watch," she murmured to the effigy. "Be my eyes in the night."

With a swirl of her red cloak, the woman hurried away, finally reaching the entrance – a rotating door that was locked for the night. Through the glass, she saw an elderly man sitting at a half-moon desk. He was reading a newspaper by the feeble lamplight, the rest of the museum swathed in shadow.

Softly, Malika tapped at the glass.

The security guard raised his head and squinted at her. "We're closed," he barked with mild annoyance. "Come back tomorrow."

Malika tapped again.

"What the devil–" the security guard huffed. He threw down the newspaper and approached the door. But all irritation drained from his face as he peered at the woman through the glass.

"Open the door?" Malika requested lightly, widening her eyes at the old man.

Without hesitation, the guard took up his keys and let the woman in. He stepped back, instantly under her spell, his mouth hanging open as Malika closed the door behind her.

"Thank you–" Malika began, quickly searching the guard's person for a name tag. "Thank you, George," she said, smiling demurely.

"Mm… gg…" the guard called George mumbled, unable to form anything more than clumsy sounds. Malika daintily extended a hand, and the guard took it, falling to one knee in front of her. He was mature in years, probably in his early sixties, so it took some effort, but he got there eventually.

"What a gentleman," Malika teased, and her brittle laughter glanced off the marble pillars, echoing up into the foyer ceiling.

"Wh–what," the guard began. He cleared his throat. "What can I do to be of service?"

Malika craned her head back to take in the full grandeur of the foyer. It was narrow but high, framed by sweeping symmetrical staircases. Gilded pillars bore the full weight of an elaborate ceiling. It resembled a chamber of the Gods.

"There's something here that I need," she began. "It'll be old. Small. Easily mistaken for a European relic. Or perhaps African."

"The Rome room," grunted the guard, already staggering to his feet and shuffling over to a set of stairs.

Malika followed him, gliding over the marble floor, her pallid complexion giving her the appearance of one of the museum's statues brought to life. Together, they descended the stone steps, passing under a sign that read Rome and Ancient Sudan, and walked down a bright white corridor that shimmered under the glow of numerous spotlights.

In the museum's empty after hours, when the buzz of flocking tourists had long since fallen into a hush, every footstep rang out sharply. The collections huddled in their glass cases, peculiarly purposeless in these twilight hours when there was nobody to observe them or wonder at their links to an ancient world.

But Malika was looking. Eagerly and with purpose. She pored over every chipped bit of china, every rusted tool, every worn item of clothing. These were relics from a time long before she'd gasped her first breath. They were a novelty, objects older than even she, and they aroused her curiosity. The pages of man's history were filled with barbaric deeds; the Romans had been particularly bloodthirsty. Malika would have liked to have lived then.

More than just momentary interest thrilled the Familiar's senses, though. Somewhere here was the Rewe; that most prized artefact so integral to Diltraa's designs. She wouldn't fail him a second time.

The room was entirely white and Malika stood out like a pricked finger in the middle of it. Red and raw and out of place.

The guard stopped at the back of the Roman collection.

Malika sidled up next to him and gazed through the glass. It was a display crammed with unusual objects. And there it was.

Set amongst various pottery vessels, lamps and a Roman folding penknife was what she sought: an unremarkable, squat bowl. It had been wrongly attributed to the Romans thanks to its faded, almost illegible markings, not to mention its likeness to some Roman pottery, and placed here along with other ancient artefacts from that period.

Except Malika knew what it really was. She pressed her palms to the pane of glass and beamed.

"Yes," she murmured, her breath steaming up the pane. "This is it. Open it."

The guard took up his keys once more and opened a tiny lock in the bottom of the cabinet. He slid open the glass front and Malika reached in to extract the bowl.

"Your jacket," she requested silkily.

Without blinking, the guard shrugged off his jacket and offered it to her, his face drawn tight with the desire to please. Malika took it and wrapped the bowl up.

"You've been most helpful, George," she said, offering the man a coy smile.

George blushed and grinned sheepishly, shoving his hands into his pockets.

Malika moved in and pressed her lips to his, kissing him softly.

George sighed and his eyes rolled back in his head.

He was dead before he hit the floor.

Back out in the night air, Malika purred to herself and cradled the Rewe in the security guard's jacket. She reached the top of the museum's front steps and paused. A smirk teasing the corners of her lips, she returned to the plinths where the stone lions rested.

She hissed strange words rebelliously.

Quietly at first, the lions began to shudder and vibrate. In seconds, their unnatural juddering was making a thunderous din, almost like the sound of a train's engine picking up speed.

Laughing with malevolent glee, Malika swept away from the statues and stepped out onto Trumpington Street.

When the woman had finally disappeared down the cobbled street and been swallowed by the night's shadows, an almighty explosion rocked the museum and the twin lions erupted into clouds of alabaster dust.

★

The rail track stretched on for an eternity, making a point on the horizon. It was night, and blue fog spun eerily through the air.

He ran, but he didn't seem to be getting anywhere. Panic spurred him onwards, though from where that sickening sense of urgency had come he wasn't sure. He felt sticky, heavy, hot. His heart hammered frantically in his chest, and he could barely see as he stumbled down the track.

All he knew was that he had to get away. Soft rustles crunched behind him, but he dared not look back. He didn't want to know what it was. He ran. And ran. His limbs ached and he seemed to be going in slow motion.

It was as if he was running through air thick with syrup, and it took every ounce of his strength to press onward.

Something rattled.

He let out a muted whimper.

What was it? What did it want from him?

The rattling grew louder.

Confused and blinded by panic, his boot caught on one of the rungs of the track and he fell forward, crashing onto the hard metal with a grunt. Groaning, he rolled over.

The thing bore down on him with fangs and claws that flashed red.

He screamed.

"Mum!"

Nicholas jerked upright in bed. The dream lingered and he didn't know where he was.

Next to him the cat raised its head, observing the panting, sweaty boy. And there was another watching him. As Nicholas's eyes grew accustomed to the dark, and the nightmare drifted up through the ceiling, he made out the shape of a woman sitting at the end of his bed.

"M–mum?" he croaked.

"No," a delicate voice replied. "It's me Nicholas, your godmother."

It all came flooding back. Nicholas sagged.

"I didn't mean to disturb you. You looked like you were having a bad dream."

"I was."

Nicholas felt suddenly embarrassed. He pushed a hand through his knotted hair.

The cat stretched on the bed, flexing its claws. It got to its feet and lumbered over to the woman, rubbing its head against her leg.

"I see you brought a friend with you."

"Yes," Nicholas replied. As the haze of sleep lifted, his curiosity stirred.

He watched Jessica raise a hand above the cat's head and hold it there. A judder travelled through the mattress, but as quickly as it had started, it was gone.

As if satisfied, Jessica scratched behind one of the cat's ears. It purred appreciatively.

"So you are my godmother, then?" he asked.

"In a manner of speaking," she confirmed mellifluously. "My old name was Jessica Bell, though I've been afforded many others since that one. It was your parents wish that, should anything ever happen to them, you be brought here to me." She paused as the cat flopped stupidly onto the duvet, and then added: "I'm sorry for your loss, Nicholas. I lost my mother when I was young, too. There are still days I don't remember; the hard ones when you almost feel like you've died yourself."

Nicholas's intrigue grew with every soft utterance that drifted up from the foot of the bed. Jessica wasn't at all what he'd been expecting. He'd imagined his godmother to be older, sterner – an image that was fortified by the sight of the manor house. Then Jessica had answered the door and smashed his expectations to pieces.

"I hope you will be comfortable living here," Jessica said, "though I admit there's not much for a child to occupy himself with."

"But… I don't understand," Nicholas said, ignoring the 'child' part of her sentence. "You're barely older than me, how can you be my godmother?"

"There is much to explain," Jessica replied.

She spoke as if she were older. Nicholas wasn't sure if she was being pretentious, or if that was just her way. There was something about her, though. Something he couldn't put his finger on.

"I understand that you have many questions," the woman said, "and I will happily answer them for you. But first you must eat and replenish your strength. Come."

She rose from the bed. Nicholas watched her go. Then, realising how hungry he was, he scrambled to his feet and followed her out of the room. The cat trotted after them.

CHAPTER TEN
LIBERTY

SAM PONDERED THE LITTLE HOUSE. UNLIKE its frowning terraced siblings, care had been taken over it and it radiated a quiet resilience. A rose bush with waxen flowers hugged the wall face, thickening protectively over the doorway, and a flowerpot on the downstairs window bustled with brightly-coloured Busy Lizzies.

The elderly man rubbed his bleary eyes – he'd barely slept a wink that night. After leaving Nicholas at Jessica's, he'd trudged back through the snow to a nearby village (though not *that* village, that would never do) and caught a taxi back to Cambridge. It had cost him a pretty penny, but he was grateful that the driver had agreed to the trip at all, considering the distance. Being old sometimes had its benefits; the young man had clearly taken pity on him. Sam chuckled inwardly at how dishevelled he must have appeared – he'd freshened up at Jessica's house before leaving, but he still must have looked a sight, especially after the attack on the bus.

Still, he'd arrived home at a reasonable hour. But he'd spent the rest of the evening in the attic rifling through old files and newspaper clippings, searching for anything that might help him get to the bottom of who that woman had been. He'd even cracked open a few of Judith's old cabinets, which he rarely permitted himself to do.

This was desperate, though. He was certain the red-haired harlot had survived the shotgun wounds; he'd encountered enough wicked things in his time to know it took more than a few bullets to stop the servants of the Dark Prophets. No matter how many clippings he pored over, though, his research had surrendered nothing useful, as he'd expected – he'd never encountered anything quite like the woman on the bus. That fact was unnerving in itself.

And then there was Nicholas. Sam couldn't help but feel guilty about unloading him on Jessica, even if it had been Max's wish. Had the circumstances been different, he'd have gladly taken the lad in. Given the present climate, though, not to mention the fact that the Prophets were actively hunting him, that was an impossibility.

Sam pushed these worries aside as he trudged down the neatly-gravelled path, resolving to concentrate on the matter at hand. He tapped a silver knocker.

Within seconds the door handle rattled and Sam peered down at the small figure who appeared to greet him.

It was a six-year-old girl, her bushy black hair plaited and beaded to keep it out of her face. Her skin was a mocha shade and she was snuggled up in a fluffy purple jumper. She smiled impishly up at the old man on the doorstep, eyes not without a sparkle of mischief.

"Hello there," Sam greeted her.

"Francesca! What have I told you about answering the door?"

The front door was pulled fully open by a tall, dark-skinned figure.

"Oh," the newcomer uttered. "Mr Wilkins, what a nice surprise."

Sam smiled. "I am honoured to be able to surprise you, Liberty."

Francesca looked up at her mother. "It was only Uncle Sam," she said, pushing out her bottom lip.

The woman named Liberty merely smiled and put a hand on her daughter's head. "Won't you come in, Mr Wilkins."

"Very kind of you," Sam said, removing his hat as he crossed the threshold. "Though I must again insist that you call me Sam – makes me feel far less ancient."

"Forgive me," Liberty said. Her daughter galloped down the hall, then crouched behind a potted plant to stare out at the elderly visitor. She snarled like a jungle cat.

"Come through," Liberty said. "I've just got to finish Fran's lunch."

"Ah, young stomachs must not be kept grumbling."

Sam winked at Francesca and followed Liberty into the kitchen. She started buttering bread at the counter while Sam seated himself at the table; his usual spot. In a corner, the TV played a news report about a missing child.

"That thing looks old."

Francesca had come after them and was gazing enviously at the fedora in Sam's hand. The elderly man's eyebrows twitched and he placed the hat on the girl's head. It was comically over–sized, but she beamed with delight.

"I'm just like you!" she proclaimed, striking a pose.

"That you are!" Sam laughed. In a secretive tone, the old man added: "You know, that's a very important hat."

The girl's eyebrows disappeared under the brim of the fedora. "It is?"

"Oh yes," Sam said sincerely, his eyes glittering. "It's very old, you see. Older than you, even."

"How much older? I'm six."

"You're a mere sapling in comparison my dear child," Sam laughed. "The hat you are now wearing–" he touched the brim affectionately for a second "–once belonged to my father. He gave it to me on my twenty-first birthday, his most prized possession, now mine. The stories this hat could tell, should it be given the chance…" He let his breath out dramatically.

Francesca's eyes swelled and her mouth opened a fraction.

"What stories?" she whispered.

"Oh I couldn't possibly," Sam said. "Unless…" He shook his head and looked away. "No, you wouldn't be interested in that."

Francesca's eyes were almost popping out of their sockets. "I would! I would!" She stamped her foot. "Tell me!"

Sam raised his eyebrows in mock surprise. "Oh, well if you insist." He leaned in to her. "In his youth," he began slowly, "my father fancied himself as something of a secret agent. He also fancied himself a few drinks here and there, which meant that he was a frequent visitor to our local, the Dog and Partridge. Scandalous business often took place there, scandalous. And the company left a little to be desired; but then my father always had a soft spot for an old dog with a tragic tale." Sam's brow furrowed disapprovingly at this. "On one such visit, my father caught whiff of what he considered to be a plot to knock off the pub's landlord. Seems Mr Barker had a bit of a flair for gambling, though unfortunately for him he wasn't particularly good at it. He owed money, quite a bit if my father overheard correctly. Mr Barker had failed to pay up, and a previous threat was to be carried out that very night."

"They were going to shoot him!" Francesca exclaimed.

Sam nodded soberly. "Just so. They waited until the locals had departed for bed before making their move. My father sat still and quiet in a dark corner; perhaps the rogues didn't consider him a threat, or perhaps they had failed to notice him. They paid him little heed, either way. My father looked on as two men approached Mr Barker from behind, both pulling pistols from their pockets. But as they took aim at the landlord's back a quite remarkable thing happened."

"What?"

Sam paused. "There was an earthquake," he revealed. "The first for many years, and it was a belter. Nothing matches mother nature's rage when she has an itch to scratch." He paused dramatically once more. "Well, you can imagine the destruction, practically half the street collapsed; and with it the Dog and Partridge. Mr Barker, the two rogues and, of course, my father, were buried in the rubble. Locals rescued Mr Barker and his potential assassins from the wreckage. My father, however, was nowhere to be found."

Francesca's elfin features became confused.

"He was there alright, but buried so deeply nobody could see him," Sam said.

"Did he die?"

"As luck would have it, it was my father's love for the drink that saved him in the end," Sam said, the corners of his eyes crinkling. "He was so well known in local circles that when people were giving up and going home, it was an object lying in the rubble that alerted them to his presence amid the debris."

Sam touched the fedora again, remembering. "This hat. A regular at the pub recognised my father's hat, and dug deeper into the wreckage. A few feet in he found my father – unconscious and bruised, but very much alive."

Francesca strained to look up at the hat on her head, going cross-eyed in the process.

Sam sucked in a deep breath. "So, you see, this hat is very special indeed. It can be credited with saving a man's life, among other things. It has certainly been a good luck charm for me – you don't make it to seventy in this day and age without a certain amount of good fortune."

"Has it saved you from an earthquake as well, Uncle Sam?" Francesca asked.

"Come on Francesca, lunch is ready."

Liberty placed a plate on the kitchen table.

"I believe we'll leave another story for another day," Sam said softly, removing the hat and straining to stand back up again. His knees popped.

Francesca went reluctantly round the table and was just about to clamber onto a chair when–

"Stop right there, young lady," Liberty said suddenly. Francesca paused, turning an innocent look on her mother.

"Give it back," Liberty said sternly.

Sam's bemused gaze drifted between mother and daughter. Stubbornly, Francesca stuck out her bottom lip, then her shoulders slumped and from the sleeve of her oversized jumper she produced a small, shiny object.

"Give it back to Mr Wilkins and say you're sorry," Liberty instructed.

Sheepishly, Francesca plodded over to Sam and offered up the object. It was a little gold pocket watch. Sam stared at it incredulously, shoving a hand into his trouser pocket. It was empty.

"Sorry Uncle Sam," Francesca mumbled, almost inaudibly. Sam took the watch from her and the girl flitted quickly to the other side of the kitchen table.

"Incredible," the old man murmured, tittering with delight. "The little devil! You've got your hands full there, Liberty." He pocketed his watch, shaking his head in astonishment.

"Don't I know it," Liberty said. She handed him a steaming mug. "You look like you needed this."

"Ah, one of your magic potions," Sam said, taking it gratefully. He hadn't even noticed her making it as he told Francesca his story.

"Let's go into the lounge," Liberty said. "Francesca, I'll be watching you through the hatch. No funny business."

Francesca pouted and Sam winked at her as he followed Liberty down the hall. He sniffed the contents of his mug. The scent of blackberries thrilled his nostrils. He'd built up the courage to ask Liberty what she put in her brews only once, and she'd said something flippant about pixie dust and frogspawn. If he sniffed hard enough, he was sure he could detect a hint of cinnamon, but other than that he was at a loss. All he knew for certain was that Liberty's remedies always made his fingers and toes tingle pleasantly.

She was a Sensitive. Many assumed she was merely a good judge of character, but her abilities went far beyond that. 'Sensitive' was a fitting word for what she could do. Her senses were sharper than others; a gift she'd inherited from her father. Of course, she was also a Sentinel – a rare combination that made her an invaluable ally.

"How you spoil me," Sam said, taking an appreciative sip of his brew as they went into the living room.

"What brings you here, Mr Wilkins? I trust this isn't simply a social call."

Liberty perched on the arm of the sofa. She was all arms and legs. An older, leaner version of her daughter.

"You're hurt," she added, noticing the red seam running down the side of his face.

Sam put a hand to his cheek. "I had a minor incident with a rather unpleasant woman," he told her.

"Still breaking hearts?"

"Bones more like." He dropped his hand, meeting her gaze. "You have sensed the change, I am sure."

Liberty nodded. "It feels like something's waking up," she said simply.

Sam sighed. He went to the window where the dreamcatcher twirled and touched the curving frame. "We've laboured so hard to prevent their return. Centuries of vigilance and sacrifice, and yet still things have slipped through the cracks."

Sam regarded the dreamcatcher a moment longer. He sipped the herbal broth, the warmth spreading right to his fingertips.

"Has anybody you know been harmed?" he asked, easing himself onto the window seat.

"My mother's friend," Liberty said, "he was killed a fortnight back. A neighbour got him in his sleep."

"Harvester?"

Liberty nodded. "As far as we can tell. She's long gone, though. No doubt joining the ranks."

"And your mother?"

"Shaken, but fine. Dread to think what she'd have done if the Harvester had come back. Not sure who I'd have pitied more."

Sam nodded. "Most I've spoken with are retreating from their everyday lives in fear of attack. It's infuriating, though necessary, I think. Anything to elude a Harvester. Which brings me to why I am here…" He broke off, adding: "Other than for the pleasure of your company."

"Mine and my thieving daughter's." Liberty smiled wryly.

"Quite." Growing serious again, Sam continued: "A friend of mine, Richard Walden, was attacked earlier this week. The thing is, he isn't dead… not yet anyway. This attack was different. Both he and his wife survived, she entirely unharmed."

"An attack, but no deaths," Liberty mused. "That is odd, especially if a Harvester was responsible. They're not exactly celebrated for their compassion."

"Indeed. And while there exists even the smallest glimmer of hope that Richard might recover, I have taken it upon myself to do everything I can to help. Any information he has might prove vital."

"You want me to come with you to see him," Liberty noted.

"If you have the time. I understand it is an enormous favour to ask, but–"

"I'll come," Liberty interrupted. "Anything I can do to help. Besides, I know how much you despise asking favours, Mr Wilkins. It would take something of vast importance to drag you here."

"Sam, please," the old man corrected with infinite patience.

Liberty turned suddenly to the TV. She reached for the remote and turned it on.

"The break-in, we're told, took place at 11.35pm last night," a pretty news reporter was saying. She was standing in front of the Fitzwilliam Museum, huddled in a winter coat. "Though police are unable to give full details of the events at this early stage, these crime scene tents—" the camera panned to reveal a couple of big white canopies "—have been erected as examinations continue on the remains of the museum's famous lion statues. They are now little more than piles of rubble. An act of vandalism, or something altogether more sinister? It's too early to say. Perhaps the saddest part of this most unusual of stories is the death of a sixty-five-year-old security guard who has yet to be named. His body was removed from the scene first thing this morning. He is believed to have suffered a heart attack."

"What is going on at the moment?" Liberty wondered out loud, turning the TV off again. "First that missing child, now this. Cambridge is turning into a war zone."

"Missing child?"

"A boy disappeared two days ago," Liberty told the old man. "Eight years old. He was out walking the dog with his aunt on the Gog Magog Downs, and he just vanished. No trace of him."

"What a week," Sam tutted. "Think the two are related? The break-in and the missing child?"

"Too early to tell," Liberty said. "I'll see if I can stop by the museum at some point as well. As for Richard, I'm free in the morning; I can drop Francesca at my mother's."

Sam's face flooded with gratitude.

"Tomorrow, then," he said.

CHAPTER ELEVEN
The Sentinels

NICHOLAS FOLLOWED JESSICA AS SHE MADE her way down the stairs and into the vast, circular lobby. He stared up at the round window in the ceiling, his mouth gaping open. Feeling dizzy, the boy hurried after Jessica and they moved down a number of hallways. The house was like a maze; bigger than it looked on the outside, if that was possible, and there were more doors than he could count. As they moved through it, he became quickly disorientated, as if the house itself wanted to confuse him.

Finally they entered a cosy parlour. A fire blazed in the hearth and before the fireplace a low table had been laid with a silver tray bearing food and drink. It was only when he saw the food that Nicholas realised just how hungry he really was.

"Go ahead," Jessica said, having noted his eagerness.

"Cheers."

Nicholas sat on the floor in front of the table, digging into a plate of cooked meat and vegetables.

Jessica seated herself on the nearby sofa, watching him patiently. There was a contented air about her, a constant smile in her eyes.

"You were hungry," she observed, watching the cat as it entered the room. It had clearly tired of exploring. Jessica took a saucer of milk from the table and placed it on the floor. The cat ran keenly to it, lapping loudly.

"Do you live alone?" Nicholas asked between mouthfuls.

"I do," Jessica nodded.

"It's a big house to live alone in," Nicholas said. "Must get lonely."

"I have grown accustomed to my own company," Jessica stated. "Besides, I am not alone here for long, I have visitors now and again." She paused. "The house belonged to a friend of mine a long time ago. I spent much of my youth here, and grew up under her care. When she was gone, I inherited it. I suppose I don't feel alone here because this is where I have always been."

"You talk like you're older," the boy observed.

Jessica merely smiled.

"Where's Sam?" Nicholas asked, realising that he hadn't seen the elderly man since falling asleep.

"He had to leave," Jessica told him. "He is a very busy man, as I'm sure you are aware."

"He never stays still for long, I don't know how he does it."

"You will see him again soon."

Having finished its milk, the cat moved over to the fireplace, purring as it licked its whiskers. Then it rolled onto its side and began its ritual of self-cleaning, preening its jet-black fur with experienced proficiency.

"How did you know my parents?" Nicholas asked. He speared a piece of white meat and chewed on it. "They never mentioned you to me, not even once. But you're my godmother."

"Complicated relations," Jessica murmured. She seemed to become mesmerised by the flames frolicking in the hearth. "There is no simple way for me to explain." Her gaze met Nicholas's. "You have questions, I know. And I have much to tell you."

Nicholas rested the knife and fork on the plate, suddenly stuffed.

"Sam wouldn't tell me anything," he said, fighting the drowsiness that inevitably came with a full belly.

"Do not hold that against him," Jessica said softly. "There is a time and place for certain things. You asked how I knew your parents. They were fine people. I met them years ago, long before you were born, before they were even married." She raised a hand as Nicholas opened his mouth to speak. "They belonged to a different world, Nicholas. But I think you have suspected that. They belonged to my world."

Nicholas resisted unleashing the torrent of questions that were building up in his throat. He sat quietly and watched the elfin woman on the sofa take up a glass of water.

"Picture the ocean, if you will. The surface is a place inhabited by birds and fishermen and revellers," she said. "They live in the sun, breathing the air, mostly ignorant of that which resides below. There is a divide, and below the rippling waters dwell the monsters of the deep. This is the world that we inhabit, so close to the ordinary, and yet always just out of sight; always apart."

Nicholas nodded, understanding. "The Sentinels."

"The Sentinels," Jessica echoed. The firelight twinkled in the gold thread of her dress and she looked almost inhuman. She set the glass back down on the table.

"What is a Sentinel?" she said, as if reading his mind. "A Sentinel is a guard. A detective. A killer. There are Sentinels stationed all over the world, watching for the dark creatures that inhabit the night. It is a Sentinel's duty to destroy those creatures, to protect the weak and the vulnerable. The world you come from knows nothing of the Sentinels and their cause. It is perhaps a thankless existence, but their duties must be carried out nonetheless."

"My parents… they were Sentinels. And Sam?"

"Yes. As were their parents before them, and theirs before them, stretching all the way back into the youth of the world, when the sun was new and the land rich with possibilities."

"I never knew my grandparents," Nicholas said. "They died when I was young."

"As is often the way. The Sentinel life is one fraught with risk, something you have experienced in the past weeks. Ordinary people are ignorant of the dangers that surround them every day, heartbeats away. It is the job of the Sentinel to keep watch, to enter the shadows where the everyman dares not tread, to eradicate any threat that may be uncovered there."

"What sort of threats?" Nicholas asked. "Why don't people know about them?"

"People see what they want to see," Jessica explained. "The world that you grew up in, protected from the Sentinel way, is ordered very specifically. That world depends on a delicate equilibrium. For example, it is taken as a fact of nature that humans are the most intelligent beings walking the Earth. Now, this may not necessarily be true, but people depend on this belief to go about their daily lives. The everyman believes that he, and nothing else, is the controller of his own destiny. Anything that happens that is not of his doing is accredited to chance, luck – good or bad – and that ominous being 'God'."

She stopped, casting Nicholas a look.

"Perhaps I am losing you, and none of this is really important. You must forgive me; I tend to wander off in my thoughts. A consequence of living alone, I'm sure."

"It's okay," Nicholas said. "I think I sort of get it. You're saying that people like to think that they're in control of their lives, but they aren't. The Sentinels are the ones who make sure that nothing hurts them… us. But… what is it that's so dangerous? What are the Sentinels watching for?"

"Just as there is a barrier between the Sentinels and the ordinary people, so too is there a barrier between our world and an uglier place." Jessica's face darkened. "Terrible things were banished from this plane of existence centuries ago, but they are forever seeking ways to get back in. Call them what you will; evil spirits, devils, monsters, demons, they all add up to the same. They are the emissaries of the Dark Prophets."

"Prophets?"

Jessica nodded, her expression grave. "As in all things, there is a hierarchy. At the very top reside the Dark Prophets, the foulest of all creatures whose sole purpose is to destroy. They are forever fighting to reclaim the Earth, to fashion it in their own corrupt image. The Prophets are served by their Adepts, the strongest of all demons, and the Adepts in turn are served by their faithful Familiars. Most demons reside in the Other World, but Familiars are often humans who have sold their souls for dark powers."

Nicholas's head was spinning.

"These Prophets," he said, "what are they?"

"Nobody knows for certain. They were defeated centuries ago by the Trinity, the divine figures whom all Sentinels bow to and revere."

"Are you a Sentinel?" Nicholas asked.

Jessica pondered this before answering. "Yes and no," she responded finally. "I was not born into Sentinel ancestry, though I have been a part of it for a long time. In the old tongue they call me the *Vaktarin*;

the Guardian. I watch over the community, act as council and guide, aid when bid. I am a site for refuge and sanctuary. It is my magic that protects this house from evil forces. My place is here and I will never leave."

"And that's why I'm here?"

"It is. As well as Anita and Max being dear friends, you are a Sentinel yourself. The godmother business is just a way of getting around the paperwork that non-Sentinel men love so much," Jessica said. She paused, offering him a knowing smile before adding: "Did Sam tell you the name of this place?"

He shook his head.

"It's called Hallow House," the woman told him. "Years ago, it was occupied by your ancestors, and it has retained that name ever since. So, you see, your arrival here is almost prophetic – you're home, Nicholas."

"My ancestors owned this place?" Nicholas marvelled, peering around the parlour. "They must've been loaded."

Jessica laughed. The ring of it made the hairs on Nicholas's arms stand on end.

"I still don't understand why my parents never told me any of this," he said.

Jessica nodded sadly. "They were dreamers," she explained gently. "They wanted you to live out your childhood free from the knowledge of sinister, ugly things. You would have found out in your sixteenth year, as is tradition in the more progressive corners of the community."

"I'll be sixteen in a few weeks," Nicholas murmured regretfully. "They should have said something."

"They couldn't have known they wouldn't be here for you now." Jessica took on a faraway look. "You have come to me in a time of change and uncertainty; I fear that we are on the brink of war. Only time will tell. The weather is a sign. Balances are shifting; the equilibrium is becoming distorted. The seasons do not remember where they belong – already a manner of madness is slipping into the world." She stopped abruptly, appearing to remember her company. "I do not mean to scare you, I apologise. I forget how strange and new this must be; I have lived it for so long."

As Nicholas looked at her, he could see that she was not as youthful as her delicate features suggested. There was something old about her, something brittle. She was porcelain. Hardened but fragile. She had witnessed and survived a lot. As he contemplated her pale features, Nicholas could tell that Jessica had faced horrific things; he could see the mark that they had left on her. Before he could stop himself, he found himself asking: "How – how old are you?"

The despondency lifted immediately from the woman's face and the familiar chiming laugh spilled from her throat.

"I have lost count of the years," she said. "There have been so many. Let us say I am older than I look and leave it at that."

"There's one more thing I need to ask," Nicholas ventured.

Jessica smiled. "Please ask it."

Nicholas struggled to find the words. "There was a woman who attacked Sam and me," he started. "She was strange, not like normal people. She was one of those evil things, wasn't she?"

"Yes, I believe she was."

"She said things to me," Nicholas continued. "That I was… different, a threat. She said I was dangerous." As he said this, the boy thought Jessica looked briefly troubled. She blinked and the look was gone. "And I've sort of felt… strange things. Before we were attacked I think I knew it was going to happen. And I heard whispers back at home, there was this weird thing with cows, and I found a secret room…"

Jessica sat quietly, listening. Then she realised that the boy had stopped talking and was watching her, waiting for a response.

"There are some Sentinels," she began carefully, "with certain qualities, certain gifts. Some call them Sensitives. It is possible that you have inherited abilities that allow you to sense things that others cannot. One of your distant relatives was extremely powerful, as a matter of fact." She gave the briefest of pauses before continuing: "As to the woman, I believe that she referred to the Sentinel community as a threat, not you personally. All evil considers the Sentinels dangerous."

Nicholas let this information sink in. "But… abilities? What–?"

"They are nothing to fear," Jessica assured, leaning towards him in earnest. "They are as natural to you as breathing. Let them be and as you mature you may learn to control them, use them." She touched the hair that lay over her shoulders and sighed, standing. "All this talk has left me weary, I must rest. Please, use the house as you will, roam wherever you desire. All I ask is that you do not leave the grounds. I think you understand why."

With that, she drifted from the room.

Nicholas sat motionless for a while, his mind reeling with all that he had learnt. After all this time, after Sam's refusal to answer Nicholas's questions, after all of his suspicions and frustrations, now he had answers.

It felt strangely anti-climactic, and yet exhilarating at the same time. A cynical voice nagged at the back of his mind, though. Could everything Jessica had said really be true? Sentinels and demons and psychics? Divine beings called the Trinity, and twisted monsters called Dark Prophets?

If it was true, it was surely the best-kept secret in the history of the world. An entire community right under society's nose, completely invisible and unseen. He thought of the Government. The Prime Minister. The President of the United States. Were they all oblivious to the Sentinels? Did they know nothing about any of this? Nicholas found it hard to believe. As he struggled to reconcile the two worlds – the one he'd grown up in and the one Jessica had described – the only thing he could do was look at what he knew as fact.

His parents' secret study. The books about Sentinels. The dreams. The sleepwalking. How he'd known that somebody was following the bus. The whispers. The strange weather.

All things he'd experienced first hand. All things that matched up with what Jessica had said.

After it all, his thoughts returned to his parents. He'd always considered them the most normal and unsurprising of people. According to Jessica, they had been supernatural demon hunters. The thought left him with a bittersweet feeling, one of pride intermingled with regret. He wished that he could have known them as they really were. It should have been them who told him fantastical stories, not Sam.

He lay back on the carpet, the cat dozing next to him. The warmth of the fire soothed him, and Nicholas spent the rest of the afternoon lounging there, attempting to make sense of everything that had landed him in a rambling manor house out in the middle of nowhere.

★

Lucy Walden sat in the dusky surroundings. It was another cold evening, but it could have been midnight, or midday for all that it mattered to her. She hadn't left the house since the day the doctor turned their lives upside down, and the longer she stayed huddled away, the less inviting the outside world seemed. Of course, the outside world had become a bleaker place since the attack. They were being used as a cautionary tale for the rest of the community, no doubt, and Lucy could imagine what they were all whispering.

"Trust nobody, little ones. Not even those you hold dear. Just look at those Waldens – they trusted their family doctor and now look at them."

They had been foolish. All of them, including Lucy, and she knew it. This wouldn't have happened in the past, not when the Sentinel laws had been stricter. Back then, Sentinels were forbidden from conducting business or social affairs outside of the community; the Sentinel's only business should be safeguarding the world from the terrors that ordinary people knew nothing about. But, as with most things, time ushered in a new order. The Sentinels had relaxed. They thought that everything was under control; they had a handle on the forces that for so long had battled to free themselves, and so life became a new place for discovery. A Sentinel could get a job, explore passions, befriend neighbours. And why shouldn't they? They were human like everybody else, made of the same blood and flesh, and with their own hopes and dreams. Why should they fight for the rest of the civilised world simply because their ancestry dictated it?

The new system worked for a time. The Sentinels were not scattered and fragmented by their new freedom; they had always been an organised people. There were weekly meets, and should an event occur that required their full attention, their jobs and lives could wait. But when things grow quiet, it is easy to forget. When past battles against unnameable terror are replaced with the daily battles of everyday life, the mind can grow cluttered with new priorities.

This was the environment that Lucy and Richard had grown up in, with their lives governed at a comfortable distance by the Sentinel laws, afforded enough independence to live as they wished. It was a cruel twist of fate that had landed them in their current miserable position, but Lucy couldn't help feeling that they had brought it on themselves. If they hadn't become so relaxed – others would call it complacent – then perhaps they would have been alerted before any tragedies occurred.

"Oh Richard," she murmured, clasping his clammy hand in her own as she sat at the bedside. He was so still. The only sign that he was alive was the laboured rise and fall of his chest, which barely disturbed the sheets laid over him.

"What are we going to do?"

Lucy wondered if he could hear her, somewhere, deep in the fog of the coma. She was sure she'd read somewhere that certain comatose people were able to register the voice of a loved one. She hoped that Richard was one of those people. Looking at her husband, sadness washed over her.

Anger came with it. They were good people. They had never knowingly hurt anybody save the odd Harvester, but there was certainly nothing good about them. What had they done to deserve this? Lucy didn't suppose she would trust anybody ever again. She bowed her head, letting her forehead rest on the bed sheet.

Then she frowned. Something was different. She lifted her head.

"Richard?" she whispered. His breathing had changed. She was sure of it; she had sat here long enough to know. She stared at her husband's face, part hopeful, part scared.

Richard lay still as ever, but as she watched him uncertainly his eyes flickered behind the lids.

"Richard?" she repeated, louder this time, squeezing his hand.

The eyes flickered again and finally, painstakingly, the man's dry lips parted.

"Lucy," he uttered weakly.

Lucy's heart leapt into her throat.

"Richard!" She clutched tightly at his hand. "Oh, Richard."

Her husband's eyelids shuddered sluggishly and then opened.

"Lucy," he croaked. "Where are you? I can't see you."

CHAPTER TWELVE
THE PENTAGON ROOM

AUDREY JONES SWEPT HER FEET FORWARD and rocked up into the air, ignoring the wind as it nipped at her cheeks. She wasn't bothered by the cold. Quite the opposite; it meant that she could play on the swings for as long as she wanted. All the other kids were being kept inside, out of the unnatural weather.

The weather wasn't the only reason other children were being kept in their homes, though. Everybody was hiding away because of what had happened to Raj Gupta, too. Audrey didn't really understand what all the fuss was about. That Raj kid had been stupid enough to wander off into a field during a snowstorm and was found frozen stiff two days later by a farmer. Dead as a doornail. Audrey had heard her mum on the phone to Sophia's mum, who was sure that there was something more to it – why had Raj wandered off from his aunt in the first place?

Audrey hadn't liked Raj anyway. He'd kicked a ball in her face that time in a sports lesson. Her nose had bled for ages. No, Audrey had no intention of staying inside because of something stupid Raj had done, which is why she'd slipped out to the park when her mother was busy chatting to one of her men on the internet.

As she pushed herself higher on the swing, the girl noticed something strange. There was another child in the playground, there, by the slide. Stranger still, he wasn't running about or playing, he was just standing there, staring at her.

Audrey eyed the newcomer. Even from here she could tell there was something wrong with him.

He smiled at her, but the smile wasn't right somehow. It looked stretched. Abnormal.

"What you doing?" the boy asked, sidling up to the swings. He was probably about the same age as her, eight or nine, but he didn't have a winter coat on and his skin was grey as the sky.

Audrey decided to ignore him. She thrust her feet out, swinging higher still.

"Bet I can get higher'n you," the boy said.

Audrey scowled. "Bet you can't," she said, watching the trees as they bobbed up and down in front of her.

"I'll prove it."

"No."

"Go on."

"No."

Audrey swung on, showing off now, willing the swing higher with every shove of her stockinged legs. The boy watched her with odd, glassy eyes that made her skin crawl. Finally, Audrey couldn't bare him looking at her anymore. She hopped off the swing.

"Where you going?" the boy asked.

"Home," she huffed.

"Don't you want to see that dead dog everybody's been talking about?"

Audrey, who was heading resolutely toward the park's exit, slowed slightly.

"What dead dog?" she asked doubtfully.

"Some dog got frozen out by the river there," the other child said, pointing back past the swings to a bushy area that led out into the countryside. "Probably a stray. Everybody's seen it. It's sick."

"You're making it up," Audrey said, certain that if there really was something that grisly round here, she'd have been the first to know about it. "There's no dead dog."

"There is. You can see its brain through its nose; it snapped off in the cold."

The boy giggled wickedly.

Audrey had stopped walking now. She looked at the boy, who was wearing a devious, expectant little grin.

"Can you really see its brain?" she ventured. The boy nodded quickly.

"Show me," the girl ordered, pushing past him to start in the direction that he'd pointed.

Not smiling anymore, but instead dabbing his chapped lips with his tongue, hungry for young flesh, Diltraa led Audrey Jones off into the wilderness and to her doom.

★

Up close it resembled nothing more than a capricious scattering of dots, as if a dozen cans of paint had simultaneously exploded. But when Nicholas stepped back, allowing his eyes to wander over the surface of the painting, it was a masterpiece. How anybody could produce anything quite so emotive out of a collection of coloured dots was beyond him.

The two enormous canvasses were the only things that occupied the poky room. The house seemed to be filled with odd little rooms like this, tucked away in funny corners, perhaps the result of an indecisive architect.

It was Nicholas's first full day at Hallow House and he'd spent it exploring his new home. He'd discovered the hard way that it was easy to get lost here. There were strange marvels everywhere. In the statue-lined hallways, great vases were filled with peculiar dried flowers, and huge, polished boulders were strewn about the place like dozing armadillos. Then there was the glass cabinet that contained the bones of a colossal beast. Nicholas had never seen anything like it. At first he'd thought it was a dinosaur, but then he remembered what Jessica had said about evil forces – "the monsters of the deep" – and wondered if this was some kind of malevolent creature.

Elsewhere, he'd uncovered a handful of strange rooms and cramped corridors that he didn't suppose had been used by anybody for quite some time. There were rooms with no windows, rooms with nothing but windows, rooms filled with mysterious objects draped in big white sheets.

Then there was this room. It was a circular turret with dark panelled wood walls. A small chandelier was suspended from the ceiling, spilling light onto the two paintings.

The first was of a woman in her late sixties, he guessed, wearing a simple black dress and an expression that was supremely sour. Black hair, shot through with flecks of silver, curled neatly on her head but failed to soften the woman's stony grimace. Her sharp green eyes stared right out of the painting; if Nicholas hadn't known better he would have sworn she was looking right at him. Whoever she was, she was a severe-looking individual, and Nicholas pitied anybody who'd ever come across her on a dark night.

The second painting was more inviting. Two young women and a man danced in a circle, their heads thrown back in mirth. The wind tugged playfully at the girls' white dresses and one of them hitched up her hem to kick her legs out gaily. Wreaths of bright flowers had been threaded into the blonde-white ringlets of their hair, while their skin was fair almost to the point of translucency. The man was dressed in a blue tunic, clutching the girls' hands as they spun about, bathing in the gracious rays of the sun.

Nicholas could almost hear their joyful cries as they frolicked barefoot in the grass. He wondered who these sprightly individuals were, and how they were connected to the grim-faced woman that was their neighbour. There must be a connection, if not with her, then at least with Jessica. Nicholas mulled this over; somehow the two dancing women reminded him of Jessica.

Something rubbed against his leg and he found the cat staring up at him. "Where've you been?" the boy said, bending down to scoop the animal up into his arms. The cat purred as he fondled its ears, shoving its head into his hand.

"Let's get out of here shall we?" Nicholas said, eyeing the scowling old lady. He went out onto the dimly-lit landing. He was on the second floor, and if he peered over the banister he could see right into the circular lobby below. From this height, Nicholas could trace the twisting design of the marble floor – it appeared to consist of three intertwining sections that coalesced in the centre around a six-pointed star.

The sound of voices echoed into the lobby. Surprised, Nicholas crouched down, holding the cat tightly to him. He hadn't seen Jessica since that morning, when she'd given him a brief tour of the house –

including the kitchen, where a pantry was full of food, and the sunny conservatory. He'd used the shower in the bathroom adjoining his bedroom to wash away the dirt of the bus crash.

Jessica hadn't mentioned that they would be receiving guests, though, and he'd not heard anybody else come into the house. So who was talking?

There came the sound of footsteps and Nicholas pressed his forehead against the banister rail, straining to see into the lobby.

Jessica glided across the marble floor, talking in a hushed tone. A second figure appeared behind her – a tall stranger wearing a hooded black cloak. Jessica spoke quietly to the newcomer, and then they both disappeared through a doorway.

What's going on? Nicholas thought. Who could this newcomer be? Another Sentinel? Unable to contain his curiosity, the boy hurried down to the lobby. The cat squirmed in his grasp so he dropped it to the floor.

A light burned in one of the passageways beyond the circular foyer and Nicholas skulked quietly after Jessica. He'd crept around his own house many times at night and he knew that he could move about unheard if he concentrated. He stepped lightly, brushing a hand along the wall for balance.

This part of the house seemed older and the few lamps lining the walls were not lit. Finally, the boy came to the spot where the sole flickering light originated – it pushed its way through the crack of a peeling old door that had been left slightly ajar. Nicholas recognised this door. He'd tried to open it earlier in the day, but it had been locked. Blood thumping in his ears, he eased in to the stare through the gap.

It was another one of those strange little rooms. Though plain in decor, this one, a parlour, perhaps, was shaped like a pentagon, its five walls making it distinct from the other rooms in Hallow House. The smell of damp was all-consuming. It was clear this place had been locked up for quite some time. Nicholas realised that this was the one part of the house that truly showed its age. Broken cobwebs quivered in the corners and there was a layer of dust covering everything. Even the surface of the walls had chipped away to reveal the plaster underneath, like a picked scab.

Standing before a round table, her back to him, Jessica glowed in the sputtering candlelight.

"I have seen the boy," a deep, male voice rumbled, resonating hollowly in the confined space.

The figure in the black robes lingered in one of the room's furthest corners. He was unnervingly still. Nicholas frowned. There was something wrong with the hooded stranger's face. It was emotionless and sallow, fixed in a perpetual expression of indifference. Then the boy realised what was wrong – it wasn't a face at all, but a mask. For a moment, the shadows that twitched across its smooth surface had afforded the visor a life-like appearance.

"And?"

This time it was Jessica who spoke.

"He is emotional."

Jessica didn't move a muscle. "He mourns," she reasoned. "He has endured much in these past weeks. For now he is grieving, but he has strength."

"You like him," the figure observed. "Be careful. You must not let your feelings muddy the truth – if the boy isn't capable of what is required, he must be dismissed."

Nicholas's stomach gave a little flip. What were they talking about? Whatever it was, the boy took an instant dislike to the stranger. He spoke in clipped, self-important tones. There was an air of the military about him. And what was with the mask? Nicholas wanted to see the stranger's face, but all that was visible behind the mask was the eyes. Nicholas remembered his mother telling him that eyes were the windows to the soul. The newcomer's were shards of black glass.

"Do you have news from the community?" Jessica asked.

"There is panic," the hooded figure told her, though he sounded resigned to what he had witnessed. "Nobody anticipated this; not even the Sensitives. Naturally they sensed something, but this was beyond prediction." The figure paused before continuing darkly: "Cambridge has been particularly active. Strange things are happening there. Missing children, a break-in at the museum. Attacks on Sentinel families."

"But that's where Nicholas has come from," Jessica started. "What do you—"

"We cannot stand about debating the 'whats' and 'ifs' of the situation," the figure snapped. "You're delaying."

"I'm not." Jessica sounded annoyed. Nicholas was surprised that she could be riled in that way. She'd seemed so composed with him.

"What are we to do?" Jessica asked finally.

"The moon is waxing," the figure told her. "It's time to put your studies into practice."

Jessica moved – and Nicholas nearly cried out in shock.

A skull was grinning at him.

There, in a chair pushed up to the circular table, sat a withered old corpse. Its taut skin was papery, while a mound of black and silver curls tumbled down into the empty eye sockets – which gaped right at him.

Nicholas put a hand over his mouth to muffle his breathing, which suddenly seemed to be huffing loudly from his throat. He wondered if Jessica could hear the blood pumping in his ears. What the hell was going on?

"Tonight?" Jessica said. She eyed the cadaver. It was still wearing the clothes it had died in. The necklaces and rings adorning its throat and bony fingers were dull with age. "I'm not ready."

"You will have to be," the figure told her bluntly. "If we are to stand any chance against those in the service of the Dark Prophets, we'll need any aid that is available to us. You have studied the conjuration for long enough, and she has been trapped for far too long. She will prove a powerful ally, especially with regard to the boy. It is time to release her."

Even from here Jessica looked nervous, and Nicholas started to feel uneasy. He'd known Jessica for only the briefest of moments, but she'd seemed so serene, possessing wisdom beyond her youthful appearance. Now, a fracture in her confidence had appeared, and for once she was acting as young as she looked. As Jessica regarded the cloaked figure in the corner, Nicholas realised that she was scared.

Something touched Nicholas's leg and he stifled another yell, gripping the doorframe to stop himself tumbling into the candlelit parlour. It was the cat again.

"Shhh," Nicholas warned it, shoving it away from the door. Then he turned back to the room. The cloaked figure handed Jessica a small velvet pouch.

"Focus," he told her. "You have trained long for this. It must not fail."

Jessica clutched the velvet pouch before her and swallowed. The figure retreated into the shadows in the corner of the room.

Jessica closed her eyes. She drew in a deep breath, letting it out slowly before pulling on the gold cord that bound the pouch. Reaching inside, she fingered the contents and withdrew her hand. Then she began to murmur deferentially, humming foreign-sounding words.

The candles guttered and then flamed higher.

Nicholas quivered. The words were needling at his skin. He could feel them crackling through the atmosphere, elongating and settling. Goosebumps prickled down his arms.

In the room, the wooden chandelier began to spin. It whirled faster and faster. The candle flames merged to become a gyrating circle of fire. A spinning halo above.

Jessica fixed her gaze on the corpse.

She threw her hand out, scattering dry powder into the air. As it fell and met the candles, they sputtered and flashed. The flames flickered black.

An unnatural wind groaned. It unsettled Jessica's hair and ruffled the folds of her dress.

Nicholas watched on, his nose twitching as the dust gusted through the gap in the door. What sort of words was Jessica speaking? And what had turned the flames black like that? He didn't like it. A part of him wanted to shout out; to storm into the room and – what? Shake Jessica out of whatever madness had gripped her? Something stopped him. Perhaps it was fear. Or curiosity. Whatever it was, Nicholas barely moved, barely breathed, both horrified and thrilled.

Jessica stretched her hands up to the ceiling. Above, the halo of light span faster.

"Return!" she beseeched. "Awaken. Remember. Live!"

The walls trembled.

In the corner, the masked figure stood motionless. Sinister and snake-like. Black eyes glittering at Jessica.

Nicholas caught his breath as he noticed a small furry shape crouched on the floor by the table. The cat had moved towards the commotion, its own inquisitiveness getting the better of it. It sniffed at the incensed air, its head moving in circles as it followed the course of the rotating chandelier.

"Get back here," Nicholas hissed at it.

"Return!" Jessica cried.

There came a crackle of thunder and sparks danced about the spinning halo.

With an almighty crunch the ceiling split, a jagged line zigzagging from wall to wall, and the wooden floorboards sagged with a groan.

The sparks were alive, swarming through the air.

They fizzed down from the chandelier and flickered in between Jessica's hands.

Nicholas watched as a sudden change came over the cat. Its hackles raised and it squashed itself up against the wall behind it. A low growl burred from the back of its throat and it let out an uneasy *hisssssss*.

Jessica's concentration seemed to falter. She turned toward the cat.

The last thing Nicholas saw before the explosion of light was a black cat with its ears flattened against its skull.

A concussive pulse of energy blasted through the room.

Nicholas was hurled back and hit the floor.

A blanket of white light smothered him.

He couldn't see. His ears were ringing. For a moment he thought that he was blind for good and panic snatched at him. Then the white haze began to clear and the ringing in his ears slowly subsided. He lay there for a moment, crumpled, a ball of nerves. Part of him dared not look back into the room for fear of what he might find. It had sounded like a bomb had gone off. But he had to look.

Steadying himself against the doorframe, he peered through the crack once more.

Jessica stood blinking. On the other side of the room, the masked figure crouched low, those dark eyes swivelling uneasily. The candles had all gusted out and a ghostly calm rested over the parlour.

"What devilry is this?"

A terse voice shattered the silence.

Nicholas looked about uncertainly at this new voice. He didn't recognise it. It sounded like an old woman.

In the room, Jessica stiffened. Her eyes flashed to the corpse and she frowned when she saw that it was as lifeless as ever. She looked confused, searching for the owner of those brusque tones, and her gaze finally rested, incredulously, on the cat. It was peering at its meagre surroundings with renewed interest. Perhaps it was a mere trick of the light, but it seemed that irregular flashes of silver had appeared in its jet-black fur.

Jessica watched the animal, finally finding her voice.

"Isabel?" she uttered doubtfully.

The cat looked at her, *really* looked at her, and there was a flicker of recognition in its marble-like eyes.

Then the animal opened its mouth and said: "Jessica? What–?"

Jessica flinched. In his corner, the masked figure rose.

"What is happening?" the cat demanded. It seemed to notice the corpse at the table for the first time and its tail began lashing irritably. Ears flattened.

"What is this?" the cat demanded again, the cracked voice choking.

Jessica stared at the talking feline. Then a grin spread across her face and she clapped her hands joyfully.

"It worked!" she rejoiced. "Not quite how I expected, but... look at you! You're here!"

The animal glared at her. "Well of course I'm here," it snapped. Then it hesitated, as if realising that something wasn't quite right. It was talking up at Jessica – that in itself was odd. The creature appraised the room and seemed to become aware that everything was bigger than it ought to be. It blinked, looked down where two furry black paws rested. The cat's eyes widened in horror and a growl rumbled through it – which only served to cause it even greater disquiet.

"What–?" it stuttered. "What is this?"

Jessica took a quick step toward the animal, but it recoiled.

"Isabel–" Jessica began.

"What have you done?" the cat shrieked. Disgusted and humiliated, it turned tail and fled.

The animal streaked past Nicholas and out of sight. For a moment the boy stood motionless, his mind reeling. What had he just witnessed? He was certain that the cat – his cat – had just spoken. Not only spoken, but spoken with the voice of an old woman. Before he could think anything more, Nicholas realised that Jessica might chase after the animal and discover him. He turned and hurried quickly down the hallway.

Back in his bedroom, he paced the floor.

The cat had spoken. *The cat had spoken.*

Those four words repeated in his head over and over, until he almost believed that it was perfectly normal for a cat to speak. But it wasn't. It most certainly and absolutely wasn't.

★

Lucy Walden hadn't slept since the attack. No, that wasn't completely true. There had been moments. Snatches here and there, when the exhaustion and worry had become so great that her body merely slumped into slumber against her will. They were tortured moments where the real and the imagined morphed together, and she had dreamt disturbing dreams of sightless monsters and suffocating bed sheets.

Richard knew this because she'd told him when he woke up. When Richard had finally stirred, Lucy told him she had thought that was a dream, too. It hadn't been a dream, though. Richard had woken up, and he was conscious, and he had spoken. He was drained and his vision was impaired, his eyes still a milky white after the attack, but he was awake.

So for the first time in what to her must have felt a very long while, Lucy slept. She slept deeply, worn out and relieved, curled up next to him.

On that chill night, she slept so soundly that when Richard stirred next to her, she didn't feel it.

He lay there, his pale eyes open, blankly staring up at the ceiling. Slowly he sat up, slid his legs over the side of the bed and eased his weight onto them. He moved over to the bedroom door and unhooked his dressing gown, shrugging into it. Then he went out onto the dark landing.

He moved quietly, steadily. He stopped momentarily in an open doorway. There, in the room beyond, his father lay in bed, soft snores rising from his throat. Richard regarded him momentarily with his peculiar, colourless eyes. Then he moved off down the landing once more.

Outside, it was bitterly cold. The layers of snow had hardened and become ice, shimmering on the garden path. Richard stepped out of the back door, his bare feet crunching on the frozen path. He didn't notice.

Despite the snowy deposits that proliferated in the garden, it was unnervingly dark, with only the light of the moon punching a ragged hole in a cloud.

Richard made his way into the garden, coming to a small shed. He stopped and his breath curled out in a mist.

There came the softest of sounds, then a figure stepped out from behind the shed. It was a woman in a red dress. Her pale skin gleamed in the moonlight and Richard's breath caught in his throat.

"Hello Richard," the woman purred. "My name's Malika."

"Hello," Richard returned simply.

"Did you sleep well?" Malika asked conversationally. She trailed a finger down one of the shed's windowpanes, forging a line through the frost.

"I feel like I slept a hundred years," Richard said. "I feel different."

"Yes," Malika said. She licked the ice from her finger, taking a step closer to him. "You have been chosen," she told him. "You are one of few, but you will become one of many."

"You work for Them," Richard said.

A corner of the woman's lips curled upward.

"You know what you must do," she said. "Listen to the voice that speaks from within." She raised a hand and held her palm over his eyes. When she removed it, his eyes were back to normal.

Richard blinked, his pupils focussing.

"You have been a Sentinel since birth, tied up by their rules and rituals. It is time to break free, to fashion yourself anew."

"It is my time to evolve," Richard said.

"You may call it that," Malika told him. "But do not forget who you once were. Use that information; it is vital. It is why you have been chosen."

Richard nodded, understanding.

"Move about on the inside, be our hands and eyes there," Malika hummed. "It is time to bring about the fall of the Sentinels."

Richard nodded. He turned to look up at the house where his family slept.

CHAPTER THIRTEEN
In The Garden Of Norlath

NICHOLAS BARELY SLEPT THAT NIGHT. He lay staring up at the ceiling, jumbled thoughts tumbling in his mind. So much had happened in the past week, so many odd things. He felt completely out of control. It seemed like everything was happening either to or around him, and he just wanted to slam his foot down on some sort of cosmic brake pedal and bring everything screaming to a halt.

That wasn't an option, of course. Most worryingly, the catalogue of oddness only appeared to be swelling in size. The weird weather, the midnight stroll, the bus, the Sentinels and now, inexplicably, magic and a talking cat.

It was at 4 a.m, as the darkness deepened in the silence of his new room, that Nicholas happened upon a particularly disturbing theory. What if he'd imagined it all? He'd heard that people who'd recently gone through traumatic experiences – say, a death in the family – were susceptible to peculiar dreams and a detachment from reality. There was a difference, though, he reasoned, between forgetting what day it was and thinking you've seen a cat talk.

Had he imagined everything he'd witnessed in that strange pentagon-shaped room? Perhaps he really had lost it. Lying with only his thoughts for company, the events started to become hazy. Nicholas's mind swam with all that he'd learnt. He thought about the Sentinels, and what Jessica had said about a world hiding behind the every day. Then there was what the masked figure had said about strange things happening in Cambridge. What sort of strange things? Nicholas grew even more anxious. Had he made a horrible mistake coming here? What if something happened to Sam? Or Tabatha?

Half dreaming, half thinking, Nicholas twisted and turned in the bed sheets, dipping in and out of wakefulness. For a moment, he was sure he'd seen his mother standing by the bedside, but as he'd reached out a hand to her, she'd vanished, been absorbed by the shadows.

By the time dawn finally edged through a gap in his curtains, Nicholas didn't know what was real and what wasn't. Only one thing was certain: he hadn't seen the cat all night.

Unable to lie thinking any longer, Nicholas dragged himself out of bed and went to the window, parting the heavy curtains to squint out at the frosty countryside. From here he could see for what seemed like miles; the house really was in the middle of nowhere. There was no other sign of life, though. Not even the sun could penetrate the dense clouds pleated above.

In the bathroom connected to his room, Nicholas got into the shower, hoping that the warm water would wash away the confusion. When he emerged from the steamed-up bathroom, he felt refreshed and hungry.

He pulled a t-shirt, jumper and a pair of trousers from his suitcase. As he dressed, he noticed his backpack poking out from beneath the bed. He grabbed it and reached inside, pulling out the velvet box that he'd discovered in his parents' hidden room. He'd almost forgotten about it. Flipping it over in his hands he scrutinised it once more.

"There's got to be a way to open the stupid thing," he mumbled to himself. Next time he saw Jessica he'd ask her about it.

But Jessica was nowhere to be found that morning, either. As he traipsed the hallways, Nicholas could find no sign of her – or the cat for that matter. It was deathly quiet, and the boy realised that he almost missed Tabatha's clatter and commotion. Only almost though, because she'd been a massive pain in the backside as well.

Not that Nicholas didn't find Hallow House intriguing. There was something about the place. Despite the building's utter stillness, Nicholas sensed life here. The lives of those who had been here before permeated everything: the scuffs on the walls, a bowed floorboard that had curved under centuries of footfall, books with folded over pages stacked neatly in corners. There had been life here, he sensed, and passion. It had been home.

In a corner of the house near to the living room, Nicholas entered the kitchen. It was toasty warm and spotless, with a flagstone floor and exposed beams in the ceiling. The pantry was packed with food, and Nicholas made himself some porridge using the immense, old-fashioned stove.

Full and restless, he roamed the quiet halls, considering what Jessica had told him about Sensitives. Could he really possess such gifts? Did that explain the way he'd been feeling since his parents' deaths? The whispers? The way he inexplicably knew things; how he'd known something was going to happen on the bus? What had the cloaked figure said to Jessica?

"*If the boy isn't capable of what is required.*"

Nicholas was sure there was more to Jessica's explanation. And, he thought with growing agitation, if he was in fact Sensitive, why couldn't he find that damned cat?

Resolving to get to the bottom of last night's strange activities, Nicholas returned to the dank corridor he'd followed Jessica down the previous evening. He approached the door that led to the pentagon-shaped parlour and was frustrated to find that it was locked once more. Nicholas ran his fingers along the cracks in the doorframe, but it was useless. Then, without really knowing why, he found himself pressing his palms against the aged wood, and he closed his eyes in concentration.

"Get away from there," came a low whisper.

Startled, Nicholas spun away from the door, only just catching sight of a black tail as it whipped around a corner. That voice. It had been the same dissenting voice he'd heard last night. The old woman.

Without pausing, he gave chase, turning corner after blind corner until he eventually skidded into a corridor with brilliant white walls. At the far end, a pair of high, double doors, were enclosed by sturdy, bleached pillars. Nicholas's breaths echoed in the stark space and he approached the doors, surprised that he'd not yet come across this part of the house.

He eased open one of the doors, and light spilled across his face, along with a potent, heady fragrance. His nostrils thrilled at the delicate perfume and he could taste the myriad of scents on his lips. Images of spring and laughter flew unbidden to his mind.

As his eyes adjusted to the light, Nicholas became confused. It appeared that he'd stumbled outside. Before him, verdant leaves shimmered and beckoned, while giant trees towered upwards, their branches reaching out to him in welcome. There was no snow here, though, and there, high up as far as Nicholas could see, was a glass firmament. The boy's eyes grew wide with astonishment.

It was a garden. But this was unlike any garden Nicholas had ever seen. While the snow-ravaged terrain of the outside world was battling crippling frost, here life was thriving. Wildflowers fashioned their own multi-coloured carpets across the ground, creating a sea of colour and texture that bubbled around the trunks of the trees. The boy drank in the greenery, finding the scents intoxicating, and he ambled into the garden, dazzled by the bustle of colour.

Here and there, fragments of flint and cement jutted from the wilderness. They seemed out of place, as if they'd fallen from the sky and been embraced by the wildlife. The further Nicholas went, the larger the stony edifices became; some even had large gaps that looked like they had once housed doors and windows.

The boy paused as he felt a familiar prickle across the nape of his neck, as if there were eyes upon him. He searched the foliage for another, and then he saw her.

Jessica appeared from behind a maple tree mere feet away. The golden locks of her hair shimmered, but there was something different about her. Her silken dress was grubby, and there was mud smeared on her bare knees.

"Hi," Nicholas said, surprised at the woman's appearance. What had happened to the immaculate, composed creature he'd met only a couple of days ago?

Jessica pushed her way through the garden. She seemed agitated. One of her hands was balled up in a fist by her side, while the other snatched up handfuls of the vegetation before tossing it distractedly to the ground.

"Norlath," the woman said in a tight, desperate voice. "Have you seen Norlath? She was just here, not a moment ago."

Nicholas frowned.

"I– I don't know who that is," he said. Jessica was right in front of him now and suddenly looked very small. A lost little girl.

She cast a furtive glance about her, and put a hand to her head, scratching at her scalp with her fingernails. "She was here," she muttered. "She was just here, but I can't find her. There was something I needed to tell her. It was important. The flowers were talking again and I had to tell her, because it was so marvellous. Black-eyed Susan and Sweet William, they were singing to one another."

"I've not seen anybody," Nicholas told her truthfully, thinking of the big empty house he'd just wandered through. "Is everything alright?"

Jessica peered up at the canopy of leaves above her and began to whisper to herself. "All in the downs the fleet was moored, banners waving in the wind. When Black-eyed Susan came aboard, and eyed the burly men. 'Tell me ye sailors, tell me true, if my Sweet William sails with you…'"

Her breath caught in her throat and Jessica scrambled up to Nicholas, seizing the front of his jumper in her fists.

"You have to help me," she pleaded, staring up at him, her eyes wide and glassy. The boy could see his own startled face reflected in them. "Please, please," she begged.

"I'll help you," Nicholas said, upset by the change in the woman. "Just tell me what to do."

Jessica collapsed against the boy. "Maybe you shouldn't be here," she hissed, her hot breath tickling his bare neck. "There are things here. Scratching around, pushing their way out of the ground. They'll eat your tongue."

Nicholas didn't know what to do. He thought about putting his arms around her, attempting to comfort her because she was obviously upset, but it didn't feel right.

"The world…" Jessica murmured sorrowfully into his shoulder. "It's flailing and falling. The oceans spill over and shrivel and the air grows thick with poisonous waste. There are screams, but nobody hears them, and we all stand around laughing and playing like naïve children, unaware of the seeds. Death is coming. The end…"

"Jessica," a snobby voice retorted, cutting off the woman's ramblings. "What the devil are you doing?"

Jessica fell away from the boy.

"Isabel," she mumbled, brushing absentmindedly at the folds of her dress. Nicholas turned in the direction of that snooty voice and found that the cat was watching them, its gold-flecked eyes both suspicious and arrogant.

"D—did you just speak?" he said to the animal. The creature shot him a disdainful glare, and Jessica seized her chance.

"I'm sorry," she said quietly, suddenly more lucid than she had been only a moment before. "I'm sorry." In a flutter of grubby white she was gone.

"What have you done?"

The cat was addressing Nicholas now, squinting balefully out from the shade of a bush. Its tail danced like a live wire, unsettling a crop of diamond-shaped leaves.

"What have I done?" Nicholas retaliated. "She's the one acting nuts!"

"You provoked her," the animal continued, though now there was doubt in her voice.

"I barely said a word," Nicholas said miserably. He stopped short, adding apprehensively: "And why can you talk? Cats aren't supposed to be able to do that."

"I'm not a cat," said the cat. Nicholas's cynical stare prompted it to add: "Not normally, anyway. This is but a temporary… inconvenience."

"I'll say."

"Don't mumble," said the cat. It drew itself deeper into the protective shade of the plant. With Jessica gone, it seemed suddenly aware of how exposed it was out here in the garden, and its eyes flashed uneasily up at the trees before returning to the curly-haired boy.

"Who are you?" Nicholas asked, his interest growing. "What are you doing here?"

"I'm Isabel," the cat returned distractedly. "And I might ask the same of you. This is no place for children."

"I'm staying here," Nicholas said, choosing to ignore the insult. "I thought I was the only one, but Jessica mentioned somebody else, Norlath or something. She said she was looking for her."

The cat gave as close to a tut as it could muster.

"Norlath's gone, has been for many an age," it said bluntly. "This was her garden. She was obsessed with it. Consumed her life."

"Why would Jessica be looking for her if she's gone?" Nicholas asked, still unnerved by the woman's strange behaviour, not to mention the cat's sudden eloquence.

Isabel didn't have an answer for that. Instead, she started licking her front paw. Then, thinking better of it, she sat up straight and fixed her piercing gaze on the boy.

"You still haven't told me what you're doing here," she said.

It was a good thing that she'd spoken because in that brief moment of silence Nicholas had been given time to realise that he was having a conversation with a feline, a thought that was making him feel decidedly unwell.

"Right now, this place is all I've got," Nicholas told her.

"What a sad existence you must lead."

"Better than some," Nicholas shot back. "Besides, I like it here."

"Like it?" the cat retorted. "What is here for you? Cobwebs and melancholy? You should be out gambling with your years, causing mischief, fighting other street urchins for scraps and vittles... or whatever folly young boys meddle in nowadays."

"You're one to talk," the boy said, the novelty of their conversation wearing thin. The creature's consistently bristling tone was annoying. "You're a cat!"

"You really don't know much, do you child?" sighed the creature under the bush.

"I'd know a lot more if everybody wasn't so bloody secretive around here!" Nicholas yelled.

"Petulant, too, I see," the cat noted snidely.

That was it. He'd had enough. Sick of the miserly creature and her barbed tongue, Nicholas kicked a clump of dirt in the animal's direction and stomped back towards the house.

As Isabel ranted and raved behind him – spitting insults he was sure hadn't been used in at least a century – he burst into the white corridor and slammed the door shut behind him.

CHAPTER FOURTEEN
NOWHERE IS SAFE NOW

SAM EASED THE MORRIS MINOR TO the kerb. Its engine spluttered as it slowed and the radio, through which Frank Sinatra had been softly crooning 'A Foggy Day', shuddered into silence.

In the passenger seat, Liberty unclipped her seatbelt and went to open the car door.

"Ahem."

Sam cleared his throat disapprovingly, stopping her mid-motion. He got out of the car, crunched a path through the snow and opened Liberty's door for her.

"M'lady," he said.

Liberty stepped out.

"You consider me a lady, how remarkably misinformed you are."

She had twisted ribbons of brown suede through her hair, affixing little beads with white feathers to the tips of her braids. Sam didn't find the result wholly displeasing to the eye. Of course, fashion was a mystery to him.

He locked the car.

"Quiet, isn't it?" Liberty commented. She was peering down the snow-swathed street. Sam thought he saw her shiver, then huddle deeper into her winter coat.

It was mid-morning, and she was right; the world was eerily quiet. When the freak snowstorms had first blustered in, there had been a sudden rush of activity. Children had been bundled up in their coats, retrieved from the backs of cupboards after only the briefest of reprieves.

There had been snowball fights and snowmen and Sam's neighbour had dressed up in a red suit and donned a fake beard just for the fun of it.

There had been a peculiar thrill to seeing snow during the summer. But as the bitter weather persisted, the children returned to their homes. Few now ventured out into the unnatural cold, save those forced to by work and responsibility. People were becoming as bitter as the present climate, grimly waiting for the summer to return.

"Quiet as the grave," Sam agreed. "I suppose everybody is toasting their feet in front of a nice fire." He stamped his boots enviously. Beside him, Liberty peered up at the house they had parked by and Sam wondered if she was already sensing the trouble awaiting them.

He went to the front door and was just about to knock when–

"No."

Liberty was frowning, half squinting at the house as if attempting to read its mood. She tilted her head.

"Something's not right."

Sam nodded. "I know, but we can't let that stop us," he said.

"Use your key."

He didn't bother to ask how she knew that he had a spare for the Walden's. Some people might find Liberty's gift unsettling or intrusive. In fact, this had been the case on more than one occasion. Sam, however, admired her for it. She couldn't help the things that she felt.

He fished around in his pocket and pulled out a crammed key chain. He singled one out and pushed it into the lock.

The air in the hall was stale and Sam felt a twinge of unease. Things had certainly changed in recent weeks. Lucy Walden was one of the most house-proud women he'd ever met, even more so than his Judith, bless her soul. He had often teased Lucy for her obsessive cleanliness, once commenting that there would be a frost in hell before any dust settled on her surfaces. There was a horrible irony in that now. The morning's mail lay unattended on the doormat, while a potted plant near the stairs drooped, neglected.

Sam peered at Liberty. Her eyes were impossibly large in the dim light. It was a familiar look. Sam had been there when she was born and he'd watched her grow into a confident young woman. It hadn't always been that way, though. He remembered her teenage years all too well.

Her abilities had made school a nightmare. She'd come home stoic and tight-lipped more than once when he was there, shutting herself in her room.

Luckily, her father – Sam's friend Alastair – shared her gifts and had taught her the best he could. Sam remembered how Alastair had explained what being a Sensitive was like. Alastair had once owned a battered old television set. It had never worked properly. The aerial had to be resting at just the right angle to display a fuzz-free picture. Alastair likened Sensitives to that television set. There were signals in the air and Sensitives were the receiver. Mostly the signals were emotions, feelings; sometimes they were images and facts. Like the aerial, Sensitives had to find just the right frequency.

Liberty took a breath beside him and Sam left her to work her magic. She didn't like interruptions.

He opened a door. It had once been a lounge, but it was almost impossible to tell that now. Slashes had been gouged into the wallpaper and the chimney breast had been attacked with such aggression that half of it had collapsed into the room, bringing with it a layer of soot that smothered everything.

Anything that could be ruined had been. It looked as if a demented animal had been let loose on the room.

"What the–?" Sam began. "Trinity spare us. What could have done this?"

He tensed.

A noise came from above.

The creak of a floorboard.

"I don't like it," Liberty said.

"Can't say I disagree," Sam murmured. He couldn't take his eyes off the living room. What could have done this? He answered his own question with a single word: *Harvester*. Liberty looked at him and nodded.

"Trap?" Sam said in a hushed voice.

"It's not a trap if we know it's a trap," Liberty replied.

"One way to be certain."

He went to the kitchen and took out a knife, then headed for the stairs. Liberty went after him and together they made a stealthy ascent.

The landing was deserted.

Sam took a few furtive steps, coming to Patrick Walden's bedroom. The door was only slightly ajar, so Sam eased it open.

Even as his fingers touched the wood, Liberty let out a little moan.

This room had been relatively untouched by whatever furious force had destroyed the living room. Nothing seemed to be out of place here. Except for the bed.

A figure lay in it, motionless. The crisp white sheets were splashed with red.

Sam shuddered. He leaned on the doorframe.

"Patrick."

"Killed while he slept," Liberty muttered. "Cowards."

For a fleeting moment, as the grief overwhelmed him, Sam wondered what Liberty sensed from the dead – if anything. Was it as if they were asleep? Perhaps a groggy blur of dreaming? Or was there simply nothing? An empty space where once life had been?

Another noise snapped Sam to his senses. It was closer this time, coming from further down the landing.

He turned toward it, anger boiling through him. Whatever had done this was still in the house, he was sure of it. Had the doctor Lucy told him about returned to complete what he had started? Sam's jaw set and his fist squeezed the knife.

Liberty placed a hand on his arm. He didn't look at her.

"Too many have been killed now," he growled. "I won't suffer the monster to live."

"Trap," Liberty reminded him gently.

"The last he will set."

Sam moved down the landing, toward the scuffling sound, and threw open Richard and Lucy's bedroom door.

Nothing. No sign of life here either. Or death, for that matter. A small relief.

The room was, unsurprisingly, in a shambles. The bed was flipped over so that the bed frame lay atop the mattress. One of the windows had been smashed and some of the carpet had come up off the floorboards.

Sam scrutinised the debris. There had to be something here that would provide some clue as to what had happened.

Where were Richard and Lucy?

Another noise.

Sam stiffened and looked at the wardrobe in the corner of the room, the one thing still standing where it was supposed to.

Liberty appeared next to him.

"Somebody's in there," she said quietly.

Sam nodded and inwardly kicked himself. Why hadn't he brought his rifle? He reminded himself that he hadn't been expecting this. But then, the world was going to hell right now, wasn't it? He should have been more prepared. The words the red-headed vixen had spat at him on the bus echoed in his ears.

"You're losing your touch."

And she had winked.

Sam puffed out his chest and strode up to the wardrobe. He reached for one of the doors, but before he had the chance to touch it, the door crashed open in his face and a screaming creature burst out at him.

Something sharp glinted in its hand.

It fell on the old man with haunted eyes and raised the shining object–

"Lucy!"

The creature stopped at the sound of its name, straining to look at who had shouted.

"S–Sam," she trembled.

Lucy Walden fell away from him, dropping the knife to the floor. She backed up against the wardrobe, shaking uncontrollably.

"Lucy," Sam said, his voice filled with concern. He eased himself up from the floor. The woman was a mess; still in her pyjamas, her honey-coloured hair wild. There were grazes on her arms.

Sam moved toward her.

Lucy cringed away. "I–I almost… I almost–" she stammered, her eyes fixed on the knife on the carpet.

"No harm done," Sam assured her. "Look at me, right as rain."

She wouldn't look at him, though. Her troubled gaze lingered on the knife and she was still shaking. She seemed to be deeply traumatised. *What has she been through?* A horrible thought struck him. What if she had done something to Richard and Patrick? What if she had killed her father-in-law? Sam pushed the disturbing notion away, not wanting to believe it.

He cupped her chin.

"Lucy."

Finally she looked at him.

The tears came.

"Sam," she whispered. "You shouldn't have come back."

"Where's Richard?" Sam asked. "What happened here?"

"Richard," Lucy whimpered.

Sam wrapped his arms around her and she sagged against him, not bothered by his scratchy grey suit. Only a few days had passed since Sam left the Waldens to accompany Nicholas, and although he'd hardly left Richard and Lucy in the happiest of circumstances, what he had returned to was almost beyond comprehension. He swept Lucy's hair out of her face.

She was terrified, that much he could tell. She clung to him like a child who was afraid of the dark.

"Lucy," he appealed softly. "If you can tell me anything…"

Lucy gave no response; she simply leant into Sam's shoulder despairingly.

He bent to look at Liberty. She was occupied with other things. He wondered if she could sense anything. He wasn't Sensitive, but even he could feel the anxious energies throbbing through the house.

Liberty pressed a hand to her head, as if it was pounding, and Sam dreaded to think what she was picking up. She closed her eyes, a pained expression twisting her pretty face. Then her eyes snapped open.

"It gestated here," she murmured.

"Gestated?"

"The thing that did this," Liberty answered. "While the man slept. It seized hold, sank in deep, spread roots."

"Richard–" Sam began.

"Don't you know it's rude to talk about somebody behind their back?"

A voice punctured the air.

Lucy let out a cry, thrusting away from Sam and wedging herself into the space between the wardrobe and the wall.

There was a figure in the doorway.

"Didn't take you for a gossip, old boy," it said.

It took Sam a few moments to realise just who this scruffy figure was. In the end it was the familiar brown eyes that gave the newcomer's identity away. If the change that Sam had witnessed in Richard days ago had been difficult to stomach, what he was confronted with now made that pale in comparison.

Richard had never been a man possessed of particular presence or poise. He was a gentle, unassuming soul. It was therefore all the more chilling to see him now. Richard lounged against the doorframe, face gaunt and fixed with a sly smile. Days without shaving had encouraged the growth of a bristly mesh of a beard, which matched his greasy brown hair. His shirt was blood-spattered and his eyes glinted like steel. He wasn't wearing his glasses anymore.

"Quite a reunion," he snorted. "Alone in my bedroom with two women, Samuel! What would dear Judith say?"

"Richard–" Sam began, confused.

"No," Liberty broke in.

Richard gave the dark-skinned woman a withering glance.

"Is this who you brought to save me, friend? A witch? I feel I should be offended."

Sam's face was a picture of bewilderment as he stared at the other man. There wasn't a shred left of the Richard he had known.

"You," he finally croaked. "You did all of this."

Richard eased away from the doorframe, arms crossed.

"Oh, come, come," he chided. "Senility really is setting in, isn't it? Do I need to spell it out for you? Treat you like an invalid?" He snorted in contempt. "I had quite enough of that with Dad."

Sam's initial surprise faded as new, hotter emotions stirred.

"You killed your father," he said. "You destroyed your home. Look what you've done to your wife."

"A shame that you find this all so disagreeable," Richard sighed. "I had hoped we could work together. Side by side, like the good old days. Starsky and Hutch. Butch Cassidy and the Sundance Kid."

"It was the doctor," Liberty interrupted. "He did something to him."

"Speak again, witch, and I'll cleave the tongue from your mouth," Richard snapped.

He took a step toward Sam and the older man saw that he was trembling. Not from the cold. He was excited. Richard was enjoying this.

"Tell me, Samuel," the scraggly man began, scratching the coarse pattern of hair at his throat. "Are your wits sharp enough to take me, do you think? I'm not so sure."

"Don't engage with him," Liberty said. "He—"

Before she could finish the sentence, Richard had leapt across the room with such speed that it caught them all off guard. He dealt a blow to the side of Sam's head, sending the old man crashing into the wardrobe.

Sam's vision exploded in stars. They fizzed and his ears rang.

When the stars finally popped and cleared, he saw that Richard and Liberty had tumbled onto the upturned bed. Richard was on top of her, squeezing her throat in his hands.

For a moment their eyes locked; Liberty's wide with surprise, Richard's bloodshot. Then with surprising strength, Liberty bucked beneath him and Richard was thrown across the room, hitting the far wall and tumbling to the floor.

Sam attempted to get up, but wooziness overcame him and he sucked air in, biting back the bile. When he glanced up again, he saw that Richard was already rising from where he'd landed.

"Interesting," he grinned. "You found a feisty one, Sam."

Liberty didn't take her eyes off him.

"Sam," she said. "Are you okay?"

Sam couldn't speak.

"What to do now, witch? What's running through that pretty head?" he heard Richard goad. The man considered her for a moment. Then he whispered, "Am I fast enough? Can I get the knife? Is Sam okay?"

"Stop!" Liberty yelled. She had put a hand to her head.

In that instant the figure pounced at her again, striking her jaw. Liberty fell to the floor.

Sam's vision swam and he watched in a daze as the pair tussled. They seemed evenly matched. He cursed himself. What did he think he was doing? Just two days ago he'd been in a bus crash. Now he was being thrown into wardrobes. Even a young man would have trouble recovering from that. Fear blazed into frustration. His body was too old for this, even if his mind was still sharp. He breathed deeply. He was no good to anybody like this. As he attempted to tap into some inner well of strength, he heard another crash and saw Liberty tumble across the floor. She seized the kitchen knife from where it had fallen earlier.

Leaping to her feet, she struck out with it and sliced Richard's arm. She seemed to have been aiming for his chest.

As the slathering man swung for her, Liberty seized his bleeding arm and sent him crashing into the wall once more.

Now! Sam thought. *Get up now!*

But his body didn't respond.

Helplessly he watched Richard go for Liberty again, hurling her across the bed, where she landed in a heap near the window. She looked dazed, and Sam saw Richard swipe the knife from the carpet. He reached down and dragged Liberty to her feet, clutching at her throat with his free hand.

Sam didn't hear what he hissed at her.

As he prepared to launch himself from the floor, a blurry form suddenly darted past him and Sam started in surprise.

It was Lucy. She had emerged from her hiding place between the wall and the wardrobe.

"You're not him!" she screamed, bowling into the man who had once been her husband. "YOU'RE NOT HIM!"

Richard let out a strangled cry, caught off guard. He crashed backwards, straight through the smashed window.

Sam heard the sound of shattered glass raining down on the patio, and then a muted *whump*.

Lucy stood staring out the window, grasping the sill for support.

Liberty looked on her last legs as she heaved herself to her feet and put an arm around the trembling woman.

Finally the nausea lessened and Sam struggled up from where he had landed by the wardrobe. Every inch of him ached as he went to the window.

"You okay?" Liberty asked.

Sam didn't answer, ashamed at his inability to help. Instead, he peered down at the patio.

"Gone," he muttered. "We must find him."

"He's injured," Liberty said, searching the garden. "He won't be bothering us again today."

She hesitated. Sam followed her gaze to the garden shed.

"What is it?" he asked.

"Something else was here," Liberty murmured. "It visited Richard."

"Can you sense anymore?"

"It…" Liberty started falteringly. "It pretends to be a woman. Red hair…" She touched her forehead, blinking. It looked like she was going to throw up. "It… calls itself…"

Sam didn't like this. "Liberty," he said.

Liberty squeezed her eyes shut.

"Malika," she purred. "She was here with Richard. She and the doctor, I see them together in a dark room…" Liberty pushed her hand against her forehead.

Sam took her arm. "Liberty," he said softly.

At his warm touch, the pain seemed to ease and Liberty blinked out of whatever the daydream had been.

"You alright?" he asked.

Liberty nodded.

"So we have a name for her," he mused, tracing the healing scratch on his cheek. "If she's been here, we must get away. Lucy, we'll take you to your sister's."

Lucy didn't seem to hear him. She stared out at the sky, lost in the horror of the situation.

"Will she be safe there?" Liberty asked.

"Nowhere is safe now," Sam said darkly.

CHAPTER FIFTEEN
Reynolds And Rumours

Dusk came. As the snow-encrusted terrain hardened about Hallow House, a fire crackled in the parlour. Nicholas slumped dozing on the sofa. The previous restless nights had finally caught up with him and he slept soundly, the firewood softly popping in the background.

Jessica watched the boy from the parlour door. For some reason, she felt guilty, but she wasn't sure why. Something to do with a garden. Whatever it was, it couldn't be very important. It was so difficult to remember everything these days.

She sighed.

Everything was changing. Already the atmosphere in the house was different. Simply having another presence here – one so full of youth and inquisitiveness, and as yet unscarred by the wars of her world – had unsettled the fabrics of her home. Revitalised them. Nudged them out of their centuries-long slumber.

As she looked on, the woman's fragile countenance grew uneasy. Despite the flickering firelight she appeared as pale as a ghost. She hadn't expected her houseguest to carry with him such change. Not so suddenly. Deep down she felt the compulsion to protect him, to shelter him from the horrors that awaited him. Already he had encountered a servant of the Prophets and been lucky to live. She knew, though, that any energy spent endeavouring to protect the boy would ultimately prove wasted. The darkness was rolling in as sure as the chill fogs, and one day he'd be forced to face it.

Jessica glided from the room. The uncountable years of waiting and wondering suddenly seemed to have flashed by. What had she been doing with herself all that time? It was an unnerving thought.

The woman shook herself. The time had come to face down one particular demon from her past. Purposefully, she moved down the hall, ignoring the sightless eyes of the statues as she passed them, ignoring also the blinding light of the setting sun as it sliced in through the windows. Soon enough she came to a little unlit stairway and ascended to the first floor.

Jessica could feel a change in herself. Those pockets of moments she'd shared with the boy had stirred memories. With them came pains that Jessica thought she had banished forever. Unpleasant jolts from years long lost were surfacing; ghoulish reminders of the time that she had come from.

The woman shuddered.

There were things that she yearned to forget, to bury forever, but such escape was denied her. While she quietly shouldered the burdens of her past, the demands of the present grew ever more pregnant in her mind.

Winding her way down the landing, Jessica passed a large open dining area. A lavish table had been laid with polished silver cutlery. The dying sunlight spilled in through the balcony doors, and the filtered blue light curved across the intricate display. It almost seemed the table had been set for an eerie midnight dinner party. Jessica almost giggled at the uncanny notion. But she resisted. Now was not the time.

Finally the woman came to the door she had been seeking. It was already open a fraction; another had recently entered. Bracing herself, Jessica nudged open the door and moved inside.

She felt like she had stepped into a painting of the past. The bedroom remained unaffected by the time that had steadily progressed beyond its walls; nothing had been touched during its prior resident's absence. The air was heavy with the scent of herbs and dried flowers, and a glittering dust lay over all.

It was a noble room lavishly furnished. Rich indigo curtains adorned the tall, slender windows, and were fashioned in loops about the four-poster bed. The ceiling was made of leather mache and a sizeable armchair had been set by the window. At its side was a little round table with half-finished embroidery resting on top.

Jessica regarded the room with fascination. It had been an age since she last set foot in here. Back when Isabel had first disappeared, the same night that Jessica had encountered the raven, she had lain across this bed and sobbed for her mentor, as if an outpouring of emotion might bring her back. After that terrible night, she had closed the door and never returned. It was as if closing the door had created a vacuum, and time had stopped within.

The room had been waiting; it seemed to know that one day Isabel would return.

Except the black cat was nowhere to be seen.

"Isabel?" Jessica ventured softly.

There was a muted shuffling sound, but Jessica couldn't tell where it was coming from. Then a voice said: "Leave me be, child."

Jessica realised that the voice was coming from near the armchair. "Isabel, where are you?"

"I wish to be alone," grumbled the aged voice. "Leave me where I might wallow in my misery."

Jessica's eyebrows rose. "Wallow?" she demanded. "The Isabel I once knew would wallow in nothing, least of all self-pity."

"Have I no cause for self-pity?" Isabel regaled. Finally Jessica could see her. There, in the gap between the bottom of a monstrous wardrobe and the floor, the faint light picked out the thin whiskers of a cat.

"Wallow, indeed," it muttered. "I shall wallow all that I wish, and I would quite prefer to do it alone!"

"That much at least has not changed," Jessica mitigated, allowing herself a sly smile. "You were never much for company."

The eyes under the wardrobe closed dejectedly and the cat rested its head on its front paws. Jessica reclined into the armchair.

"You wish to be alone," she mused, glancing at the half-completed embroidery resting on the table-top. It depicted a scenic summer's day, except the flowers sat waiting to have their petals stitched with colour, and a wheeling bird in the cross-hatched blue sky had only half a wing. "You have no questions for me whatsoever? Not one?"

There came no response.

"You wouldn't believe how the world has changed in your absence," Jessica continued conversationally, taking up the embroidery and threading a petal. "It's been five hundred years. There are no horses and carriages. Now they have busses and cars and trains. They even have vehicles that can fly. And then there's space. Can you believe they put a man on the moon?"

"Impossible," Isabel grunted.

"In our time, perhaps, but not now. There's technology now. People can't live without it. It's berserk, and also quite wonderful. There's surgery, proper surgeons, not the barbarians of our time. They save lives with machines and medicine."

"Save lives? So Man has finally accomplished his ambition to become God."

"If that's how you want to look at it," Jessica responded mildly. "It isn't Man you should be concerned with, though. The agents of the Dark Prophets are rousing, even now Sentinel voices are being silenced by their blades."

"You should have left me dead," the cat said wearily.

"Maybe I should have!" Jessica erupted. She slammed the embroidery down on the table. "Maybe I should've left you rotting in that room for another five hundred years – it might have improved your mood!"

The cat emitted a low growl. "You've got your wits back this evening," it observed.

"What do you mean?" Jessica asked.

"Only this afternoon you were ranting at the boy and carrying on like a lunatic," Isabel said drearily.

Jessica's shoulders sagged and she trembled slightly. "I…" she murmured. "I have moments, I think…" Then, regretting her earlier outburst, she added quietly: "Isabel, I'm sorry. I know this isn't ideal, exactly. But you're here now. And… I want to atone for what happened that night. The night you died."

"Leave it in the past," came the cracked reply.

"It's not that easy," Jessica maintained. She brushed her fingers over the soft silk of her dress, a clean one, not the muddy embarrassment she'd found herself in earlier. "The guilt over that night has never left me. I feel like some of me died with you."

"Leave it in the past," Isabel repeated, almost tenderly this time. "You were not responsible for your actions. I… forgive you."

Jessica shivered, her old mentor's words chipping at the centuries-held remorse, though they could never relieve it completely. She blinked back the tears, determining to change the subject.

"You've met Nicholas," she said.

"The boy?" Isabel's haughtiness returned. "You're a fool to have a child in the house."

"He's not just any child," Jessica said casually, reclining back in the armchair. "He's the one Esus has searched for."

As Jessica had expected, that got the creature's attention. Without thinking, Isabel emerged, startled, from under the wardrobe. "Him?" she ventured. "The curly-haired nuisance with the quick temper? He's the one Esus talked about all those years hence?"

Jessica nodded, her expression brightening. How odd it was to see her old mentor's voice speaking through the cat. This wasn't what she had planned, but it was something. Maybe everything was going to be okay after all. With Isabel back, the odds had tipped ever so slightly in their favour. Isabel knew things that maybe even Esus didn't.

"Esus is certain?" the cat asked.

"As certain as he can be," Jessica said. "And the boy's actions speak for themselves. There's no doubt he's no ordinary child."

"Then all is not lost," Isabel barked. "We finally have him. We must begin training at once!" Rallied by the news, the cat forgot her misery and hopped up onto the bed, the fading sunlight picking out the white in her fur. She clawed at the bed sheets absentmindedly.

"He needs time," Jessica cautioned.

"Time?" Isabel scoffed. "Have we not wasted enough of it?"

"He's not yet sixteen," Jessica reasoned, "and he's only recently suffered a terrible loss. His parents. He's new to the Sentinel calling. Apply pressure now and he may break."

"If he breaks, he's not the one."

"We have time enough," Jessica persevered. "Still Esus searches for the other. She remains lost to us. But Nicholas could prove pivotal in that regard." She raised herself from the seat and turned to peer out of the window, resting a hand on the windowsill. "We must tread with care. Even the smallest stumble could result in ruin. You must acclimatise yourself, this world is far removed from the one you remember."

"Not only the world has changed," Isabel noted, scrutinising the girl at the window.

"Five hundred years will do that to a person." Jessica smiled sadly. "Let me tell you about Nicholas."

★

Nicholas yawned and stretched out on the sofa. He rubbed at his eyes. How long had he slept for? The clock above the fireplace read five past six. He'd been out for almost three hours. That was strange even for him. The house seemed to have that effect, though – it was so hushed here that it was easy to nod off. It almost invited it.

As Nicholas pulled himself up, he knocked something off the sofa onto the floor. It was a volume of *The Sentinel Chronicles*. Several other books were scattered around the boy. He'd taken them all from the library that he'd stumbled across after his encounter with Jessica and the cat. Each tome was full of strange tales that he found almost impossible to believe, tales of battles and monsters. The detail was almost forensic.

Stranger still, despite the library being filled with volumes of *The Sentinel Chronicles*, there only seemed to be one period of time not covered by the dusty digest. The Sentinels seemed to have commenced recording their history in the year 1600, and that massive library was rammed with row upon row of leather-bound tomes, some spanning entire years, others mere months. From 1600 until present day, though, only August 1997 was missing. Nicholas wouldn't have noticed, except for the fact that he was born in that very month.

At first, the boy had shrugged off the coincidence, but he couldn't let it lie. Why that month, out of all the months since 1600? What could have happened in August 1997 to cause a sudden break in the records? Of course, it was possible that particular volume had simply gone missing, lost to time. But the coincidence felt significant somehow.

Nicholas pushed a hand through his dark, curly hair and yawned again. What now? He was bored of reading. Maybe he'd go find the cat – though he didn't fancy another tongue-lashing. He didn't remember ever feeling so tired in his life. He needed fresh air.

Except Jessica had forbidden him from leaving the house. Where was she now, though? He'd not seen her since the garden, an encounter that had left him unsettled and confused. She hadn't seemed herself at all – right down to that strange, child-like voice. Being under Jessica's care suddenly didn't feel quite so safe. Nicholas was annoyed; more oddness, more secrets and more things that he wasn't being told. Maybe it was time he had a few secrets of his own. Maybe he'd go outside and simply neglect to tell Jessica. It was only fair.

Energised by this new, insidious idea, Nicholas left the parlour and went to the entrance hall. Without hesitating, he moved to the oak front door and went to draw back the bolts.

"Where do you think you're going?"

A prickly voice rang out behind him.

Nicholas froze. He turned slowly and there was the cat, perched on a small mauve armchair in the corner, squinting at him with sallow eyes as sharp and bright as that detestable voice.

"There's something–" Nicholas started, then realised there was no point in lying. "I fancy a bit of fresh air is all."

"Out of the question," Isabel retorted. "You're not to leave the house, I'm sure you've been told."

"You going to stop me?" Nicholas challenged. He reached for the door handle.

"Ungrateful urchin!"

Nicholas cried out as claws raked into his ankle, and he fell away from the door, rubbing at his leg where the cat had scratched him.

"You– you scratched me!" he yelled at the animal, which had now seated itself directly in front of the door.

"You gave me no option," Isabel replied indifferently.

"You can't do that! You can't just attack people for no reason!"

"You're not to leave the house," Isabel repeated.

Nicholas clenched his fists, barely able to control his anger.

"In my day, children did as they were bid," Isabel maintained gravely.

"At least I'm not a bitter old woman who spent her entire life locked up in this house hating everybody and everything!" Nicholas jibed back.

The cat faltered. "How did you–?" Isabel began, but Nicholas had seized on her surprise and pushed past her, shoving her aside with his foot as he drew back a big, heavy bolt and flung the front door open. A freezing flurry of air blasted him in the face, but Nicholas didn't stop, rushing out to meet the twilight world.

Trudging into the snowy countryside, Nicholas's heart hammered in his chest. He'd been cooped up for so long that the fresh air made him dizzy. It felt good, though; so good that he nearly didn't feel the cold. Pulling the sleeves of his jumper down, the boy clenched them in his fists and stomped off into the countryside. He knew he was being foolish, that Jessica had warned him against leaving the house, but he couldn't stand it any longer. The house made him tired and lethargic, and he felt like he was forgetting things. Important things like his parents, his life before this madness.

Now that he was outside he felt instantly better, like he could breathe again.

After a while, Nicholas became aware of a soft pitter-patter as tiny, tentative paws traced his footsteps. He didn't acknowledge the noise, didn't care if Isabel was following him. He wound his way between two fields, cheeks burning in the bitter air. A twig cracked on the ground behind him and, out of the corner of one eye, Nicholas caught sight of a black shape moving alongside him.

Without moving to face his unwanted companion, the boy said: "You didn't have to follow me."

"You gave me no choice," Isabel returned. She sounded out of breath, but her usually snooty tone had evaporated. She would never admit it, but getting out of the house had probably done her a world of good, too. "Where exactly do you intend on going?"

"Nowhere," Nicholas shrugged. "Anywhere. Just out of that place." He felt himself inexplicably softening toward the pitiful creature. He shouldn't have shouted at her like that. He'd never shouted at anybody in that way before. His voice had sounded tight and strange.

"What was wrong with Jessica today?" Nicholas asked the cat. No reply came. "You don't know, do you?"

"No," Isabel relented finally, confirming his suspicions. Nicholas should have revelled in the haughty little animal's inability to explain

Jessica's behaviour. Instead, her sudden ignorance – after previously having an answer for everything – only deepened the boy's concern for his godmother.

They continued on, the odd duo. A boy and his cat, pressing between bushes and moving across the snow-clad land. The dusky countryside seemed to greet them merrily, the sky blushing hot pink as the sun sank behind the trees.

Moving past a little outcrop of greenery, Nicholas found himself suddenly bathed in artificial light. He'd stumbled upon a suburban street.

"Orville," Isabel said, hopping up onto a stone wall and trotting alongside him.

"What?"

"The village, it's called Orville, or was in my time," the cat explained. "I'm surprised it has survived the years."

Up ahead, the sound of laughter trickled into the evening air, and Nicholas wandered toward the cheerful hum. Eventually he reached what must be the village's small high street. Here, the shrieking and whooping poured out from an old-fashioned pub called The Red Lion, which was nestled at the heart of Orville.

The village was a twee place with shops that still bore hand painted signs and took pride in bijou window displays. In the snow, it looked like the kind of place that usually featured on biscuit tins, with its old-fashioned lampposts and bright red post boxes. It reminded Nicholas of some of the little hamlets that surrounded Cambridge. Except instead of comforting him, there was something about the village that unnerved him.

"The tavern's altered none," Isabel remarked, eyeing The Red Lion with ill-concealed contempt.

"You mean you weren't a drinker in your time?"

Isabel shot him a glare. "Filthy beggars," she condemned. "Shameless what they got up to in there. I wouldn't pass its threshold if the Trinity themselves bade it."

"What is it with this Trinity?" Nicholas asked. Before Isabel could reply, the boy gave a grunt as a man bowled into him. Nicholas staggered backwards, but the stranger kept walking as if nothing had happened. He pretended he hadn't even seen the boy.

"Don't worry about me," Nicholas called after him.

"What did I tell you?" Isabel gave a satisfied sniff. "The people of Orville always were too big for their boots. At least their neighbours in Fratton had manners, basic though they might've been."

"Can't say I disagree," Nicholas mumbled. He stared about the picture perfect hamlet with its antiquated buildings and frosty veneer. He didn't like it. There was a disquieting ambience about the place. It was too neat, too quiet, too perfect. Though the notion seemed ridiculous, it felt almost like the village itself was watching him. "Let's get out of here."

"Wait."

Nicholas looked at the cat, which was perched motionless on the wall, her fur prickling. She sniffed the air, her small head darting this way and that as she picked up an assortment of scents.

"There's a strange odour," she said.

"I've not showered for a while," Nicholas quipped. He was uneasy, too, though. The hair on the back of his neck shivered and rose, and Nicholas's stomach gave an uneasy twinge.

Almost at the same time, the boy and the cat turned toward a poky alleyway on the other side of the road.

An involuntary chill bristled through Nicholas.

There, in the darkness of the passageway, a sinewy shape was tensed. Its gleaming red eyes were fixed intently on him.

"There's something—" Nicholas started, but before he could finish the thought, the thing in the shadows let out a blistering, inhuman screech and hurtled into the street.

"RUN!" Isabel yowled.

Nicholas didn't stop to get a better look at whatever had made that nerve-shredding cry. Kicking snow up, he sprinted down the high street, righting himself as the ice endeavoured to slip him up. Behind him, colossal claws clattered against the cobbled road, and the sound was accompanied by the wheeze of massive lungs expanding and contracting. He spurred himself on.

"Boy!" Isabel's voice cried out nearby. "The tavern!"

As the boy reached The Red Lion, one of the pub's patrons stepped out into the street and Nicholas grabbed a hold of the man's shoulders.

"Help," the boy panted. "You have to help us. Please, something's after us."

But there was something wrong with the man. As Nicholas stared into his face, the stranger blanched. He stared blindly into Nicholas's eyes, his mouth sagging stupidly.

"Please!" Nicholas screamed, shaking him. The stranger let out a strangled yelp and collapsed backward into the pub, slamming the door shut. Nicholas threw himself against it, hammering on the wood with his fists. "Let us in!"

Before he knew what was happening, there was a searing pain in his leg, and the pavement rushed up to meet him. Nicholas hit the ground with a thud that forced the air out of his lungs. Gasping, he pushed himself onto his back. But it was too late.

There at his feet, an immense, muscular thing opened a mouth filled with razor fangs. It was the ugliest thing Nicholas had ever seen, somewhere between a giant dog and a hulking reptile, both scaly and hairy with big scarlet eyes that glistened as they glowered hungrily at him. It was an abhorrent, repulsive thing; something that shouldn't exist, couldn't exist. A massive, misshapen head extended into a snorting snout. The nostrils flared as they sucked up Nicholas's scent, and a tremble rippled down the beast's scaly back, all the way down to its thick, trunk-like tail.

The beast snarled, a string of saliva escaping its snapping jaws as it climbed on top of the boy. Nicholas tried to squirm away, but the abomination was so heavy he could barely move.

"No! NO!" Nicholas yelled.

The creature pushed its dripping muzzle right up into the boy's face, its hot breath steaming into Nicholas's nostrils. He gagged, and the beast opened its massive maw, preparing to snap it shut around the boy's head.

"Nicholas!"

As Nicholas squeezed his eyes shut against the rows of piercing incisors, he felt the monster shudder and convulse. It emitted an outraged squeal, then the weight was lifted and Nicholas was free. He clambered to his feet, seeing that the monster had rounded on Isabel; she had sunk her claws into its alligator-like tail.

"Run child!" the cat urged. The beast thrashed at the irksome feline, and Isabel was flung into the snowy road.

Gripped by some kind of primitive impulse, Nicholas leapt at the creature, kicking it in the side where he hoped its ribs were. The beast howled and a claw flashed in the lamplight, slicing into Nicholas's arm. The boy gasped and staggered away, hurrying towards Isabel. Together, they stumbled down the street, a clatter of claws telling them that the creature was giving chase once more.

Then, out of nowhere, a voice yelled: "In here!"

A hand grabbed Nicholas by the scruff of the neck, dragging him backwards, in from the street, away from the gnashing jaws. The boy collapsed panting onto a wooden floor as his rescuer banged a door shut and hastily locked it.

"Th– th–" Nicholas wheezed, "Thank you."

The newcomer – a short, stocky man – peered through a tiny window in the door. Scrabbling sounds came through the wood – along with a breathy snort – and then abruptly ceased.

Finally, the stranger at the door relaxed.

"I think it's gone," he said. "You're safe now."

He went to Nicholas, reaching out a hand to help him up. Nicholas took it, pulling himself to his feet.

"Are you hurt?" the man asked with concern, squinting at the boy from behind a pair of round spectacles. He was thickset and sturdy with an open, friendly countenance and a large belly that ballooned his knitted jumper out of shape.

"No, I don't think so," Nicholas said, inspecting his arm through the tatters of his sleeve. "It's just a scratch."

"And your furry friend?"

Isabel was sitting on a counter, her eyes saucering with worry.

"She looks fine," Nicholas said.

"You were lucky," the man told him, moving to the counter and reaching out a hand to stroke the cat. Isabel hissed at the stranger and dodged the offending digits, pattering soundlessly over to the window to peer outside. "That thing's killed here more than once," the man continued, unfazed by the cat's caginess. "It's a good job I was working late."

As Nicholas's breathing evened, he became aware that they were in a shop. This wasn't any ordinary shop, though. A dreamcatcher display twirled and twinkled in the window, while giant peacock feathers filled an ornate ceramic vase in the corner. There were strange bowls and shelves lined with pestle and mortars. Tribal masks dangled from the dado rail. Behind the dark wood counter, yet more shelves reached right up to the ceiling and were stacked with row upon row of curious little jars. Next to Nicholas a tall cabinet was filled with jagged, glittering crystals of all shapes, sizes and colours. It was a hodgepodge of a place, so overstuffed with remarkable, curiosity-baiting objects that it felt somehow cosy.

"What is this place?" Nicholas asked, touching a dried-out iguana that sat with its tongue perpetually flickering out of its mouth atop the crystal cabinet.

"My little home away from home," the man said. "My shop, Rumours."

"Is it a–" Nicholas paused, knowing it sounded stupid. "A magic shop or something?"

"I prefer the term apothecary, but that'll do," the man said. He extended his hand again and smiled a wide, warm smile. "I'm Reynolds. Melvin Reynolds."

Nicholas went to the counter and shook his hand. "Nicholas."

"Well, Nicholas, let's take a look at that arm of yours, shall we?"

Nicholas nodded and placed his arm on the worktop, letting Reynolds peel the shredded jumper sleeve back. The boy winced as the drying blood pulled at the hairs.

"Mind telling me what you were doing out after dark like that?" Reynolds asked, inspecting Nicholas's arm.

"I was–" Nicholas began, but a warning grumble from Isabel stopped him.

"What's got his goat?" Reynolds peered at the cat over the rim of his glasses.

"I don't know, and he's a she," Nicholas said. "Isabel."

"Right, yes. Funny name for a cat," Reynolds observed genially. "You're right, it's just a scratch. Nothing a bit of warm water can't put right. Wait here, I won't be a tick."

The man disappeared through some curtains at the back of the shop.

Isabel hopped back onto the counter. "We must return to the house," she hissed at Nicholas.

"Chill out," Nicholas said. "We're safe here. He's nice, he saved us."

"We won't be safe until we're with Jessica," the cat persisted.

"Shhh, he's coming back."

Reynolds emerged from behind the curtains carrying a yellow washing up bowl. He set it on the worktop and rolled his sleeves up.

Nicholas froze. There, on the man's forearm, was a raven tattoo. The boy looked at Isabel to see if she'd noticed, but the cat was busily watching out the window.

"Here," Reynolds said, dipping a clean cloth into the water and squeezing off the excess. "Let me." Carefully he began to clean the scratches on Nicholas's arm. The cloth came away stained red.

"What was that thing?" Nicholas ventured. "The thing that attacked us." His insides were trembling. This stranger who had saved him was another Sentinel. Had to be. Who else would have a raven marked on their skin? Especially a raven that matched exactly the design from the covers of *The Sentinel Chronicles*.

"Garm," Reynolds replied with a sigh. "A creature of the old days."

"A monster, you mean."

"That works, too," Reynolds nodded.

"It's my second," Nicholas told him, recalling Malika. "They're getting worse." Isabel sounded another warning grumble, but Nicholas didn't pay it any notice.

"Why hasn't anybody stopped it?" he continued.

"Oh, I've tried," Reynolds assured him, rinsing the cloth and drying Nicholas's arm with a towel. "Not easy to kill Garm, as I'm sure you've noticed. The villagers are in denial. They've been out hunting foxes and bears. I'd like to see a fox that can rip a man's head off."

"Not sure I would," Nicholas muttered. Reynolds laughed.

"You're alright, lad," he grinned, patting the boy roughly on the back. "Men twice your size would've collapsed and sobbed at the sight of that beast. You've got pluck."

Nicholas didn't particularly agree with that. If it hadn't been for Isabel, he'd be sitting in that monster's digestive tract right about now.

The boy ripped the bloody sleeve off his jumper.

"How about the leg?" Reynolds asked. Nicholas looked down, seeing that his trouser leg had been shredded when that thing, Garm, had grabbed him outside the pub.

"It's fine," Nicholas said. He caught Reynolds's eye. The desperation to ask if he was a Sentinel filled up his chest. But he didn't know what to say. He knew how secretive the Sentinels were. The moment passed.

"You believe in all this magic stuff then?" Nicholas asked, admiring the shelves behind the counter.

"Well, not fairies and pixies and leprechauns, if that's what you're thinking," Reynolds replied with a wry smirk. "But yes, the elements, nature, cause and effect, chaos and balance. They're all important. Not to get too 'flower power' about it."

Nicholas smiled. "You actually sounded sane when you said that," he said.

"Fairies are just for fun," Reynolds explained. "Monsters are the things you want to keep an eye out for."

A plaintive cry interrupted their conversation. At the shop door, Isabel was scratching at the wood.

"Looks like Isabel wants to go home," Reynolds said, striding over to the shopfront.

"Do you think it's safe now?" Nicholas asked.

"I'd say so." Reynolds peered through the door's porthole again. "Garm doesn't stick around in the village for too long. He hates the smell, I'd say. Best you hurry back before it gets too dark out there. I'll walk you."

Reynolds escorted them through the village. He loaned Nicholas a jacket, and was wearing a big winter coat himself. It had a hood fringed with fur, which made him look like an Arctic explorer.

"You're new around here, aren't you?" he said.

"It's that obvious?" Nicholas asked. He noticed that Isabel was limping slightly as she hurried along next to him. She wouldn't let him pick her up, though, hissing if he tried.

"Aye, you look far too normal to be from Orville," Reynolds commented. "And talk about bad luck – it normally takes people at least a few days before they spot Garm. Where you staying?"

Somehow Nicholas knew he shouldn't mention Hallow House. It didn't feel right. Even if Reynolds was a Sentinel, divulging personal information like that felt wrong. He was getting good at this secrets thing.

"Fratton," the boy said, naming the nearby village that Isabel had mentioned earlier. "Got family there."

"Nicer place'n this," Reynolds said wistfully. "You're lucky on that count."

Nicholas nodded, feeling guilty at the lie and finding he couldn't look at the man.

Reynolds didn't ask any more, perhaps sensing his young companion's reticence. Instead, he told the boy about Orville's history, how witchcraft had always been linked to the village, even now. "It's a strange place, to be sure," the man nodded. "Strange things seem to gravitate towards it. Well, here we are."

They'd arrived at the little street that Nicholas and Isabel had first stumbled upon. Ahead of them, the countryside huddled under a leaden sky.

"Know your way from here?" Reynolds asked.

"Yeah, cheers," Nicholas said. "For, y'know…"

"Any time," Reynolds said, winking at him. "You be careful." And then he was gone, striding back into Orville, the snow crunching under his boots.

Nicholas and Isabel lumbered through the chill countryside. They didn't talk, instead listening out for any sign of Garm. They needn't have worried; soon they were back at Hallow House, the large oaken door bolted once more against the terrors that the night had surrendered.

Isabel broke the silence. "Give me your word that's the last time you leave the house," she said.

"What?"

"You see now why you must remain here," the cat pressed. "We were lucky the Reynolds man came to our aid. I dread to think what could have happened if he hadn't."

"I liked him," Nicholas said. "He reminded me of somebody. Didn't you see his tattoo? I think he was a Sentinel."

"Be that as it may, you're not to leave the house again," Isabel asserted. "You've seen what horrors lie waiting. The house protects you while you're within its walls; no evil can pass its threshold uninvited. Outside you're vulnerable to a great many dangers."

"I don't care. I want to see him again."

"Stop being so selfish," Isabel retorted, jumping onto the mauve armchair. "There's more at play here than your feelings. Swear it."

"I–" Nicholas began angrily.

"Swear it!" Isabel shrieked. "Or I'll find a way to bind you here myself."

"Fine!" Nicholas yelled. "I'll stay here, and I'll wallow and be miserable just like you!" He trudged off down the hallway, leaving the cat alone in the entrance hall.

CHAPTER SIXTEEN
Blood

THE SECOND SAM STEPPED THROUGH THE front door, he knew something was wrong. The atmosphere in the murky hallway was different, unsettled. Sam had lived here alone long enough to know that something wasn't right. As he hovered in the open doorway, barely breathing, he was sure of it: somebody had been here.

The elderly man stood and listened. No noise. He set his keys on the small table just inside the door and eased the door shut behind him. His shoulders tensed as he lingered in the hall, his ears ringing with the silence. He paced slowly into the living room, then the kitchen.

Nothing.

The back door was still securely locked. All the windows were sealed tight.

Still, something was wrong. Something felt out of place. Frowning to himself, Sam went back into the living room. He surveyed the light brown three-piece-suite which was still ornamented with the cushions that Judith had made, his gaze moving over to the fireplace. Then he saw it. Propped up on the mantelpiece above the hearth. His wallet.

Sam hurried over and took up the battered leather holder, turning it over in his hands. He'd lost it that day on the bus, when he'd struggled with the woman. Malika. Yet here it was, back in his house, as if it had followed him home of its own accord.

If his wits hadn't been sharper, Sam probably wouldn't have noticed the wallet for days. Whoever had placed it there knew he was no simpleton, though. They were counting on him finding it, and their message couldn't have been any clearer – we know where you live, and we can get you whenever we want.

Sam shuddered, his unease quickly budding into resentment. Who was the culprit, that harlot from the bus? Richard? Another Harvester? For a moment, the old man considered leaving, getting out of here. But his anger and pride refused to let him. This was his house, his home. If anybody wanted to take him out, they might as well do it here, and he'd happily challenge any intruder to a fight.

Besides, as he'd told Liberty, nowhere was safe now.

Liberty! After he'd made a quick check upstairs to be absolutely certain that his unwelcome visitor was no longer around, Sam picked up the phone.

"Liberty," he breathed, relieved when she answered.

"Sam, are you okay?"

"Yes, yes," he said. "Are you?"

"Of course."

"Francesca?"

"She's asleep. Sam, what's going on?"

"Nothing. Nothing." Suddenly he felt foolish. But at least Liberty was alright. It was just him, then, that they'd visited. Was that a good thing? Sam assured Liberty that everything was fine and then replaced the receiver.

He made himself dinner. Though his appetite had all but vanished, he forced down two sausages and some mashed potatoes, almost in defiance of anybody who could even now be watching him through the windows, savouring his discomfort.

He was exhausted, physically and mentally. The encounter with Richard that day had left him shaken and drained. He really was getting sentimental in his old age. Unanswered questions rattled around inside the old man's head, refusing to settle until they'd found answers. What on Earth could have changed Richard like that? The doctor? It had to be. At least Lucy was with her sister now; he'd managed to save *somebody*.

As the old man poured himself a rare brandy from a decanter in the living room, he plucked a framed photo from the mantelpiece, the very frame that he'd found his wallet resting against. A curly haired, sixty-year-old woman with kind eyes beamed out at him.

"Oh Judith," Sam murmured, taking another sip of brandy. "What am I going to do?"

He replaced the frame, and wondered if there was any saving Richard. Was his friend gone for good? Or could he be brought back from the brink of whatever madness had taken hold of him?

It was late when Sam contemplated going to bed. He'd not slept well in the years since his wife's death, and he'd slept even worse in the aftermath of Anita and Max's murders.

Murder.

Strange that he'd not connected that word to their deaths before now. Even if the news reports were adamant the train wreck had been a horrible accident, there was no escaping the truth. Nicholas's parents had been murdered. Sam couldn't help wondering if he was next. The fact that his intruder hadn't been here when he'd gotten home offered some small comfort. If they'd decided to toy with him for a while first, he could probably sleep easy tonight.

Sam had just finished washing up and was switching off the kitchen light when a crash from outside made him jump. In the darkness, the old man hurried to the cupboard under the stairs, dragged out his suitcase and quickly assembled his shotgun. By the time he got to the back door, all was quiet again. His heart thrashing against his ribs, Sam peered out into the night. Nothing.

Cursing his nerves, the elderly man double-checked the door was locked and trudged shakily into the living room. It had probably been a fox knocking over a bin. Still, his reaction to the noise was sign enough that the intruder had done its job. Sam was on edge.

Flicking off the living room light, he lowered himself into his favourite armchair and prepared to wait the night out.

★

Sam awoke with a start. He'd dropped off in the chair, the gun still clasped in his lap. The moon edged in through the living room window, casting everything in a ghostly pallor.

Then he felt the eyes on him, and instinctively Sam flipped the gun up, ready to fire.

"Who's there?" he barked.

The sound of his own voice aggravated him. It was the voice of a scared pensioner.

"Peace, brother," a deep voice throbbed in the dark.

As Sam's eyes adjusted, he picked out the figure in the corner of the room. It stood still as a statue, wearing a cloak of shadows.

"Esus," Sam choked, lowering the barrel. The moonlight picked out the familiar metal mask.

"My apologies for the intrusion," Esus said. "It was not my intention to alarm you."

"I'm just an old man with jangly nerves," Sam replied wearily. He tried to relax into the armchair, the gun at his side, but Esus's presence always made him uneasy. That voice seemed to echo inside his own skull, as if Esus was occupying the same cramped space as his nervously-huddled thoughts.

"What brings you?" Sam asked

"There's word you're on the trail of something," the figure said.

"You might say that," Sam nodded. "Though just what I'm on the trail of I couldn't tell you."

"Richard Walden."

Even the sound of his name made Sam's stomach twist into knots.

"Yes." The elderly man rubbed his forehead. "Yes, Richard. He was attacked by a Harvester, and suddenly he's different. He's acting like one of them."

"He's not the first," Esus's voice rumbled, filling the murky living room. Sam could feel the voice vibrating in his gut now. It got everywhere, creeping and polluting.

"There are others in Oxford and Manchester, but mostly here. You must double your efforts. This madness started here, in Cambridge. Something's hunting out there, too. It's targeting children. Already three have perished."

"And there was the break-in at the museum," Sam added with a somnolent nod. "And Richard, and the attack on Nicholas, not to mention Anita and Max."

"It's all connected," his visitor intoned. "You're closer than anyone to the truth. You must persist."

Sam stared up at that impassive mask. The black eyes pierced deep inside of him and he felt wearier than ever. "I'm a decrepit old bag of bones," he sighed. "What can I do?"

"Doubt before the dawn," the phantom mused. "You must see that you, and only you, are capable of resolving this. You've been at the centre of it from the beginning. Ever since your wife first met Anita and Max Hallow. Doubt not. Be vigilant. And persist. May the Trinity watch over you."

With that, Esus melted into the shadows.

Drawing a grateful breath, Sam found he was alone once more.

★

Nicholas stuffed another pair of trousers into his suitcase and squeezed it shut, zipping it up hurriedly. Enough was enough. All night he'd lain awake, replaying the evening's events on the blank canvas of the dark ceiling. The creature Garm, the shopkeeper and his raven tattoo, Isabel forbidding him from ever leaving the house again.

After thinking himself into a corner, he'd resolved that it was time to take matters into his own hands. At first light he'd thrown back the covers and decided to get the hell out of this place.

When Sam had suggested coming here, Nicholas had stupidly agreed, lost in the fog of grief, curious about the secretive godmother, eager to escape his parents' memory-heavy house. But it had been wrong. If anything, this place was worse than home. Nicholas felt like the old, desolate manor had swallowed him whole and was slowly digesting him, reducing him to nothing. He'd been put here to be forgotten about, and he was forgetting.

Anger scorched through him; anger at Sam, anger at that wretched godmother. And most of all, anger at his parents for leaving him. He couldn't even look at photos of them anymore. Their faces only stirred up confused emotions that tumbled furiously, poking at his insides like thorns.

Still, if he could get back to Cambridge, the house on Midsummer Common was still there, as far as he knew. Sam would have to cut through a lot of red tape to sell it, and even if it had been put on the market, there was nothing stopping Nicholas from squatting there for a while. Just long enough to plan his next move.

Yes, that's what he'd do. First, he'd go to Reynolds or that other village Isabel had mentioned, Fratton, and figure out a way back to Cambridge – back to his old house, back to a world that didn't include talking cats and strange masked visitors. Back to normality.

The boy pulled on his coat and seized his suitcase. He was just heading for the bedroom door when he stopped.

There, sat in the doorway, was the cat.

"Nicholas," it said, and for once that aged voice wasn't patronising. It creaked softly, knowing.

"I'm leaving," Nicholas said. "Don't try and stop me."

The cat blinked, but didn't move. "I think we both know I couldn't stop you," it said tiredly. "But before you go, I want to show you something."

"I'm not interested," Nicholas said. "I don't care. I'm sick of this place. You're all a bunch of nuts. I'm going." He pushed past her into the hall, dragging his suitcase behind him.

Isabel turned and padded after him. "It'll only take a second," she called. "Do you really want to leave here never knowing who you are?"

Nicholas stopped warily. "What do you mean?" he asked, suspiciously.

"Follow me," Isabel said plainly. She trotted down the stairs and out of sight.

Nicholas struggled with himself. *Who he really was.* What did she mean? Part of him didn't care, was sick of the riddles and half-answers, just wanted to get away from here as fast as possible. But the other part – the part that had helped him find his parents' secret room – willed him to swallow his pride and go after the cat. Sighing, Nicholas dropped the suitcase and chased after her.

"In here," the cat said when Nicholas had caught up. She nodded at a closed door, which the boy pushed open. They went inside, and Nicholas found they were in the painting room.

The circular alcove that contained those two strange canvasses – one depicting a crotchety old woman, the other two girls and a young man spinning joyfully in the sun's warm rays. The chandelier above shone down on the twin canvasses, and the dancers revelled in its light.

Isabel sat beneath the portrait of the woman and stared up at it. Her whiskers bristled and she said: "Isabel Hallow."

"What?"

"That's her name," the cat explained, craning to look up at the wrinkled woman with the curled black hair and thin, pressed lips. "Isabel Hallow."

"What's that got to do with anything?"

Nicholas's patience was fast waning, but what the cat said next took him by surprise.

"She's me," Isabel said simply. "I'm her, and she's me. She's who I used to be, once upon a time."

"Oh," Nicholas said. And suddenly it fit, that brittle voice, the grave expression of the painted woman, those merciless eyes. He could see it exactly. The odd animal suddenly seemed to make a fraction more sense.

"I was a miserable, bitter thing, as you were right to point out," the cat continued, still peering up at the canvas. "My brother never liked me. My parents thought me a bore. My only friend was my nanny. She's the one who raised me, taught me things my parents could never have understood." Nicholas edged further into the room behind the animal, intrigued. "It was a different time, a horrible time. The rich were rich and the poor were miserable. And my parents were despicable. I was glad when they died. Glad but lonely, because suddenly the house was quieter than I'd ever imagined it could be."

"It was like that after my parents died, too," Nicholas said softly. "I couldn't wait to get away."

"And you found yourself here," Isabel laughed, but there was no mirth in the sound. "How sorry you must have felt."

A silence fell between them. Then the cat looked at the boy.

"Hallow," she said, her whiskers trembling. One of her ears twitched of its own accord as if swatting at a fly. "It's your surname, too."

The boy nodded.

"Then we're related somehow. My brother married as soon as he could and left this place. He had many children. You're no doubt of his lineage, though I don't see any of him in you. Apart from your temper, perhaps."

Nicholas smirked at that, unable to stop himself. "Dad had a temper," he said. "Sometimes we'd wind him up so much he wouldn't speak to us for days. He made it too easy." It felt odd talking about him as if he were gone. Because he was gone, Nicholas had to remind himself. But, perversely, talking about his dad almost made him feel alive again.

"You were a handful," Isabel noted. "I'm not surprised."

"And you're not?" Nicholas shot back. He stopped, suddenly aware that this was the first conversation he'd had with Isabel that didn't involve shouting and jutting egos. It felt different. Less lonely. His anger had subsided and he almost felt human again, like he could think clearly for the first time in days.

"You," he began. "You were dead, weren't you?"

Isabel sniffed, and her tail whipped behind her in agitation. "Yes, I suppose I was," she said.

"But you came back. Jessica brought you back."

"Yes."

"So… it's possible," Nicholas said. "People can come back."

"No."

"They can! Because you're here," the boy persisted, stepping into the shaft of light cast by the chandelier. "If you found a way back after being dead for hundreds of years, that means anybody can!"

"There were very specific circumstances," Isabel said, her tail still sweeping the floor. "I was trapped in that room, like a cork in a bottle. I was dead, but not in the way that most are dead. I was still here."

"That doesn't make any sense."

Nicholas felt himself getting irritated again, felt the pressure building in his chest.

"Don't get all het up," Isabel snapped. "I'm here. And I shouldn't be. But I am. That doesn't change anything about your parents, so don't start getting any silly ideas."

Nicholas slid down the wall until he was slumped on the floor, his jacket puffing up around him. He picked at a stone that was caught in the sole of his shoe. Another thing that he didn't understand. It would take years to get to grips with the strange workings of the Sentinels and their laws, and he was so behind. Light years behind. It was like he was on a treadmill that stretched for miles, and no matter how hard or fast he ran, he'd never get to the end.

The boy flicked the stone across the floor. "What did you mean earlier?" he said. "About who I am?"

Isabel went to chase the stone, then seemed to decide against it. She sat with her front paws together, the chandelier casting a circle of light around her. Staring at the boy with half-closed eyes, her little, triangular nose moved nervously.

"Well?" Nicholas said. "What's the matter, cat got your tongue?"

"You're more than a Sentinel," Isabel complied eventually, disregarding the bad joke.

"What does that mean?" Nicholas demanded, though he was now more curious than annoyed.

"Esus has never divulged the full facts," Isabel said. "But you're, Trinity forbid, *special*. That's why you're here. That's why you're being protected."

"Esus? He was here the night you—" Nicholas paused. "You know. Arrived."

Isabel's tail batted the floor. "Esus," she burred, rolling the sound around her mouth, feeling it properly for the first time in centuries. "He is our protector. When I was alive, he came to me and reminded me of my calling. My parents, ignorant fools, ignored theirs. They used this house as a place for revelry and parties, forgetting its significance. Esus came to me after their deaths, and I received him gladly."

"He looks like he'd kill somebody in their sleep," Nicholas said.

"Blasphemy!" Isabel cried in outrage. Her tail made a *whump* as it hit the floor. "His is the purist of souls. He is our cherished guide and guard. Speak ill of him and have him cleave the malicious tongue from your mouth."

"Woah, okay," Nicholas held his hands up. "Don't get your whiskers in a twist. This is all new to me."

Isabel licked a paw and rubbed it absentmindedly across her muzzle. "You won't see him often," she continued resignedly. "He travels from place to place, wherever he's most needed. If you see him, you're either in trouble, or soon will be."

"I hope I never see him again, then," Nicholas muttered. "And what do you mean 'special'? There's nothing special about me."

"You're meant for something," Isabel said. "'Destiny' is a detestable word – how can anything ever be destined? Far too many variables in life – but I'm sorry to say it best applies here. You entered the world for a reason."

"What reason?" Nicholas demanded hungrily. This was more like it. He knew that Jessica was holding out on him. Even as she'd explained the Sentinels and their cause, he'd sensed there was something else that she was keeping from him. Sensed. Sensitives. "Jessica said I could be a Sensitive," the boy said, searching the cat's furry features for a confirmation.

Isabel heaved out a puff of air. "Who knows?" she sighed. "That much I was never informed of. But now you see why you must–" she broke off, then more tactfully continued, "why it would be best for you to remain here."

Nicholas smirked at Isabel's attempt at diplomacy – he didn't expect she'd had much practice. So they thought he was special? That explained a lot. What that red–haired woman had said to him on the bus, for a start. *"I can smell it on you; in your veins, your skin, your hair. You're different."* Different. Special. At school, those words meant bad things. Here, among the Sentinels, maybe they meant something good. Maybe he hadn't been put here to forget and be forgotten. Perhaps he was merely waiting, on standby for something that was just over the horizon.

"I'll stay," the boy said finally. "But I want to go back to Rumours and see Reynolds again."

"Out of the question!" Isabel snapped. "It is too dangerous."

"He was a Sentinel, I know it!" Nicholas maintained. "And those people in the village. You're just going to let them face that monster alone?"

"I won't allow you to go back there. You very nearly didn't survive the first time."

"Like I need your permission," Nicholas returned sulkily. "I'm going back and that's it."

"Wretched Hallow blood," Isabel grumbled, emitting a low rumble of disapproval. "If your mind's decided, there's nothing I can do. Not like this, anyway."

"Good."

"If you insist on this ridiculous escapade, though, you'll need some form of protection."

"There's a suit of armour in the hall," Nicholas suggested helpfully.

"I see wits haven't sharpened any in my absence." Isabel got to her feet and trotted over to her portrait. "This painting. Open it."

"Huh?"

"Don't sit there like an idle cow, help me," Isabel said. "There's a latch on the right, release it and open the painting."

Nicholas jumped up and ran his fingers up the side of the frame.

"Are you sure there—" he began doubtfully, but then he felt it. A small metal catch that flicked up easily. The enormous portrait began to swing away from the wall, revealing behind it a stone archway that was completely covered in a net of cobwebs.

"Am I the only one who doesn't have their own secret door?" the boy said, brushing away the mesh of sticky webbing and rubbing the remnants on his trousers.

"Follow me."

Isabel hurried into the wall of blackness beyond the arch. Nicholas chased after the soft pitter-patter of her paws on bare flagstones. The dank stink of mould rushed into his nostrils and almost immediately the boy crashed into something hard and metallic. He swore. The word echoed in what must be a cramped space with a high ceiling.

"There, the lamp," Isabel's voice rang out in the murk.

"Not all of us can see in the dark, you know," Nicholas muttered, rubbing at his sore knee. He fumbled away from whatever he'd tripped over and felt along the damp, rocky wall, finding an iron lamp set into the stone. He twisted the little knob beneath it, prepared to berate Isabel — how could something this old possibly still work? — when a bright flame erupted within the glass.

Light stretched across the rough, craggy walls, illuminating a poky little room that consisted solely of shelf upon stony shelf, reaching up to an impossibly lofty ceiling. They were cluttered with all manner of odds and ends. It was a treasure trove, circular like the painting room, the bending shelves arranged around a giant iron cauldron that sat on the stone floor. That must be what he'd tripped over in the dark.

The room smelt damp and disused, but under the wet tang of rot there was the faint scent of herbs and dried flowers.

"What is this place?" Nicholas breathed, slowly getting used to the dank air.

"My collection," Isabel said, hopping up onto a shelf. She sat next to a grinning cow skull. "There, by the runes, do you see it?"

"See what?" Nicholas mumbled. He skirted around the cauldron, eying it distrustfully, and began to search the shelf that Isabel had nodded to. Runes were scattered everywhere, their strange angular symbols meaning nothing to him, and there, resting in a special upright stand, was a knife. Not just any knife, but an ornate, delicate weapon entirely carved from something that resembled ivory. A metal sheath protected the blade, while rune-like symbols had been etched carefully into the handle.

"Take it," Isabel said.

"What is it?" Nicholas asked, taking a hold of the carved handle and lifting the dagger from its stand. It was disarmingly light.

"A bone dagger," Isabel said, "carved from the horn of the demon Druj centuries ago by my ancestors. The Drujblade is a formidable weapon – many fell beasts has it slain through the years."

Nicholas carefully removed the sheath, revealing a blade hewn from the same dark bone as the handle. Its jagged teeth were dangerously sharp, and it was inscribed with words that he didn't recognise.

"Feels like it'd snap if anybody tried to use it," the boy said, slashing it tentatively through the air.

"No such thing could ever happen," Isabel scoffed. "'Tis more powerful than it looks. Many have used it against the evil things of nighttime and nightmare. And be careful, it's an antique, you know."

Nicholas stopped when his enthusiastic thrusting caused him to bump into the cauldron again. He quickly re-sheathed the blade.

"This'll definitely do some damage to Garm," he said, admiring the ancient weapon.

"Pray it doesn't come to that," Isabel said sternly. Nicholas only grinned.

CHAPTER SEVENTEEN
FIGHTING

MELVIN REYNOLDS GREETED HIM WITH AN enthusiastic slap on the back.

"The monster slayer returns!"

Nicholas staggered into the shop, Reynolds' animated welcome almost causing him to crash into a case full of animal skulls. Instead, he merely bumped it and the skulls skittered nervously on their shelves.

It was as fusty as ever inside Rumours, but Nicholas preferred that to the oddly-sterile atmosphere of Hallow House. He was just glad to be out again – and this time there hadn't been any cat scratches involved. Orville was still unsettling, though. Even more so in the daylight, if that was possible. Without the soupy darkness it was dazzling, and more unnervingly perfect than it had been the previous evening. The snowy high street was crisp and polished, gleaming like a new button. It was also disturbingly quiet. Aside from a few stragglers in the distance, there was nobody on the street. Nicholas wondered if they were all nursing sore heads after the exploits of the Red Lion.

"You've caught me at the perfect moment," Reynolds boomed. He was surprisingly loud. "I've just put the kettle on. Having a slow day. You'll have a cuppa, won't you?"

"Yeah," Nicholas said. He handed over the coat that the shop owner had loaned him. "Cheers for this."

"Oh that old thing? You should've dumped it in the bin on the way over," Reynolds said dismissively. He threw it onto the counter. "Ah, I see Isabel's in a brighter mood today."

He was being facetious.

Isabel had skulked silently in behind Nicholas and was perched at the window again, glaring suspiciously out at the high street. Her gift for unfriendliness was really something, Nicholas thought. At least she'd let him come back to the village. She'd barely put up a fight at all; though she had insisted that he wear the Drujblade. It was attached to his belt in a leather holder, concealed beneath a baggy hoodie.

"After you," Reynolds said, drawing aside the frayed brown curtain at the back of the shop. He was wearing a knitted jumper, and the ribbed columns of brown and mauve were stretched at the seams by his generous belly.

Nicholas ducked through. The back room was toasty and dark. It smelt like old cigars and boot polish, mixed with the sweeter bouquet of pine cones. It had been furnished as a kind of living room. Second-hand armchairs were studded with cigarette burns and a tattered old rug hugged an even tattier carpet. Unusual artwork hung on the walls, and there was a poster that contained a quote from Henry James' *The Portrait of a Lady*: "There are few hours in life more agreeable than the hour dedicated to the ceremony known as afternoon tea." A little set of wooden stairs led up to what must be the flat above the shop.

"I'm afraid builder's tea's the best I can do," Reynolds apologised, plodding over to the sink in the corner. It was piled high with crockery. An assortment of plates was doing a reasonable impression of the Leaning Tower of Pisa.

Nicholas wandered over to one of the armchairs. Beside it rested a glass-fronted cabinet, inside of which a number of books dozed lazily against one another. They looked very old. *The Complete Grimm's Fairy Tales. Stories or Fairy Tales from Past Times: Tales of Mother Goose. The Complete Works Of Hans Christian Anderson.*

"You like fairytales?" the boy asked.

Reynolds was fishing dirty crockery out of the sink and rinsing it under the tap.

"'Like' might be a bit of a strong description," he mused, using the sleeve of his jumper to wipe the rim of a mug. "I studied them for a time. They're fascinating – almost as fascinating as the people who told them. Did you know that there were actually nine Grimm siblings? And the brothers Grimm didn't just tell fairy tales, they also started work on an enormous German dictionary that wouldn't be completed until 120 years later. Not by them, of course."

"I always liked Little Red Riding Hood," Nicholas said, though the thought of that particular story made his chest constrict. He couldn't help but be reminded of the woman from the bus.

"Ha!" Reynolds scoffed, bowling over to the armchairs with a tray. He set it down on the book cabinet with a clink. "You want to read the original," he said, his dark eyes twinkling as he poured the tea. "You won't sleep for a month."

"Why not?"

"Charles Perrault's version from 1697 pre-dates the Grimms' and, shall we say, contains less savoury imagery." Reynolds paused, seeing that Nicholas wanted to know more. "Think of it this way," he continued. "A young woman is devoured by a 'big bad wolf'… In French, a girl becomes a woman when *elle avoit vû le loup*, or 'she has seen the wolf'." He left the suggestion dangling in the air.

"Doesn't sound like something kids should read," Nicholas said, cradling a chipped mug in his hands.

"Fairytales aren't for kids," Reynolds replied, sitting down with a huff. He took a great swill of his tea and exhaled a loud, lip-smacking "aaaah".

"C.S Lewis knew that," the shopkeeper added. "He's the one who said: 'When I became a man, I put away childish things, including the fear of childishness and the desire to be very grown up.' Fairytales are about the dangers of the adult world. Adults should study them just as much as kids."

Nicholas nodded thoughtfully. His mother had hated fairytales. He'd always assumed she was just squeamish, but now that he knew about her 'other' life, he wondered if there was something else to it. Fairytales were about monsters. Perhaps his mother had simply had enough of them; she didn't need stories to remind her about things that ate little children.

He realised his shoulders had stiffened and he'd retreated into his thoughts again. Funny how no matter where he was or what he was talking about, the subject always drew him back to his parents. A sucking whirlpool of grief had opened in his chest when they had died and its current often dragged him inside. Deeper into himself. Away from reality. Whatever 'reality' was now. He attempted to shake off the numbness, gripped the mug a little tighter.

"Seen that Garm thing again?" he asked the shopkeeper.

"Nah," Reynolds breathed, the sound blasting from deep in his gut. "It'll be off nursing its pride after it failed to eat you for dinner."

"I would've given it indigestion," Nicholas said.

"Out of spite," Reynolds laughed.

Nicholas nodded.

"How long has it been hunting round here?" he asked.

Reynolds raised his eyes to the ceiling. The circular discs of his glasses caught the light.

"Four, five… Seven weeks maybe," he said finally.

"Seven weeks! Why hasn't anybody done anything about it?"

"Fear," Reynolds said simply, batting a hand at the air. He reclined in the armchair, resting his mug on his stomach. "They're simple folk round here. Quiet folk. They wouldn't know the first thing about demons."

"And you do?"

Nicholas was wary of asking Reynolds outright about the Sentinels. For some reason it felt like a dirty word. A sinister word. *Sentinel*. He was only just getting used to it himself. It was one of those words that felt heavy. If you uttered it, it clunked to the floor and sat there.

"More'n I'd like to," Reynolds sighed. He tapped his temple. "There's stuff in here I'd rather not know, truth be told. Demons that paralyse their prey with a stinger. Others that devour you whole and digest you alive over a period of days."

"Nice."

"Why else do you think people turn them into fairytales. Deny their existence? It's too much to accept. Demons on the six o'clock news? Now that would be interesting."

Nicholas laughed.

"'A Kaijo demon is on the loose in the Norfolk Broads,'" Reynolds intoned, impersonating a news reporter. "'Police have advised people not to panic, and not to approach the Kaijo under any circumstances. Unless they want to see what their entrails look like. Now onto the weather…'"

Nicholas almost snorted his tea through his nose. He spluttered and wiped his mouth with his sleeve.

"So what do we do about it?" he asked.

"We?" Reynolds looked taken aback.

"The Garm," Nicholas persisted. "We need to stop it."

"Lad, there can't be any 'we' where demons are concerned."

"Of course there can."

Reynolds leaned forward in the armchair.

"Boy," he said slowly. "This isn't like hunting foxes. There's no horse-riding or fancy red jackets or 'tally-ho, old boy!' These are wild things from another world and they'd sooner gut you as look at you."

"I know that."

Reynolds held his gaze, not blinking for a very long time. He seemed to be having an internal wrestling match with his conscience.

"Why do you want to hunt it?" he asked. His voice was unnervingly, uncharacteristically soft.

Nicholas peered down into his mug, hunched over it like a fortune teller.

"Dunno," he said, jerking one of his shoulders.

Reynolds steepled his fingers over his own cup.

"People fight for lots of reasons," he began quietly. "If you separate out the details, though, it generally boils down to three things: duty, self-defence and revenge."

The boy's crop of curly hair barely moved as he raised his eyes to peer at the shopkeeper's fingers. He couldn't meet his gaze.

"There's an elusive fourth, though," the shopkeeper continued. "It's most common in young men. It's the most dangerous of them all, because what drives these young men isn't a sense of duty, or a need for self-preservation, or even a desire for vengeance. It's a yearning to destroy – not others, but themselves. To find an end. A peace."

The room fell silent.

"Nicholas," Reynolds said. "Why is it you want to fight?"

Finally, Nicholas looked at the shopkeeper. There was kindness in that big, red-cheeked face. Without saying anything, Nicholas tugged at his sleeve to reveal the bandage that Reynolds had put there.

"I know what that thing can do, and I don't care. I want to help you kill it."

The boy paused.

"There's nothing else. I think… I think this is what my parents would want me to do."

Reynolds's gaze was unwavering. At last, he released a breath.

"If you lose an arm, I shan't be the one carrying it to the hospital for you," the shopkeeper said.

"Then I won't lose an arm."

Reynolds peered at the boy out of the corners of his eyes. Nicholas couldn't tell if he thought he was mad, or if he was admiring his courage. Probably the former.

"Alright," the shopkeeper finally said, setting his mug down on the tray with a bang. "Tomorrow we go hunting."

CHAPTER EIGHTEEN
The Ectomunicator

'Cold claims lives' declared the front page of the *Cambridge News*. According to the article, more elderly people had died in this snowy summer than in the last two winters combined. Frozen pipes, swollen electricity bills, bad road conditions. All were being blamed, while certain angry fingers were being jabbed at the Environment Agency for failing to warn about the effects of global warming.

Sam tutted and shook his head, his breath frosting in the air. That headline seemed particularly insensitive considering they'd found the body of another dead child yesterday; another boy. Young too. Unimaginably young. Though Sam had felt disheartened and drained the previous evening, the discovery of the dead boy had doubled his resolve to get to the bottom of whatever was happening in Cambridge. Esus was right. Though he was loath to admit it, Sam was the closest to all of it. Richard had made sure of that. He had to do something.

"Things are going to pot, Judith," the old man muttered. "No two ways around it." He shivered.

Outside the Fitzwilliam Museum, Trumpington Street was eerily quiet. Four days had passed since the disturbance at the museum, and only the odd straggler had braved the iced-over roads to sneak a glimpse at the plinths where the famous lions had once rested.

Sam scanned the remainder of the front-page articles. The only other thing of note was a small story reporting that travel agents had seen a "phenomenal rise in last minute holiday bookings", which surely accounted for the lack of people milling about on the streets. Those who hadn't planned any time away this summer were now hastily booking last minute flights to exotic locales in pursuit of warmth. Sam's friend, Geraldine Adams, had done as much. She was a doctor, and he'd attempted to get in touch with her after Richard was attacked – she might know something about Snelling and what he'd done. The receptionist had informed him that Dr Adams and her husband were away for the next couple of days.

Sam didn't blame them; he'd probably have done the same if it weren't for more pressing matters.

He tossed the paper into a nearby bin as he spotted Liberty approaching. She looked tired.

"Been burning the midnight oil, Ms Rayne?" Sam greeted her.

"Midnight would've been an early one," the woman replied drily. She cradled a Styrofoam cup in her gloved hands and sipped her coffee. "I've been trying every trick in the book to get a fix on Richard, but he's moving around so much it's damn near impossible. I've trawled every text I could get my hands on. Even cracked open a box of my dad's old things; Mum wasn't too pleased about that. But I've never heard of a Harvester turning somebody like that. Not overnight. Not ever, if the lack of information in the books is anything to go by."

"This is dangerous new territory, to be sure," Sam breathed. He turned to look at the museum. The grand stone building looked colder than ever, hunched under the slate sky. Unusually, the overhead lights behind the columns were on, and the friendly glow spilled out into Trumpington Street, as if attempting to cheer those who had ventured into the city centre.

"You think the break-in has something to do with Richard?" Liberty ventured. Sam was grateful that she didn't ask him about the frantic phone call he'd made the previous evening. She was perhaps hoping to spare him any embarrassment. She probably knew that, if it was important, he'd tell her.

"I'm hoping you can answer that," Sam replied. "The police are clueless I'm afraid; the few remaining contacts I have there aren't talking. There's word of CCTV footage, but I've not been able to get my hands on it yet."

Liberty handed him her coffee.

"Help yourself," she said, "you look how I feel."

She took a hold of the ice-encrusted railings that surrounded the museum. Sam watched her focus on the steps that led up to the entrance and even out her breathing.

"Yes," she said almost immediately. "The woman. Malika. She went up these steps."

Liberty's breathing slowed further still.

"She left this way, too, through these gates. And… the lions." Liberty turned her head. "The lions were just for fun."

"Anything else?" Sam probed. "What brought her here?"

Liberty closed her eyes. "She's cradling something," she said. "A jacket… and something else. It looks like some kind of dish. Very old." Releasing the railings, Liberty took back her coffee. "That's all there is," she sighed. "Without getting inside, that's all I've got."

"Shame," Sam tutted. "Seems we're ten steps behind her again. Come on."

Together they moved away from the museum and its mysteries, and Liberty slipped her arm through Sam's as they trudged down the snowy path. For once he didn't shake it off in embarrassment.

"Maybe we shouldn't be focussing on her so much," Sam pondered, stomping his feet to get the blood flowing. "We need to change how we're looking at this."

"I'm open to suggestions."

"Richard, he's the key," Sam mused. "Malika helped the doctor corrupt him, which means he's now even more of a threat than she is."

Liberty nodded. "Not only is he a maniac with an insatiable bloodlust, he's a man on the inside."

"She already has the Harvesters in the palm of her hand, and now she has a corrupted Sentinel," Sam said, his voice catching with unease. "He knows everything about us. Everything. How we work. How we're organised. How we'd retaliate if attacked. He's perfectly positioned to cause grave damage."

"So where does he start?" Liberty said.

Sam stopped in his tracks.

Further up the street, he thought he'd seen a small child watching them. How long the youngster had been there he couldn't guess, and he was gone before Sam got much of a look at him. But it had definitely been a boy. Dressed in a suit. And he'd been smiling in a way that made Sam's stomach shrivel queasily.

"Sam?" Liberty looked at him. She followed his gaze down the street.

There was nobody there.

"I– I could've sworn," Sam began. "There was something–" Then he shook himself. "Never mind." He motioned to the Morris Minor at the kerb. "Get in. I've got an idea."

They drove back to Sam's house without talking. Sam had known Liberty for long enough that he didn't feel the need to fill the silences. And she was polite enough not to pry, though she could surely sense something was troubling him. Sam pitied anybody who tried to untangle his current knot of thoughts. He remembered that Liberty had previously confessed to occasionally slipping into somebody's mind without meaning to. "Channel-surfing" was what she'd called it; the ability to absent-mindedly flick between her own thoughts and somebody else's.

Sam didn't have anything to hide, though. For the most part. There was a certain something that could prove devastating if revealed, though, and Sam shoved that thought away. Of course, he knew he could trust Liberty. After his wife Judith had died, he'd spent a lot of time at the Rayne family dinner table. They were a good sort and he'd found comfort in the bustle of their family home. Then when Liberty's father had passed, Sam and Liberty had grown closer still. Sam realised she was the closest friend he had who had evaded the Harvesters thus far. He had to make sure it stayed that way.

When they got to Sam's house, he let them both in and barely paused to hurl his fedora at the coat stand before hurrying up the stairs. With Liberty behind him, Sam pulled a cord attached to the landing ceiling, from which a collapsible ladder dropped down. The old man swiftly climbed and Liberty clambered up at his heels.

Like the rest of the house, the attic was immaculate. It had been semi-converted into a small but functional office. Boxes were neatly stacked under the sloping roof and the drawers of two filing cabinets were neatly packed with important files. There was even a beautiful old rosewood wardrobe standing against the tallest wall which was lined with vintage fur coats and attractive dinner dresses, all wrapped up in plastic. All once worn by Judith.

"Here we are," Sam sighed, plonking himself down at an ancient mahogany bureau. He clicked on a lamp, illuminating a bulky object that rested on the desktop, draped in a white dust cover. Liberty stood behind him as he pushed back a portion of the protective sheet.

It was a smart, well-preserved apparatus; a mass of bright brass cogs and wheels. An old-fashioned set of keys – almost like those of an upmarket typewriter – were embellished with letters, numbers and symbols, and the strange mechanism shone like new, though it was obviously extremely old.

"What is it?" Liberty asked.

"An Ectomunicator," Sam told her proudly. He pulled a pair of reading glasses from his shirt pocket and blinked through them, mole-like, at the machine. "Every Sentinel family used to have one. Some people called them 'talkies', like the movies, because of what they were used for. We called ours Crosby." He gave one of the keys an affectionate polish with the cuff of his sleeve. "Didn't we, eh Crosby?"

"I've never seen anything like it," Liberty said, admiring the antediluvian device. "Never even heard of them."

"People stopped using them years ago," Sam said with a shrug. "They use spirit frequencies or some such to carry messages. I never really understood how they worked. We used them to communicate, but then somebody found out that kids were receiving Sentinel messages through their Ouija boards, so Ectomunicators were abandoned. By then we had telephones and telegrams, of course, so it wasn't a great loss. I always loved Crosby, though. I'd beg my father to let me send messages when the occasion arose."

For a moment Sam was lost in memory, his dry lips crinkled in a semi smile. Then he remembered that they had pulled Crosby out of retirement for a reason and he threw off the rest of the dust cover.

"There," he breathed, almost despondently now, as he uncovered what he'd hoped he wouldn't find. At the top of the Ectomunicator, a faded brown scroll of paper like a receipt roll curled up out of the guts of the machine. There were characters marked on the paper in dark ink. Tearing the scroll from the device, Sam moved over to the bare bulb that hung from the ceiling.

"It's from him. Richard." He tutted as he squinted at the message. "See there, the ID number in the top corner, unique to him. His father must've kept his old talkie and shown Richard how to use it." Sam studied the manuscript. "This was sent in the small hours of this morning. Richard must have doubled back to his house to send it."

"What does it say?"

Liberty peered over the old man's shoulder.

"'Emergency,'" Sam read slowly. "'Sentinel summit. St. John's Baptist Church. Tonight. 10.30. Urgent. Trinity blessings.' That's how we used to sign off." Sam's forehead creased into a frown. Something about the message was nagging him, but he was too rattled to figure out what.

"He's setting a trap," Liberty murmured. "They'll be like lambs to the slaughter. How many people do you reckon still use their talkie things?"

"Not many," Sam said, his glasses slipping to the end of his nose, "but enough to spread the word by more contemporary means, I'd imagine."

Liberty rushed to the desk. "Can we send a message? Tell people to stay away?" she demanded, seating herself in front of the archaic mechanism.

"We can, though there's no guarantee anybody will receive it in time."

"Better that than nothing," Liberty persisted. "How does this thing work?"

Sam went over, peering down at Crosby affectionately.

"Press the key with the house picture first," he instructed patiently, wetting his lips in excitement. He looked younger suddenly, the memories of his youth a little fresher in the presence of the brass apparatus. "That's the one that tells the receiver who's sent the message." He watched Liberty locate the right key and press it. It gave a tiny tinkle. "Now type the message."

Liberty read aloud as she pressed each of the keys, which all emitted jingles of differing pitch. "'Warning,'" she read. "'Stay away from St.

John's Baptist Church. Seized by Harvesters. Await further notice.' Is that enough, do you think?"

"I'd say so," Sam said encouragingly. "Now press the key with the wings icon, that says you're sending it. And then type '5, 6, 2, 9', that's the code for Cambridge. Every Sentinel with an active talkie in Cambridgeshire will receive it."

Liberty followed his instructions. As soon as she pushed down the final '9' key, the mechanics inside the Ectomunicator began to whir, and the cogs and wheels span. The desk trembled beneath the mechanism, and it gave a final *ping!* before falling silent.

"Done," Sam said, removing his glasses. "Now we wait."

Liberty raised herself out of the chair. "I'll ask Mum to keep hold of Fran again tonight, she's already there now," she said. "Come fetch me tonight. We'll go to the church."

"Are you sure? It could be quite dangerous."

"It'll definitely be dangerous," Liberty said sternly, "and I have no intention of letting you go there alone."

"Who said anything–" Sam began, but Liberty's no-nonsense glare caused his protestations to swiftly die.

"Tonight," Liberty said.

"Yes, tonight," Sam echoed softly.

They climbed back down the ladder and began to descend the staircase. They were almost at the foot of the stairs when Sam noticed Liberty grip the banister rail until her knuckles turned white.

"Liberty?" he began, but then he felt it, too.

A chill prickled the air and pressed right into his heart.

Warily, they peered through the railings into the dim living room, where a silhouette stared back, and a pair of cat-like eyes flashed.

"Won't you join us?" purred a voice that Sam recognised. The woman. The snake-like curls of her hair.

Sam felt a stab in his gut at the sight of her, as if she'd buried something sharp in him. But she was still by the mantelpiece, resting a slender arm against it.

Sam and Liberty remained on the stairs, transfixed by the outline of the woman. As Sam's eyes adjusted to the murk of the afternoon light, he saw that her white teeth were gleaming in a sultry grin.

"Here I was looking forward to a catch up," the woman burred in mock disappointment. "It appears you're not as pleased to see me as I am you. You break my heart."

"You have no heart, wench," Sam said evenly, having found his voice.

"You've been close enough to say that with certainty," Malika returned silkily. She trailed a finger across the exposed skin of her shoulder, then down to where her heart should be.

"*Enough*," guttered another voice.

Sam shuddered at the sound. It vibrated through his bones.

"*Join us.*"

Though every muscle in his body screamed against it, Sam found himself following Liberty down the stairs to the living room doorway. The room was awash in gloomy half-light as the dismal afternoon gave way to an equally morose evening. As the few dying rays of the sun pushed through the netting at the window, they framed a child, who stood with his back to them.

A boy.

His hands were clasped confidently behind him.

"*So this is the pair who've been causing me so many problems,*" rattled that tremulous voice. The boy turned and looked Sam in the eye. It was the boy from the street, the one Sam had caught sight of earlier.

What was wrong with him?

The boy's pupils were milky white and his skin looked parched, like it was drying from the inside out, and flaked away in pieces.

"What are you doing in my house?" Sam breathed.

The boy's cracked lips twitched into a grimace. "*You have something we want,*" he stated simply.

"There's nothing here of value," Sam assured him, his voice level, though his insides were shuddering. "Take whatever you want."

Those eyes. Those swirling, bone-white eyes. They were like blocks of ice, and the coldness they emanated drew him in, made him weary and heavy, forced him to feel every one of his seventy-one years.

"Going to stop us, Sammy?" came a third voice.

Sam shook himself out of the daze.

There was Richard, reclined lazily in his armchair. He was wearing

Sam's fedora, which cast his gaunt, bearded face in shadow. He was twisting a bloody knife in one hand.

"I always fancied this for myself," the man sneered, running his fingers along the brim of the hat.

"Richard," Sam said.

"Richard's dead," the other man spat, his spindly frame tensing in the chair.

"I hope that's true," Sam replied. He eyed the knife. "The Richard I knew would never kill harmless children."

Richard let out a roaring laugh and stabbed the blade into the arm of the chair. "I wish I'd had the pleasure," he said, practically drooling at the prospect. "Sadly, they were not mine for the taking."

"*Enough*," the boy by the window rasped. Though he barely moved a muscle, his presence filled the entire room. He shot Malika a look. "*Take her.*"

Malika's dress whispered snake-like rustles as she approached Liberty. Even as she reached for the woman's arm, though, Liberty struck out with her fist and caught Malika in the jaw. The red-haired woman's eyes burned bright with admiration.

"Feisty," she said, touching her jaw. "Can't wait to see what breaks you."

She flew at Liberty in a flash of glittering crimson, scratching and punching, a blur of frenzied movement.

"Liberty," Sam began, but before he could go to her aid, Richard sprung at him and forced the old man up against a wall.

"Come old boy, hold me," Richard hissed, pressing a bony arm into Sam's throat.

The two women crashed into the living room wall, dislodging a painting. Liberty spun to face her attacker, fist raised, which was when she made her fatal mistake.

She looked into Malika's eyes.

Liberty's cry of agony made Sam blanch. What was happening? Malika wasn't touching her, but Liberty's face had crumpled in pain. Her eyes were wide, unblinking. She was caught in Malika's malevolent glare.

"Yesssss," the red-haired creature hissed.

"Liberty!" Sam yelled, squirming in Richard's grasp.

"Not yet," Richard jeered through clenched teeth, his putrid breath blasting in Sam's face. "You and me, we're staying right here. Won't that be nice?"

"I-I-" Liberty was trying to speak, but she couldn't form the words. She swayed unsteadily.

"You're mine," Malika said softly, persuasively.

Liberty's face became blank. The pained creases evened out and she stood still, her eyes never leaving Malika.

"*Come*," the boy commanded, leaving the living room. Sam heard him open the front door and trudge out into the snow. He watched as Malika moved after him, Liberty mindlessly following her.

"Liberty!" he cried again, struggling against Richard. But he was helpless in the other man's grip. Liberty couldn't even turn to look at him as she went out into the hallway.

"Shame I didn't get to play with the old man," Malika purred from the door, glancing at Sam over her bare shoulder.

"Make it slow," she told Richard.

Then the front door slammed and Sam was alone in the living room with Richard.

CHAPTER NINETEEN
Hunting

Nicholas squeezed one eye shut and focused on the tree. Then he pulled the trigger. The rifle bucked alarmingly in his hands and the sound of the shot exploded deafeningly in his right ear.

Beside him, Melvin Reynolds let loose a jubilant hoot and slapped Nicholas roughly on the shoulder. "Nice shot!" he hollered. "You swear you've never used one of these before?"

His ear still ringing, Nicholas shook his head. His cheeks were flushed and his heart was hammering like he'd just cleared the finish line at a marathon – it was as if the gunshot had jumbled his insides up and they were hopping around trying to return to their rightful positions. He hadn't expected firing a gun to make him feel like that. Powerful and in control. It felt dangerous somehow, as if he shouldn't feel that way.

The boy stared at a tree not twenty feet away. There, in a sheet of paper nailed to the trunk, was a ragged bullet hole.

"If we come across Garm, I'll let you do the shooting," Reynolds declared, though Nicholas suspected he was joking. He handed back the weapon.

The woods were peaceful at this time of day. It was gone lunchtime, but there was barely any sun and the trees were gathering together against the frosty weather. Bundled up in his coat, Nicholas could barely feel the cold. Maybe it was the exhilaration of the hunt that was keeping him warm. The boy watched Reynolds as he discharged the used cartridge from the rifle and replaced it with a new one. He was an unusual man – large in every sense of the word. He wasn't as tall as Nicholas, but he was easily twice as wide. There was a strange mix of the delicate and the savage in him. Just when Nicholas thought he'd figured him out, Reynolds said or did something that surprised him. This morning was a perfect example. Before they'd taken to the woods in search of Garm, Nicholas had found Reynolds hunched over the shop counter at Rumours, his eyes magnified to almost ten times their normal size by a pair of bizarre metal goggles.

"Just taking a look through my collection," the shopkeeper had said, holding up what looked like a postage stamp. Sat on the worktop in front of him was a scuffed cardboard box packed with hundreds of similar little squares.

"You collect stamps?" Nicholas asked.

"Give me some credit," Reynolds returned drily. "Here, look." He slipped the lenses off and handed them to Nicholas. Putting on the over-sized glasses, the boy picked up one of the stamp-like squares. Except through the magnifying lenses, he could see now that it was a painting of a beach. The detail was remarkable – everything from a striped red and white deckchair to tiny, speck-like seagulls had been carefully inscribed in the miniature canvas.

"It's a painting," the boy marvelled.

Reynolds smiled. "Art has many forms," he said. "This one is my favourite. It makes us appreciate that not everything is what it seems, and that even the smallest of things can surrender the most surprising of wonders."

Now, lost in the dense forests that enclosed Orville like a prickly, protective wreath, Nicholas realised that it was Reynolds's inscrutability that he liked. From discussing art to hunting the beast Garm and using a tree as target practice, Nicholas never knew what he was going to do next. He found himself wondering if all Sentinels were this unpredictable. Could they all turn their hand to whatever their work required? Could his father have taken up a rifle and shot a hole in that target? Again, that sucking feeling of regret created a vacuum in his chest, and Nicholas attempted to swallow it down, force himself to remain in the present. It was so easy to get lost in the memories, and he'd always been inclined to daydreaming. He watched Reynolds working at the rifle and pushed thoughts of his parents away.

Isabel observed the pair from a log. She wasn't happy with the child's decision to leave the house again, and she made her feelings abundantly clear. Begrudgingly, she'd insisted that if Nicholas really had to take to the woods with the shopkeeper, he must keep the dagger with him at all times. Accepting this as a reasonable price for his freedom, the boy had strapped it to his belt, and now the cold metal sheath of the Drujblade dug reassuringly into his thigh.

The cat looked up as birds that had been startled by the gunfire returned to their roosts, wittering at one another in irritation. Without knowing why, she began pondering what blackbird tasted like, and, horrified, quickly banished the unwelcome thought.

"Where do you suppose he is?" Nicholas asked. "Garm."

Reynolds gave the firearm a check over. Nicholas noticed that he'd discarded the red and gold cartridge case on the ground and the boy retrieved it, turning it over in his hands. It was still warm.

"Damned if I know," Reynolds said. "Been sweeping the forest every morning for a month without any luck."

"Do you think he goes underground?" Nicholas asked, casting about the forest. The leaves rustled against one another above his head. "Maybe he burrows like a rabbit."

"If he does, he hides the holes well," Reynolds commented. He raised the rifle and aimed it at the paper nailed to the tree. "Gives us time for a little target practice," he added. "Besides, the sound of gunfire should tempt him out."

"It wouldn't scare him off?" Nicholas asked, watching the other man. He was overweight yet surprisingly nimble. He used his ample belly as a rest for the rifle.

"Nah. He's been shot before, knows it doesn't do much." Reynolds shrugged his shoulder, jiggling a large blade that was slung over his back on a strap, like a quiver of arrows. "That's what the knife's for."

He fired at the target, making a second tattered hole in the paper. The crack of the gunshot echoed through the trees, and the birds scattered into the air once more, shrieking their annoyance. Isabel eyed them distrustfully.

Reynolds sat down on a log with a sigh and pulled a yellow rag from his pocket. Carefully, he began to clean the rifle.

Nicholas perched on a tree stump opposite him, and knew this was his moment. "You're a Sentinel, aren't you?" he asked the man.

Reynolds didn't seem surprised by the question. He carried on cleaning, his chubby fingers working efficiently over the weapon.

"Wondered how long it'd be before you asked," he commented jovially, immersed in the task. "What gave it away?"

"The tattoo," Nicholas said. "I saw it the other day when you rolled your sleeves up. It's a Sentinel mark isn't it?"

"Aye," Reynolds said. "Only some of us get them nowadays. They're a tradition more than a requirement. They're always on the right forearm, too – the fighting arm."

"Dad didn't have one," Nicholas mused. "Probably thought it'd hurt too much."

"So you're part of the brotherhood, too," Reynolds observed. "Knew no ordinary boy could come away from a clash with Garm quite so unshaken."

Nicholas smiled, pleased that he might even partially resemble a Sentinel, even if this was all so new and confusing.

"There are more like Garm, aren't there? Monsters or whatever they are."

"Garm's a cuddly puppy compared to some of the things I've seen over the years," Reynolds replied soberly. "There are others, aye, all over. That's what the Sentinels are for. Things like Garm are always wriggling through the gaps, finding a way into our world, tempted by the smells and the promise of blood. I imagine our world's a sight more pleasant than whatever hell dimension he's clawed his way out of."

"And there are different types?"

"More'n you could ever imagine. They're all different. There are some, like the Garm, that live on instinct alone. They're wild animals only stronger, viler, deadlier. You've heard of Bigfoot? The beast of Bodmin? They're all monsters that have been spotted, caught in the act. Normally they're pretty good at staying out of sight."

"So most demons just want to eat you?"

Reynolds chuckled. "For the most part, But then there are the Adepts. They're just as hideous, only they have a calculating intelligence – they'll *tell* you they're killing you as they do it."

Nicholas remembered what Jessica had said about demons being banished centuries ago. Where had they been banished to? And how did they get back in?

"How many are there?" he asked.

"How long's a piece of string?" Reynolds asked back. "They're always finding cracks in our reality and forcing their way through. Impossible to count them."

Nicholas nodded faintly and let this sink in. The casual manner in which both Reynolds and Jessica talked about such otherworldly things still made him uncomfortable. He decided to steer the conversation into less uncomfortable terrain. "Have you always lived out here?" he asked.

"Aye, ever since I was a boy. My uncle raised me. Hard man, fiercely traditional. Taught me everything I know about fighting. Rumours used to be his. Except back then it was an armoury. Can't say I ever had much taste for weapons, though." Reynolds paused, perhaps aware that he was contradicting himself as he sat diligently polishing the rifle. "Old habits die hard, I suppose."

"Your uncle's not around anymore, though?" Nicholas asked.

"Oh no, he's been underground for years."

"The people in the village," Nicholas began, "they're… odd."

From her log, Isabel sniffed in what Nicholas knew was her usual disdainful manner. Reynolds didn't notice.

"You could say that," he nodded. "Orville can do that to people. Sometimes a place has a soul, and Orville's is a troubled one, no doubt about it. It has a bloodier history than most, and that history can rub off on the people who live here. Terrible things have happened here. Things that'd turn your hair white." He set the rifle aside. "That'll do. What say we head back to the shop and get a bite to eat?" He patted his generous belly. "Makes for hungry work, this hunting."

Nicholas laughed. They hadn't exactly done much hunting, but he wouldn't say no to a steaming cup of hot chocolate to bring the warmth back into his fingers. Reynolds reached for the rifle, then stopped when he saw Isabel. Her ears were flat against her skull, and she was staring off into the distance, sniffing the air curiously.

"What you picking up, then?" Reynolds murmured. The cat didn't seem to hear him. A faint breeze ruffled her fur, making it almost stand on end.

Nicholas was looking at her as well now.

"Think she's picked up his scent?" he asked eagerly. "Isabel, what is it?"

The cat looked at him, and the boy knew that she'd sensed something even if she daren't voice it in front of Reynolds. Then he heard it. A stealthy cracking of twigs that only got louder with each second that passed.

Instinctively, Nicholas wrapped his fingers around the Drujblade sheathed at his side. Reynolds seized the rifle, spinning down onto one knee and resting the gun on the log he'd just been using as a bench.

"Here he comes," Reynolds breathed in a low voice.

Between the trees Nicholas saw a great, hulking shape galloping toward them, crashing through the greenery and kicking up dirty snow as it came. He tensed, standing behind Reynolds with Isabel at his side. The cat moved close to Nicholas.

With a throaty squeal, Garm broke into their little clearing. In the daylight, the creature was even more hideous, scrabbling in the dirt with powerful, sinewy limbs. Its scales were a dull green, the patches of fur that erupted in spikes along its spine the same brown as the mud, and the swivelling eyes were a vibrant red – the red of blood.

Without pausing, Reynolds fired into the mountain of muscle and the Garm snorted tetchily, barely noticing the bullet as it rebounded off its scaly armour. Reynolds fired again, but the monster kept coming, its slimy tongue lolling out of its incisor-lined mouth. The shopkeeper didn't have time to reload the rifle before the creature was upon him.

As he watched the foul beast throw itself at Reynolds, Nicholas suddenly snapped to his senses. Yelling, he hurled himself at the monster, raising the Drujblade and sinking it into the Garm's massive front leg, which was pinning Reynolds to the snowy ground. Yellow sparks spewed into the air as the blade penetrated Garm's armour, and a piercing shriek erupted from the monster's gullet. It backed off, scraping away from the pair through the mud and snow. Its red eyes burning hate, it licked at the wound and trilled phlegmy comfort sounds to itself.

Nicholas helped Reynolds to his feet, and the man turned breathlessly to him.

"Run," he panted.

"But–" Nicholas began in protest. Reynolds held up a hand to silence him as he wrenched his own blade from his back. Wielding it in front of him like a sword, he squared up to the Garm, which was already recovering and setting its devious sights on them.

"Get out of here, boy," Reynolds yelled. "RUN!"

Confused and disappointed, Nicholas backed slowly away from the shopkeeper. He'd thought they would defeat the beast together, but now he saw he'd been stupid to think that Reynolds would let a boy get in the way of his conquest. Nicholas lingered by the log that Isabel was perched on, desperate to see Reynolds in action. A Sentinel in action.

"GO!" Reynolds commanded huskily, and Nicholas didn't dare defy him. He seized Isabel in his arms and hurtled through the woods.

For once, the cat didn't complain, sinking her claws into the boy's thick jacket and clinging on fearfully. As they reached the outskirts of the village, a horrendous scream sliced through the woods.

"Reynolds!"

Nicholas skidded to a halt. That scream. Reynolds was hurt, maybe even killed.

Isabel seemed to read the boy's thoughts.

"We can't go back," she insisted quickly. "We must return to the house at once. That beast will be the death of us."

"We can't just leave him out there in the woods," Nicholas reasoned defiantly. "That thing will kill him!"

"Not our problem," Isabel said. She squirmed out of the boy's grasp and landed noiselessly on the ground. "Come, child," she urged, already hastening in the direction of the Orville high street.

Dragging his heels, Nicholas went after her. He stopped as they came to the street, where a handful of people were bustling about, braving the snow in order to shop for supplies. A thought struck him, and Nicholas hurried over to a burly bald man who was coming along the pavement.

"Please," the boy said. "You have to help us. The thing in the woods, it's got Reynolds."

The burly man didn't seem to notice him, though, and carried on down the high street as if Nicholas hadn't spoken at all. Cursing the insolence of the Orville folk, Nicholas rushed up to the next person he saw – a middle-aged woman with short black hair and a puffy blue winter coat who was carrying a full bag of groceries.

"Please," Nicholas began again with growing desperation. "Please, can you help us?" The woman ignored him and, frustrated, Nicholas seized her by the arm. "Please," he begged. "There's something in the woods and it's going to kill Reynolds."

The woman stared fearfully at him, just as the man at the Red Lion had done the previous day.

Nicholas squeezed her arm encouragingly, tried to soften his voice. "Is there anybody who can help us?" he pleaded.

The woman only gasped in horror, staring right through him as if he were nothing more than vapour. Dropping her groceries, she let out a shriek and jerked her arm free, scrabbling down the street away from him.

"They can't see you, child," Isabel said slowly.

Puzzled, Nicholas looked down at her. "What? What do you mean?"

"Isn't it obvious?" the cat said, casting an appraising look at the people in the street. "This is no normal village. I don't know what's happened here, but I doubt anybody who lives here can see outsiders. They certainly can't see you or I. Come, we must leave this damned place."

Baffled, Nicholas stared apprehensively at the villagers going about their business. They couldn't see him? They could certainly feel his touch, maybe even hear his voice, so why couldn't they see him? He shivered, recalling how he'd felt when they'd first stumbled upon the village. That feeling of unease, almost like the place itself was aware of him.

"Nicholas!"

The boy snapped back to reality as the gruff voice cried his name. It was Reynolds!

Nicholas turned to see the shopkeeper staggering down the street toward him. His face was covered in blood and he was limping, his left trouser leg tattered and stained.

"The shop," Reynolds huffed, sweat running down his face, mingling with the blood. "We have to get to the shop. I lost the gun. And the blade. That hellbeast's stronger than I thought. I wounded it, but it'll be after our innards now more than ever."

"No," Nicholas said. He didn't want to stay in the village any longer than he had to – especially after what Isabel had just said. "We should go to the house. Come on."

Isabel shot the boy a glare, but Nicholas didn't stop to argue, putting an arm around Reynolds' waist and shouldering the man's weight. Considering Reynolds' ample girth, it took a concerted effort, and together they stumbled through the village.

"Come on!" Nicholas yelled at the cat and Isabel hurried after.

As they hastened out into the fields, that familiar wheezing screech sounded through the trees, and all three of them broke into a run.

"I could've helped," Nicholas panted, struggling as Reynolds' arm dug into his shoulder. "Back in the woods. Why wouldn't you let me?"

Reynolds winced as pain shot up his leg. "I…" he gasped. "I… wanted to… protect you."

"I don't need protecting," Nicholas cried. "Why does everybody think I need so much protection?" If the shopkeeper hadn't been in such bad shape, he'd have suggested going back and finishing off the monster instead of fleeing to the house. He knew, though, that Reynolds wouldn't allow it, especially with that leg.

Another inhuman scream sounded, closer this time, and Nicholas attempted to quicken his pace, pulling Reynolds with him.

The house appeared before them and they hurried to it.

Letting go of Reynolds, Nicholas raced up the steps and threw open the front door. The shopkeeper was right behind him, but he tripped on the top step and tumbled to his knees.

"Come on!" Nicholas cried. He grabbed the man's hand and hauled him inside.

"Thanks," Reynolds huffed. He pushed Nicholas away from the door and turned just as the Garm monster launched itself up the steps. It ignored Isabel, who was still at the foot of the stairs, and its claws scraped against the stone like metal.

It went to hurl itself through the door when Reynolds suddenly straightened, threw his arms up and bellowed "STOP!"

The beast skidded to a halt on the top step and glowered up at the man. Nicholas stared on incredulously as the monster's behaviour changed completely. Its ruby eyes became meek and docile as they blinked dopily up at Reynolds, and it sat there obediently, as if awaiting a command.

"Good Garm," Reynolds soothed, peering down at the massive beast. He reached out and patted him on the snout. The creature gave an affectionate snort.

"I think you've earned your supper," Reynolds cooed. "How do you like the sound of cat?"

The Garm tilted its head and saliva oozed out of the corner of its gaping maw.

"Go get her," Reynolds commanded encouragingly. An excited squeal escaped the monster's throat, and it whirled about on the steps, rushing clumsily down to where Isabel was sitting, still panting and breathless.

"Reynolds?" Nicholas began unsurely. "What's going on?" He stepped backwards slowly, disturbed by the way the man had suddenly changed.

"Why don't you just call me Snelling from now on?" the other man said, leering at the boy. "I always preferred that name."

CHAPTER TWENTY
HARVESTERS

SAM'S HEAD STRUCK THE FLOOR WITH a sickening crack and immediately the world began to spin. The old man heaved himself woozily onto his hands and knees and attempted to get up, but a boot dug him hard in the ribs and he collapsed against the floor once more.

"Oh, come, come, old man," a venomous voice goaded over his shoulder. "I thought you had a little more fight in you than that."

They were still in the living room. Sam's head pounded dully, as if at any moment it was going to implode, and blood wept from a cut above his right eye, half blinding him. He gasped in short, sharp breaths, his ribs screaming, every inch of his body aching. In the back of his mind, a tiny voice considered the possibility that this was it; he was done for. He didn't want to think that way, wouldn't have done even five years ago, but he was too old for this sort of thing now.

"You–" stuttered the old man with effort. "You're a coward."

Richard threw his head back and howled with laughter. "Words can't hurt me now," the scruffy man sneered. "That's okay, though. Words are all you've got. You're feeble. Pathetic. Should've been put out to pasture years ago. He was only friends with you out of pity, you know. He hated you. Couldn't wait for you to cark it and end your ceaseless meddling."

Sam tried to shut out the needling words, but they jabbed at their intended mark like pokers. Even if this thing that used to be Richard was no longer his friend, he knew exactly where the sore spots were.

Steel-like hands seized the elderly man's shoulders and suddenly

Sam was being dragged to his feet. He was spun to face Richard and the older man stared blearily into that smirking, bearded face. The afternoon sun had almost entirely sunk below the window frame and the shadows distorted themselves across Richard's stiff, skeletal features. His hair was lank and greasy, and he looked meaner than ever.

"This is just the beginning, Sam," he goaded. "We're everywhere, and with each sunrise our numbers swell. The Sentinels will join us or die screaming."

"N–never," Sam muttered, wiping at his bloody eye.

"The Dark Prophets are mustering their strength," Richard said. He put a grubby finger to his lips. "Shhh, listen," he whispered, cupping a hand to his ear. "Can you hear that? That silence? It's the sound of defeat. The fight is already over." He scratched his beard thoughtfully. "I'll give you a sporting chance. If you can land one hit, I'll let you have it. Go on – in the name of sportsmanship."

Sam swayed unsteadily. Pain ran jaggedly down his right leg where Richard had kicked it moments before. In front of him, the other man hopped about like his veins were crackling with electricity instead of blood. He couldn't stay still for more than a second.

His head throbbing, Sam wracked his brain for a way out of this. What in this room or the next could save him? Then he had it. The knife. The one that Richard had sunk into the arm of the chair earlier. It was still there, and Sam was standing right next to the chair. Could he move fast enough? Sam doubted it, but if he could get in just one good hit, it might buy him the time he needed to snatch the blade up.

Still swaying, Sam attempted to focus his mind, push every angry thought he could muster down the length of his arm to gather in a ball in his fist. He gritted his teeth, then swung his fist up with as much furious energy as he could.

Richard was too fast. He blocked the punch easily, and landed a hard smack to Sam's left temple. The old man went down again. He coughed, tasted carpet and blood. As he heard Richard pace toward him, though, he realised through the daze of pain and exhaustion that he'd landed right by the armchair. Rallying his strength once more, he flailed a hand upward, gripped the blade's handle, and wrenched it free from the chair.

It wasn't a moment too soon. Rolling over onto his back, Sam raised the knife just as Richard threw himself at the old man. Sam slashed the blade in an arc in front of him, and Richard only just managed to dodge its bite. The knife still caught his arm, though, and Richard snorted, recoiling from the contact.

Head clearing slightly in the wake of this small victory, Sam wobbled to his feet and clutched the blade before him. Richard ignored his bleeding arm and stared Sam down like a mad dog, not sure how to react now that the odds had changed.

"Richard," Sam panted. "Stop this. Whatever it is that's got you, you can free yourself from it. You're stronger than it."

Blood trickled down Richard's forearm and dripped onto the living room carpet. "Richard's dead," he told the other man coolly. "He died in that sad little house of his, and it's a good thing. He was a waste of space, a snivelling lowlife who spent his entire life in the shadows of others, too afraid to take credit for anything."

"You're a good man," Sam persisted, his shoulders sagging with fatigue. He could barely keep the knife pointed at Richard. "A smart man. You can come back from this." His voice was desperate now. "You have to fight."

"RICHARD'S GONE!" the other man bellowed, and he bowled into Sam. Together they hurtled through an open doorway into the kitchen where they collided with the kitchen table. Richard pummelled Sam in the stomach with his fists, and the old man grunted, slashing out with the knife. It sunk into Richard's abdomen and Richard yowled. Sam shoved the man away from him and got behind the table.

"Please, Richard," Sam pleaded, the hand gripping the knife now slick with the other man's blood. Richard shot him a deadly stare, then leapt up onto the table. He kicked Sam in the jaw, and the old man crashed against the sideboard, knocking the toaster and kettle onto the floor. Richard jumped on top of him, forcing Sam down onto the linoleum, gripping the old man's throat with his dirty fingers. He squeezed.

"How much fun do you think they're having with her right now?" he teased, pushing his face so close to Sam's that his stale breath violated his nostrils. "The black witch. After I've dealt with you, I think I'll go and get some of that for myself. I'll bet she squeals."

Sam battered feebly at the vice-like grip at his throat, but Richard was too strong. The clamp of his rough fingers crushed his windpipe and he couldn't breathe. The blood pumped deafeningly in his temples and everything started to go fuzzy.

"Nnnn," Sam gurgled. Richard batted the old man's flapping arms away as if he were swatting at a bad smell.

"I'll bet she's as feisty elsewhere as she was with her fists," Richard drooled, revelling in his power over the nuisance pensioner.

Sam's hands beat against the linoleum floor, questing for the knife, which he'd dropped in the scuffle. Then his fingers grazed something – the metallic kettle. As he felt himself starting to lose consciousness, he gripped the handle and swung the kettle at Richard's head. It made a dull clunk, and Richard rolled heavily off him. Sam wheezed in a welcome breath, spluttering as his lungs filled with air.

Richard sprawled on the floor in a daze, blood splattered across his face.

The kettle trembled in Sam's fingers as he heaved himself up, and the other man looked at him with scared eyes.

"Sam," Richard choked. "Sam…"

The old man's heart leapt. It sounded just like the Richard he knew. His friend. He softened, went to move toward the fallen man. In an instant, Richard's features contorted and he bared his teeth in a snarl. He lashed out with his bloodied hands, clawing the air in desperation, clutching for the old man.

Sam brought the kettle down on his skull. It made an upsetting squelch. Driven by blind hatred now, he lifted it and brought it smashing down again. And again. And again, venting his anger at the thing that had destroyed his friend until it wasn't moving anymore.

Finally, shattered, the old man dropped the kettle and collapsed onto the kitchen floor.

With Richard's lifeless body pooling blood across the white linoleum, Sam slipped into unconsciousness.

He wasn't sure how long he was out for, but when he came to it was dark. Richard's dead eyes stared accusingly through the gloom at him and Sam turned away. He struggled to his feet, sucking the air in sharply as pain spiked at his ribs. He limped to the kitchen sink, took a dirty mug from the side and filled it with water, gulping down three cups before his mouth stopped tasting like blood and sandpaper. Then he opened the cupboard by the sink and retrieved a first aid kit.

For half an hour he cleaned and bandaged himself, put a plaster over the cut above his right eye. He'd done this before, but that didn't lessen the sting of the antiseptic wipes. One thing drove him: Liberty. They had her. Where they'd taken her he couldn't guess. Liberty had sensed Malika's presence at the museum, but why would they return there? Malika had already obtained what she needed from that place. Richard's home was a tip. He only had one option. The church from the Ecto message. St. John's Baptist Church. Even if Liberty wasn't there, somebody at the church might know where she had been taken.

With this vague plan filling him with purpose, Sam shakily retrieved his fedora from the living room floor where it had fallen during the fight. In the hall, he plucked his coat from the stand and gingerly pulled it on. Then he grabbed his keys and went out into the cold.

Twenty minutes later he was driving down a quiet country lane with his headlights off. He was a few miles outside the city, out in the darkening countryside. The only lights brimmed from the stars and the warm orange glow of the city at the bottom of the hill.

Sam parked behind a large hedge and got out into the snow. He'd have to walk the final mile to the church if he didn't want to be seen. Pulling his collar up, he seized his rifle from the back seat and hunched into the wind.

★

Liberty came to with a start. A smell of damp and mould hit her solidly. The cloying reek curled up into her nostrils and she gagged, tying to put her hand to her face. Except she couldn't. Her hands were chained. Confused, she tugged at her restraints, but they held fast.

"Sam?" she called. Her voice echoed up into what must be a high ceiling, getting lost above her head.

Where was she?

It was too dark to see anything, and deathly quiet. Only her own short, nervous breaths came to her ears. She attempted to

218

calm herself. Centre her mind. Where was she? She could feel dirt beneath her. She was crouched in it on her knees. Liberty tried to focus, but the blackness was so thick, so absolute that it choked her, and she stared wildly into the nothingness that pressed suffocatingly around her.

She tried to remember how she'd arrived here, but there was nothing. She had a vague recollection of a woman and lots of shouting. The insistent pounding in her head hinted that she'd come to blows with somebody, but other than that…

A faint shuffling sounded nearby, and Liberty turned her head in its direction.

"Hello?" she called. Her voice disappeared up into the invisible ceiling once more.

There came a high-pitched chuckle, and Liberty stiffened.

"Malika?" she ventured uneasily, attempting to blink away the dark.

"You know my name," a soft voice whispered. It was so close that Liberty felt the warm breath caress her neck. Every hair on her body stood on end and Liberty cringed away, attempted to wrestle free from the chains. It was useless.

"What fun we're going to have!" called Malika, her jubilant voice now further away. It glanced off hidden surfaces and battered Liberty from all sides.

"You're the final piece!" the voice rang. "Always two, there have to be two."

Liberty shrank into herself, attempted to block out the witch's goading words. She evened out her breathing and reached out with her mind, striving to sense where she was.

There was something wrong. She couldn't sense anything at all.

It was as if some dark magic had shackled her mind, just like the chains that fettered her wrists. Liberty suddenly felt very cold and very alone. This had never happened before. There were people who referred to her abilities as a sixth sense, and Liberty had used them often as just that – another set of eyes and ears, another way of deciphering the world. Now even that had been denied her.

"Don't worry," Malika's voice called merrily. "It's not long now. Not long at all. Soon it'll be time to play. Aren't you excited?"

Liberty didn't answer. She closed her eyes against the darkness and waited.

★

It was quiet as the grave. Sam crouched behind a low stone wall and hazarded a swift glance over the top. There was the church. The bell tower spire jabbed up at the wintry sky, as if attempting to spear the heavy clouds that had rolled in, and the trees that lined the gravel path wore their snow-white coats with conviction.

Sam frowned. There was something about this place that was nagging at him. Had been ever since he'd read the note from the Ecto. What was it? Then it struck him like a slap to the cheek. Of course! St. John's Baptist Church. It was the very same building that Nicholas had sleepwalked to in the middle of the night a week ago. The old man shivered. If ever he'd needed a demonstration of Nicholas's latent abilities, that was the one to beat.

The old man didn't have time to marvel at the boy's talents, though. If anything, the knowledge that Nicholas had been here filled him with dread. Nicholas's burgeoning abilities had drawn him here against his will, which meant that something very powerful must be here, waiting. It had probably been here all along.

Sam couldn't see anybody, though. The church appeared as deserted and derelict as ever. Its front doors were boarded over with graffiti-stained panels of wood, and the building was still. It made Sam nervous.

Had the warning that Liberty sent over the Ecto reached the other Sentinels? Was that the reason the site remained abandoned? Or had Sam simply missed whatever activity had taken place here? Hoping it was the former, Sam crept towards the building, moving around its considerable bulk until he was at a side door. He tried the handle. Locked. Sam kept going, reaching the immense graveyard at the back of the church. It stretched out as far as he could see, a jumble of dark stones. Still no sign of life. Sam cursed under his breath. Then froze.

There. A flicker. Through the drunken muddle of headstones, off to one side of the cemetery, there was a glimmer of light. Sam watched, waited, but the light didn't move. Carefully, he made his way through the graveyard, picking his way in between the tipsy stones. Then he saw where the light was coming from – a mausoleum. It was pushing its way out from the inside of a grand old mausoleum, through a crack in the ancient door.

Two men stood either side of the entrance. One had a scar running from his chin to the back of his head. The other was younger but had a steely glint in his single eye.

Harvesters, Sam thought. They couldn't be anything else. What were they doing guarding a mausoleum?

Sam pressed close to a stone, his shoulder disturbing the snow that had crusted over it. What if Liberty was in there? Grimly, Sam realised there was nothing for it – he had to get inside the crypt. He was too beaten up to take on both of the Harvesters, though. His skull still pounded and his ribs felt, if not broken, then severely bruised. How to get inside? The Harvesters prowled about outside the decrepit tomb, panther-like in their movements.

Sam fumbled about on the ground and soon found what he was looking for. His hand closed around a small rock. When he was sure the guards weren't looking in his direction, he hurled the stone into another part of the graveyard, away from the mausoleum.

The rock cracked against a headstone, and the sound rang sharply into the night.

The heads of both guards snapped in the rock's direction. They shared a steely look, then the one with the scarred face took off through the cemetery.

"A classic never dies," Sam breathed to himself. "Maybe you're not too old for this, old boy."

Keeping low, he hurried between the headstones and then around the side of the mausoleum. Bracing himself, Sam took a breath, then hurtled around the corner, shoving the butt of the rifle into the face of the younger, one-eyed Harvester.

The guard didn't even have a chance to cry out, falling unconscious to the ground, an ugly welt rising on his forehead. Not wasting a moment, Sam dashed into the mausoleum and hid behind the rusted metal door. How long did he have before the other guard returned and found his comrade cataleptic? Not long. He'd just take a quick look then get out of there.

Except there was nothing in the mausoleum. Flames guttered in iron holders bolted to the crumbling walls, but other than a great sarcophagus in the centre of the cramped space, there was nothing here.

Sam edged over to the tomb, which lay open, and his eyebrows raised in surprise. Within the stone coffin, a flight of stairs led down into darkness.

Sam eyed the door of the mausoleum and knew he had no choice.

No turning back now, Judith.

Treading as lightly as he could, he descended into the gloom. Below, more lights flickered, leading the way to the foot of the stairs. Sam dreaded to think what was waiting for him down there. His hands clamped around the rifle in preparation, ready to fire if necessary. He hoped he wouldn't have to resort to that just yet – the sound of a gunshot would no doubt attract more trouble than he was looking for.

How much more trouble could I possibly get into, though?

The steps came to an end and Sam was relieved to find that this entrance was not guarded. Out of the corner of his eye, though, he sensed movement, and pushed his back up against a nearby pillar. Stalking in between the stone columns were mean-looking figures carrying blades of varying sizes. More Harvesters. There were easily a dozen of them, some muscular, some rake-thin and lithe, all slithering through the shadows like animals of prey.

They're uglier than I remember.

There came a faint murmuring sound from up ahead. Squeezing the rifle tighter still, Sam kept an eye on the moving silhouettes as they patrolled the underground tomb and hopped to the next pillar. He repeated this action until finally he was as near to the murmurs as he dared stray. Tentatively, he edged around the pillar.

Malika was kneeling, prostrated, in front of a massive stone effigy – a snarling sculpture of a fearsome, devil-like entity. In the guttering firelight, the coarse features seemed to move. The woman's back was to Sam, and she was whispering reverently, her head bowed in quiet prayer.

Beside the sculpture stood the demon child. It wore the same blank, emotionless expression that sent chills down Sam's spine. Flanking him were two further Harvesters, their gazes averted respectfully from whatever Malika was doing.

And there, just in front of the effigy was Liberty. Her hands were chained to a little circular table that was barely a foot off the ground. She was slumped on the dusty floor in front of it. A gag had been stuffed into her mouth. Sam started when he realised that Liberty was staring right at him. She looked terrified.

Malika's dress whirled about her in a fan as she moved away from the image of her god, and Sam saw that in her hands she was clasping a rough, ancient-looking bowl. Barely even registering Liberty's presence, the flame-haired woman hummed to herself as she set the artefact down on the circular table.

"It is time," she said with a slow smile. She seated herself opposite Liberty, and yanked the woman's restraints so that her hands were on the table. "Play nice," Malika cautioned, seizing a hold of the Sensitive's hands, holding them firmly either side of the bowl. She tossed her head back, her red curls shimmering in the firelight, and began to chant in a strange tongue that Sam didn't recognise.

He raised the rifle, preparing to fire at the witch.

"What do we have here, then?"

Sam tensed at the voice.

Behind him, two shadows broke into the light and Sam reacted too slowly as the one-eyed Harvester snatched the rifle from him and tossed it out of reach.

"Did nobody ever teach you that spying on people is rude?" the Harvester sneered. He seized Sam by his collar and threw him against a pillar. The old man struck the column and landed on the floor with a thud. He looked up just in time to see the other Harvester, the one with the scar, emerge from behind another column. Together, the two of them grinned like hyenas, their lips curling back threateningly in silent snarls.

One-Eye cracked his knuckles in front of him, and now that he was closer, Sam's insides gave a jolt. He knew him. He wasn't a Harvester at all. He was a Sentinel. Except the last time Sam had seen him, he'd had the use of both of his eyes. His name was Vincent Carmac; he was a local boy whose father worked in the bakery on Nuffield Road.

"Vincent," Sam gasped in horror, getting to his feet.

"Sammy Wilkins," snarled the man with the scar. "You should've said you wanted to come along. You would've been more than welcome."

Horrified, Sam realised that he knew him, too. Jack Davies from Great Shelford, one of the villages on the outskirts of Cambridge. They'd been turned, just like Richard – and their faces now bore the scars of the fights that had robbed them of their sanity.

Sam shook his head in disbelief. This couldn't be. Would the nightmare never end?

"Jack," Sam uttered, crestfallen. "What have they done to you?"

"I'm free, Sammy," Jack replied arrogantly. "I've never felt better."

Sam heard Liberty groaning by the effigy and cast a wary look over his shoulder. The woman's face was gaunt and her eyes were rolling in her head. Whatever Malika was using her for, Liberty was fighting it with everything she had.

The bowl at the centre of the table was trembling, and within it, black liquid was swirling like a vortex. A sluicing breeze had stirred between the pillars, and it whistled through the underground tomb, shrieking like dead voices.

"Thought you'd get the better of us, eh Sammy?" Jack rasped.

Next to him, Vincent dabbed at the welt on his forehead. "The old man's getting nosy," he spat. "Shoving that beak where it don't belong. Think we should put it out of joint for him, stop it straying again."

Jack nodded, grinning. "What do you think, Sammy boy?" he goaded. "We were promised blood today, but we've yet to see a drop. You could say we're very, very thirsty."

The ground began to shudder and rock beneath them, but the ex-Sentinels didn't appear to notice. The firelight flickered madly in their eyes. Sam wondered if they were as lost as Richard had been.

"What did this to you?" he demanded.

"Look at that face, Vince," Jack laughed. "Did you ever see anything stupider? He looks like he's seen a ghost."

"Woooooooo!" Vincent murmured in a ghost–like voice. "Afraid we're gonna steal your pension, Sammy?"

The earth trembled under their feet, and Malika's cries resounded through the tomb. As the wind turned into a ferocious howl, Sam found he had to shout to be heard.

"You can stop this!" he cried. "Remember who you are! You have to remember!"

Vincent cupped a hand to his ear and pretended he couldn't hear him. "What's that old fella?" he called. "Think I need my ear trumpet, not catching a word!"

Sam pressed his back against the pillar and, despairing, knew there was no reasoning with them. He'd been unable to save Richard, and he wouldn't be able to save Jack and Vincent, either. Whatever had seized control of their bodies had long since killed them.

With a sinking feeling in his stomach, the old man realised there was only way out of this – either they were going to kill him, or he was going to have to kill them. What could he do, though? They were both much younger and fitter than he was. Where had the rifle gone? Sam cast about, seeing the butt of the weapon poking out from behind a column a few feet away. Too far to run for it. He was going to have to fight. He reached into his pocket – luckily, he'd not come unprepared.

"No more talk?" Jack yelled, feigning hurt.

"Yeah, you've gone awful quiet," Vince agreed. "Not like you at all – life and soul of the party, that Sammy Wilkins. Just like his poor dead wife. She threw quite a party in her day – all the trimmings. Shame, I miss her cooking – can't say the same about her face."

Jack broke down into a fit of giggles and slapped Vince on the back. "Bit harsh, there, Vince," he laughed, then fixed Sam with a sympathetic stare. "We're not all that bad, you know, Sammy. We'll give you a chance. Get down on your knees and beg for your life. We'll listen."

Sam stared him down. "It's you who'll be begging," he said coolly. Under his breath he added: "Trinity forgive me." Then he pulled his hand from his pocket and hurled his secret weapon at the slathering thing that had once been Jack.

It was a small cotton pouch – Sam's very own creation, something he had used only twice before in his entire life, and only then during the most desperate of situations. The pouch exploded in Jack's face, and he was engulfed in a cloud of white powder. It blasted into his mouth and eyes. Immediately, horrific blisters erupted across the man's skin and, agonised, Jack gagged and retched, clawing at his throat as he fell to his knees.

Vincent shoved him out of the way and charged at Sam. The old man was already running for the rifle, and he cried out as Vincent tackled him to the ground, mere inches from the firearm.

Sam kicked out with his feet as he groped for the gun, his bruised ribs screaming at the strain. Finally it was in his hands and he whipped it around, jabbing it into Vincent's cheek. He pulled the trigger.

Normally, the shot would have resounded loudly through this hollow space. Instead, the sound was swallowed by a terrible tremor that clapped through the subterranean grotto like thunder.

Sam staggered across the bucking ground.

"I'm sorry," he uttered to the fallen men. Jack's body gave a few final jerks as the white powder consumed him, burning and gnawing at him, and then he was still. It was a gruesome way to die, which was why Sam used the packets so sparingly. He only ever turned to them in desperation.

Clinging to the pillars for support, he staggered away from the dead Sentinels and fell against the stone column that he'd hidden behind before.

In front of the effigy, Malika was screeching alien words and Liberty looked as if she was about to vomit. The demon child watched from its place by the sculpture, unblinking as the wind tugged at its scuffed suit.

Realising that it was now or never, Sam raised the rifle and took aim at Malika's head.

Before he could pull the trigger, a heavy hand grabbed his shoulder and Sam found himself staring into the face of a third guard. Reacting quickly, the old man bucked the butt of the rifle upwards and smashed it into the guard's nose. Blood spurted onto his coat and Sam raised the rifle again, bringing it down with a crack on the man's skull. The guard collapsed solidly to the ground.

Sam turned to aim again, but there came a blast of flaming light and Malika's voice fell silent.

The earth stopped trembling. All was still.

Sam's mouth fell open in horror. There, a fiery shaft of light spiralled up from the bowl, twisting into the ether. It eddied delicately, ripples of heat shimmering seductively in the air.

Malika released Liberty's hands and the Sensitive slumped backwards, her eyes closed. Malika got to her feet, her cat–like eyes staring into the blinding light without blinking. A tiny hand touched hers and Malika looked down to see that Diltraa was holding on to her.

Finally, the demon child smiled, and its skin split and ruptured.

Aghast, Sam watched as the woman and the boy stepped up onto the low table and disappeared into the shimmering radiance. Then they were gone.

The portal flashed and died.

Not wasting a moment, Sam charged at the two Harvesters still flanking the demonic sculpture. He hurled his final two pouches in their faces. Like Jack, they collapsed squirming to their knees, their features bubbling and blistering hideously. Their hands clawed at the air as the foul substance consumed them. Then they hit the floor and were still.

Sam hurried over to Liberty, freeing her from her shackles. She could barely open her eyes, and she was mumbling quietly to herself. Her wrists were bloodied, scraped raw from where the chains had dug into her flesh – no doubt she'd made it worse by struggling against them.

A yell sounded behind Sam and another Harvester flew at him. The old man lashed out with the chains and his attacker went down. With growing dismay, Sam watched as yet more of the vile things emerged from the shadows and made their way between the pillars toward them. There were at least a dozen of them, each one more cruel–looking than the last.

"Come on!" he urged Liberty, looping an arm around her and helping her to her feet. "Help me, we need to get to the door."

Liberty leaned against him, barely able to lift her head, but she found her feet and together they staggered between the pillars. With the rifle still in his free hand, Sam prepared to fire at anything that moved.

A female Harvester with broken teeth blocked their path, and Sam pulled the trigger.

Blood spurted across one of the stone columns.

"Come on, come on..."

Sam pulled Liberty with him, his arm wrapped around her waist. They reached the door that led to the steps, and Sam helped Liberty lean against the wall. Quickly, he reloaded the rifle – just in time to shoot dead two more Harvesters who had emerged from the shadows. He loaded the rifle again, and then rushed to Liberty, who was clinging to the wall.

"Steps," he told her. "Come on, climb."

Somewhere deep in the woman's mind, the words seemed to reach her, and slowly they began to ascend.

Something whistled through the air and a curved blade embedded itself in the wall next to Sam's head. The old man turned to see another female Harvester charging up the steps behind them. Sam struck out with his foot, kicking the monster in the jaw, and she tumbled back down into the darkness with an angry cry.

At last, they were at the top of the steps.

"Grab the edge," Sam told Liberty. "Pull yourself over."

Liberty reached up and seized the lip of the sarcophagus, heaving herself onto the edge. Sam pushed her up by the legs, and Liberty went over the top. The old man threw his rifle over and then pulled himself up, his ribs screaming at the exertion. He dropped down into the mausoleum and rushed over to the coffin's huge, stone lid. Grinding his teeth with the effort, he put all of his weight behind it, but his ribs were too painful and the lid refused to move.

There came the sound of footsteps ringing against the stairs below, and Sam braced himself for the worst.

Then, inexplicably, the great slab shifted. Astounded, Sam saw that Liberty had come to his aid, despite her sorry state. Together they heaved the lid round and with a crunch it shut. Liberty collapsed to the floor, exhausted.

Muted, angry thuds resounded from inside the sarcophagus as the trapped Harvesters attempted to beat their way out. It was no use, though. They were trapped.

"Let's get you out of here," Sam said to Liberty, helping her to her feet again.

"My hero," she murmured, wrapping an arm around his waist.

They emerged into the night and Sam drew in a grateful breath of fresh air, welcoming it after the stuffy underground crypt. That had been too close. He tried not to think about the smoking ruin of Jack's burnt face, but the image clung to him unforgivingly.

Sam paused, suddenly aware that somebody – or something – was watching them.

Then he saw it. Perched on a nearby gravestone was a raven. It observed the old man with dark, interested eyes.

"Fly!" Sam yelled, waving his free arm at the bird. "Go!"

The raven emitted a terse *caww!* and took to the air.

CHAPTER TWENTY-ONE
Old Enemies

"What's going on?" Nicholas demanded, his back pressed up against the wall. His mind reeled as he attempted to make sense of what had just happened. It felt like the floor of the house was tipping underneath him, and he was sliding helplessly toward the squat man by the front door.

Reynolds. The monster Garm had obeyed him like a puppy, like it knew him, and now Reynolds was sneering maliciously at him with viper–like lips.

He'd called himself Snelling.

"Reynolds—" the boy began, but the other man cut him off.

"Snelling," he corrected coarsely, slinging his jacket to the floor and rolling his sleeves up. "Do you believe that the name makes the man?" he continued pensively. "I must admit, I quite enjoyed being Melvin Reynolds. He seemed like a good egg. And I was rather pleased to find I hadn't lost my touch with a rifle." He paused and looked almost wistful. "I was Snelling for so long, though, I became quite used to it. Rather missed him when Melvin was around."

Nicholas was chilled by the aloof stranger that he found himself with.

"Who are you?" he pressed anxiously.

"Ah, the idiocy of youth," Snelling spat in a voice that sounded nothing like Reynolds. He dabbed at the fake blood on his face with a handkerchief, cleaning it away. "How remarkably naïve you are. And how quickly you fell for Melvin. Not that I can blame you – he was rather likeable, wasn't he? With his crystals and his curious little potions and his fairytale theories." He appraised the boy. "They say the future of the world rests on your shoulders, boy. Ha! What a world that will be."

"I–I don't understand," Nicholas stammered, still baffled by the man's transformation. There wasn't a shred of the man he'd known as Reynolds left – the vile brute in front of him had swallowed him up, destroyed him from the inside out. Had it all been a trick? Nicholas couldn't believe that somebody could so convincingly play a role like that, so easily conceal the boiling revulsion that Snelling was directing at him with those squinting, pig–like eyes.

The other man stood blocking the front door. The injuries that he'd faked in the village were forgotten, and he clutched his fleshy hands together, cracking his knuckles with excitement.

"Where are my manners?" he drawled with false civility. "I should be thanking you for inviting me into this most hallowed of abodes. I must admit, I wasn't entirely certain it would work, but that was a risk we were willing to take." The podgy figure puffed himself up, talking more to himself than the boy. He drank in the entrance hall, as if quenching a lifetime of thirsty curiosity. "The house protects itself from the likes of us. But in you, we discovered an exception to the rule. You invited me in of your own volition. Quite astonishing, really."

"But," Nicholas continued in disbelief, "you're a Sentinel. You've got the tattoo, you knew things. Your uncle…"

Snelling's chubby cheeks glowed scarlet and he let loose a wicked cackle.

"You mean this?"

He tugged at his shirt sleeve to expose the raven inked on his forearm. With a leer he licked the tip of his thumb and then smeared the black ink across his skin. "Just a little something I picked up along the way." He winked. "Of course, it was lucky for me that you came to the village at all. That was a worry to begin with. Then I realised that all teenage boys are the same – lock them up in a secluded ruin like this and they'll soon be foraging for ways out. It'd be like trying to cage a baboon. And then all it took was an attack by Garm and you were mine. He's quite tame, really. Docile as a dog if you feed him the right thing."

The Garm was Snelling's pet?

As the feelings of surprise began to wane, Nicholas felt foolish. Used. He shouldn't have been so stupid. Jessica had warned him against leaving the house, now he knew why. The evil she'd talked about hadn't just referred to monsters like the Garm. It was everywhere, hiding in plain sight, corrupting and persuading. He'd brought it right to her and let it into her home. The fear and guilt mingled inside of him and, with alarm, Nicholas realised there was nobody to rescue him as Sam had done before.

"Get out!" the boy shouted. "Get out of here!"

Snelling moved his head slowly from side-to-side.

"Oh no," he said softly, his eyes shining balefully at Nicholas. "We're going to go for a little tour of the house, and you're going to be the guide."

"We're not going anywhere!" Nicholas said firmly. Though Snelling could conventionally be regarded as a comical figure – a podgy ball of flesh with stocky legs and a thinning crop of hair – those eyes contained real danger. His mere presence was intimidating, and Nicholas felt young and stupid. He cursed how quickly he had taken to Melvin Reynolds. How was he to know? Could anybody blame him for latching onto the first sane thing that had presented itself since his parents' deaths? Bitterly, he realised even that had been a lie, a grand ruse, and he'd fallen for it like a needy child. Now he was the only thing standing in the way of this deceitful wretch and whatever he was planning. That thought alone spurred him on.

"You're going to get out of here or–"

"Or what?" snapped Snelling.

Adrenaline flooding through him, Nicholas shrugged out of his jacket. His heart thrashed against his ribs and he couldn't form a single clear thought. He was a ball of tensed muscle and instinct, his skin clammy in anticipation as he waited for the other man to make the first move.

Snelling grinned sadistically at the challenge.

"Let's see you try, boy," he smirked, raising his right hand.

Nicholas faltered. There, the other man had fitted a shiny metallic device. Nicholas didn't know what it was – it looked like a futuristic glove inset with tiny amber jewels. It gleamed in the shallow lamplight. Disregarding the strange device, the boy flew at the flabby man, ready to seize hold of him and force him out of the front door.

There came a concussive pulse of blinding light and something pummelled into Nicholas's chest, knocking the wind out of him.

He flew backwards, colliding with the wall and sliding to the floor.

Gasping like a fish, Nicholas sprawled where he had landed. Before he had a chance to get to his feet, Snelling was on him, his free hand clenched around the boy's throat. He was surprisingly strong.

"Come on, boy," Snelling spat, grabbing Nicholas by the collar, "you're taking me to the five-walled room – you know the one I mean. We're going to have some fun, you and I."

The boy was wrenched to his feet and shoved through the double doors into the lobby.

★

Isabel shivered and shrank into the shadows. Darkness had fallen and still the unclean beast was on her trail. She cursed her lot – in her time, she'd have made short work of such an abomination. Still, she had been pleasantly surprised at just how swiftly this nimble new body moved, and the speed with which she'd sprung out into the frostbitten countryside must have surprised even Garm.

Crouching under a bush, gathering her breath, Isabel contemplated her fate. They'd been fools to trust the Reynolds man. She'd watched from outside the house as the shopkeeper's demeanour changed the second he'd stepped over the threshold. He'd spoken to the Garm beast like one does a household pet, and the monstrous brute had actually obeyed his command.

The cat's hackles quivered at the memory.

Now he was in the house with Nicholas. That had been his plan all along, no doubt – to breach the boundaries of Hallow House. Isabel wondered what the Reynolds man really was. He could be anything. There were plenty of things desperate to infiltrate the Hallow residence, to get their filthy claws on its many wonders. None had succeeded before. None save one, and that monster was long gone.

Isabel tensed. Heavy footsteps vibrated through the freezing ground, and she heard exhausted lungs gulping in massive breaths.

The cat peered out through the leaves, grateful for her newfound night vision – how sharp everything looked even at this late hour.

Garm had returned. Its scaly, trunk-like tail swayed through the air and its misshapen snout shovelled through the dirt in search of its prey's scent. Those blood red eyes pierced the dark, and Isabel cringed back in fear. The creature was easily ten times her size. What chance had she against it?

The Garm stopped suddenly and lifted its monstrous head. Its great nostrils expanded and contracted. The fringes of fur along its back shivered with delight and it emitted an elated screech as those scarlet eyes burned in Isabel's direction.

Not giving the brute a chance to corner her, Isabel sprang from her hiding place.

"Come, then, fetid hellbeast!" she shrieked. "Let us dance!"

In a blur of black and silver fur, she whisked through the night, leaping over stones and bounding through bushes.

The beast thrashed after her and its hot breath blasted against the cat's tail. Isabel spurred herself on, dashing from side to side. Together, the bizarre pair tore through the countryside, and the monster's gleeful screams echoed through the dark.

Finally, Isabel caught sight of the house as it reared up out of the night. Its windows radiated warm light and once again she cursed her lack of opposable digits. How on Earth was she to get inside? She didn't have time to think, as at that moment the Garm swiped out a huge, razor-clawed paw and nearly lopped off the top of her tail.

Isabel flew at the house and seized her only option – the trellis that hugged the brick wall. She sank her claws into the mesh of wood and plant, hauling herself up as fast as she could. Below, Garm attempted to do the same, but the monster's great bulk made it impossible. It collapsed onto the ground, scrabbling angrily around in the dirt, then prowled back and forth in irritation. Its disappointed, hungry whimpers made Isabel's fur bristle.

"No cat for you this eve, swine!" Isabel taunted, leaping onto a windowsill three storeys up. The cat stalked along the ledge and peered into the room beyond the glass. It was too dark to make out more than the shapes of a few chairs and a table, but the door was open a crack, letting in some light from the landing.

Dejected, Isabel perched there and did the only thing she could — she mewed as loudly as possible, praying that somebody would hear.

★

A hand shoved Nicholas in the back and the boy spun to face Snelling.

"Do that once more and I'll break your nose," he yelled, clenching his fists at his side.

Snelling was in too good a mood to take the boy's threat seriously, merely snorting in response. "The room," he urged ravenously. "Is it close?"

Nicholas eyed the gleaming metallic gauntlet, which Snelling was holding in front of him threateningly, and nodded dejectedly. He turned to lead him down the dusty old corridor. His chest still throbbed painfully where the crackling light had struck him and he moved sluggishly, woozily leading Snelling through Hallow House. He'd lost the Drujblade in the scuffle in the entrance hall, and he felt useless without it.

Where was Jessica? Surely she'd heard the commotion? Nicholas had considered yelling out her name, or even escaping into the confusing warren of the house. Something about Snelling convinced him not to — the piggish wretch was dangerous; no doubt he'd find a way to make things a lot worse if Nicholas didn't co-operate.

At last the boy stopped outside an old, dark wood door that was peeling with age.

"This is it," he said miserably.

Snelling looked at the door, unable to hide his excitement. "Yes, yes," he hissed, licking his lips. "Open it."

"I can't, it's locked."

Snelling shot the boy an irritated look. He shoved Nicholas out of the way to try the handle himself. Finding it locked, he spat in annoyance. After a moment's thought, he seized the handle with the gauntlet and squeezed.

Nicholas's eyes widened as a sizzling sound filled the darkened hallway, and the door handle blushed a violent red. Snelling began to sweat, great drops sliding down his forehead, and then he wrenched the melted door handle clean away. Eagerly, the flabby man dropped the hunk of twisted metal to the floor and opened the door.

The smell of decay and dust was overpowering. Snelling seized Nicholas by the arm and shoved him into the pentagon room, then drew the door to behind them.

In the gloom, Nicholas eyed the dusty corpse still grinning in the chair. He gave a start when he remembered it was Isabel's withered form, and averted his eyes. She wouldn't want him to see her like this. Now he came to think of it, what kind of person left a corpse rotting in a chair like that? Nicholas's unease about Jessica deepened and he hoped he'd get the chance to ask her about it.

Snelling was muttering animatedly to himself, fishing around in his pockets. He wiped at his sweaty face and the sheer elation pinched into his chubby, crowded features was terrifying. Nicholas pushed himself up into one of the room's many corners, watching nervously.

The parlour was still in ruins after Jessica's earlier summoning spell. Above, the ceiling sagged sorrowfully and the wooden chandelier dangled precariously, three of its chains broken. Nicholas wondered what would happen should it suddenly fall on Snelling's head.

The other man barely noticed Nicholas as he went about his work. He lit the candles already in the room, then placed three objects on the circular table at the room's centre. A knife, a strange velvet pouch, and a stout bottle made of green glass. All were set down reverently.

Snelling wiped at his sweaty forehead once more and peered at his watch.

"Five minutes," he said to himself. "We made it just in time. Diltraa will be pleased."

Filled with feelings of doom, Nicholas knew nobody was going to stop Snelling. Loneliness welled up inside of him, that familiar hollow feeling that had overwhelmed him in the wake of his parents' deaths, and Nicholas almost surrendered to it.

Then something struck him. What would Sam do? The boy knew the answer without even thinking – he'd fight with every scrap of energy he had in him, just as he had on the bus. Sam wouldn't sit back while somebody like Snelling seized control, and neither would Nicholas. The boy eyed the knife on the tabletop. If he could just get close enough to snatch it away before Snelling saw him. This time he'd catch him off guard – and he'd have to kill him with it. Somehow, he had to distract the despicable man.

"The villagers," Nicholas said suddenly.

"Eh?" Snelling barked. He seemed to have forgotten the boy was there.

"The villagers," Nicholas repeated, moving casually away from the wall. "You were trying to help them. Save them from that thing."

Snelling's top lip curled upwards in scorn. "Boy, you're even thicker than I give you credit for," he scoffed, the loose skin under his chin shuddering. "Is there nothing rattling around in that skull of yours?"

"That Garm thing was killing villagers," Nicholas continued, "and you said you'd been hunting it. Was all of that a lie, too?"

Snelling regarded the boy icily. "Do you know what Garm eats?" he spat with relish, spittle dribbling down his chin. "Souls. That's why he loved Orville so."

Nicholas had almost managed to reach the table, but this new bit of information threw him. "Why?" he asked, genuinely intrigued.

"It's a dead town," Snelling explained in a detached voice. "Packed full of dead souls."

Nicholas studied the other man's fleshy face and wondered if he was lying. Everything Snelling had said as Melvin Reynolds had probably been a lie. Then Nicholas recalled how nobody in Orville had been able to see him. They'd stared right through him, even as he'd screamed in their faces.

"They're all dead?" he said slowly.

"I'm not surprised she hasn't told you," Snelling sneered. "She's probably been sitting on that dirty little secret for years."

"Who? Who are you talking about?"

"Why, Jessica," the chubby man said, savouring the confused look on Nicholas's face. "She's the one who destroyed that place, did something terrible there. It killed everybody. Every living soul perished in that forsaken place." He paused, smiling a toothy, rapturous grin. "At least Garm appreciates the place. To him, there's nothing tastier than a tortured soul. All that pent up hatred and anger, distilled into its purest form over the years like a fine cabernet. The older the soul, the more delicious. He's enjoyed hunting them down all these weeks, never seen him so wild and malevolent." The man paused. "Don't think he's ever tasted cat before," he added nastily. "He probably gobbled Isabel up in one go, snapped her little cat bones like twigs."

Nicholas balked at the thought – against Garm, Isabel was as helpless as a butterfly. He dared to hope that she was okay, that she'd managed to evade the hellbeast. She was a tough one, after all; maybe even right this minute she was running to Jessica for help. But then… could Jessica help? Snelling had just accused her of a massacre. After their encounter in the garden, when Jessica had seemed to be teetering on the knife edge of sanity, Nicholas didn't know who to believe anymore.

Determined, the boy's hands curled into fists at his side and he eyed the knife on the table. He didn't fancy getting hit with another pulse from that glove, but he had to do something. Like a soldier plucking up the courage to leap over the trenches, Nicholas felt the pressure building in his chest, felt the blood thundering in his ears, and with a cry he hurled himself at Snelling.

The man threw both his arms up and Nicholas clenched the wrist with the metallic gauntlet, forcing it away from him. Then he kneed the fat man in the groin and elbowed him in the ribs. Snelling spluttered and coughed.

"You… you spiteful brat," he gasped, clutching at his chunky side. He attempted to squirm free, but Nicholas had worked himself up into a frenzy. He clamped his hands around both of the squat man's wrists, staring into his face with pure hatred.

"Not so cocky now, are you?" the boy panted.

Snelling thrashed about like a mad pig and together they crashed against the table. In its chair, the shrunken corpse pitched forward, a toothy, smirking witness to the brawl. Nicholas ignored the cavernous eye sockets and went to reach for the knife.

It was a fatal mistake. As he released his grip on one of Snelling's hands, the other man lashed out, seizing Nicholas's hair until the boy's eyes watered. Wrenching the gauntlet free, Snelling forced it against

Nicholas's chest. A blinding, white-hot force barrelled into his ribcage and the boy hurtled back through the air, landing in a heap on the floor.

Crumpled and in agony, the pentagon room became nothing more than a faint blur as Nicholas dipped in and out of consciousness. Only dimly aware of what was going on, he felt Snelling drag him across the dusty floor. Then he was heaved unceremoniously into something upright and hard, and his arms and legs were bound.

"Be thankful you're needed alive, boy," Snelling's voice hissed in his ear. "If it was up to me, you'd be in pieces by now."

Nicholas attempted to raise his head, but it was suddenly made of lead. He struggled against his body's pounding complaints, blinked open his eyes, tried to focus. His vision swam frighteningly, but he was able to discern that he'd been strapped to a chair in a corner of the room. Opposite him, Snelling had returned to his spot by the table.

"Sit back and watch, boy," he snarled. "You're about to witness the true extent of our power. When the time comes, you'll beg for your pathetic life on your knees."

Dismissing the boy, Snelling took up the knife and held his hand over the shallow bowl on the tabletop. Without flinching, he dragged the blade over the palm of his hand. Instantly, blood welled in the crevices and he squeezed his hand into a fist, smiling triumphantly as his blood dripped into the bowl.

Dismally, Nicholas struggled against his restraints, but they held fast. Every muscle in his body throbbed dully, sluggish and spent after the second gauntlet blast. Grimly the boy realised there was nothing he could do.

Setting the knife aside, Snelling pressed a finger into his bloody palm and drew a peculiar symbol on his forehead. He began muttering strange words, and Nicholas cringed away from the sounds. The words reverberated deafeningly inside his skull. They were ugly and evil, charged with ancient power, and the boy's ears rang as Snelling uttered them.

Still murmuring, Snelling uncorked the green bottle and poured a slick, gloopy black liquid into the bowl. Through his daze, Nicholas saw the liquid moving of its own accord, circling the bowl's rim and bubbling poisonously.

Snelling looked ill. He was sweating profusely, beads of perspiration clinging to his flabby face. Dark bags bulged under his eyes. Yet he continued ardently, shrieking those ugly words. As he took up the velvet pouch, the floorboards quivered and bucked underfoot, and an unnatural wind blew into existence. Screaming now, Snelling tossed the contents of the pouch into the bowl – it looked like a glittering powder – and sparks danced across the black liquid, spitting and fizzing like fireworks.

As the wind shrilled in Nicholas's ears, the entire room came alive. The walls rocked back and forth as if they were made of nothing but paper and the floor convulsed. Whatever Snelling was doing, it was affecting the very fabrics of the house, causing them to strain violently apart and then spring back together.

Just when Nicholas thought he was going to vomit, the sparks hopping around the inside of the bowl blazed higher and there came a mighty explosion. Searing heat caressed Nicholas's cheeks and a wall of fire shot up from the bowl. Yet instead of burning itself out, the column twisted and turned, a mixture of fire and light, threads of yellow forking through its murky depths.

Snelling threw his arms wide as if to embrace the funnel of blistering light, tossing back his head to let loose a screaming whoop of delight.

It was the last thing he would ever do.

As the dazzling light flickered and pulsed, an explosion of flame scorched through the air and blasted right through him, consuming the man whole. In an instant he was gone, reduced to a pile of smouldering ash. Only one thing survived the furious discharge – the gauntlet crashed to the floor, scattering the cinders that only moments before been Snelling.

The room fell silent. Nicholas sat frozen in the chair, mesmerised by the sputtering luminescence that was spiralling in the centre of the room. It had stabilised, and now the column of light was almost tranquil.

Nicholas sat watching, transfixed and horrified, flushed by the fierce luminescence. He blinked and shook his head. Perhaps he was imagining things, but it seemed a shape was forming in the rolling crimson curtains. Before his eyes, a vague shadow took form and slowly became more solid with every second that passed.

Then somebody stepped out of the fire and onto the tabletop.

It was like a nightmare born flesh. The woman. He recognised her. It was the woman from the bus. His insides squirmed uneasily, both aroused by and terrified of her. Where had she come from? What was she doing? As she stepped elegantly down from the table, the enchanting creature reached up and helped a smaller figure onto the floor. A boy, ashen and ill-looking, dressed in a black suit.

The boy looked at him and Nicholas cried out. Those piercing white eyes scorched into him and horrific images flashed in his mind.

Hellfire and erupting volcanoes, children lying dead and frozen in the countryside, animals with their insides spilling from their buckled bodies.

The beast's named burned into him. *Diltraa.* It had done all of that. Killed children. Drained them for its own needs. Destroyed them so it might live.

Nicholas howled.

"You have done well, Malika."

An arcane voice sliced through the depraved visions like a wet blade, and Nicholas was free of them. The little boy was still looking at him, and those icy eyes stabbed right into his gut.

"So, this is the child."

Nicholas cowered as the boy approached him, curiosity warping his sallow features. No, it wasn't just curiosity contorting the boy's face. Somehow he looked wrong, as if the bones of his skull were being pushed from the inside out, stretched beyond their means by something awful under the surface. Nicholas felt immediately repulsed, like he was looking at something that shouldn't exist, something that defied the laws of nature.

As the boy got closer, Nicholas saw that his skin was flaking away in pieces, exposing raw, dried-out flesh beneath. And always the empty white eyes were on him, turning his muscles to stone.

"Nicholassss," the little boy rasped. He reached out a shrivelled grey hand and pushed Nicholas's chin up with his index finger. Nicholas felt caged by the boy's soft, probing glare. *"Handsome child, by man's measure. Seems Snelling's been having some fun with you."*

"Snelling's dead," surged a caramel voice.

Behind Diltraa, the red-haired woman it had called Malika scraped at the ash-strewn floor with a delicate shoe. "Burnt to a crisp," she noted. Stooping, Malika fished the gauntlet out of the charred residue and slipped it into the folds of her dress.

"Such is the price," Diltraa wheezed in a non-committal tone. *"He was not built to work such potent forces. Unlike this one."*

Dry lips peeled into a smile.

"You don't even know what you're capable of, do you human child?"

Nicholas stared blankly back, the scarlet blaze of the portal making him nauseous. Or maybe it was the way that the boy was looking at him that made him feel sick. There was a covetous leer on those rind-like lips, and though Diltraa's face was falling apart in pieces, Nicholas read confidence and triumph there.

"We'll speak again," Diltraa promised. *"For now, there are other things to attend to. I'll leave you in good company."*

The eyes released him and Nicholas took a welcome breath. It had felt like he was being strangled. He watched the boy go to the door, shoot a brief, jagged look in Malika's direction, then disappear into the hall, closing the door behind him.

Malika stepped forward. The candlelight caressed her slender form and she sashayed slowly toward Nicholas, biting her bottom lip.

"Look at me, child," she purred.

In the chair, Nicholas attempted to avoid her gaze. Heat seemed to come off her and he felt like he was burning up. He recalled only faintly what had happened on the bus that day – that feeling of rapture that had bubbled over him in a warm, welcoming rush. It had been like a soothing, smothering embrace. He didn't trust himself.

Malika crouched before him, touched his knee. Behind her, the portal flickered and died.

"Nicholas," she soothed. "I have something very important to tell you. But I need you to look at me."

Nicholas struggled against her, but the woman's will was strong, that voice so tender and inviting. Nicholas shook his head, squeezed his eyes shut.

"Get away from me," he warned.

"There's no need to be afraid," Malika assured him. "I'm not going to hurt you; that's the last thing I want to do. Look at me so that I know you believe me. You know you want to." Nicholas fought against it, but Malika's caressing words were too seductive. Unable to take it anymore, the boy relented.

He opened his eyes and his breath caught in his throat.

"Mum," he croaked.

Before him, Anita Hallow smiled kindly and stroked his cheek.

"Nicholas," she said softly, her pretty face framed by dark brown curls. "I've missed you so much."

Confusion flickered across Nicholas's face. Something wasn't right. What had he just been doing? A minute ago he'd been afraid, he was sure of it, but now he couldn't remember why. Hadn't there been somebody else here? He stared into his mother's open, familiar face, her green eyes crinkled in the corners just as he remembered them, and he surrendered to the promise of her comfort.

"Mum!" he cried again, wrenching at the restraints. "What are you doing here? It's not safe."

Anita nodded, sadness in her eyes. "I know," she said sombrely. "You must forgive me, Nicholas. I've put you in terrible danger. Your father and I both have. We wanted the best for you and we thought we were protecting you by sending you here."

"What do you mean?" Nicholas asked.

Anita clutched at the boy's bound hands, entwining her fingers with his.

"We had to go off in secret," she explained, desperate for him to understand. "We couldn't tell anybody, not even you. But our work is over now and we can go home. All three of us. Would you like that?"

Nicholas's eyes shone with tears and he nodded.

"We can be a family again, you, me and your father," Anita promised. "Just like before. We can be happy again."

"Yes," Nicholas murmured.

Anita blinked back the tears and threw her arms around her son. Nicholas pressed his face into her shoulder, smelling her – that familiar scent of heather, her favourite perfume. Everything was going to be okay. His parents were back and all this craziness was finally going to end. He didn't have to stay here with Jessica, stranded in the middle of nowhere, lonely and miserable. His mother had come back for him. She hadn't forgotten about him. She still loved him. Tears rolled down the boy's face.

"Mum," he whispered. "I thought you were dead."

"I know," Anita said, wiping the tears from his cheeks. "I'm sorry you had to go through that, I truly am. I hope I can make it up to you."

Nicholas nodded.

"There's something we have to do first, before we can go home," Anita said urgently. She began swiftly untying the restraints that bound Nicholas's arms and legs to the chair.

"What? What do we have to do?"

"It's Jessica," Anita told him darkly, finished with the restraints. "We have to stop Jessica."

"Stop her from doing what?" Nicholas asked. He rubbed at his wrists.

"She's a very bad woman," his mother replied, her expression deadly serious. "She's done terrible things."

"What?" Nicholas said, unable to believe it. "What kind of things?"

Anita bit her lip. "She's… she's killed children," she said. "Poor, innocent babes. She snatched their lives away before they'd even had a chance to live. She must be stopped."

Nicholas frowned, still unsure.

"She's strange," he said, "but has she really killed children?"

Anita stroked Nicholas's cheek once more.

"That's what I love about you," she smiled, running her hand affectionately through his hair. "You've always seen the good in people. I know this is difficult but you have to believe me. That woman has committed the most terrible of deeds."

Anita paused before determining grimly: "Nicholas, we're going to have to kill her."

CHAPTER TWENTY-TWO
DEVASTATION

DILTRAA STALKED THE HALLS OF HALLOW House with a look of rapture splitting his slowly-cracking features. Everything was going according to plan. Five hundred years he'd waited for this. The creature's bone-white eyes flashed at the memory, peering up at the sightless statues that guarded the grand hallway. He passed unnoticed beneath their noses and his small, inconspicuous form continued through the house.

Moving silently through the lobby, Diltraa swept stealthily down another hall, this one bronzed by subdued lamplight that made everything glow softly. With his head held high, the demon child appraised the surroundings, a supercilious air about him.

These were the sacred spaces within the Sentinel keep, then. These antiquated halls, filled with long-forgotten treasures, all sealed behind glass. A look of disgust crossed the child's face, but that quickly vanished when he came to what he had been seeking.

"There you are," Diltraa trilled. Head tilted to one side, he peered up at an immense glass box that rested on a mahogany base. Within the cabinet, the skeleton of a mighty beast was posed as if in battle, its huge, knuckled front claws – easily the size of a man's head – swiping through the air. Its emaciated jaw stretched wide in a noiseless roar.

The demon child reached out an ashen hand and tapped the glass lightly. The glass shivered and then shattered into pieces, shards tinkling across the marble floor.

With infinite care, Diltraa reached up and touched the front leg of the hulking skeletal frame. Immediately, the child's body began to convulse. He retched and shuddered, and pieces of skin and dried flesh fell away in great chunks.

Diltraa discarded the dead child's body and it crumpled to the floor.

Out of the wreckage a slimy, stunted abomination crawled. Spindly and shrunken, it resembled a four-legged spider as it hopped up into the cabinet. Scaling the great skeleton, ribbons of wet flesh flew from the parasite's back and latched onto the ancient bones. Slowly, the demon lord called Diltraa reclaimed its true form, many years after the torturous event that had robbed it of these very bones.

The creature emitted a shrill cackle that echoed portentously down the wide corridor, and the house itself shuddered.

★

Jessica was sitting on a stone bench in Norlath's garden when Nicholas found her. She seemed lost in thought, listening to the plants as they rustled their soft whispers.

Only when he was almost upon her did Jessica snap from her reveries and turn to acknowledge him.

"Nicholas," she said warmly, then frowned. She looked him over, then peered past him at his mother, who lingered behind him. "Nicholas, who is this?"

He answered stonily. "She's come back," he said. "She's told me everything."

"Whatever do you mean?" Jessica asked, her gaze flitting between the woman and the boy.

Nicholas didn't know why she was acting so confused, surely she knew that one day somebody would come to stop her. To make her pay for what she'd done. The mesh of lies clung to him and he couldn't even feel them.

"What has she told you?" Jessica prompted nervously.

"Everything," Nicholas replied coldly. "There's no use pretending anymore. I know what you've done."

His voice didn't sound like his own, as if somebody was moving his mouth for him.

Jessica took a step toward him, but Nicholas shrank back.

"Stay there," he warned, and his fist tightened around a dagger. He had retrieved the Drujblade from the entrance hall, where he'd lost it during his confrontation with Snelling. Now he held it fast, knowing what he must do, even if his insides were shuddering. He cast a look back at his mother and Anita nodded encouragingly, her lips pressed together tightly. He drew strength from her.

"Go on, Nicholas," she said softly. "You know you must."

Nicholas turned back to Jessica.

"I–" he began, then stopped, realising he had no idea what to say. He just had to take the blade and put it in her throat, like his mother had told him. Why was it so difficult? Something didn't feel right. But the boy didn't question his mother's words; such was his desperation to have her back. He shoved away the doubt, returned to the welcome certainty of his mother's assurances. He had to do this. Then everything would be okay again. They'd go home and be a family. None of this madness would matter anymore.

Gritting his teeth, the boy seized Jessica by the arm.

"You've done terrible things," he told her, echoing Malika's words, unaware that they weren't his own.

Jessica's eyes grew wide.

"Nicholas, you're hurting me," she said, attempting to struggle free. He squeezed tighter still.

Jessica looked at his mother. "What have you done to him?" she cried. Then to Nicholas: "You have to fight it! What you're doing isn't right. Listen to yourself. Who do you think she is?"

He ignored her strange behaviour.

"She's come back for me. Everything's going to be okay again."

Jessica looked at him and her expression changed. It flooded with sudden sympathy, though Nicholas didn't know why.

"Your mother," she whispered. "You think she's your mother." Her voice filled with fresh urgency. "She's not, Nicholas. You have to believe me. Everything she's said is a lie. Remember what you asked me before? About sensing things? Use that now, free yourself from whatever spell she's cast over you."

"What about the people you've killed?" Nicholas shouted. His head was pounding. Confusion exploded into anger.

"The village! All those villagers. What did you do to them?"
Jessica's face hardened.

"No, Nicholas," she said firmly. "That was nobody's fault."

"It was you!" Nicholas bellowed, crushing her arm in his fist. "You killed them all!"

"NO!" Jessica yelled, her eyes glassy with tears.

"What did you do to them?"

"I didn't do anything," Jessica persisted, pleading with him now. "Nobody did anything to them. Please stop."

"Tell me!"

"Nicholas, please," Jessica begged. Tears streamed down her face, but he didn't care. He was sick of the lies, the deceit. He needed answers, and if this was the only way, so be it.

"What happened in Orville?" Nicholas demanded. He raised the knife and pressed it against her throat. "What killed those people?"

"Not yet," his mother warned him gently from behind. "Don't kill her yet. We need her to talk first."

"What killed those people?" Nicholas repeated, pressing the blade against Jessica's skin.

As if unable to bear it any longer, Jessica let out a pained shriek.

"You!" she cried. Her shoulders sagged and she stared wildly into his eyes. "You did, Nicholas," she told him. "You were born there, almost sixteen years ago. And your birth was a beautiful thing. A terrible thing. Such power never comes into the world without a price, and the occupants of Orville paid that price for you with their lives."

"No," Nicholas murmured. "I was born in Cambridge. My parents told me." His hand was shaking, weighed down by the Drujblade. It suddenly felt as heavy as a sledgehammer.

Jessica shook her head. "No," she whispered. "You were born here and taken away for safety. Such was the force of your entrance into this world that it nearly destroyed the entire village. It became frozen in time, caused a tear in reality, and every soul that lived there was caught like a fly in a web. They're dead, but they continue to live undead lives, caught there for all eternity." She grabbed Nicholas's arms. "It's not your fault. You're meant for great things, Nicholas. You're special."

Nicholas pushed the woman away, the bitter tang of the truth snapping the chains that had bound him. Gone were the feelings of warmth and comfort. Reality crashed down on him like a freezing wave and he spluttered as if rising from the cold depths of the sea, raw and exhausted. He whirled around, finally seeing the red-haired woman for who she really was.

She was standing right where his mother had been not a moment before.

"You," he said.

Malika merely smirked.

"A pity," the woman drawled. "I had hoped you would be the one to kill her. There would have been such poetry to it. You'd have been one of us forever. How we yearned to welcome you into our fold. You have such power at your fingertips. It seems I'll have to finish the witch myself."

Nicholas put himself between the two women. "No," he said.

The red-haired woman laughed and the plants around her shivered. "And they say chivalry is dead," she teased.

At that moment, a guttural roar blasted into the still garden. The woman's smile widened and she threw a look back at the garden doors.

"Oh dear, Daddy's woken up," she smiled. "Doesn't sound happy, does he?"

Nicholas listened as destructive sounds echoed from within the house, and Jessica flinched beside him. Then the doors were ripped from their frame and hurled high over their heads into the foliage.

Nicholas's heart leapt into his throat. A hunched, repugnant creature like nothing he had ever seen was revealed in the doorway.

It filled the entire doorframe with its gangling form. Slimy, copper-coloured skin was stretched tight over jutting bones. The monster looked like a giant insect, twice as tall as a man and with elongated limbs that were easily twice as powerful. Bone protuberances stuck out from the creature's elbows, shoulders and knees, knotted knobs of bone that looked tough and durable. Worst by far, though, was the beast's countenance. Enormous horns protruded from a high, wide forehead, and it had only slits where the nose should be. At the centre of those craggy features, twin orbs of ice-white burned into Nicholas's soul and the demon gnashed its enormous, razor-sharp teeth eagerly.

"**Nicholasssss,**" it hissed.

"It's the boy," Nicholas said, recognising the inhuman glow of those terrible eyes. He put an arm out protectively towards Jessica and saw that she was trembling with terror.

"No!" the woman gasped. "NO!" Petrified at the sight of this fresh nightmare, she fell to her knees, clutching her hands together before her.

The beast lumbered over on its awkward, wiry limbs, using its long front legs like an ape might. It shifted its weight skilfully, trampling flowers and bushes, tearing trees from the earth and hurling them out of its path.

Then, finally, it was towering over Nicholas and Jessica, its great shadow falling like a shroud. The fusty stench of charred coals came off the beast and Nicholas had to fight not to gag.

"**Jessica,**" the demon drooled, its incisor-lined mouth lolling open. Colossal fangs dripped with black saliva and a forked tongue flickered in the air. "**How long it's been. You haven't aged a day. Tell me, do I look any different?**"

Jessica didn't seem able to answer. Her face was a picture of horror. As Nicholas looked on helplessly, their doom seemed inevitable.

★

18 August, 1589

As the storm raged outside, Jessica and Isabel sat hand-in-hand. The sapphire portal coiled delicately between them, pulsing with the glow of a thousand stars. The light reflected in Isabel's many rings and bracelets, and Jessica watched, wide-eyed, as a man's features strained through the luminescence.

"*There is another here…*" throbbed the despondent voice of Harold Baxter, the spirit caught within the gateway.

"There are two of you?"

Isabel wasn't able to conceal her surprise, and Jessica grew nervous.

"*I… I don't know who it is. They wish to speak.*"

"There's somebody with him?" Jessica hazarded quietly.

Isabel squeezed Jessica's hand reassuringly, which only served to increase the young woman's alarm – Isabel wasn't exactly one for offering comfort.

"It can happen on occasion," the old woman explained. "Brace yourself." Then, addressing the spirit called Harold, she commanded: "Allow him entrance."

Immediately the gateway changed. There was blazing red fire. Sheets of heat blasted up the column, choking the pure radiance that had been softly glowing there. Jessica cringed away, her brow immediately prickling with sweat.

"Don't move," Isabel ordered her. "This entity bears much anger. Be strong and we shall withstand it." She addressed the furious wall of fire at the centre of the table. "Tell me your name."

"Free me."

The voice made Jessica's head pound.

"We are here to guide you. Accept our help or leave this place," Isabel ordered.

Her words went unheeded, for at that moment a feral howl screeched from within the portal, and a form ripped clean through the column of fire.

Slithering from the tabletop onto the floor, the bent, deformed figure spluttered and slowly uncurled itself.

Jessica screamed.

It looked like an emissary of Satan. Long, spindly limbs stretched and unfurled, and thin, copper skin strained over gnarled, bony protuberances. The stench of burning coals was suffocating and the monster filled the corner of the room, its horned head scraping the ceiling.

Jessica wrenched her hands free of Isabel's. Immediately, the portal spluttered and died, plunging the room into darkness.

"What have we done?" Isabel's voice croaked.

A spluttering cackle echoed from the corner.

As Jessica's eyes grew accustomed to the gloom, a cruel mouth filled with razor teeth smirked at her. Bone-white eyes flashed frigidly, scouring the pentagon-shaped parlour, and Jessica shuddered as the creature's icy stare raked through her.

"The world has changed little," the fiend rasped. *"Still over-pompous mortals meddle in powers too potent for their brittle minds."*

Jessica recoiled. The urge to run threatened to overpower her. Voices of reason toiled sluggishly in the back of her mind. For the first time in her life, Jessica knew that Isabel had no control over what was happening, and she would have fled, but her entire body was frozen in fear.

"Be gone!" Isabel shrieked, rounding on the hulking shape. She seized one of her necklaces and brandished a pentagon star in front of her. "I expel you from this plane! Leave this place!"

A forked tongue lashed at the air.

"Banish me? You believe you possess such power, enervated crone? Many lifetimes has it taken to find a way back into this pitiful world. Do you expect me to cower before your feeble totems?"

"What is it that you want?" Isabel demanded, still clutching the necklace before her.

"Death, agony, chaos," the demon drooled. *"The Dark Prophets will rise, and the Trinity shall be blasted into oblivion. There, they'll rot until the end of days."*

Isabel was unable to conceal her alarm.

"What are you?" she challenged.

"Diltraa," the monster spat. Its pointed teeth glinted like metal. *"Demon of the Eld Regions."*

"D–demon?"

Jessica couldn't stop the hoarse whisper escaping her lips. At the sound, Diltraa turned to behold her, and its ugly countenance twisted with maniacal glee.

"A young one! I adore the young ones," the demon cackled, and hot breath steamed from its viper-like nostrils. The stink of burning flesh overwhelmed the room. *"I shall peel the skin from you inch by inch, little one."*

"Leave her be!" Isabel yelled, but the demon ignored her objection. It hobbled across the room on elongated limbs and dragged Jessica from her chair. Screaming, Jessica felt the revolting thing's abrasive skin graze against her own, and a massive claw clamped around her throat. The stench of burnt cinders flooded her nostrils.

Isabel jumped to her feet, reaching up to her hair and wrenching free a long, mean-looking hairpin.

"Wait," Diltraa hissed, raising its horned head and sucking in the air through its nostrils. *"There is power here."*

The creature scrutinised the room. Its shooting glare saw right through the walls, searching. Then the beast let loose an elated crow.

"Can it be?" it hooted jubilantly. *"Can I have breached the very stronghold that so many others have failed to enter?"*

The head swivelled to stare at Isabel and the ugly, jutting features appeared to see her in a new light.

"I'd know that stench anywhere," Diltraa spat. *"Sentinel scum. Filthy parasite. What luck this is! When I'm finished with the child, I'll gladly tear you into a thousand pieces and feed you to the hounds of Hell. This house is the Sentinel keep! It shall be my new fortress and seed evil through the world of Man."*

The fog of fear was smothering Jessica, but then something so unexpected happened that she was jerked back into the present.

Isabel hooted loudly.

"Demon of the Eld Regions, did you say?"

The old woman let out another roar of laughter.

"I heard your kind were all scum-eating, slow-festering maggots! All talk and no spine!"

Diltraa's eyes blazed at Isabel.

"What say you?" Diltraa snarled. Its teeth gnashed in irritation.

Jessica's insides felt like they were turning in on themselves. What was Isabel doing? She glared at her guardian, dumbfounded, and saw that a pale confidence had stretched across her mentor's wrinkled features.

"You are nothing to this world," Isabel stated matter-of-factly, shrugging her shoulders. "How do you account for your kind's effortless expulsion from this plane all those centuries ago? Make threats all you want – a hearty laugh would do me a world of good!"

A trembling snarl vibrated from the demon's throat. Slowly it appeared to be escalating in size. Its eyes raged white fire.

"Your lunacy reveals itself, witch," the beast rasped. *"We were not expelled. There are ways in and out of this world that you could never*

fathom. How easily I intercepted your gateway, forced my way back into this wretched plane. Others shall do the same, and it will rain blood for a century!"

Jessica was cast aside. She collapsed against the wall.

Diltraa's lanky frame loomed over Isabel and Jessica watched the old woman become lost in the white pools of the demon's eyes. The nothingness that filled them seemed to draw her in, mesmerising and murderous. The old woman let out a sudden cry of pain and clutched at her chest, as if an iron fist had clamped around her heart. She let out another strangled cry, collapsing back into the chair.

"Isabel!" Jessica shouted. "No!"

Isabel forced her eyes open and drew a laboured breath.

"Go!" she gasped. Horrendous, cramping pain seemed to have seized her body and she convulsed alarmingly.

"No!" Jessica cried, tears coming. "I won't leave you!"

In desperation she searched the room for something – *anything!* – that would help them. Then she saw it. The iron candle holder that had toppled over in a corner of the room. With the demon concentrating on Isabel, Jessica darted over and seized the metal stand. She plucked the candles from their holders, revealing short, vicious-looking spikes.

Diltraa's pitiless gaze fell down on Isabel and a forked tongue flickered from the fiend's mouth again, greedily consuming her terror.

"Your fear is glorious," the demon gurgled.

Anger and loathing like nothing Jessica had ever felt before coursed through her. She gripped the candle holder tight and charged at the demon, plunging the metal stand into its back.

The creature emitted a strangled screech and the teeth of the holder speared clean through it, buckling its back before bursting out the other side.

Diltraa gasped and gagged, floundering across the floor. It writhed like a stranded fish.

Jessica hurried to Isabel's side, dodging the demon's flailing limbs.

"Isabel, are you okay?" she panted.

Isabel took Jessica's hand and nodded, attempting to catch her breath.

"I knew you had it in you," she coughed.

Together they watched the demon crush itself into the corner, curling its limbs up like a dying spider. Black blood spilled across the floorboards and Diltraa thrashed its elongated limbs, squirming in agony.

"Not so easily…" it crowed, *"…shall I leave this world."* The creature fixed its scorching gaze on Jessica and rasped: ***"You!"***

As Jessica stared into those bottomless pits, she felt her own will shrivel into nothingness, only to be replaced with a spearing determination.

"NOW!" Diltraa shrieked. It let loose a guttural hoot.

The girl moved like a puppet, reaching out for Isabel's throat.

"Jessica," Isabel cried, "what are you doing?"

Jessica's hands wrapped about Isabel's neck.

"Stop," Isabel choked. "Jessica, no!"

But Jessica had no control over her actions. She squeezed tighter, clamping the crone's shrivelled neck between her hands.

Isabel gripped Jessica's arms in vain, tried to prise her hands free, but it was futile. She scratched at the girl's skin, but Jessica didn't even flinch. With cold detachment, she wrung the old woman's neck and Diltraa gargled with glee until, finally, the demon perished in a pool of its own putrid blood.

Only then did Jessica return to her senses.

Too late, she realised what she had done.

★

"Diltraa…" Jessica spluttered. "I–I killed you."

Beside her, Nicholas looked confused, still clutching the Drujblade in readiness.

The demon called Diltraa cackled.

"Where do you suppose a demon goes when it dies?" the creature rasped scornfully. ***"That is why Man will never prevail. Knock us down, destroy us, and we'll keep clawing our way back out of Hell. Surrender now, Sentinel pig."***

"NO!" Nicholas shouted. He grabbed Jessica by the arm, this time protectively, and wielded the Drujblade in front of him. "Stay back!" he cried.

The demon stared down at him reproachfully.

"Boy," it rasped. *"Your bravery is admirable, but you're on the wrong side of this battle."*

Nicholas began to back away from the monster, pulling Jessica with him. Diltraa threw out a sinewy limb to stop them, razor-like claws slicing for their necks. Instinctively, Nicholas jabbed out with the blade and golden sparks erupted where the bone dagger sliced into the demon's flesh.

Diltraa howled, enraged, and arched away from the weapon. Nicholas seized his moment and turned, dragging Jessica away through the garden. They disappeared into the undergrowth.

"Malika!" Diltraa's gurgling voice rang out behind him. *"Find them!"*

"Come on," Nicholas urged, charging through the garden with Jessica, batting massive leaves out of the way as he pulled the woman after him. He pushed deeper and deeper into the garden, further than he'd been before, losing himself in the greenery. Only when he couldn't run anymore did he stop. They hid within the sheltering bows of a willow tree, which rested at the lip of a large pond.

"Jessica, what are we going to do?" Nicholas panted.

The woman turned away from him.

"Jessica!" Nicholas persisted. "You know what that thing is, don't you? What are we going to do? How can we stop it?"

"I can't," Jessica whispered. "I can't stop it. It's too powerful."

Nicholas pulled her round to face him. "That's rubbish!" he said in a low hiss.

"You've faced things like that before, I know you have. We have to fight it. We can't just give in."

But that's exactly what it looked like Jessica wanted to do.

"I'm so tired," she said, her hair falling across her face. She broke free of the boy's grip and trudged over to where the willow's slender branches hung like a curtain to the garden floor. She brushed her hands over the leaves.

There came the distant sound of trees being torn from the ground and a bleak howl tore through the garden.

Malika's euphoric chuckles echoed somewhere.

"Nicholas!" she called mockingly. "I've got a message from mummy! Don't you want to know what it is?"

She sounded close.

Nicholas ignored her and stared down at the dagger in his hand. The Drujblade. Isabel had said it was a formidable weapon; it had slain "many fell beasts", in her words. Diltraa certainly hadn't liked it very much. The boy looked over at Jessica and knew it was up to him.

He had to kill the monster himself.

"Stay here," he murmured to her.

The woman didn't seem to hear him.

"Oh Norlath," she hummed quietly, still playing with the tree's leaves.

Nicholas parted the vine-like branches of the willow tree and looked out into the garden. All was peaceful. The wide pond reflected an upside-down version of the world, blossoms spinning and twirling across its mirror-like surface.

The boy stepped out from the tree's protective umbrella and picked his way between the tree trunks.

In the evening gloom, it was difficult to see the ground, so he treaded carefully, mindful of the twigs underfoot, which might reveal his whereabouts to the monster.

Had the situation been less treacherous, he'd be deliberating over what Jessica had said about the village and his birth. He was so focussed, though, that such troubling revelations didn't bother him. The boy skulked onward, ready for anything.

At last he was back in the clearing near the door, where the flowers pooled across the ground in multicoloured congregations. There was no sign of the beast.

"Boy," purred a voice.

Nicholas spun around and found himself face to face with Malika.

"Are you certain this is the path for you?" she entreated softly. "There are such wonders in the world, such sensations I long to share with you."

The boy stared into the dazzling depths of her eyes, saw magic spark and shimmer there. Now, though, he was immune to her seductive charms. She had exploited his private pain. His anger was still fresh.

Nicholas felt the hatred gather in his chest, smouldering heavily there. Somehow, he found himself reaching out from the place where the rage throbbed, stretching malevolently for the red-haired woman with his mind.

Before she had a chance to take a step toward him, Malika froze and seemed to realise that something was wrong. An invisible, spiking shard pierced the front of her skull and suddenly something was groping around inside.

Nicholas didn't know what he was doing, but it felt as natural as breathing. He strained against the defences of the woman's mind, easily swept them aside and unlocked the mysteries twitching there. He saw men and women falling at Malika's feet, felt her pride and arrogance as she cut them down, slashed their throats and left them naked in the rain. Her laughter echoed in his head, but separate from him, something he could control.

The boy pushed deeper, and there she was, in a car with a man. A waiter. He was drunk, driving erratically, buoyed by her presence, whooping as she nibbled on his ear and whispered tenderly to him. Then the car ran off the road and into the countryside. Suddenly it was on a rail track, bouncing fitfully over the tracks before screeching to a halt. Malika dug her claws into the waiter's throat and tossed him over the bridge into the water below. Then she watched from the shadows as a train ploughed into the car, and hundreds of souls plunged to their deaths, wailing as they fell.

"You killed them," Nicholas gasped. "You put the car there."

Malika was on her knees now, bent awkwardly on the ground, her hands buried in her snake-like hair.

Nicholas couldn't stop. Fury drove him and the boy dug ferociously into Malika's mind. It was wartime. Great fires raged as planes whirred overhead. Then they were in a market square. A man was being hanged, but before he dropped through the trapdoor, he looked at Malika with accusatory eyes. Now, inexplicably, they were back in the pentagon room, the very room that Nicholas had been in this evening. Except this wasn't a memory from today. It was older. Malika was shivering naked in the corner of the room, scared and confused…

Surprised by this last image, Nicholas jerked away, releasing his hold on the woman.

"What…? What did you…?" Malika garbled. She let out a tortured cry, scrambled to her feet and fled the garden.

Nicholas couldn't believe what he'd seen. That woman. Malika. She had been responsible for his parents' deaths. She had orchestrated the train wreck and watched gleefully as every person onboard perished. For weeks now, the authorities had been clueless – and now he knew the truth.

"Nicholas!" came a voice, and the boy whirled around to see Isabel bounding across the grass toward him.

"You're alright," the cat shouted happily. Behind her, a dark shadow swept into the garden. Nicholas recognised the glinting silver mask that belonged to Esus.

"Child," the figure boomed. "Much has happened this night. Never before have these walls been breached. We must act fast."

"Where did he come from?" Nicholas asked Isabel, eyeing the masked figure distrustfully.

"Esus killed Garm," the cat explained. "He's come to help. Where is Jessica?"

A scream rang out across the garden.

"Jessica!" Nicholas cried. Without thinking, he hastened back into the garden, bolting through the undergrowth toward that pitiful sound.

"Nicholas, wait!" Isabel's voice called out after him, but Nicholas didn't hear it. He rushed between the trees, swiping plants out of the way and leaping over fallen logs. The garden had been devastated by Diltraa. The demon had taken its insatiable rage out on just about every plant that Nicholas passed, and the garden was in tatters, shredded beyond recognition.

Another scream sounded and Nicholas quickened his pace, bounding through the shrubbery. For some reason, Jessica felt like his responsibility. Not half an hour ago he'd held a knife to her throat and was going to kill her. Perhaps it was guilt driving him – he had to atone for what he'd done to her while under Malika's influence. But he'd seen a different side to Jessica tonight, as well. She was wise and old, but fragile, too. She needed protecting.

The boy hurried back to where he'd left Jessica and skidded to a halt in the dirt. The willow tree had been ripped to pieces. Its earth-caked roots lay exposed and there was the demon, clutching Jessica in its claws, holding her off the ground.

"Tell me!" Diltraa burbled. *"Tell me where the Trinity are!"*

The creature's hideousness struck Nicholas anew and his inner resolve weakened. The monster's ribs strained against the thin, rough skin that encased its towering frame and it was huge, its stretched limbs spider-like. The stink of charred flesh hung in the air.

Seeing the look of panic on Jessica's face, Nicholas clenched his teeth.

"Hey!" he yelled.

The demon's eyes wheeled in the boy's direction, set in the centre of that bony, low-browed face.

"If I was that ugly I'd be angry too!"

Diltraa snarled in annoyance at the interruption and hurled Jessica to the ground. It rounded on Nicholas.

The demon's insect-like limbs carried it to the boy with horrific speed and Nicholas struck out with the Drujblade as the creature's shadow loomed over him. Diltraa crowed wickedly, dodging the blow and slammed a barbarous arm into the boy's chest.

With a cry, Nicholas went hurtling through the air. He landed with a great splash in the pond.

The demon returned its attention to Jessica.

"Tell me!" it bellowed, and Jessica threw her hands to her ears at the terrible sound, squatting on the ground. *"Pitiful worm, writhing in the mud! No wonder the cracks are opening up like great sores, no wonder the Sentinels are being trampled like bugs. Pathetic whelp!"*

"Jessica Bell!" an aged voice shrieked. "What on Earth are you doing?"

As he clambered out of the pond, Nicholas saw Isabel hurry up to Jessica.

Startled, Jessica slowly unclamped her hands from her ears.

"Isabel," she whimpered.

The cat nudged at her with one of its front paws, its tiny feline features bunched up into a furry frown.

"You're not going to let that bag of bones talk to you like that, are you?" Isabel demanded, her golden eyes flashing up at the demon. "We've defeated it once, we'll damn well do it again!"

Nicholas watched as Jessica slowly began to rise from the ground. She seemed to have discovered some hidden strength within. As if refusing to bend to the demon's insidious will, she pulled herself to her feet and stared defiantly into the repugnant creature's face.

"Time has passed, demon," she said, a cold self-assurance replacing the fear that she had surrendered to. "Much has changed. The Trinity sleep and they will never awaken to the sounds of your callous tones. They are safe, hidden from the world. You'll never know of their whereabouts, nor will they know of you."

Frenzy boiling in its eyes, Diltraa made to lunge for the woman, but a sharp pain made the demon shriek out instead.

Nicholas had sunk the Drujblade into the demon's bony leg. Golden sparks spewed from that spot as the magic blade dug into the demon's flesh.

Diltraa lashed out, its cloven hoof striking Nicholas in the chest. The boy hit the ground, then clambered to his feet again and doggedly seized the blade's handle, wrenching it free. He stabbed the creature again, black blood spurting from the wound.

Diltraa emitted a horrific yowl and struck out with his front claws, swiping at the boy. Nicholas dodged out of the way. Raising the blade again, he sliced off one of the looming claws. It landed on the ground with a thud, still twitching, dark blood oozing around it.

"That's it!" Isabel whooped. "Get him, boy! Cut the foul beast down to size!"

As the demon shrieked in agony, Nicholas flew at it again, hacking and slashing with the Drujblade, gold sparks dancing about him. Gory sores opened up in the beast's torso and the boy was showered in sticky black blood.

"DIE!" Diltraa howled, striking out with its remaining claw.

Nicholas flew through the air and hit a tree trunk, the back of his head cracking dully against the tough bark. Unsteady, his skull throbbing, he slumped to the ground. What happened next all flickered before his drooping eyelids in a blur.

Esus swept in front of him, his black robes billowing.

"The knife," the masked figure hissed, and though it took a great deal of effort, Nicholas raised his bloodied hand and offered up the Drujblade.

Snatching the dagger from him, Esus darted over to the beast that was Diltraa and mounted it, scaling those gangly limbs like they were footholds on a mountainside. Nicholas's eyes closed heavily and the next thing he saw was Esus slamming the Drujblade into the back of the demon's neck and twisting ferociously. Then he seized the horned cranium with his gloved hands and tore it clean off.

The dismembered head squelched to the ground, the tongue lolling from its mouth, and Esus rode the collapsing demon's frame until it, too, struck the earth.

"Nicholas," Isabel cried, rushing to his side. She pawed at his leg, licking his hand before she could stop herself.

"I'm just going to… lie here for a moment," Nicholas murmured.

Then he slumped into unconsciousness.

★

Nicholas was in bed. As he'd rolled in and out of wakefulness, Jessica had treated his wounds, washed away the demon blood and helped him under the covers. The fight was over. They had won. Tomorrow was going to be a busy day. The boy's dreams would be far from peaceful tonight.

At the doorway, Jessica watched until she was sure he was asleep.

When she saw that his eyes were moving slowly behind the lids, she stepped into the room, sidling up to the bed.

"He fought well."

A deep rumble of a voice.

Jessica looked over to the open window. There, in a dark corner of the room, was Esus.

She nodded.

"There is much for him to learn," the shadow said. "You will begin training at once."

"Yes," Jessica said. "He is ready."

Esus made no reply.

In a swirl of black radiance his robed body buckled and became smoke. Feathers sprouted out of nowhere and from the dark cloud a raven flew to the windowsill. The bird Esus squawked then flitted from the window, disappearing into the night.

Jessica returned her attention to the sleeping figure in the bed. A secretive smile on her lips, she placed a book at the boy's bedside. On its spine, silver letters caught the light: *The Sentinel Chronicles – August 1997.* Pausing a moment to stroke the boy's hair, she went to the door.

Curled up at Nicholas's side, Isabel heaved a deep sigh and purred proudly.

Outside, great storm clouds split open and the rain began to fall.

EPILOGUE

FOR NOW, SHE SLEPT. SHE KNEW nothing of all that had occurred mere miles away. Her dreams passed unblemished by any notion of the horror that was carefully, watchfully feeling its way into the world. She knew nothing of the Sentinels, nor the Harvesters, nor of the forces that even now were seeking her out in the black of night. Seconds, hours, days, weeks. All mere heartbeats. They would find her, and she would know nothing of their coming. For now, peacefully, she slept.

The Sentinels will return in *Ruins*.